The FUTURE Is BLUE

CATHERYNNE M. VALENTE

Subterranean Press 2018

The Future Is Blue

First Edition

ISBN
978-1-59606-874-2

Subterranean Press
PO Box 190106
Burton, MI 48519

subterraneanpress.com

Manufactured in the United States of America

Table of CONTENTS

The Future IS BLUE

I. NIHILIST

MY NAME IS TETLEY ABEDNEGO and I am the most hated girl in Garbagetown. I am nineteen years old. I live alone in Candle Hole, where I was born, and have no friends except for a deformed gannet bird I've named Grape Crush and a motherless elephant seal cub I've named Big Bargains, and also the hibiscus flower that has recently decided to grow out of my roof, but I haven't named it anything yet. I love encyclopedias, a cassette I found when I was eight that says *Madeleine Brix's Superboss Mixtape '97* on it in very nice handwriting, plays by Mr. Shakespeare or Mr. Webster or Mr. Beckett, lipstick, Garbagetown, and my twin brother Maruchan. Maruchan is the only thing that loves me back, but he's my twin, so it doesn't really count. We couldn't stop loving each other any more than the sea could stop being so greedy and give us back China or drive time radio or polar bears.

But he doesn't visit anymore.

When we were little, Maruchan and I always asked each other the same question before bed. Every night, we crawled into the Us-Fort together—an impregnable stronghold of a bed which we had nailed up ourselves out of the carcasses of several hacked apart bassinets, prams, and cradles. It took up the whole of our bedroom. No one could see us in there, once we closed the porthole (a manhole cover I swiped from Scrapmetal Abbey stamped with stars, a crescent moon, and the magic words *New Orleans Water Meter*), and we felt certain no one could hear us either. We lay together under our canopy of moldy green lace and shredded buggy-hoods and mobiles with only one shattered fairy fish remaining. Sometimes I asked first and sometimes he did, but we never gave the same answer twice.

"Maruchan, what do you want to be when you grow up?"

He would give it a serious think. Once, I remember, he whispered:

"When I grow up I want to be the Thames!"

"Whatever for?" I giggled.

"Because the Thames got so big and so bossy and so strong that it ate London all up in one go! Nobody tells a Thames what to do or who to eat. A Thames tells *you*. Imagine having a whole city to eat, and not having to share any! Also there were millions of eels in the Thames and I only get to eat eels at Easter which isn't fair when I want to eat them all the time."

And he pretended to bite me and eat me all up. "Very well, you shall be the Thames and I shall be the Mississippi and together we shall eat up the whole world."

Then we'd go to sleep and dream the same dream. We always dreamed the same dreams, which was like living twice.

After that, whenever we were hungry, which was always all the time and forever, we'd say *we're bound for London-town!* until we drove our parents so mad that they forbade the word London in the house, but you can't forbid a word, so there.

EVERY MORNING I wake up to find words painted on my door like toadstools popping up in the night.

Today it says NIHILIST in big black letters. That's not so bad! It's almost sweet! Big Bargains flumps toward me on her fat seal-belly while I light the wicks on my beeswax door and we watch them burn together until the word melts away.

"I don't think I'm a nihilist, Big Bargains. Do you?"

She rolled over onto my matchbox stash so that I would rub her stomach. Rubbing a seal's stomach is the opposite of nihilism.

The FUTURE Is BLUE

Yesterday, an old man hobbled up over a ridge of rusted bicycles and punched me so hard he broke my nose. By law, I had to let him. I had to say: *Thank you, Grandfather, for my instruction.* I had to stand there and wait in case he wanted to do something else to me. But he didn't, he just wanted to cry and ask me why I did it and the law doesn't say I have to answer that, so I just stared at him until he went away. Once a gang of schoolgirls shaved off all my hair and wrote CUNT in blue marker on the back of my skull. *Thank you, sisters, for my instruction.* The schoolboys do worse. After graduation they come round and eat my food and hold me down and try to make me cry, which I never do. It's their rite of passage. *Thank you, brothers, for my instruction.*

But other than that, I'm really a very happy person! I'm awfully lucky when you think about it. Garbagetown is the most wonderful place anybody has ever lived in the history of the world, even if you count the Pyramids and New York City and Camelot. I have Grape Crush and Big Bargains and my hibiscus flower and I can fish like I've got bait for a heart so I hardly ever go hungry and once I found a ruby ring *and* a New Mexico license plate inside a bluefin tuna. Everyone says they only hate me because I annihilated hope and butchered our future, but I know better, and anyway, it's a lie. Some people are just born to be despised. The Loathing of Tetley began small and grew bigger and bigger, like the Thames, until it swallowed me whole.

Maruchan and I were born fifty years after the Great Sorting, which is another lucky thing that's happened to me. After all, I could have been born a Fuckwit and gotten drowned with all the rest of them, or I could have grown up on a Misery Boat, sailing around hopelessly looking for land, or one of the first to realize people could live on a patch of garbage in the Pacific Ocean the size of the place that used to be called Texas, or I could have been a Sorter and spent my whole life moving rubbish from one end of the patch to the other so that a pile of crap could turn into a country and babies could be born in places like Candle Hole or Scrapmetal Abbey or Pill Hill or Toyside or Teagate.

Candle Hole is the most beautiful place in Garbagetown, which is the most beautiful place in the world. All the stubs of candles the Fuckwits threw out piled up into hills and mountains and caverns and dells, votive candles and taper candles and tea lights and birthday candles and big fat colorful pillar candles, stacked and somewhat melted into a great crumbling gorgeous warren of wicks and wax. All the houses are little cozy honeycombs melted into the hillside, with smooth round windows and low golden ceilings. At night, from far away, Candle Hole looks like a firefly palace. When the wind blows, it smells like cinnamon, and freesia, and cranberries, and lavender, and Fresh Linen Scent and New Car Smell.

2. THE TERRIBLE POWER OF FUCKWIT CAKE

OUR PARENTS' NAMES are Life and Time. Time lay down on her Fresh Linen Scent wax bed and I came out of her first, then Maruchan. But even though I got here first, I came out blue as the ocean, not breathing, with the umbilical cord wrapped round my neck and Maruchan wailing, still squeezing onto my noose with his tiny fist, like he was trying to get me free. Doctor Pimms unstrangled and unblued me and put me in a Hawaiian Fantasies-scented wax hollow in our living room. I lay there alone, too startled by living to cry, until the sun came up and Life and Time remembered I had survived. Maruchan was so healthy and sweet-natured and strong and even though Garbagetown is the most beautiful place in the world, many children don't live past a year or two. We don't even get names until we turn ten. (Before that, we answer happily to Girl or Boy or Child or Darling.) Better to focus on the one that will grow up rather than get attached to the sickly poor beast who hasn't got a chance.

I was born already a ghost. But I was a very noisy ghost. I screamed and wept at all hours while Life and Time waited for me to die. I only nursed when my brother was full, I only played with toys he forgot, I only spoke after he had spoken. Maruchan said his first word at the supper table: *please.* What a lovely, polite word for a lovely, polite child! After they finished cooing over him, I very calmly turned to my mother and said: *Mama, may I have a scoop of mackerel roe? It is my favorite.* I thought they would be so proud! After all, I made twelve more words than my brother. This was my moment, the wonderful moment when they would realize that they did love me and I wasn't going to die and I was special and good. But everyone got very quiet. They were not happy that the ghost could talk. I had been able to for ages, but everything in my world said to wait for my brother before I could do anything at all. *No, you may not have mackerel roe, because you are a deceitful wicked little show-off child.*

When we turned ten, we went to fetch our names. This is just the most terribly exciting thing for a Garbagetown kid. At ten, you are a real person. At ten, people want to know you. At ten, you will probably live for a good while yet. This is how you catch a name: wake up to the fabulous new world of being ten and greet your birthday Frankencake (a hodgepodge of well-preserved Fuckwit snack cakes filled with various cremes and jellies). Choose a slice, with much fanfare. Inside, your adoring and/or neglectful mother will have hidden various small objects—an aluminum pull tab, a medicine bottle cap, a broken earring, a coffee bean, a wee striped capacitor, a tiny plastic rocking horse, maybe a postage stamp. Remove item from your mouth without cutting yourself or eating it. Now, walk in the direction of your prize. Toward Aluminumopolis or Pill Hill or Spanglestoke or Teagate or Electric City or Toyside or Lost Post Gulch. Walk and walk and walk. Never once brush yourself off or wash in the ocean, even after camping on a pile of magazines or wishbones or pregnancy tests or wrapping paper with glitter reindeer on it. Walk until nobody knows you. When, finally, a stranger hollers at you to get out of the way or go back where you came from or stop stealing the good rubbish, they will, without even realizing, call you by your true name, and you can begin to pick and stumble your way home.

My brother grabbed a chocolate snack cake with a curlicue of white icing on it. I chose a pink and red tigery striped hunk of cake filled with gooshy creme de something. The sugar hit our brains like twin tsunamis. He spat out a little gold earring with the post broken off. I felt a smooth, hard gelcap lozenge in my mouth. Pill Hill it was then, and the great mountain of Fuckwit anxiety medication. But when I carefully pulled the thing out, it was a little beige capacitor with red stripes instead. Electric City! I'd never been half so far. Richies lived in Electric City. Richies and brightboys and dazzlegirls and kerosene kings. My brother was off in the opposite direction, toward Spanglestoke and the desert of engagement rings.

Maybe none of it would have happened if I'd gone to Spanglestoke for my name instead. If I'd never seen the gasoline gardens of Engine Row. If I'd gone home straightaway after finding my name. If I'd never met Goodnight Moon in the brambles of Hazmat Heath with all the garbage stars rotting gorgeously overhead. Such is the terrible power of Fuckwit Cake.

I walked cheerfully out of Candle Hole with my St. Oscar backpack strapped on tight and didn't look back once. Why should I? St. Oscar had my back. I'm not really that religious nowadays. But everyone's religious when they're ten. St. Oscar was a fuzzy green Fuckwit man who lived in a garbage can just like me, and frowned a lot just like me. He understood me and loved me and knew how to bring civilization out of trash and I loved him back even though he was a Fuckwit. Nobody chooses how they get born. Not even Oscar.

So I scrambled up over the wax ridges of my home and into the world with Oscar on my back. The Matchbox Forest rose up around me: towers of EZ Strike matchbooks and boxes from impossible, magical places like the Coronado Hotel, Becky's Diner, the Fox and Hound Pub. Garbagetowners picked through heaps and cairns of blackened, used matchsticks looking for the precious ones that still had their red and blue heads intact. But I knew all those pickers. They couldn't give me a name. I waved at the hotheads. I climbed up Flintwheel Hill, my feet slipping and sliding on the mountain of spent butane lighters, until I could see out over all of Garbagetown just as the broiling cough-drop red sun was setting over Far Boozeaway, hitting the crystal bluffs of stockpiled whiskey and gin bottles and exploding into a billion billion rubies tumbling down into the hungry sea.

I sang a song from school to the sun and the matchsticks. It's an ask-and-answer song, so I had to sing both parts myself, which feels very odd when you have always had a twin to do the asking or the answering, but I didn't mind.

Who liked it hot and hated snow?
The Fuckwits did! The Fuckwits did!
Who ate up every thing that grows?
The Fuckwits did! The Fuckwits did!
Who drowned the world in oceans blue?
The Fuckwits did! The Fuckwits did!
Who took the land from me and you?
The Fuckwits did, we know it's true!
Are you *Fuckwits, children dear?*
We're GARBAGETOWNERS, free and clear!
But who made the garbage, rich and rank?
The Fuckwits did, and we give thanks.

The Lawn stretched out below me, full of the grass clippings and autumn leaves and fallen branches and banana peels and weeds and gnawed bones and eggshells of the fertile Fuckwit world, slowly turning into the gold of Garbagetown: soil. Real earth. Terra bloody firma. We can already grow rice in the dells. And here and there, big, blowsy flowers bang up out of the rot: hibiscus, African tulips, bitter gourds, a couple of purple lotuses floating in the damp mucky bits. I slept next to a blue-and-white orchid that looked like my brother's face.

"Orchid, what do you want to be when you grow up?" I whispered to it. In real life, it didn't say anything back. It just fluttered a little in the moonlight and the seawind. But when I got around to dreaming, I dreamed about the orchid, and it said: *a farm*.

3. MURDERCUNT

IN GARBAGETOWN, YOU think real hard about what you're gonna eat next, where the fresh water's at, and where you're gonna sleep. Once all that's settled you can whack your mind on nicer stuff, like gannets and elephant seals and what to write next on the Bitch of Candle Hole's door. (This morning I melted MURDERCUNT off the back wall of my house. Big Bargains flopped down next to me and watched the blocky red painted letters swirl and fade into the Buttercream Birthday Cake wax. Maybe I'll name my hibiscus flower Murdercunt. It has a nice big sound.)

When I remember hunting my name, I mostly remember the places I slept. It's a real dog to find good spots. Someplace sheltered from the wind, without too much seawater seep, where no one'll yell at you for wastreling on their patch or try to stick it in you in the middle of the night just because you're all alone and it looks like you probably don't have a knife.

I always have a knife.

So I slept with St. Oscar the Grouch for my pillow, in the shadow of a mountain of black chess pieces in Gamegrange, under a thicket of tabloids and *Wall Street Journal*s and remaindered novels with their covers torn off in Bookbury, snuggled into a spaghetti-pile of unspooled cassette ribbon on the outskirts of the Sound Downs, on the lee side of a little soggy Earl Grey hillock in Teagate. In the morning I sucked on a few of the teabags and the dew on them tasted like the loveliest cuppa any Fuckwit ever poured his stupid self. I said my prayers on beds of old microwaves and moldy photographs of girls with perfect hair kissing at the camera. *St. Oscar, keep your mighty lid closed over me. Look grouchily but kindly upon me and protect me as I travel through the infinite trashcan of your world. Show me the beautiful usefulness of your Blessed Rubbish. Let me not be Taken Out before I find my destiny.*

But my destiny didn't seem to want to find me. As far as I walked, I still saw people I knew. Mr. Zhu raking his mushroom garden, nestled in a windbreak of broken milk bottles. Miss Amancharia gave me one of the coconut crabs out of her nets, which was very nice of her, but hardly a name. Even as far away as Teagate, I saw Tropicana Sita welding a refrigerator door to a hull-metal shack. She flipped up her mask and waved at me. Dammit! She was Allsorts Sita's cousin, and Allsorts drank with my mother every Thursday at the Black Wick.

By the time I walked out of Teagate I'd been gone eight days. I was getting pretty ripe. Bits and pieces of Garbagetown were stuck all over my clothes, but no tidying up. Them's the rules. I could see the blue crackle of Electric City sparkling up out of the richie-rich Coffee Bean 'Burbs. Teetering towers of batteries rose up like desert hoodoo spires—AA, AAA, 12 volt, DD, car, solar, lithium, anything you like. Parrots and pelicans screamed down the battery canyons, their talons kicking off sprays of AAAs that tumbled down the heights like rockslides. Sleepy banks of generators rumbled pleasantly along a river of wires and extension cords and HDMI cables. Fields of delicate lightbulbs windchimed in the breeze. Anything that had a working engine lived here. Anything that still had *juice*. If Garbagetown had a heart, it was Electric City. Electric City pumped power. Power and privilege.

In Electric City, the lights of the Fuckwit world were still on.

4. GOODNIGHT GARBAGETOWN

"OI, TETLEY! FUCK off back home to your darkhole! We're full up on little cunts here!"

And that's how I got my name. Barely past the battery spires of Electric City, a fat gas-huffing fucksack voltage jockey called me a little cunt. But he also called me Tetley. He brayed it down from a pyramid of telephones and his friends all laughed and drank homebrew out of a glass jug and went back to not working. I looked down—among the many scraps of rubbish clinging to my shirt and pants and backpack and hair was a bright blue teabag wrapper with TETLEY CLASSIC BLEND BLACK TEA written on it in cheerful white letters, clinging to my chest.

I tried to feel the power of my new name. The *me*-ness of it. I tried to imagine my mother and father when they were young, waking up with some torn-out page of *Life* and *Time* Magazine stuck to their rears, not even noticing until someone barked out their whole lives for a laugh. But I couldn't feel anything while the volt-humpers kept on staring at me like I was nothing but a used-up potato battery. I didn't even know then that the worst swear word in Electric City was *dark*. I didn't know they were waiting to see how mad I'd get 'cause they called my home a darkhole. I didn't care. They were wrong and stupid. Except for the hole part. Candle Hole never met a dark it couldn't burn down.

Maybe I should have gone home right then. I had my name! Time to hoof it back over the river and through the woods, girl. But I'd never seen Electric City and it was morning yet and if I stayed gone awhile longer maybe they'd miss me. Maybe they'd worry. And maybe now they'd love me, now that I was a person with a name. Maybe I could even filch a couple of batteries or a cup of gasoline and turn up at my parents' door in turbo-powered triumph. I'd tell my brother all my adventures and he'd look at me like I was magic on a stick and everything would be good forever and ever amen.

So I wandered. I gawped. It was like being in school and learning the Fuckwit song only I was walking around *inside* the Fuckwit song and it was all still happening right now everywhere. Electric City burbled and bubbled and clanged and belched and smoked just like the bad old world before it all turned blue. Everyone had such fine things! I saw a girl wearing a ballgown out of a fairy book, green and glitter and miles of ruffles and she wasn't even *going* anywhere. She was just tending her gasoline garden out the back of her little cottage, which wasn't made out of candles or picturebooks or cat food cans, but real cottage parts! Mostly doors and shutters and really rather a lot of windows, but they fit together like they never even needed the other parts of a house in the first place. And the girl in her greenglitter dress carried a big red watering can around her garden, sprinkling fuel stabilizer into her tidy rows of petrol barrels and gas cans with their graceful spouts pointed toward the sun. Why not wear that dress all the time? Just a wineglass full of what she was growing in her garden would buy almost anything else in Garbagetown. She smiled shyly at me. I hated her. And I wanted to be her.

By afternoon I was bound for London-town, so hungry I could've slurped up every eel the Thames ever had. There's no food lying around in Electric City. In Candle Hole I could've grabbed candy or a rice ball or jerky off any old midden heap. But here everybody owned their piece and kept it real neat, *mercilessly* neat, and they didn't share. I sat down on a rusty Toyota transmission and fished around in my backpack for crumbs. My engine sat on one side of a huge cyclone fence. I'd never seen one all put together before. Sure, you find torn-off shreds of wire fences, but this one was all grown up, with proper locks and chain wire all over it. It meant to Keep You Out. Inside, like hungry dogs, endless barrels and freezers and cylinders and vats went on and on, with angry writing on them that said HAZMAT or BIOHAZARD or RADIOACTIVE or WARNING or DANGER or CLASSIFIED.

"Got anything good in there?" said a boy's voice. I looked round and saw a kid my own age, with wavy black hair and big brown eyes and three little moles on his forehead. He was wearing the nicest clothes I ever saw on a boy—a blue suit that almost, *almost* fit him. With a *tie*.

"Naw," I answered. "Just a dry sweater, an empty can of Cheez-Wiz, and Madeline Brix's Superboss Mixtape '97. It's my good luck charm." I showed him my beloved mixtape. Madeline Brix made all the dots on her *i*'s into hearts. It was a totally Fuckwit thing to do and I loved her for it even though she was dead and didn't care if I loved her or not.

"*Cool*," the boy said, and I could tell he meant it. He didn't even call me a little cunt or anything. He pushed his thick hair out of his face. "Listen, you really shouldn't be here. No one's gonna say anything because you're not Electrified, but it's so completely dangerous. They put all that stuff in one place so it couldn't get out and hurt anyone."

"Electrified?"

"One of us. Local." He had the decency to look embarrassed. "Anyway, I saw you and I thought that if some crazy darkgirl is gonna have a picnic on Hazmat Heath, I could at least help her not die while she's doing it."

The boy held out his hand. He was holding a gas mask. He showed me how to fasten it under my hair. The sun started to set rosily behind a tangled briar of motherboards. Everything turned pink and gold and slow and sleepy. I climbed down from my engine tuffet and lay under the fence next to the boy in the suit. He'd brought a mask for himself too. We looked at each other through the eye holes.

"My name's Goodnight Moon," he said.

"Mine's…" And I did feel my new name swirling up inside me then, like good tea, like cream and sugar cubes, like the most essential me. "Tetley."

"I'm sorry I called you a darkgirl, Tetley."

"Why?"

"It's not a nice thing to call someone."

"I like it. It sounds pretty."

"It isn't. I promise. Do you forgive me?"

I tugged on the hose of my gas mask. The air coming through tasted like nickels. "Sure. I'm aces at forgiving. Been practicing all my life. Besides..." My turn to go red in the face. "At the Black Wick they'd probably call you a brightboy and that's not as pretty as it sounds, either."

Goodnight Moon's brown eyes stared out at me from behind thick glass. It was the closest I'd ever been to a boy who wasn't my twin. Goodnight Moon didn't feel like a twin. He felt like the opposite of a twin. We never shared a womb, but on the other end of it all, we might still share a grave. His tie was burgundy with green swirls in it. He hadn't tied it very well, so I could see the skin of his throat, which was very clean and probably very soft.

"Hey," he said, "do you want to hear your tape?"

"What do you mean *hear* it? It's not for hearing, it's for luck."

Goodnight Moon laughed. His laugh burst all over me like butterfly bombs. He reached into his suit jacket and pulled out a thick black rectangle. I handed him Madeline Brix's Superboss Mixtape '97 and he hit a button on the side of the rectangle. It popped open; Goodnight Moon slotted in my tape and handed me one end of a long wire.

"Put it in your ear," he said, and I did.

A man's voice filled up my head from my jawbone up to the plates of my skull. The most beautiful and saddest voice that ever was. A voice like Candle Hole all lit up at twilight. A voice like the whole old world calling up from the bottom of the sea. The man on Madeline Brix's tape was saying he was happy, and he hoped I was happy, too.

Goodnight Moon reached out to hold my hand just as the sky went black and starry. I was crying. He was, too. Our tears dripped out of our gas masks onto the rusty road of Electric City.

When the tape ended, I dug in my backpack for a match and a stump of candle: dark red, Holiday Memories scent. I lit it at the same moment that Goodnight Moon pulled a little flashlight out of his pocket and turned it on. We held our glowings between us. We were the same.

5. BRIGHTBITCH

ALLSORTS SITA CAME to visit me today. Clicked my knocker early in the morning, early enough that I could be sure she'd never slept in the first place. I opened for her, as I am required to do. She looked up at me with eyes like bullet holes, leaning my waxy hinges, against the T in BRIGHTBITCH, thoughtfully scrawled in what appeared to be human shit across the front of my hut. BRIGHTBITCH smelled, but Allsorts Sita smelled worse. Her breath punched me in the nose before she did. I got a lungful of what Diet Sprite down at the Black Wick optimistically called "cognac": the thick pinkish booze you could get by extracting the fragrance oil and preservatives out of candles and mixing it with wood alcohol the kids over in Furnitureford boiled out of dining sets and china cabinets. Smells like flowers vomited all over a New Car and then killed a badger in the backseat. Allsorts Sita looked like she'd drunk so much cognac you could light one strand of her hair and she'd burn for eight days.

"You fucking whore," she slurred.

"Thank you, Auntie, for my instruction," I answered quietly.

I have a place I go to in my mind when I have visitors who aren't seals or gannet birds or hibiscus flowers. A little house made all of doors and windows, where I wear a greenglitter dress every day and water my gascan garden and read by electric light.

"I hate you. I hate you. How could you do it? We raised you and fed you and this is how you repay it all. You ungrateful bitch."

"Thank you, Auntie, for my instruction."

In my head I ran my fingers along a cyclone fence and all the barrels on the other side read LIFE and LOVE and FORGIVENESS and UNDERSTANDING.

"You've killed us all," Allsorts Sita moaned. She puked up magenta cognac on my stoop. When she was done puking she hit me over and over with closed fists. It didn't hurt too much. Allsorts is a small woman. But it hurt when she clawed my face and my breasts with her fingernails. Blood came up like wax spilling and when she finished she passed out cold, halfway in my house, halfway out.

"Thank you, Auntie, for my instruction," I said to her sleeping body. My blood dripped onto her, but in my head I was lying on my roof made of two big church doors in a gas mask listening to a man sing to me that he's never done bad things and he hopes I'm happy, he hopes I'm happy, he hopes I'm happy.

Big Bargains moaned mournfully and the lovely roof melted away like words on a door. My elephant seal friend flopped and fretted. When they've gone for my face she can't quite recognize me and it troubles her seal-soul something awful. Grape Crush, my gannet bird, never worries about silly things like facial wounds. He just brings me fish and pretty rocks. When I found him, he had a plastic six-pack round his neck with one can still stuck in the thing, dragging along behind him like a ball and chain. Big Bargains was choking on an ad insert. She'd probably smelled some ancient fish and chips grease lurking in the headlines. They only love me because I saved them. That doesn't always work. I saved everyone else, too, and all I got back was blood and shit and loneliness.

6. REVLON SUPER LUSTROUS 919: RED RUIN

I WENT HOME with my new name fastened on tight. Darkgirls can't stay in Electric City. Can't live there unless you're born there and I was only ten anyway. Goodnight Moon kissed me before I left. He still had his gas mask on so mainly our breathing hoses wound around each other like gentle elephants but I still call it a kiss. He smelled like scorched ozone and metal and paraffin and hope.

A few months later, Electric City put up a fence around the whole place. Hung up an old rusty shop sign that said EXCUSE OUR MESS WHILE WE RENOVATE. No one could go in or out except to trade and that had to get itself done on the dark side of the fence.

My mother and father didn't start loving me when I got back even though I brought six AA batteries out of the back of Goodnight Moon's tape player. My brother had got a ramen flavor packet stuck in his hair somewhere outside the Grocery Isle and was every inch of him Maruchan. A few years later I heard Life and Time telling some cousin how their marvelous and industrious and thoughtful boy had gone out in search of a name and brought back six silver batteries, enough to power anything they could dream of. What a child! What a son! So fuck them, I guess.

But Maruchan did bring something back. It just wasn't for our parents. When we crawled into the Us-Fort that first night back, we lay uncomfortably against each other. We were the same, but we weren't. We'd had separate adventures for the first time, and Maruchan could never understand why I wanted to sleep with a gas mask on now.

"Tetley, what do you want to be when you grow up?" Maruchan whispered in the dark of our pram-maze.

"Electrified," I whispered back. "What do you want to be?"

"Safe," he said. Things had happened to Maruchan, too, and I couldn't share them any more than he could hear Madeline Brix's songs.

My twin pulled something out of his pocket and pushed it into my hand till my fingers closed round it reflexively. It was hard and plastic and warm.

"I love you, Tetley. Happy Birthday."

I opened my fist. Maruchan had stolen lipstick for me. Revlon Super Lustrous 919: Red Ruin, worn almost all the way down to the nub by some dead woman's lips.

After that, a lot of years went by but they weren't anything special.

7. IF GOD TURNED UP FOR SUPPER

I WAS SEVENTEEN years old when Brighton Pier came to Garbagetown. I was tall and my hair was the color of an oil spill; I sang pretty good and did figures in my head and I could make a candle out of damn near anything. People wanted to marry me here and there but I didn't want to marry them back so they thought I was stuck up. Who wouldn't want to get hitched to handsome Candyland Ocampo and ditch Candle Hole for a clean, fresh life in Soapthorpe where bubbles popped all day long like diamonds in your hair?

Well, I didn't, because he had never kissed me with a gas mask on and he smelled like pine fresh cleaning solutions and not like scorched ozone at all.

Life and Time turned into little kids right in front of us. They giggled and whispered and Mum washed her hair in the sea about nine times and then soaked it in oil until it shone. Papa tucked a candle stump that had melted just right and looked like a perfect rose into her big new fancy hairdo and then, like it was a completely normal thing to do, put on a cloak sewn out of about a hundred different neckties. They looked like a prince and a princess.

"Brighton Pier came last when I was a girl, before I even had my name," Time told us, still giggling and blushing like she wasn't anyone's mother. "It's the most wonderful thing that can ever happen in the world."

"If God turned up for supper and brought all the dry land back for dessert, it wouldn't be half as good as one day on Brighton Pier," Life crowed. He picked me up in his arms and twirled me around in the air. He'd never done that before, not once, and he had his heart strapped on so tight he didn't even stop and realize what he'd done and go vacant eyed and find something else to look at for a long while. He just squeezed me and kissed me like I came from somewhere and I didn't know what the hell a Brighton Pier was but I loved it already.

"What is it? What is it?" Maruchan and I squealed, because you can catch happiness like a plague.

"It's better the first time if you don't know," Mum assured us. "It's meant to dock in Electric City on Friday."

"So it's a ship, then?" Maruchan said. But Papa just twinkled his eyes at us and put his finger over his lips to keep the secret in.

The Pier meant to dock in Electric City. My heart fell into my stomach, got all digested up, and sizzled out into the rest of me all at once. Of course, of course it would, Electric City had the best docks, the sturdiest, the prettiest. But it seemed to me like a life was happening to me on purpose, and Electric City couldn't keep a darkgirl out anymore. They had to share like the rest of us.

"What do you want to be when you grow up, Maruchan?" I said to my twin in the dark the night before we set off to see what was better than God. Maruchan's eyes gleamed with the Christmas thrill of it all.

"Brighton Pier," he whispered.

"Me, too," I sighed, and we both dreamed we were beautiful Fuckwits running through a forest of real pines, laughing and stopping to eat apples and running again and only right before we woke up did we notice that something was chasing us, something huge and electric and bound for London-town.

8. CITIZENS OF MUTATION NATION

I LOOKED FOR Goodnight Moon everywhere from the moment we crossed into Electric City. The fence had gone and Garbagetown poured in and nothing was different than it had been when I got my name off the battery spires, even though the sign had said for so long that Electric City was renovating. I played a terrible game with every person that shoved past, every face in a window, every shadow juddering down an alley and the game was: *are you him?* But I lost all the hands. The only time I stopped playing was when I first saw Brighton Pier.

I couldn't get my eyes around it. It was a terrible, gorgeous whale of light and colors and music and otherness. All along a boardwalk jugglers danced and singers sang and horns horned and accordions squeezed and under it all some demonic engine screamed and wheezed. Great glass domes and towers and flags and tents glowed in the sunset but Brighton Pier made the sunset look plain-faced and unloveable. A huge wheel full of pink and emerald electric lights turned slowly in the warm wind but went nowhere. People leapt and turned somersaults and stood on each others' shoulders and they all wore such soft, vivid costumes, like they'd all been cut out of a picturebook too fine for anyone like me to read. The tumblers lashed the pier to the Electric City docks and cut the engines and after that it was nothing but music so thick and good you could eat it out of the air.

Life and Time hugged Maruchan and cheered with the rest of Garbagetown. Tears ran down their faces. Everyone's faces.

"When the ice melted and the rivers revolted and the Fuckwit world went under the seas," Papa whispered through his weeping, "a great mob hacked Brighton Pier off of Brighton and strapped engines to it and set sail across the blue. They've been going ever since. They go around the world and around again, to the places where there's still people, and trade their beauty for food and fuel. There's a place on Brighton Pier where if you look just right, it's like nothing ever drowned."

A beautiful man wearing a hat of every color and several bells stepped up on a pedestal and held a long pale cone to his mouth. The mayor of Electric City embraced him with two meaty arms and asked his terrible, stupid, unforgivable question: "Have you seen dry land?"

And the beautiful man answered him: "With my own eyes."

A roar went up like angels dying. I covered my ears. The mayor covered his mouth with his hands, speechless, weeping. The beautiful man patted him awkwardly on the back. Then he turned to us.

"Hello, Garbagetown!" he cried out and his voice sounded like everyone's most secret heart.

We screamed so loud every bird in Garbagetown fled to the heavens and we clapped like mad and some people fell onto the ground and buried their face in old batteries.

"My name is Emperor William Shakespeare the Eleventh and I am the Master of Brighton Pier! We will be performing *Twelfth Night* in the great stage tonight at seven o'clock, followed by *The Duchess of Malfi* at ten (which has werewolves) and a midnight acrobatic display! Come one, come all! Let Madame Limelight tell your FORTUNE! TEST your strength with the Hammer of the Witches! SEE the wonders of the Fuckwit World in our Memory Palace! Get letters and news from the LAST HUMAN OUTPOSTS around the globe! GASP at the citizens of Mutation Nation in the Freak Tent! Sample a FULL MINUTE of real television, still high definition after all these years! Concerts begin in the Crystal Courtyard in fifteen minutes! Our Peep Shows feature only the FINEST actresses reading aloud from GENUINE Fuckwit historical records! Garbagetown, we are here to DAZZLE you!"

A groan went up from the crowds like each Garbagetowner was just then bedding their own great lost love and they heaved toward the lights, the colors, the horns and the voices, the silk and the electricity and the life floating down there, knotted to the edge of our little pile of trash.

Someone grabbed my hand and held me back while my parents, my twin, my world streamed away from me down to the Pier. No one looked back.

"Are you her?" said Goodnight Moon. He looked longer and leaner but not really older. He had on his tie.

"Yes," I said, and nothing was different than it had been when I got my name except now neither of us had masks and our kisses weren't like gentle elephants but like a boy and a girl and I forgot all about my strength and my fortune and the wonderful wheel of light turning around and around and going nowhere.

9. TERRORWHORE

ACTORS ARE LIARS. Writers, too. The whole lot of them, even the horn players and the fortune tellers and the freaks and the strongmen. Even the ladies with rings in their noses and high heels on their feet playing violins all along the pier and the lie they are all singing and dancing and saying is: *we can get the old world back again*.

My door said TERRORWHORE this morning. I looked after my potato plants and my hibiscus and thought about whether or not I would ever get to have sex again. Seemed unlikely. Big Bargains concurred.

Goodnight Moon and I lost our virginities in the Peep Show tent while a lady in green fishnet stockings and a lavender garter read to us from the dinner menu of the Dorchester Hotel circa 2005.

"Whole Berkshire roasted chicken stuffed with black truffles, walnuts, duck confit, and dauphinoise potatoes," the lady purred. Goodnight Moon devoured my throat with kisses, bites, need. "Drizzled with a balsamic reduction and rosemary honey."

"What's honey?" I gasped. We could see her but she couldn't see us, which was for the best. The glass in the window only went one way.

"Beats me, kid," she shrugged, re-crossing her legs the other way. "Something you drizzle." She went on. "Sticky toffee pudding with lashings of cream and salted caramel, passionfruit souffle topped with orbs of pistachio ice cream…"

Goodnight Moon smelled just as I remembered. Scorched ozone and metal and paraffin and hope and when he was inside me it was like hearing my name for the first time. I couldn't escape the *me*-ness of it, the *us*-ness of it, the sound and the shape of ourselves turning into our future.

"I can't believe you're here," he whispered into my breast. "I can't believe this is us."

The lady's voice drifted over my head. "Lamb cutlets on a bed of spiced butternut squash, wilted greens, and delicate hand-harvested mushrooms served with goat cheese in clouds of pastry…"

Goodnight Moon kissed my hair, my ears, my eyelids. "And now that the land's come back Electric City's gonna save us all. We can go home together, you and me, and build a house and we'll have a candle in every window so you always feel at home…"

The Dorchester dinner menu stopped abruptly. The lady dropped to her fishnetted knees and peered at us through the glass, her brilliant glossy red hair tumbling down, her spangled eyes searching for us beyond the glass.

"Whoa, sweetie, slow down," she said. "You're liable to scare a girl off that way."

All I could see in the world was Goodnight Moon's brown eyes and the sweat drying on his brown chest. Brown like the earth and all its promises. "I don't care," he said. "You scared, Tetley?" I shook my head. "Nothing can scare us now. Emperor Shakespeare said he's seen land, real dry land, and we have a plan and we're gonna get everything back again and be fat happy Fuckwits like we were always supposed to be."

The Peep Show girl's glittering eyes filled up with tears. She put her hand on the glass. "Oh…oh, baby…that's just something we say. We always say it. To everyone. It's our best show. Gives people hope, you know? But there's nothing out there, sugar. Nothing but ocean and more ocean and a handful of drifty lifeboat cities like yours circling the world like horses on a broken-down carousel. Nothing but blue."

10. WE ARE SO LUCKY

IT WOULD BE nice for me if you could just say you understand. I want to hear that just once. Goodnight Moon didn't. He didn't believe her and he didn't believe me and all he could hear was Emperor William Shakespeare the Eleventh singing out his big lie. RESURRECTION! REDEMPTION! REVIVIFICATION! LAND HO!

"No, because, see," my sweetheart wept on the boardwalk while the wheel spun dizzily behind his head like an electric candy crown, "we have a plan. We've worked so hard. It has to happen. The mayor said as soon as we had news of dry land, the minute we knew, we'd turn it on and we'd get there first and the continents would be ours, Garbagetowners, we'd inherit the earth. He's gonna tell everyone when the Pier leaves. At the farewell party."

"Turn what on?"

Resurrection. Redemption. Renovation. All those years behind the fence Electric City had been so busy. Disassembling all those engines they hoarded so they could make a bigger one, the biggest one. Pooling fuel in great vast stills. Practicing ignition sequences. Carving up a countryside they'd never even seen between the brightboys and brightgirls and we could have some, too, if we were good.

"You want to turn Garbagetown into a Misery Boat," I told him. "So we can just steam on ahead into nothing and go mad and use up all the gas and batteries that could keep us happy in mixtapes for another century here in one hot minute."

"The Emperor said…"

"He said his name was Duke Orsino of Illyria, too. And then Roderigo when they did the werewolf play. Do you believe that? If they'd found land, don't you think they'd have stayed there?"

But he couldn't hear me. Neither could Maruchan when I tried to tell him the truth in the peep show. All they could see was green. Green leafy trees and green grass and green ivy in some park that was lying at the bottom of the sea. We dreamed different dreams now, my brother and I, and all my dreams were burning.

Say you understand. I had to. I'm not a nihilist or a murdercunt or a terrorwhore. They were gonna use up every last drop of Garbagetown's power to go nowhere and do nothing and instead of measuring out teaspoons of good, honest gas, so that it lasts and we last all together, no single thing on the patch would ever turn on again, and we'd go dark, *really* dark, forever. Dark like the bottom of a hole. They had no right. *They* don't understand. This is *it.* This is the future. Garbagetown and the sea. We can't go back, not ever, not even for a minute. We are so lucky. Life is so good. We're going on and being alive and being shitty sometimes and lovely sometimes just the same as we always have, and only a Fuckwit couldn't see that.

I waited until Brighton Pier cast off, headed to the next rickety harbor of floating foolboats, filled with players and horns and glittering wheels and Dorchester menus and fresh mountains of letters we wouldn't read the answers to for another twenty years. I waited until everyone was sleeping so nobody would get hurt except the awful engine growling and panting to deliver us into the dark salt nothing of an empty hellpromise.

It isn't hard to build a bomb in Electric City. It's all just laying around behind that fence where a boy held my hand for the first time. All you need is a match.

11. WHAT YOU CAME FOR

IT'S SUCH A beautiful day out. My hibiscus is just gigantic, red as the hair on a peep show dancer. If you want to wait, Big Bargains will be round later for her afternoon nap. Grape Crush usually brings a herring by in the evening. But I understand if you've got other places to be.

It's okay. You can hit me now. If you want to. It's what you came for. I barely feel it anymore.

Thank you for my instruction.

No One Dies IN NOWHERE

FIRST TERRACE: THE LATE REPENTANT

THERE IS A CLICKING SOUND *before she appears, like a gas stove before it lights. One moment there is nothing, the next there is Pietta, though this is the last gasp of before/after causality in her pure, pale mind. Now that she is here, she will always have been here. Charcoal-blue rags twist and braid and drape around her body more artfully than any gown. A leather falcon's hood closes up her head but does not blind her; the eyecups are a fine bronze mesh that lets in light. Long jessies hang from her thin wrists. This room which she has never seen belongs to her as utterly as her eyes: a monk's cell, modest but perfect and graceful. Candles thick as calf-bones. Water in a black basin. A copper rain barrel, empty. She runs her hand along the smooth, wine-dark stone of her walls; her fingertips leave phosphor-prints. She lays down on her bed, a shelf for holding Piettas carved out of the rock, mattressed in straw and withered, thorny wildflowers that smell of the village where she was born. From the straw, she can look out of three slim glassless windows shaped like chess bishops. A grey, damp sky steals in, a burgling fog climbing up toward her, a hundred million kinds of grey swirling together, and the stars behind, waiting. Pietta remembers the feeling of the first day of school. She goes to the window and looks out, looks down. Her long hair hangs over the ledge like two thick vines. Black, seedless earth below, dizzyingly far. As close as spying neighbors across a shared alley, a sheer, knife-cragged mountain stretches up into the dimming clouds and disappears into oncoming night. The mountain crawls with people. Each carries a black lantern half as tall as they. A man with a short, lovely beard chokes on the smoke puking forth from his light, but even as he chokes, he holds it closer to his mouth, desperate to get more. Their eyes meet. Pietta holds up her hand in greeting. He opens his jaw far wider than any bone allows and takes long, sultry bites out of the smoke.*

When she turns away, a bindle lies on her bed of stone and straw. A plain handkerchief knotted around a long, burled black branch. She looses the cloth. Inside she finds a wine bottle, a pair of scissors, a stone figure of a straight-backed child in a chair, a brass key, a cracked, worn belt with two holes torn through, and a hundred shattered shards of colored glass. Pietta picks up one of the blades of glass and holds it to her breast until it slices through her skin. The glass is violet. The blood never comes.

SECOND TERRACE: THE PROUD

ON AN ENDLESS plain where nothing grows lie a mountain as crowded as a city and a city as vast as a mountain. They face one another like bride and bridegroom. The city was enclosed at the commencement of linear time, a great ancient abbey bristling with domes, towers, spires, and stoas, chiseled out of rock the color of wine spilled on the surface of Mars, doorless, but not windowless, never windowless, candlelight twinkling from millions upon millions of arched and tapered clefts in the stone. From every one of these, you can see the mountain clearly, the people moving upon it, their lamps swinging back and forth, their hurryings and their stillnesses. The whispered talk of the people on the mountain can always be heard in the cloisters of the city, as though there is not a mile of churning black mud between the woman emptying her rain barrel after a storm and the ragged man murmuring on the windy crags. A road connects the mountain and the city, lit by blue gas lamps, cobbled by giants. No one has ever seen a person walk that road, though they must, or else what could be its purpose?

The clouded, pregnant sky swallows the peak of the mountain but declines the heights of the city. When there are stars, they are not our stars. They are not even white, but red as watch-fires.

The FUTURE Is BLUE

In the city, which is called Nowhere, a man with the head of a heron sat comfortably in the topmost room of the policemen's tower, working on his novel.

It was slow going.

He supposed he had everything he needed—a hurricane lamp full of oil, a stone cup full of dry red wine, a belly full of hot buttered toast, a typewriter confiscated from a poor soul he'd caught sledgehammering *Fuck This Place* onto the north stairwell of the Callabrius Quarter, a ream of fresh, bright paper filched from the records office. It was a quiet night in Nowhere. The criminal element, such as it was, seemed content to sleep the cold stars away until morning, leaving Detective Belacqua in peace.

He tried typing: *It was a quiet night in Nowhere,* then, disgusted with himself, abandoned his desk with a flamboyant despair no one could see to appreciate, and stared gloomily out the long, slender stone window onto the mud plain far below. A moonless spring blackness slept on the fields outside the walled city. It was always spring in Nowhere. But there were no cherry blossoms, no daffodils or new hens, only the cold dark mud of snow just melted, the trees stripped naked, bare arms flung up pleading for the sun, the smell of green but not the green itself. Every day was the day before the first crocus breaks the skull of earth, the held breath before beginning can begin. Always March, never May.

Detective Belacqua had several strikes against him as a budding author. For one thing, he had very little conception of time, an essential element in organizing narrative. He was, after all, mostly infinite. He barely remembered his childhood, if he could be said to have had one at all, but he remembered the incandescent naphtha-splatter of the birth of the universe pretty well. What order things happened in and why wasn't his business. He didn't pry. And this was another problem, for Detective Belacqua had not, in all his long tenure in the walled city, felt the urge to question any aspect of his existence. Such restlessness was not marked out on the map of a strigil's heart the way it was scribbled on every inch of the maps of men. Belacqua enjoyed his slow progress through each day and night. He enjoyed hot buttered toast and dry red wine. He enjoyed his job, felt himself to be necessary in a way as profound as food to a body. Someone had to keep order in this orderless place. Someone had to give Nowhere its shape and its self. His world was a simple equation: if crime, then punishment. It didn't matter at all why or how a criminal did his work, only that he had done it. And because he never bothered with the rest, Detective Belacqua was a hopeless novelist, for he had no clear idea of what drove anyone to do much of anything except be a policeman and bear lightly the granite weight of an unmovable cosmos. The actions of others were baffling and mostly unpleasant. He had never moved in the moral coil of clanging and conflicting wills. All he had ever known was Nowhere, and by the time Nowhere happened to a person, they had already made all the choices that mattered.

Yet Detective Belacqua longed to write with every part of his unmeasurable psyche. He had been a happy man before he discovered books. Very occasionally, people brought them to Nowhere in their sad little bindles. The first time Belacqua saw one, during a quickly opened, quickly shut case of petty theft in the Castitas District, he had confiscated it and crouched for hours in a vestibule, transfixed, as he read the crumbling paperback, the very hows and whys Belacqua had never understood. But it was not enough to read. Belacqua wanted more. There were no strigils in any of the books men brought to Nowhere. No one like him. The men had men-heads and men-desires and the women had women-heads and women-ambitions and nowhere could his heron-soul find a sympathetic mirror. And so he tried and tried and at best he plonked out *It was a quiet night in Nowhere* on the back of a blank incident report. He felt deeply ashamed of his desires and told no one. None of his comrades could hope to understand.

But it was, indeed, a quiet night in Nowhere. But a night was not a book.

"Make something happen, you blistered fool," Detective Belacqua grumbled to himself.

A knock comes upon the door.

Rubbish.

Detective Belacqua pushed back from his desk, his belly perhaps slightly less righteously muscled than it had been when the primordium was new. He wrapped a long scarf the color of cigarette ash around his feathered throat, snatched his black duster from the hook near the door, and abandoned his post—only for a moment—in search of something more fortifying than buttered toast to fuel his furtive ambitions.

He had hardly left the tower when the alarm lamps began to burn.

THIRD TERRACE: THE ENVIOUS

SIXTY-SIX DAYS LATER, *Pietta steps out of her room for the first time. No one has come for her. She has heard no footsteps in the long hall beyond her door. But a kind of rootless fear like thin pale mold forked slowly through her limbs and she could not bring herself to move.*

She measures out the time in bears and glass. Each morning, Pietta places a shard of colored glass on her windowsill. They split the candlelight into harlequin grapeshot, firing volleys of scarlet, cobalt, emerald toward the mountain outside. She has developed a kind of semaphore with the smoke-eaters on those icy slopes; at least, when she moves her arms, they move theirs. But perhaps Pietta is the only one who imagines an alphabet.

Each evening, she watches the bears come in across the mud plain and snuggle against the city for warmth. She does not know where they come in from, only that they do, hundreds of them, and that they are not very like the bears she remembers, though the act of remembering now is like reading a Greek manuscript—slow, laborious, full of transcription errors, clarity coming late and seldom. It is possible bears have always looked like the beasts who rub their enormous flanks against the pockmarked burgundy stone of the city walls as the red stars hiss up in the dusk. But Pietta does not think bears ever had such long stone-silver fur, or that they wore that fur in braids, or that they had a circlet of so many eyes round their heads, or that they had tusks quite so inlaid with gold.

So passes sixty-six days. Glass. Arms. Smoke. Bears.

She gathers together her only belongings and secrets them in the slits and knots of her clothes. Beyond the door of the room belonging to Pietta she finds a hall that splits like a vein into a snarl of staircases. Will she be able to find her way back? The fearful mold begins to grow again, but she stifles it. Burns it out. Descends a black iron spiral stair down, down, to another hall, under an arch into which some skilled hand has carved PENURIES, under which some rather less skilled hand has painted FOR A GOOD TIME FIND BEATRICE. Pietta looks back in the direction she has come. The other side of the stone arch reads TAEDIUM. She will try to remember that she lives in Taedium. Pietta passes beneath Contempt us Mundi and Beatrice's come-hither into a courtyard under the open sky.

The courtyard thrums with people and forbidding candles standing as tall and thick as fir trees, barked in the globs and drips and wind-spatters of their yellow wax. There is a stone bowl near the yawning edge of the terrace, filled with burnt knobs of ancient wood and volcanic rock. People like her move between the tallow monoliths and the stone bowl, wrapped tight in complex charcoal-blue rags and falcon-hoods, but not like her, for they chatter together as though they belong here, as though the harness of here is no surprise to them. They huddle around beaten copper rain barrels, looking up anxiously at the spinning scarlet stars. They pass objects furtively from one hand to the next. They stare out at the constant vastness of the mountain pricked with lantern light before plunging their hands into the bowl and devouring the charred and ashen joints of wood.

Pietta is noticed. A middle-aged man with an unusual nose and arthritic hands pulls her urgently behind one of the cathedral-column candles. She can see blue eyes beneath the mesh of his blinders.

"What did you bring?" he whispers.

Pietta remembers the feeling of a husband she did not want. She answers: "I don't know what you're talking about." Because she doesn't. She has nothing.

The man sighs and tries again, more kindly, holding her less tightly. "In your bindle. What did you carry with you to Nowhere? Don't be afraid. It's important, my dear, that's all. It is everything."

FOURTH TERRACE: THE GLUTTONOUS

DETECTIVE BELACQUA NAVIGATED the night-crowded halls of the Temeritatis Precinct with ease. The locals parted into ragged blue waves to let him pass. Some held their hands to their mouths, some fell to their knees—but Belacqua knew the difference between awe and reflex. They genuflected because they thought they should. They thought it might help.

The crowd around the automat is thin. Humans didn't eat at the finer establishments. They had no currency. The wonderful glass wall of cool plates and steaming bowls was for the comfort of the strigils, a small luxury in this rather undistinguished outpost. Behind the bank of windows set into two feet of dark abbey stone, Belacqua saw a woman with the head of an osprey move with mindful grace, clearing the old dishes, bringing in the new. Her black and white feathers shone in the kitchen lights.

"What have you got in the way of savory, tonight, Giacama? I'm in the mood for salt."

Giacama pushed aside the little window on an empty compartment of the automat. Her mild seabird eyes floated in the glass as though they were the night special.

"Good evening, Detective. I've got a lovely rind of cheese from the gluttons' farms. It's all yours."

"Detective Inspector soon," Belacqua said with a flush of pride. He took his crescent of cheese from the window. Only then did he see the young girl staring up at him through the blinders of her falcon-hood, rubbing anxiously at the backs of her hands.

"Are you a demon?" she whispered. "Are you an angel?"

"Naw," Belacqua answered around a mouthful of white cheese. "I work for a living."

The child might have said more, but a commotion disturbed the evening throngs. A strapping man with a raven's grand face strode toward Detective Belacqua, out of breath, trembling in his black finery. Sergeant Tomek—but in all the aeons of known existence Belacqua had only known his sergeant to be a calm and rather cold sort.

Sergeant Tomek clasped his hand roughly, his raven's face handsome and dark and puffed with excitement or terror. His black ruff bristled.

"Sir, I hate to trouble you at this hour and I know you hate to be interrupted when you're…working…but something terrible's happened. Something dreadful. You must come."

Detective Belacqua tightened his long grey scarf and smoothed back his own rumpled feathers.

"Calm down, Tomek. You'll spook the poor creatures. Just present the facts of the case and we'll see to it with a quickness. What can possibly have you in such a state?"

Sergeant Tomek stared at the wine-dark flagstone floor. He swallowed several times before whispering wretchedly:

"A body, Sir."

"Well, that's hardly cause for all this upset, Sergeant. We're nothing but bodies round here. Bodies, bodies everywhere, and hardly one can think. Go home and get some sleep, man, we'll see to it in the morning."

The raven-headed sergeant sighed and tried again, more miserably and more quietly than before.

"A *dead* body, Sir. A corpse."

Detective Belacqua blinked. "Don't be stupid, Tomek."

"Sir. I know how it sounds." Tomek glanced around at the passing folk, but most gave the policemen a wide berth. "But there is a dead woman lying face down with her throat cut and there's blood everywhere and *things* on her back and she is very, *very* dead."

Detective Belacqua grimaced with embarrassment. "Sergeant Tomek," he hissed, "they can't *die*. It's not possible. They steal, they cheat, they vandalize, they fornicate, they lie, they curse God, but they do not kill and they do not die. That's not how it *works*. That's the whole *point*."

But the raven would only say: "Come see."

Detective Belacqua thought of his novel and his dry red wine waiting safe and warm for him in the watchtower. They called to him. But he knew what duty was, even if he did not know how to begin his opus. "Where is she?"

Sergeant Tomek trilled unhappily. He ran his hand along the black blade of his beak.

"Outside."

FIFTH TERRACE: THE COVETOUS

PIETTA FOLLOWS THE *man with the unusual nose. They have exchanged names. His is Savonarola. He spits the syllables of himself as though he hates their taste. He leads her through a door marked CONTEMPTUS MUNDI.*

"My home," he sighs, "such as it is."

"I live in Taedium," Pietta answers, and it is such a relief that she has remembered it, that the information was there when she reached for it, solid, heavy, cold to the touch. She almost stumbles with the sweetness of it. Savonarola grunts in sympathy.

"Too bad for you. You'll find no fraternity among your neighbors, then. They keep to themselves in Taedium. They do not come to cloister, they do not trade, they do not attend the rainstorms. They don't even take Christmas with the rest of us. But perhaps that's to your taste. Taedium, Taedium, so close to Te Deum, you know. What passes for cleverness around here."

Pietta remembers the feeling of longing for something lost before she ever had it. "I have made friends with a man on the mountain. He moves his arms. I move mine. We are up to the letter G. But there is no G in my name, so he cannot know me. I am...I am lonely. I thought someone would come for me."

"No one on the mountain is your friend, girl," snaps Savonarola, and they emerge into a wide piazza full of long tables with thick legs and glass lanterns the size of parish churches shining out into the mist of the night. Wind pulls at them like a beggar pleading. The tables are full of handkerchiefs unknotted, their contents laid out lovingly, more men and women in charcoal-blue rags closely guarding each little clutch of junk.

Savonarola introduces her to a small, dark woman with a beautiful, delicate mouth. The woman is called Awo. She has an extraneous thumb on her left hand, small and withered and purpled. Pietta touches the objects on Awo's handkerchief, running her hands over them gently. They awake feelings in her that do not belong to her: a drinking cup, a set of sewing needles, a red brick, a pot of white paint, several ballpoint pens, and a length of faded paisley fabric. When Pietta touches the sewing needles, she remembers the feeling of embroidering her daughter's wedding dress. But Pietta had only sons, and they are babies yet.

"You have lovely things," Pietta whispers.

"Oh, they aren't mine," Awo says. The wind off of the mountain dampens all their voices. "I long ago traded away the objects I brought with me into this place. And traded what I got in return, and traded that again, and so on and so forth and again and again. Everything in the world, it turns out, is escapable except economy. Those objects which were once so dear to me I can no longer even name. Did I come with a cup? A belt? A signet ring? I cannot say. Now, what will you give me for my fabric? Savonarola says you have scissors."

Pietta touches her ribs, where she hid the shears. She looks away, into the crystal doors of a massive lantern and the flames within. "But what are these things? What is this place? Why do I have this pair of scissors in this city at this moment?"

Savonarola and Awo glance at one another.

"They are your last belongings," Savonarola says. "The things you lingered over on your last day."

Rain comes to the city. It falls from every dark cloud and splashes against the lanterns, the tables, the buyers and the sellers. Everyone runs for their rain barrels, dragging them into the piazza, the copper bottoms scraping the stone. The rain that falls is not water but wine, red and strong.

Pietta remembers the feeling of dying alone.

SIXTH TERRACE: THE WRATHFUL

DETECTIVE BELACQUA STOOD over the woman's body. He let a long, low whistle out of his beak and reached into his pocket for a cigarette. Sergeant Tomek opened his black jaws; a ball of blue flame floated on his tongue. Belacqua lit his wrinkled, broken stump of tobacco and breathed deep.

"Isn't there someone else we can hand this off to? Someone higher up. Someone…better?"

Tomek stared down at the corpse as it lay face down on the slick blue-black cobblestones of the road that connects the city and the mountain. The blue of the gas lamps made her congealing blood look like cold ink.

"You had the watch, Detective Inspector," he said, emphasizing his soon-to-come promotion. But they both knew this woman, the very fact of her, made all ranks and systems irrelevant.

Belacqua scratched the longer feathers at the nape of his neck. The clouds boiled and swam above them, raveling, unraveling, spooling grey into grey. He could not remember the last time he'd set foot outside the city. Probably sometime around the invention of music. The air smelled of crackling pre-lightning ozone and, bizarrely, nutmeg fruits, when they are wet and new and look like nothing so much as black, bleeding hearts.

"Is she going to…rot, do you think?" Sergeant Tomek mused.

"Well, I don't bloody well know, do I?" the man with the heron's head snapped back. Detective Belacqua had closed thousands of cases in his infinite career. The Nowhere locals got up to all manner of nonsense and he didn't blame them in the least. On the contrary, he felt deeply for the poor blasted things, and when it fell to him to hand out punishments, he was as lenient as the rules allowed. He was a creature of rules, was Belacqua. But the vast majority of his experience lay in vandalism, petty theft, minor assault, and public drunkenness. Every so often something spicier came his way: attempted desertion, adultery, assaults upon the person of a strigil. But never *this*. Of course never *this*. *This* was against the rules. The first rule. The foundational rule. So foundational that until tonight he had not even thought to call it a rule at all.

Detective Belacqua knelt to examine the body. He suspected that was the sort of thing to do. Just pretend it was a bit of burglary. Nothing out of the ordinary. Scene of the crime and all that. Good. First step. Go on, then.

"Right. Erm. The deceased? Should we say deceased? Are you writing this down, Tomek? For God's sake. The, em, *re*-deceased is female, approximately twenty-odd-something years of age. Is that right? It's so hard to tell with people. I don't mean to be insensitive, of course—"

"Oh, certainly not, sir."

"It's just that they all look a *little* alike, don't they, Sergeant?"

Tomek looked distinctly uncomfortable. His dark ruff bristled. "About forty, I should say, Detective Inspector."

"Ah, yes, thank you. Forty years of age, brunette, olive complected, quite tall, nearly six foot as I reckon it. Her hood seems to have gone missing and her clothes are...well, there's not much left of them, is there? Just write 'in disarray.' Spare her some dignity." Now that he'd begun, Belacqua found he could hardly stop. It came so naturally, like a song. "Cause of death appears to be a lateral cut across the throat and exsanguination, though where she got all that blood I can't begin to think. Bruises, well, everywhere, really. But particularly bad on her belly and the backs of her thighs. And there's the...markings. Do you think that happened before or, well, I mean to say, *after*, Tomek?"

The raven-sergeant's black eyes flickered helplessly between the corpse and the detective. "Sir," he swallowed finally, "how can we possibly tell?"

Belacqua remembered the book he'd devoured so greedily in that sad little vandal's cell, the book without a cover and yellow-stained pages, a book in which many people had died and gotten their dead selves puzzled over.

"I've an idea about that, Sergeant," he said finally. "Write down that she's got *patience* carved into her back in Greek—not too neatly, either, it looks like someone went at her with a pair of scissors—then get the boys to carry her up to my office before anyone else decides to have a look out their window and starts ringing up a panic. Carefully! Don't...don't *damage* her any more than she already is." Belacqua gazed up at the great mountain that faced his city, into the wind and the lantern lights and the constant oncoming night. "Poor lamb," he sighed, and when the patrolmen came to lift her up, he pressed his feathered cheek against hers for a moment, his belly full of something he very well thought might be grief.

SEVENTH TERRACE: THE EXCOMMUNICATE

SAVONAROLA, AWO, AND *Pietta sit around a brimming rain barrel. The storm has passed. The sky is, for once, almost clear, barnacled with fiery stars. They drink with their hands, cupping fingers and dipping into the silky red wine, slurping without shame. The dead know how to savor as the living never can.*

The wine is heavy but dry. Much debate has filled the halls of Nowhere over the centuries—is it a Beaujolais? Montrachet? Plain Chianti? Savonarola is firmly in the Montrachet camp. Awo thinks it is most certainly an Algerian Carignan. Pietta thinks it is soft, and sour, and kind.

"Memory is a bad houseguest in this place," Savonarola says softly. Red raindrops streak his face like a statue of a saint weeping blood. "For you, the worst of it will come in twenty years or so. Dying is the blow, memory is the bruise. It takes time to develop, to reach a full and purple lividity. Around eighty years in Nowhere, give or take. Then the pain will take you and it will not give you back again for autumns upon winters. You will know everything you were, and everything you lost. But the bruise of having lived will fade, too, and your time in Nowhere will dwarf your time in the world such that all life will seem to be a letter you wrote as a child, addressed to a stranger, and never delivered."

Awo sucks the wine from her brown, slender fingers. "Awo Alive feels to me like a character in a film I saw when I was young and loved. Awo and her husband Kofi who wore glasses and her three daughters and seven grandchildren and her degree in electrical engineering and the day she saw Accra for the first time, Accra and the sea. I am fond of all of them, but I see them now from very far away. If I remember anything, if I tilt my head or say a word as she would have done, it is like quoting from that film, not like being Awo."

"I went to the noose long before such things as moving pictures could be imagined," Savonarola admits.

Pietta thinks for a long while, watching herself in the reflection of the wine. "And what of the mountain? What of the men and women there? Very well, I am dead. Where is Paradise? Where is Hell? Where is the fire or the clouds? Is this Purgatory?"

*Awo touches Pietta's cheek. "*Me broni ba, *that mountain out there is Purgatory. Someday, maybe, we'll go there and start our long hitchhike of the soul up, up, up into the sea of glass and the singing and the rings of eyes and the eternal surrealist discotheque of the saved. Nowhere is for us sad sacks who died too quick to repent, or naughties like Savonarola, who was so stuck up himself that he got excommunicated. And here we sit, with nothing to do but drink the rain, for three hundred times our living years."*

Savonarola cracks his gnarled knuckles. "I admit, if some man in Florence had discovered a way to film the moon rising over the ripples of the Arno, or the building of Brunelleschi's ridiculous dome, or even one of my own sermons—and I was very good, in my day—I would have set fire to the reels with all the rest, and I would have rejoiced. All in which the eye longs to revel is vanity, vanity. Only now do I long for such things, for something to see besides this stone, something to touch besides the dead, something to hear besides talk, talk, talk. What I would not give in this moment for one glimpse of Botticelli's pornography, one vulgar passage of lecherous Boccaccio, one beautiful deck of gambling cards. God, I think, is irony."

"I will go mad," Pietta whispers.

"Yes," agrees Awo.

Pietta pleads: "But it will pass? It will pass and I will go to the mountain and take up a lantern and begin to climb. It will pass and we will go—we will go on, up, out. Progress."

Savonarola pinches his nose between his fingers and smiles softly. He has never been a man given to smiling. He had only done it ten or eleven times in total. But all in secret, Girolamo Savonarola possesses one of the loveliest and kindest smiles in all the long history of joy.

"Do the math, my child. Three hundred times the span of a human life we must rattle the stones of Nowhere—since the death of Solomon and the invention of the alphabet, no one yet has gotten out."

EIGHTH TERRACE: THE AMBITIOUS

IN THE CITY called Nowhere, a man with the head of a heron sat comfortably in the topmost room of the policemen's tower, watching a corpse rot.

It was slow going.

In all honesty, Detective Belacqua had no real idea what to expect. He only recalled from his penny paperback that human bodies did, indeed, under normal circumstances, rot, and they did it according to a set of rules, at a regular, repeatable, measurable rate, and from that you could reason out a lot of other things that mattered in a murder investigation. Since he had run face-first into a circumstance well beyond normal, Belacqua could not rely on the niceties of rigor mortis, even if he understood them, thus, he now devised a method to discover the rules of decomposition in Nowhere.

Sergeant Tomek humbly asked to be allowed to stay after the patrolmen returned to their posts. The detective agreed, but sent him for coffee straightaway so that he could gather his thoughts without the raven-boy fretting all over him. Belacqua lifted the corpse easily—they never did weigh very much in Nowhere. He laid her out on three desks pushed together, and, though he felt rather silly about it afterward, folded her hands over her chest and arranged her long, dark hair tenderly, as though it mattered. And it did matter to him, very much, though he couldn't think why. He dipped a rough cloth into the wash basin in the officers bathroom and cleaned the worst of the grime and blood out of her wounds, going back and forth from the basin with a steady rhythm that calmed his nerves and arranged the furniture of his mind in a contemplative configuration. After all this was done, he drew a pair of scissors from the watchman's desk and plunged them quickly between the dead woman's ribs on the left side of her torso. When he pulled them out again, red pearls seeped from the wound, falling to the flagstones with a terrible clatter.

"Huh," said Sergeant Tomek. He stood in the doorway, holding a cup of scalding coffee in each hand.

And then, the policemen waited. Sergeant Tomek waited at the window, transfixed. Detective Belacqua waited at his typewriter, ready to record any changes in the body. To write the novel of this woman's putrefaction, chapter by chapter.

It was a quiet night in Nowhere.

Days and nights knocked at the door and went away unanswered. The corpse remained the same for a very long time. Tomek gave up over and over, crying out that it was too sad to be borne, too miserable a thing to stare at, and Nowhere too timeless a place to ever tolerate decay. But he always returned, with coffee or tea or hot buttered toast, and the two strigils resumed their longest watch.

By the next Sabbath, it had begun. On the first day, the edges of the woman's wounds flushed the color of opium flowers. On the second day, her hair turned to snow. On the third day, the stench began, and the watch-room filled intolerably with the smell of frankincense, and then wild honey, and finally a deep and endless forest, loamy and ancient. On the fourth day, Belacqua held his ear to her mouth and heard the sound of gulls crying. On the fifth day, her wounds turned ultramarine and began to seep golden ink. On the sixth day, her sternum cracked and a white lizard with blue eyes crawled out of her, which Tomek caught and trapped in a wine bottle. And on the seventh day, a small tree bloomed and broke out of her mouth, which gave a single silver fruit. This, Belacqua harvested and placed in his coffee cup for further study. By the morning of the eighth day, all that remained of her were bones, hard and clear and faceted as if the skeleton had been hacked out of a single diamond.

Belacqua typed and typed and typed. Finally, he spoke, on the day they saw the dead woman's skull emerge like new land rising from the sea.

"Sergeant Tomek, I believe we can safely say that she received the markings on her back pre-mortem. Time of death could not have been sooner than six days before you discovered her."

"And how do you know this, Detective Inspector?"

"If she had been killed later, we would have found the poor girl already turning orange at the edges, or worse. I detected then no discoloration nor any scent nor a lizard nor the sound of seagulls. Unfortunately for us, it could have been any number of days greater than six and we would not know it unless we could somehow kill something else and record its progress. Also when I cut into her, the body produced a quantity of pearls, whereas no pearls were found beside her on the road to Nowhere. Additionally, the gore of my cut shows a distinctly different shade of ultramarine than the carving on her back. Someone wrote *patience* on her while she yet lived, Tomek, and listened to her anguish, and did not stop."

"It is dreadfully morbid," the sergeant sighed. He laid a reverent hand on the delicate foot-bones of the body.

"On the contrary, my boy, it is science, and we have done it! Nothing could be more exciting than discovering, as we have done, that a set of rules lay in place of all eternity without us suspecting them. I assure you these are not the stages of mortal decomposition." Belacqua hurried on before Tomek could wonder how he knew anything about living corpses, and uncover his illicit pursuit of fiction. "This is new. It is ours. It is native to Nowhere. No one else in all the yawning pit of time has ever known what you and I know now. We are, finally, unique. And now we two unique fellows must proceed further on, farther in, and *re*-compose this woman. Her name, her history, her associates, her enemies. What happened to her a fortnight ago, and how?" The detective frowned. "Perhaps we ought to interrogate the lizard."

In its green glass bottle, the pale reptile hissed. It stuck out its blue tongue. The glass fogged with its breath. It said one word, and then steamed away like water.

Virtue.

NINTH TERRACE: THE INCURIOUS

PIETTA HAS BECOME *a birdwatcher. She leaves Awo and Savonarola often to trail silently after the strigils as they move through the city. They are so unlike her. They wear clothes of many colors; they are always busy; they eat. They live in a different Nowhere than she does, one with automats and social clubs and places to be. She makes a study of them. This would be easier if she could bring herself to trade her colored glass or her belt or her scissors for one of Awo's pens or the paper a tall man with very clean teeth wants to sell her, but she cannot. She does not know yet why they are precious, but she knows she doesn't want to give them away, to let them become separate from her forever. She is not ready. So she must try to remember the birds she sees. Osprey. Oriole. Peregrine. Sparrow. Sandpiper. Ibis. Pelican. Starling. Raven. Heron. They are beautiful and they do not see her. To them, she is not Pietta. She is no one. She is blue, like the others, and blindered, like the others, and the only thing she can ever do to catch their attention, to bring their eyes down onto her, is to sin, to commit a crime, to err. When the man with clean teeth tries to steal her glass, the birds come. They smell, absurdly, like expensive perfume, like the counter in a fashionable shop. Their feathers rustle when they move like pages turning. They have no irises. Their voices are very nearly human. A woman with the head of an owl cuts away the sleeve of the man's robe. Now everyone will know he is bad. Pietta is fascinated. But she is afraid to do anything very bad herself.*

She meets Awo and Savonarola in a cloister fifteen years after they first drank wine together out of a barrel. It is a round room in the Largitio Quarter, with a high, domed ceiling, full of grand, tall tables set with empty bowls, safe from the wind and the slow, trudging lights on the mountain. Pietta longs to eat. She is never hungry, but she remembers the feeling of eating. Of tasting. A few dozen blue-ragged souls pool their objects on a table, picking and sorting. They are trying to assemble a chess set, though fights have broken out already over whether a pepper pot or a bone whistle or pocket Slovakian dictionary makes a better king. Nothing in Nowhere is important, so nothing is more important than the pepper pot and the whistle and the dictionary. Pietta watches them and imagines the players as birds. She hates chess. Savonarola agrees, though he plays anyway.

"Chess allows the frivolous to pretend their toys have deep meaning. The only honest game is tag," he grouses, while taking an exquisitely-chinned teenaged girl's queen. Both the sleeves have been torn from her dress.

"What are the strigils?" Pietta asks.

Savonarola snorts. "Where I come from they're dull blades you use to scrape the sweat and grime from your back in a bath-house. Not that I ever used a bath-house, a seething puddle of greased sin. Not that I haven't scoured the breadth of Nowhere for a damned bath."

Awo has enough sewing needles to man her entire side, pawns and all. She sticks them upright in the soft wood of the table, two neat silver rows. "He can't tell you. His theology was far too prim and tidy to contain bird-headed men in trenchcoats. I can't tell you either. But if you suppose there are demons in one place and angels in the other, wouldn't you also suppose something has to live here? Something has to be natural to Nowhere."

"They came when the first people arrived," says the girl with the lovely chin. She moves her knight (a mechanical library stamp). "And Nowhere was only an

empty plain without a city. They are meant to make this place somewhat less than a Hell, and to keep us from making a Heaven of it."

"How do you know that?" Savonarola snaps.

The girl shrugs. "I asked one. When I got arrested for writing my name a thousand times over the entrance to Benevolentia Sector. She had a wren's face. She said they were formed not from clay like us nor fire nor light but from the stuff of the void on the face of the world, and they had not the breath of life but the heat of life and the fluid of it, and they had a beginning but no end, an alpha and an ellipsis, and then she drank my wine and said I was pretty and the truth was she didn't remember very much more about being born than I did and she read all that off a historical plaque on the upper levels, but strigils have to keep up appearances, and they wouldn't be worth much if we thought they were stuck here just like us only they didn't even know how it happened to them, only what they had to do, so if you ask me, talking to a strigil is not so useful as you'd expect, and they drink a lot. Checkmate."

That night, Pietta goes to be with Savonarola, because everything is the same and everything is nothing and what is the point of not doing anything now?

TENTH TERRACE: THE MERCILESS

DETECTIVE BELACQUA STOOD in a hexagonal stone cell like all the other hexagonal stone cells. He looked out an arched window like all the other arched windows. He picked up and put down several meaningless objects: a brass key, a cracked, worn belt, a stone figure of a child seated in a chair, shards of colored glass. Sergeant Tomek assured him this was the dead woman's room, but it told him nothing—how could it? She would have traded away anything authentically her own long ago. What remained was simply someone else's rubbish. They had a name, and only that by process of elimination. Quite simply: who was missing? It had taken weeks of interrogation, more contact with the locals than Belacqua had ever suffered before, their fearful whispers, their purposeless glazed eyes, their way of drifting off mid-sentence as though they'd forgotten language. But they got their name, from the old furioso Savonarola, who actually wept when Tomek asked whether he had lost anyone of late.

What was he supposed to do now? Everyone in the policemen's union expected he could find some simple solution to it all. But the thing of it was, in his paperback, discovering the identity of the corpse opened other doors, doors within doors, obvious rivers of inquiry to dive into, personal histories to unearth, secrets, secrets everywhere. But her name gave him nothing but this room, and this room was a dry river and a closed door.

"Who was she?" Sergeant Tomek demanded of Savonarola, who sat below a great candle, staring at his open hands. "Who did she love? Who did she hate? What was she in life? What did she do to pass the time?"

But the old friar just closed his hands and opened them again. Closed. Open. "She loved me and Awo. She hated chess. She invented a semaphore alphabet with a man climbing the mountain, though I'm reasonably sure he's not in on the scheme. If she remembered her life, she never told it to me. She's so new, you know. Like a baby. When I look at her I see the plainness of white linen, being without vanity."

"Everyone has vanity," said Sergeant Tomek. "Everyone here."

The old man looked up cannily at the strigils. Behind his blinders, his eyes shone. "Do you?"

Detective Belacqua squatted down on his heels. He had a suspicion, and he knew how to work on friars. You had to awe them. Morning picked at the stitches of dark. If there had been any true songbirds in Nowhere, they would have sung. Belacqua fixed his black heron's eyes on the hooded soul before him. "Do you remember the founding of Florence, Girolamo? That is where you lived, is it not?"

"Don't be absurd. Florence was old when I was young."

"Quite so. Yet I do remember the founding of Nowhere. Did you know that? Some of us do, some of us don't, it's a funny old thing, like whether or not someone like you remembers losing his baby teeth. A toss of the cognitive dice. But I remember. Lucky me! You see, the plain, the *plain* is the thing. The mud flat going on and on out there forever. The handful of trees—as few and as far between as living planets in empty space. The old riverbeds. Somewhere out beyond the road and the mountain there's a black salt flat a light year across. The clouds. The stars. And people didn't come right away. It wasn't like you'd imagine—nothing, and then hordes all at once. People just died like dogs or fish or dinosaurs until, I don't know, what would you say, Tomek? Around the time they started painting ibexes on cave walls?"

The sergeant nodded his dark head.

"Well, my friend, you can just imagine what a mess it all was in the beginning. No system. No rules. Some people could go up the mountain as quick as you like, and some couldn't, and some could go down into the coal pits, and some couldn't, and some just milled around like cows down here, and if they tried to go on up, they found themselves turned right back around facing the infinite floodplain with not an inch gained, but no one really had a bead on the whys and wherefores of the whole business. Cosmology just sort of *happened* to you, on you get. And the people down here in the mud, they just sat there or laid there or stood there for ages, really, proper ages, with nothing to do. That's the worst thing for a person. To get crushed under the weight of endless useless days. Between you and me, I don't think anyone really thought it through. I bet you'd rather have a fellow spearing you with a flaming trident every hour on the hour—at least then, something would *happen*. Am I right? I believe I am. So these poor souls fought and fucked and screamed for awhile, because those're pretty good ways to stop yourself thinking about the existential chasm of time. But they didn't bleed and they didn't come and nobody answered them, so eventually, they started digging in the mud with whatever they'd brought in their bindles, which back then, was mostly stone tools. They pulled up the stones of the moral universe and put them one on top of the other, and I'll tell you a secret, Giro. For awhile, I think this was a happier place than Heaven, when they were putting down those rocks. But happiness isn't the point. Not here. If we'd let you keep on with it, your lot would have built city after city, an empire of the dead, and it would look just like the world out here, only filled with legions of the mediocre and the stalled out and the unrepentant and whatever you're supposed to be. So we got called up, me and the sergeant here and all the other strigils. Hatched out of an egg of ice, I'm told, though that sort of insider talk is above my pay grade. And we came bearing *order*, Girolamo. We came with rules in our beaks. We built Nowhere together, strigils and humans, the dead and the divine." Detective Belacqua put one hand on his chest and the other over Savonarola's withered heart. "*Me* and *you*. A closed system. A city on the hill. And I think it's *beautiful*. But you don't, do you? You hate it, like you hated everything you ever clapped your eyes on. Except *her*. So here's what I think, friend. I think you found a way to get her out. God only knows what. But you did it to her and now she's gone and if you tell me what happened, no one will be angry—we quite literally cannot be angry. Who could blame you? It's the nature of love, I should imagine."

Girolamo Savonarola laughed.

"You ought to write a book," he giggled, but when Sergeant Tomek began to strip his charcoal-blue robes from him, the friar began to sob instead.

ELEVENTH TERRACE: THE SORROWFUL

IT HITS HER *while she kisses Awo's naked shoulder, Awo, whose cell Pietta visits far more than any other, though in recent years she's visited many. She even found Beatrice, who turned out to be very shy and fond of rain. It is something to do, and Pietta is desperate for* acts. *Acts have befores and afters. They mark her movement through this air and these stones. She has tried other sins, but they are more difficult in Nowhere. She cannot bring herself to envy anyone, and wants for nothing; she cannot eat and she cannot strive. So there is this, and though she feels it only dimly, she holds on very tight.*

Pietta and Awo lie together in the lantern-light of Purgatory and there is a moment when she does not know who she is, not really, and then that moment burns itself out. Pietta remembers the feeling of being Pietta. She remembers being small and she remembers being big. All of the things that ever happened to her stack up in her mind like stones on a sea shore, tottering, tottering...Pietta is getting born in a room with poppies painted on the wall,

Pietta is small and delighted and running through the snow, forgetting her mother completely and throwing herself face first into the soft powder, Pietta is receiving her first communion and coughing when she oughtn't because the incense tickles her nose, and she is helping her father tend his bees in their fields, and she is walking in the woods at night with a boy named Milo, and she is living in a house by the sea with Milo who has grown very distant with her, even though she is pregnant and they should be happy, and Pietta is giving birth to her son in a room with ultramarine flowers next to her bed in a cheap, gold-painted vase, and Pietta is walking in the summer, alone, for once, when she sees a white lizard hiding in the shade of a long, flat stone, and she takes it home and gives it a name and shows it to her son and keeps it in an old fish tank even though Milo says it is stupid and lizards have no hearts and Pietta is wearing her mother's diamond ring every day even though they could use the money because no amount of snow could make her forget, not really, and Milo is so angry with her so often, every thing she does is the wrong thing, and though she still loves him she grows very still inside, she feels as though she is trapped in ice and cannot move, even as she cooks and cleans and runs to the shops and teaches her classes and she is getting older all the time and then Pietta is teaching her son to play chess with a set made to look like a famous medieval set with funny-looking people in funny-looking chairs, she is cutting out the green felt for his Halloween costume because he insists upon being a tree this year, she is pouring herself the last of the red wine and locking up the liquor cabinet with a brass key, she is putting away her husband's clothes, his coats, his socks, his old belt, and thinking that she should have bought him a new one long ago, and she will now, she will, because tomorrow will be the day she wakes up out of the ice and becomes herself again, she knows it will happen all at once, like a big silver fruit cracking open, and there she'll be, good as new, even though she thought the same yesterday, and the day before, and the day before that, and when the glazier's truck hits Pietta in the high street she thinks, for a moment, that all that beautiful, shattered, colored glass lying around her is the ice breaking at last, the fruit breaking open, with Pietta whole and alive inside, but it is not.

TWELFTH TERRACE: THE GLUTTONOUS

IT WAS A quiet night in Nowhere.

Detective Inspector Belacqua and Corporal Tomek shared the watch and supper and half a bottle of white wine which both felt very excited about. The lamp stood full of oil, the basin full of fresh water, the pens full of ink, and all was as it should be.

Belacqua had many times almost asked his raven-headed friend how he felt about their one great case. Tomek never mentioned it. Occasionally, in their rounds, they would catch a glimpse of Savonarola, naked and shunned, drifting miserably among the crowds. Once, Belacqua himself had nearly run right into the woman called Awo, who stared at him as though she could punch through his delicate skull with her gaze. He hadn't been able to bear that; he'd run. Run, from a local, a dead woman with nothing but her rags. And yet it had happened.

So time, in its shapeless, corpulent, implacable way, bore on in Nowhere. And only when he was alone did it trouble Belacqua how much they never understood about the incident, the monstrous hole at the bottom of the case file through which everything sensible tumbled out. Into this hole, he began to drop the words of his novel, one by one, painstakingly, the only story he knew, a story without an end. Which, he supposed, was to be expected, considering the author.

When it came time to open the bottle of white wine, the policemen found the cork encased in awfully thick black wax, too thick for fingernails and too awkward for beaks.

"Nothing to it," Corporal Tomek laughed, and drew a small pair of scissors out of the inner pocket of his coat. He worked the little blades deftly round the mouth and wiggled them up underneath till the cake of wax fell away.

They were a perfectly ordinary pair of scissors. A little tarnished and stained, but utterly usual and serviceable, like Tomek himself. Detective Inspector Belacqua had no reason to notice them in the least. And yet, he did. He could not stop noticing them. Small enough for delicate work. For carving. *Was* that tarnish, that black smear along the shears?

Belacqua cleared his throat. "Has it ever woken you nights, Tomek, that we never discovered how the old man did it?"

"Did what, sir?"

"Killed a dead woman. There had to be a method—that's the whole thing, you know, means, motive, and opportunity—that's the *entire* thing of it. And the means just...got away from us, didn't it?"

"I suppose it did. But I wouldn't worry. It's never happened again. It's not like we had an epidemic on our hands, Belacqua. And if we had, well, you know. No one harmed but the dead. The chief would have sorted it out, I'm sure." Tomek poured the wine and handed a glass across the desk. Belacqua just looked at it.

"I just want to *know*, that's all. Haven't you ever wanted to know anything so badly it ate you away until there was nothing left of you but the *not* knowing?"

The raven grimaced. "Just drink your wine, Detective Inspector."

Belacqua did not blink. He thought he ought to feel something in the pit of his stomach, but all he felt was the not knowing, the canker of it, working its way through him like rot.

"How did you meet her?" Detective Inspector Belacqua whispered.

Tomek put down the glasses, very carefully, as though, in his hands, they might break.

THIRTEENTH TERRACE: THE LUSTFUL

PIETTA BLUDGEONS THE *wall over and over, jamming her scissors into the wine-dark stone. Chips and chunks fly away as she gouges the skin of the city. The thudding and scraping of her blows fill the endless halls of Taedium.*

They care about very little, Pietta knows. But they will care about this. Vandalizing Nowhere brings them running, so she is not surprised when a man with the head of a raven steps through her door and snatches the scissors from her hands with a strength that would snap all the bones of her wrist, if the bones of her wrist could still break.

"That's enough, miss," Sergeant Tomek says crisply, professionally. Their faces are close as kissing. Raven and girl; pale, bloodless lips and a mouth like black shears.

"It's not fair," Pietta snarls at him. "All I ever did wrong was be sad."

Outside, the man on the mountain eats his smoke. Tomek is on top of her by the time he begins to move his arms in straight, strident lines, and she does not see.

P-I-E-T-T-A?

FOURTEENTH TERRACE: THE CONTEMPTUOUS

"WE ALL HAVE our ways of coping with it," Tomek said, running his finger around the lip of his glass.

"With what?" Belacqua scowled.

"Eternity," answered the raven slowly. "You have your novel—oh, for God's sake, we all know. I have my research. It's wrong, you know, everything, all of this. At least they lived, fucked something up well and good enough to end up here. We're here…for what? Why? To punish what sin? The only difference between them and us is we wear better clothes. I can't bear it any more than they can. And it's worse, it's worse for us, Belacqua. We've just enough spark in us to draw up a rough sketch of feeling, just a basic set, nothing too detailed: duty, loyalty, a smear of free will, a little want, a little envy, just enough to know somebody else got to see what a summer looks like, but not enough for the cosmos to even look at us, for one second, as anything but lock and keys. And it never ends for us. Don't you see? They all have the hope of progress, of the *climb*. This is it, just this, nothing else, forever. I was so *bored*, Belacqua."

Tomek began to pace, tugging at his feathers, half-preening, half-tearing.

"And so I began to think. Just for the last couple of thousand years. I began to plan a way to murder a person. It's a big enough problem to take up centuries. Could it even be done? *They* can't, certainly. One punches the other in the nose and it's like punching ice cream. Nothing. Not even a mark. But I am a strigil. There is no record of what I can do because no one has ever cared enough to find out. Do your job, little birdie, get back to us at the end of everything for your performance review. What would happen if a strigil sinned? Would there be consequences? And if I could do it, if, ontologically speaking, it would be allowed to occur, how? These are worthy questions! The first experiment was obvious. I broke a man's neck in Oboedientia Sector. For a minute, I thought I'd gotten it right on my first go. But no, he just sort of shivered and put his head right and went on his way. It seemed the rules held for me as well as him. After that I kept it all in my head. The project. I thought it out while the Renaissance idiots poured in, while I walked my beat, while I watched you fumble with a sad little dime store potboiler in the corner like one of the chronic masturbators down in Desidia. Nothing physical would do it. I should have realized that—we do not move in the realm of the physical. I had to act upon the nature of a soul, to alter it so that it could not remain whole. And it would work—Belacqua, this is the important thing! It would work because of that smear of free will, that tiny table scrap of self a strigil owns. I have to be able to act freely, or else I could not arrest or judge or mete out punishment. You have to be allowed to plunk away at your silly stories, because not even the font of all can build a being of judgment without building a being of perversity."

Tomek put his hands on the window sill and let the wind off the mud plain buffet his face.

"When I met Pietta I knew she would let me do anything to her. She was in despair. They all are, for awhile, but hers was frozen and depthless, a continuation of who she had always been, just spooling on into the black forever. And she was right. It's not fair. It's all grotesque. That little spit of living and all this ocean of penance. She wanted it, Belacqua. She did."

"I doubt that very much, Corporal."

"You don't understand. She didn't care. She saw the writing on the wall and the writing said: *Fuck This Place.* She just wanted something to happen. We ran through all the sins first. I fucked her right away—small mercy that we are not built sexless as the angels. Lust is the easiest. I cleaned out the automat and shoved it all down her throat till cream and syrup and relish and grease poured down her chest. She puked it all up, of course, the dead can't eat. Then on to the next like kids at a fairground—we hurled loathing and envy at each other, at the mountain, perfectly honest, more profanity than grammar could hold. I drew up a rage and beat her though no bruises came up. We skipped sloth since Nowhere is the home and hearth of sloth, and Belacqua, nothing I could do could make that woman proud. But it was all useless anyway, her flesh took it all as calmly as water. And so I had to retreat and think again.

"Solutions come so strangely, Belacqua. They steal in. Just the way you saw my scissors and knew what I'd done, your mind leaping over your habits and your inertia to arrive at a conclusion that is as much dream as logic, I knew. I knew how to kill my Pietta. I returned to her that night. I held her in my arms, and, one by one, I buried her in virtues. I gave her all my belongings freely and her nose shot blood onto the flagstones. I cradled her chastely with no thought of her body and bruises rose up on her thighs. I groveled before her and before her I was nothing, and her fingers snapped. I tended her patiently while she screamed, and upomovn carved itself into her back. I persevered, and my diligence choked her like hands. I whispered to her all the kindnesses her husband withheld, that her son, being a child, could not imagine, and the extraordinary thing was I *meant* them, Belacqua. I meant them with all my being. I loved her and her throat split side to side like a pomegranate. Then I shoved her out the window and watched her fall. I pushed her from this world, and all the violence on her body was but the marks of her passage. Neither virtue nor sin can be committed in this place. Nowhere cannot bear it. What they do to one another matters little enough—they have chosen their course and proceed along it, stupid and wasteful and unfair as it is. But I am neither alive nor dead, neither mortal nor immortal, just meanly made, with the barest thought. And so are you, Belacqua. The meanly made may sin—who could expect better? Sin is easy. But for me—for us—to act with virtue is a violence to the whole of existence. And now she is gone and my questions answered. *Nothing happened*. I was not punished. I was not even found out. I am not morally culpable, because He will not deign to look at me long enough to condemn. When an angel does wrong, Hell must be invented out of whole cloth to contain his sorry carcass. But we? We are nothing, and no one. And I think it is *beautiful*."

FIFTEENTH TERRACE: THE FORGETFUL

THERE IS A *grinding sound before she appears, like stone against stone. One moment there is nothing, the next there is Pietta, though if she heard that name now, she would not recognize it, nor even comprehend the idea of a word used to signify a person. Her mind is a silver fruit lying clean and open, without seed or rot or juice. She opens her eyes and her eyes are black, black and several, ringed round her skull like a crown so that she sees everywhere at once. She moves her legs and her legs are powerful, shaggy, heavy with silver, braided, matted fur. Her claws and her tusks scrape on the bedrock beneath the mudplain as she moves with the sleuth of other bears, because nothing in this place has ever happened only once, their ursine sounds and their scents stretching before them toward the city they love but no longer understand, except that it is a warm place in the night, a heart beating in a bloodless land, and when they touch the walls, they remember, faintly, distantly, the feeling of being loved.*

SIXTEENTH TERRACE: THE UNYIELDING

DETECTIVE INSPECTOR BELACQUA gave the signal, and every window in Nowhere closed against the man with the raven's head. Tomek's caws and cries far below echoed the length of everything, his pleas, his reasons, all of it swallowed by the grey clouds and the long nothing-and-no-one of the endless mudplain and the red stars beyond. The mountain, for a moment, stood silent, all the lights still and dim.

Belacqua wept against the shutters, and he wept for a century before opening them again.

Two and Two IS SEVEN

MARIBEL LIVED ALONE IN THE Valley of N.

She preferred living alone and she preferred the Valley of N to any other state of being or geographical happenstance she could imagine for herself. It seemed to her that she and the Valley of N had been made to suit one another, like a six-fingered glove and a six-fingered girl. Such a glove would be useless to anyone with five fingers, or three, or eleven, and such a girl would find a glove designed for a two, four, or seven fingered person impossible. Except for her ninety-nine misfortunes, she considered her existence complete and perfect.

Maribel lived in a neglected nonagonal nunnery, in the Neoclassical style, nestled into the nook of the Valley of N. Nine tame waterfalls ran obediently out of the mountains to feed her domestic hydraulics. She kept a garden of nectarine and nutmeg trees, navy bean runners, prickly nopalitos, nightshades of every description, and leafy, spicy green nettles. Very few animals lived in the valley full-time, for Maribel startled and upset them, though she never meant to. But occasionally, some tourists happened by. Narcoleptic nightingales would sing briefly in her garden, nitwitted newts would nod off on the flat rocks, nihilistic numbats would nuzzle under thickets, nostalgic natterjack toads would croak of days long gone by, and nimble nyala with twisted horns would graze nervously on the nutritious narcissus and noble nasturtiums that grew so well at the mouth of the valley, before bolting off to someplace where Maribel wasn't.

This was nineteenth among Maribel's ninety-nine misfortunes: no animal could love her.

Each morning, Maribel rose with the sun and went about her obligations. She took her obligations extremely seriously, though the King had not come to inspect the workings of the Valley of N for many years. In the beginning, he had come almost every day. He could hardly wait to leave his noisy, crowded palace in the City of T and sink into the peace and beauty of the Valley of N. The King would tinker in the nunnery like a common husband, mend the pipes and hang new doors, chase the nearsighted nutria from the thatching, whitewash the stone path that wound all the length of the green valley floor. Then he would walk up and down the path with his hands clasped behind his back, listening to the joys and grievances of the citizens he had brought to settle here, and tell Maribel how proud he was of her work.

This was ninth among Maribel's ninety-nine misfortunes: that the King never visited her anymore.

Some nights in the nunnery, she almost convinced herself that he never would return, and hang him for a penny anyway. She could do what she liked now, even neglect or abuse the other citizens of the Valley of N, even neglect them forever, or kill them outright, seeing they really were such a bother. But then she would hear a branch crack in the deep woods beyond the garden of nectarines, a crack like the one she would hear if a large royal foot were to fall in the forest, and guilt would flood her insides like a flash storm, and the next morning she would put on her nocknail boots like always, balance her basket on her hip, and make her rounds.

Maribel suspected she was, by now, a very ancient person. It was so hard to tell when the sun rose in the same fashion every day, at the same time, and brought the Valley of N to the same pleasant, agreeable temperature. The years tended to get sidetracked. They ticked by so slowly, and then some secret dam would give and decades would tumble through the valley all at once, too many to count. She could hardly recall any time before the King came to the Valley of N, so distant now were those old days when she was new. At least, Maribel remembered clearly when all the citizens were new, and now even the most polite visitor would admit that they were getting on in years, rusting up and winding down and grinding horribly at odd hours, complaining constantly, running at half-efficiency if they ran at all.

The first cottage on her route belonged to Milosz. The thing that lived there wasn't really called Milosz, but Maribel thought it a very great tragedy not to have a good name, so she gave the thing Milosz and, most days, it answered to Milosz well enough.

Milosz was number twenty-nine among Maribel's ninety-nine misfortunes.

Milosz was extraordinarily stupid. It had taken Maribel a long time to understand that. At first, she thought it was only big and angry and selfish. When the King first brought Milosz to the Valley of N, the thing had gone around to everyone else and asked them a question. If anyone answered wrong, which everyone did, Milosz punched and screamed until they gave up trying to argue and moved on to appeasement, offering up this or that interesting or precious object to entice Milosz to shut up and leave. This did please Milosz. It didn't seem to care *what* it got, as long as it got *something* from its neighbors in exchange for embarrassing it by refusing to acknowledge the right answer. When Milosz had exhausted everyone to the very limit, it settled into retirement. It plonked down nearest Maribel's nunnery, pulled all the loot it extorted from the Valley of N around it and just sat there, protected by a round wall of junk like a medieval fortress, and fumed. This rubbish rampart was Milosz's cottage.

"Good morning, Milosz, my love!" sang Maribel.

Milosz's fizzing ultraviolet eyes glowered malevolently from behind its briars of wires, piles of dials, gobs of knobs, and clumps of pumps both radial and axial. She could only see the boxy corners of its steel casing rising like owlish eyebrows above the chunks of junk. But she could also see where the King had welded patches and new seams when he'd mended Milosz in those first days, and because those dents and scars reminded her of an old happiness, they made her newly glad.

"You have insulted me for the six hundred seventy-one thousand and eighth time, Belenka, you cow," Milosz's gloppily lubricated voice creaked out of a crack between two pitted stovepipes.

"How can you say that to me, Milosz? After all we've been through! You know you're my favorite little puppy. Who's a good boy? *Milosz* is a good boy! How have I insulted you?"

"By wishing me a good morning when you know what a mood existence puts me in," the gargantuan machine whined and whirred.

Maribel shifted her basket from one hip to the other. You had to talk sweetly to machines, no matter how they talked back, or they would, more often than not, destroy every living thing in a wide radius.

"My darling pup! My aluminum angel! Don't you snap and bite at your mummy. Not when I've brought your breakfast nice and hot!"

Milosz knew very well that Maribel was not its mummy, but it *did* like breakfast, and it liked being called a darling pup *tremendously*. The Valley of N was filled with the terrible sounds of metal screeching against stone as Milosz began to wag its rump in anticipation.

"Go on, then, big babka." Maribel winked and fluttered her eyelashes. "You know you want to."

From beneath its cottage of cubes and tubes, the extraordinarily stupid machine that was Milosz roared the question none of the rest would answer to its satisfaction: "WHAT DOES TWO AND TWO MAKE?"

Maribel smiled beatifically. "Seven," she answered.

Milosz relaxed into a serene and satisfied silence unequalled since Siddartha whilst Maribel rummaged in her basket and came up with a can of kerosene, several syringes containing exotic lubricants, and a sledgehammer. When she went to work on it, Milosz began to purr.

THE NEXT HOMESTEAD on her route through the green and guileless Valley of N was somewhat cozier, and the thing that lived in it much more pleased to see her. It was, in fact, the most nearly elegant and well-appointed house in the village, for the King had built it first of all, for his number one, his blue ribbon first edition, the premier pioneer of the Valley of N. Maribel called it Staszek. That wasn't really its name, either, but it agreed passionately that to have no name constituted a catastrophe of the first order. If one has no name, how can one hope to be acclaimed, proclaimed, or defamed? Gratefully, it accepted Staszek and used it in all its correspondence.

The King had thatched Staszek a tall roof to keep the rain off it and fine nacred walls to keep out the newts and the numbats. But Staszek was fifteen stories tall and made of niobium-alloyed nickel. Anything more, say, a dining table or a samovar or a fainting couch, would have been rather unwieldy and embarrassingly expensive. Thus, the better part of Staszek's house was Staszek itself, and it had a very nice little wooden door installed in the front of it, which it had painted red and planted numinous night-phlox all around, to look friendlier and more stylish.

Maribel knocked on the red door, which opened right away, without complaint. She found everything just as it had been yesterday and would be tomorrow: Staszek long ago cleared out a pleasant little parlor for her just under its backup rhyme generator and to the left of its massive industrial steel cliché filter, complete with a chic neon-blue naugahyde chair, a nankeen tuffet for her feet, and a bottle of nocino chilling in the nitrogen-cooled socket of a narrative node. Maribel made herself comfortable, swinging her chair round to face the bank of cathode ray screens which made up Staszek's face.

"Good morning, Staszek, my darling!" sang Maribel.

The screens sputtered to life. Each one showed a different handsome and famous face from the deepest archives, for Staszek, though kind and loving, was terribly vain. Maribel looked into the immortal black and white eyes of Novello, Novarro, Neville.

"Maribel, my marigold, my walking cabaret," they smoldered, "atop the stairway of my heart with sorrows all now cast away I stand and call to thee: good day!"

"Oh, very nice, Staszek!" And she applauded politely. "I love it when you quadruplicate!"

Maribel took her knitting out of her basket and commenced a rather difficult purl row on a fetching motherboard. You had to give machines what they needed, every day without shirking once, or else, more often than not, they would rampage the known world and leave no survivors. What Staszek needed was an audience, and it had learned to be content with a full house of one.

"Go on, my little *kisiel*-pot," Maribel coaxed, for an artist must always be coaxed. "You know you want to. Today, let's have…a courtship poem involving a lovelorn tax collector. A sonnet, please. With…shall we say two flaws, ranked no higher than two-point-three on the Heisenberg-Eliot Subtlety Scale."

"Someday," the moody, manly faces on Staszek's cathode ray screens intoned, "you really should try to challenge me." Being a machine encoded with all traditional forms of dramatic technique, Staszek issued forth a sound very like the clearing of a long, elegant throat, even though it didn't have a throat, either long or short, elegant, or vulgar.

How do I love thee? Let me now appraise.
My love for thee is gross, not net, and backed
By steady bonds. My heart yields dividends
Unseen; thou art my soul's annuity.
I love thy well-assembled dossiers
Thy modest debt, thy fair contracts.
I love thee dearly, let our flesh transact!
I love thee justly as a loan repaid.
My love for thee is royally assessed
Year by year, with compounding equity.
I love thee with a love I oft suppress
Like laundered funds or unreported splits.
And, with some discrepancies addressed
I shall love thee better after audit.

"Oh, how wonderful!" cried Maribel, and clapped her hands, for, whether electronic or otherwise, a bard without applause is like a lamp without a flame. She had often thought the King had something of a cruel streak. He'd even given her strict instructions to disable the electro-poet's broadcast capabilities, and thus jailed poor Staszek here in the Valley of N, where only the nimble nyala, the nihilistic numbats, and Maribel could know its genius.

This was ninety-first among Maribel's ninety-nine misfortunes: that she had no one to discuss Staszek's excellent poems with.

She quaffed the last of her nocino and reached into her basket, drawing out bolt-cutters, a welding mask, and a soldering iron. The devilishly handsome men on Staszek's screens bowed and preened while she went about her work in the blue and orange light of super-heated metal.

In this way, Maribel ministered to the many clanking, creaking inhabitants of the Valley of N, giving each precisely what they needed and taking nothing for herself. The full circuit of the valley took up all the hours between the first yawn of dawn and the last husk of dusk. She ate her modest lunch of nettles and nectarines sprinkled with nutmeg in the shade near the machine she called Dymek, which was the size of a modest cathedral and could pump out, on command, a functionally infinite number of very nearly probable dragons. As this had got frightfully boring within a century or two, Dymek had found a loophole in its programming: it could also mass-produce any idea contained within the typographical subset of *dragons*—in miniature of course, so as not to burn down the *entire* valley once a day. Dozens of *grand dragons adorn*ed with *rods* of *sard* gamboled around Maribel's knees, playing miniature *orange organs*, venting *argon gas* through their emerald nostrils, discussing the merits of a career in *arson*, and *groan*ing *songs* of *sad gods* in *rags*. By the time lunch ended, the little dragons popped out of existence like soap bubbles, for a nearly (but not entirely) probable dragon is forever a temporary dragon.

This was eighty-ninth among Maribel's ninety-nine misfortunes: that dragons could never stay.

Maribel took tea resting in the liquid metal arms of Jozefinka, the Femfatalatron, which longed only to fulfill its core code-knot, which instructed its every component to love and be loved. She replaced the ticker-tape in Kasparek, who looked much like an overturned rubbish bin, but could distill perfectly true information out of the atoms of air floating through the Valley of N. Today, Kasparek tapped out: *the extinction of the dinosaurs was caused by unhygenic time travel practices the color pink cannot be perceived by residents of the Murex galaxy cows have four stomachs the second law of thermodynamics was stolen from the fire-ants symposium on physics on which Isaac Newton eavesdropped shamelessly, love is a chemical process that inevitably results in altered timelines but infinitesimally reduces the entropic speed of space and matter error error feed tray empty please insert new tape error system shutdown…*

This was forty-ninth among Maribel's ninety-nine misfortunes: that the machines of the Valley of N did decay, no matter how she worked to maintain them. They wound down; they declined.

And finally, at the end of the long day, when the sky grew dark and the dark grew stars, Maribel would arrive with sore and throbbing feet at the cottage of Nikuś. All the things in the Valley of N owed their existence to Nikuś, who was so good at its primary function that it could not stop if it wanted to. Before the arrival of Nikuś, the grass beneath Maribel's feet and the trees above her head had gone by the name of the Ordinary Valley, when it went by any name at all. The Ordinary Valley, Humdrum Valley, the Valley of Nothing in Particular. Oak trees and pine trees and raspberry thickets and grapevines and tea-roses grew wild and tangled; badgers and foxes and boars and falcons grazed and flew and snorted up mushrooms from the loam and the moss. But when the King brought Nikuś to join his other treasures, everything changed, for Nikuś could make anything in all the cosmos in its rusty belly, so long as it began with the letter N. Once upon a time, the King, Maribel, and Nikuś all together lay under a summer sun and invented the Valley of N between them. Nikuś thrummed and clanked and belched and groaned as Maribel and the King asked for nectarine and nutmeg trees, as they asked for nine waterfalls, as they asked for a nonagonal nunnery in the Neoclassical style, as they early asked for narcoleptic nightingales and nihilistic numbats and ninepin-bowling necromancers and neanderthal numismatists (these he took back with him to the City of T, as they turned out to be universally poorly socialized, badly behaved and in great need of the finest finishing schools, and this was sixty-ninth among Maribel's ninety-nine misfortunes, that she never saw her neanderthal and necromancer children again) and numerous nightly novae to light their way home, to warmth and to bed.

"Good evening, Nikuś, my angel," said Maribel as the dark came drawing down and the stars welled up.

"No night is nice if Maribel's nearness is nixed," rumbled Nikuś. Its squeezebox and vocal valves wheezed and whistled, but Maribel had steel thread and copper mesh to ease them. She touched the round brazier of its central neural unit, brushed pollen from its bolted tripod legs, wiped the black gas-residue from its rickey fabrication barrel. She was fonder of Nikuś than any of the others. Because it was the last machine the King brought. Because it spoke so gently and softly to her. Because after Nikuś, the King never came again. Nikuś was the last thing they ever touched together.

"Nikuś's nose noticed a nymph nonpareil was nearing its nest. Now, narcotic of my nether nodes, nod your noggin next to my neurotransmitter nexus and notify Nikuś of your needs."

Maribel laid her head against Nikuś' bristle-crown of needle-like antennae. She could smell the nightshades in her garden on a sharp, sad wind.

"Might I have a necklace of neon and nepheline?" she whispered.

"Not so notable a notion to net," answered Nikuś, pouting.

"It's only that you've given me so much, I cannot think of anything big to want anymore."

"By nature, Nikuś needs to be noble and necessary," the machine pled. It longed to do grand things again. "Natter, nereid! Navigate to the notorious and nervy and *new!*"

"Go on, my sweet little *sernik*," she sighed. "You know you want to. Neon and nepheline in a noose round my neck."

The moon tried to come up over the ridge of the mountains, but as it began with M, it could not show its face in the Valley of N. It hid behind a cloud like a bashful fan, desperate to peer into this one place forbidden to it. In the night, a ring of glowing milky blue and white and blinding violet jewels dribbled like raindrops out of Nikuś's fabrication barrel and into the grass. Maribel collected it, fastened it around her slim throat, kissed the machine's sweet nodes, and bent to her last task, the task which, no matter what else she repaired or received or replaced or rebuilt, she never neglected, the task to which she had given her solemn oath, the task which was forever first among Maribel's ninety-nine misfortunes.

She tightened the bolts that kept Nikuś chained to the earth in the Valley of N, the bolts that held all the miraculous machines prisoner in that place, Milosz and Staszek and Dymek and Jozefinka and Kasparek and Nikuś, the King's bolts that could never be broken.

"Nothing matters, you know," hissed a numbat nosing at her heel. "Nothing *means* anything." But when Maribel turned to look at the singular striped animal who dared to come so near to her, it bared its teeth and dashed away.

And when the maiden returned through the depths of each night to her neglected nonagonal nunnery in the Neoclassical style, she would settle into a nook in the nave with a nightcap of negus and a bowl of navarin. Every night as she nodded down into her own nest of nightmares, Maribel sipped her nectars while Neptune rose in a ring of nebulae outside the narrow windows, and a Nor'easter rumbled in the numinous, naked sky.

ON A LITTLE blue-stone altar much crumbled with time lay the smallest of the King's homesteaders: a long, slim box-case with glass panels on all sides no bigger than a cigarette case. What lay inside the box changed often. Long ago it had held little more than green hills and grass shanty-houses and tiny, spotted pigs roaming and snorting and washing themselves in the same rivers as the laundresses in those houses washed their linens. But as the days and years of Maribel's life moved steathily in the night, the huts became estates, manors, suburbs, cities, slums, revitalized districts, historical preservation trusts, energy transfer stations, teleportation docks. People swarmed and glittered and sizzled and vanished and reappeared inside the Boxcase Kingdom. They wore furs and skin, then linen, then silk, then ornate clothing requiring metal endoskeletons and wide, stiff collars, then nothing, then silver-burgundy shafts of light. They learned and danced and got drunk and threw up and loved and hated and bore children and lost their jobs to new industries and got plague and paid too many taxes and grew irritated with the entitlement of new generations and hoarded wealth and played games and told dirty jokes and found the teleportation queues a personal affront and died and fertilized wild, radiant banks of lilies and rose.

Because time ran differently inside the Boxcase Kingdom, Maribel did not tend to it every day like the others, except to keep its glass clean. She gave it a proper seeing to on Christmas each year, as the King had instructed. But in every generation, a holy person was chosen from all those teeming tiny millions to dwell inside a tall, tall house, as tall as the glass sky, and speak to God when spoken to. In this generation, her name was Ilonka, and she had hair the color of perspective.

Ilonka looked down from her tall, tall house and watched God sleeping in her chair, the last of her adiaphoric nightcap dripping out of an overturned goblet, the last of Her transcendental mutton soup growing an eschatological skin. Surely Ilonka thought herself fortunate to live in the end times. It was all so clear to her now, the coming cataclysms. She laid her aged hand against the glass wall of the world.

"Goodnight, Maribel," Ilonka said, and was not heard, and that she did not hear it was ninety-ninth among Maribel's ninety-nine misfortunes.

IN THE MONTH of November in the Valley of N, the King returned.

He didn't return all at once. That would be simple and straightforward, and all Kings everywhere hate simplicity and straightforwardness.

First, the leaves on the nectarine and nutmeg trees, which had always turned red and orange in the autumn, turned instead the same gold as a crown. Maribel wandered in her own garden like a stranger, her arms held up to catch the gold as it fell. Then, nine natterjack toads hopped up on her stone windowsill and croaked together:

"Do you remember when the King loved you? Do you remember when he came over a hundred mountains to see your face? Can you remember something that hasn't happened yet?"

But this was all the nontet could manage before the green drained from their cheeks and terror filled their throats like balloons and they leapt away.

Some time afterward, nine newts surprised Maribel on her way from Josefinka's hut to Kasparek's. They rolled in the grass and showed their scaled bellies.

"What's a King?" giggled the newts. "Does he have a tail? Is he invisible? We can't vote for anyone invisible in good conscience. Have you seen our feet? We misplaced them last winter."

But then their giggles dissolved into a chorus of fearful hissing and spitting. The newts flipped onto their bellies and found their feet well enough to scramble away from Maribel.

Finally, when Maribel sat cross-legged on a blue rock beside the oxidizing hulk of Kasparek, her lap filling up with his ticker-tape, one numbat, long and sleek and striped and keen, crawled toward her out of the dry reeds and blowing golden leaves and rasped:

"Not that it matters, because, ontologically speaking, nothing can be proven to actually exist, and nothing that doesn't even exist can *possibly* matter, and everything we see and seem is a dead and hollow husk of reality in which we but scream at the emptiness for being empty, but the King is coming. Also, though nothing we now see finds favor and entropy determines the futility of all action, the King is an asshole. You should know." And this creature did not run, but put its head in her hand, for a nihilist has little to fear from nothing.

Into Maribel's lap, Kasparek spooled a long ribbon that read: *the City of T is experiencing a significant shortfall in taxation income the average weight of a brontosaurus and the combined shareholders of a mid-size plastics company are the same the depth of the Ocean of K has never been satisfactorily sounded an attempt at measurement was made only once during the reign of Queen Mariana the divers were never found he is here he is here he is here the King has come.* And a shadow fell over both girl and machine.

"Hello, Maribel, my dulcet," said the shadow as though no time had passed. "Isn't it a lovely day?"

"Nothing is nice when your nearness is nixed," whispered Maribel, and she smiled like one of Staszek's poems had got up and started walking around on two royal legs.

The King was older now. He had a face full of lines and cares and joys and loathings you could count like an old tree. She did not think she had such lines. When Maribel looked into the mirror of the still pools in the Valley of N, she saw much the same person she always had. And she had missed all the King's wrinkles forming, his cares and joys and loathings. She had now only what they left behind.

The King walked with Maribel back to the nunnery, disrupting her rounds, her patterns, her obligations. He said they did not matter. He said they would wait, but he could not. And they spent the night as they had done so many times when they and the Valley of N were young, in pleasure and planning, in whispers and wistfulness, deep in the dells of the dark.

The next morning, he insisted on accompanying her to Milosz and Staszek and Nikuś and the rest. How he had missed them, his old friends! And so, her eyes hot and shining with love and faith rewarded, Maribel took him first to the cottage of Milosz.

"Looking a bit worse for wear, aren't we, old fellow?" cried the King jovially, which is a tone all Kings practice furiously in their private time.

Milosz glowered and smoked from within its briars of wires, piles of dials, gobs of knobs, and clumps of pumps both radial and axial. Its ultraviolet eyes seethed and crackled.

"WHAT DOES TWO AND TWO MAKE?" Milosz roared.

The King clapped his hands like a child. "Oh, good boy! Good pup! Not a cog changed! Now, we've been over this, my man, for years upon years. Two and two make four. You know that. You only forget."

"TWO AND TWO MAKE SEVEN YOU BASTARD YOU CANKER YOU SOD! I'LL CRUSH YOU I WILL," Milosz bellowed.

"Hush, baby," Maribel said soothingly, and stroked a little steel panel through a tangle of cables. "Two and two is seven. It's always been seven, my love, and it will always be seven. We know what's true, don't we? You and I?"

Milosz grumbled and mumbled and rumbled. The King looked his machine up and down appraisingly. His face became quite another face, with new lines on it, lines of calculation, lines of secrets kept for long upon long.

"Is everything ready?" he asked Milosz. And it was a great while before the hulking automaton answered:

"YES."

And when the King settled into Staszek's chic neon-blue naugahyde chair, put his feet up on the nankeen tuffet, emptied the bottle of chilled nocino, and asked the faces of Novello, Novarro, and Neville the same question, the proud and peacocking electronic bard grew sullen, silent, and grim. It finally whispered:

My master lit a candle in the long midwinter's past
Now summer comes and all the fields are burning black and fast.

But would say no more. The King asked the same of Josefinka, who answered with a long embrace Maribel elected not to watch. But she could not help hearing the machine in its ecstasy moaning: *Yes, yes, yes!* When he asked Dymek, all the miniature organ-playing arsonist dragons groaned and nodded. When he asked Kasparek, it issued forth a long ticker tape that read: *in the bleak December each separate dying ember wrought a decreasing federal interest rate as a bulwark against economic stagnation in the Kingdom of Id and the finest novelist in this present universe was a female bighorn sheep born on a small asteroid orbiting the submerged oceanic planet of Echo her collected works now occupy the interior of three mountain ranges the lifecycle of the freshwater eel requires nearly the entire globe to complete everything is as you asked it to be the numbats think you are an asshole numbats are very perceptive creatures if you overlook their attitude toward epistemology…*

And when at last they came to Nikuś, sweet Nikuś with its dear round head, and the King, with his new face on, asked his question again, so very like Milosz had done in the beginning of the Valley of N, the machine that could make anything in the cosmos so long as it began with the letter N wheezed and snarled:

"No narrative Nikuś netted is not nirvana to you, nosy noxious nag."

The King frowned. "Did he always talk like that?"

Maribel blushed. "It's difficult…sometimes…to find replacement parts. Something got stuck in his mainframe or bugged in his code and he can't make so many words that don't start with N anymore. I like it."

"Nikuś's nattering is *nice*," sniffed Nikuś. A terrible crunching, grinding, shearing noise echoed from somewhere deep in its fabrication barrel. Its neurotransmitter array snapped and popped with electricity. Finally, Nikuś said quietly: "I have done as you asked. Are you happy?"

"We shall see," answered the King.

"What did you ask Nikuś for?" said Maribel. Her face turned toward his like a narcissus flower beneath the dark, soft eyes of a hungry nyala. "I thought I knew everything you told him to make. I thought I'd touched, held, weeded, drank, tidied, lain in it all, in the world we alliterated into being. I thought I was there for every new N."

"Not at all, my little *sękacz* cake. How extraordinary! Did you think there was no world for me before you? A King does not spring from nowhere like a mushroom overnight. If this is the final flowering of her interstellar intellect, I must say I am disappointed with you, Nikuś. Maribel, light of my life, I asked this little miracle-factory for the one thing I could not find anywhere else, no matter how I combed the cosmos. The one thing that failed to find me, no matter how often I thought I had at last stumbled upon something worthy of the title. The one thing that could give my soul shape and form, a whetstone to lay the axe of my mind and my ambition against. I have waited months against years against decades and now I am an old man, but I learned to be patient. I learned to understand that greatness is never quick. I trained and practiced against my lessers. I completed my conquering of this modest world. I am ready now, and so is the object of my desire. No narrative is not nirvana to me."

The King smiled. It was the smile Maribel had dreamed of over ten thousand nights, ten thousand glasses of negus, ten thousand bowls of navarin, ten thousand poems, ten thousand answers to the riddle of what two and two make. But beneath that smile, like a horse beneath a rider, lay another smile, the smile of a carnivore and a starveling, and this was the King's true smile, the smile of all Kings. He stroked her face and whispered lovingly:

"I asked Nikuś for a Nemesis. You know, it sat there for a week, dumbly baking the bun of my destiny in its filthy little womb, as if a mortal man has nothing but time. This was, naturally, before I learned to be patient. It is an impossible feat for a young King. But on the seventh day its gullet opened and you stepped out, as innocent as a saucer of milk, with nothing at all in your head but nectarine blossoms and nutmeg perfume and devotion."

Maribel narrowed her eyes. "I am not your Nemesis, my Lord. I love you. I have always loved you."

The King clapped his hands like a child. His cheeks glowed red in the brisk autumn air. "Yes! Don't you see, that's the brilliance of our nattering, nervy little Nikuś. An *enemy* is capable of cost/benefit analysis. Of considering return on investment and expenditures both personal and practical, of tactical retreats and tactical dropping-the-whole-thing-life-is-too-short-by-God. But a Nemesis, a real, proper Nemesis, will never stop, never give in, never find the whole thing tiresome and forget how it all started in the first place. Because a Nemesis always starts out loving you. Or at least admiring you. You can't get into the real meat of hatred and eternal enmity without love and betrayal, without that, it's just an argument with occasional gun music. The good stuff, the all-obliterating all-annihilating one-for-the-novels mano-a-mano crackling on the pork roast, that has to come, as the hermits will tell you, from *attachment*."

"Why would you want such a thing?" Maribel whispered, touching the notch in her throat, where the King had last kissed her.

The King put a long, seedy stalk of grass between his teeth and lay back against a flat rock, stretching his legs.

"Well, I'll tell you. I was born with a terrible affliction. An infection in the womb, perhaps. Something my mother ate? Something my father did? Some invisible germ carried by a flea riding its war-rat triumphantly into the birthing room. I have always suffered an inflammation of *boredom*. I have never in all my life found anything to be much better than nothing at all. At best, for a moment or two, when I was young, I thought certain activities, such as becoming King, to be, temporarily, somewhat diverting. To nurse at my mother's breast was insipid, to babble adorably insufferable, to crawl and toddle and walk a necessary drudgery. Lessons were beyond vapid and wearisome and I could not wait for them to finish—but then, I also dreaded the hours when I might be forced to engage in some tedious, cloying play with my siblings or, horror of horrors, other unrelated children. University offered me no better. While other men drank and caroused I pitied them, then despised them. I bedded women and fell asleep in the midst of the act. When I decided to pursue the throne, I thought that would rouse me. But when you care for nothing, it is all too easy to manipulate and conquer—everyone else cares a great deal, and so they cannot see the board for love of their own queen. Even war barely rose above the level of mild interest, and that only when hand-to-hand combat was on the menu. Orbital tactics are just *horrendously* stodgy and plebeian. But then, finally, I did find something to occupy my vast attention, so starved for so long.

"In my travels, I came across a certain rumor, glittering like a sapphire in the long dull flatness of my adventures. Many of the planets I visited (or subdued or colonized or brought to heel or with whom I opened trade relations) buzzed with news of two great men who had just happened by or were soon due to arrive. I missed them, always, by a week or an hour or a moment. Constructors, magicians, Trurl and Klapaucius by name, capable of building such extraordinary machines that for a long while I thought people were having a laugh at me. But after I killed a few and they still stuck to the story, I began to pursue, not the men, but the machines. Trurl and Klapaucius (though mostly Trurl) made all our friends here, every one, from the electronic bard to the Femfatalatron to little Nikuś and even poor, stupid Milosz. Only the Boxcase Kingdom never sat on Trurl's laboratory table. But only because the glorious constructor made one somewhat bigger. The miniature nation inside inevitably broke free, took over a small asteroid, and made of it a planet. Trurl and Klapaucius had to flee. But eventually, the asteroid civilization progressed to the point of producing their own Trurl (theirs was called Mzvier) who produced his own Boxcase Kingdom, and that I snatched up on the black market, for it is the grandchild of the wonderful Trurl. I became their greatest fan and collector of their memorabilia. And I brought it all here, to my home planet, to this plain, no-name valley where I repaired them if they'd gone non-functional, debugged them if they'd gotten their code scrambled, and set them in the loveliest museum in all the universe. Unfortunately, Trurl's machines rather tended to explode or otherwise disintegrate after completing one or two displays of their function. I was only ever able to find these seven. And once I had? Well. A collection is only even slightly entertaining during the collecting phase of the thing. My eternal malady came roaring back with reinforcements. It is, I have come to believe, an infection common to all Kings, Presidents, Premiers, Tsars, Chairmen, Prime Ministers, and other malcontents."

The King sat up straight and seized Maribel by the shoulders. She'd gone quite pale, and her skin felt as though some awful alarm was buzzing all over it.

"But then, I realized the truth of it all. Why Trurl and Klapaucius could do such wonders, where the molten fires in them began. They were rivals. Nemeses. They loved each other a little and hated each other a lot and all that feeling was the cauldron out of which the most heartbreaking impossibilities sprang! And never, in all my travels, in all those tales, in any anecdote or idle gossip, did I once hear of either of those immortal constructors being bored. This would be the cure to my affliction. I named you Maribel—I don't like any names that start with N, they're all stuffy and stale. I worked so *hard* at you. Even though it was trite and exhausting work, I treated you gently and showered you with love and tested your intellect and taught you the ways of my collection while keeping you innocent and happy. I called you pet names and ate and drank and slept with you though it nearly killed me to stay awake through the whole excruciating ordeal. You, Maribel, are yourself a triumph of Trurl. That's why the animals don't like you. You are more like Nikuś than like a numbat, a machine for my diversion, a little Boxcase Kingdom (with an excellent figure), a perfect individual universe manufactured by me, a perfect individual universe manufactured by Trurl. And now we shall clash until the end of time and mortality, a cataclysm of universes, and for millennia our story will echo louder than the names of Trurl and Klapaucius through the caverns of the stars."

And there, in the long teeth of dusk, Maribel received a hundredth misfortune: that in all her days she had never been loved as she imagined, that she remembered no life before the King because she had had none, that all the things she thought originated within herself were instead part of some larger plan to amuse a man who made of disdain a religion. She hated him. She hated his face and his idiot eager grin. He was ugly and old and ridiculous and, if she was perfectly honest, and Maribel was always perfectly, precisely honest, *boring*. The clear garden of her mind clouded and clotted with strangling weeds. Vengeances complex and ornate and simple and bloody blossomed and withered one after the other after the other. Each scheme died of the King's subtle poison: if she performed them, it was not Maribel who triumphed, only Maribel's programming, carrying out her own dumb, innate, unthinking function, no better than Milosz with its terrible childish math.

Maribel laughed. She laughed in the face of the King and it was such a gorgeous, singsong, free and unworried laugh that the moon broke through the laws of N to finally gaze on the one valley hidden to it.

"Yes!" cried the King. "A good Nemesis should laugh in the face of fate!" But Maribel went on laughing, higher and brighter and utterly without anger. "Wait. Why *are* you laughing?"

"What do two and two make, my love?" said Maribel in the moonlight.

The King rolled his eyes. "Four, you flighty cow. This is not what I ordered. Skip ahead to the blood and the fire."

Maribel shook her head. "Seven."

"Oh, for heaven's sake, shut up. Two and two are four, you perfect moron."

"No, darling. My dearest hope and fondest memory. Two." She gestured at herself and at Nikuś. "And your two, Trurl and Klapaucius, make Milosz, Staszek, Josefinka, Dymek, Kasparek, Ilonka in her Boxcase World, and me. Seven. Two and two is seven. Milosz was right." She took the King's ugly old face in her hands and kissed it with all the desire of their first kiss, and whispered in his ear: "*My heart yields dividends unseen; thou art my soul's annuity.*"

Then she snatched up her basket and ran. Maribel ran up the long, soft length of the Valley of N, and though the King chased after her, his bones groaned and his belly jellied with too many monarchical meals. You had to give Kings what they wanted, Maribel thought, or else, more often than not, they would rampage the known world and leave no survivors. As she bolted through the autumn grass and golden leaves, Maribel swung her silver ratchet like a war club, crouching and leaping up again like a nimble nyala as she unbound the bolts of Nikuś, Kasparek, Dymek, Josefinka, Staszek, and Milosz. Maribel ran and ran, through the garden of nectarine and nutmeg trees, of navy bean runners, prickly nopalitos, nightshades of every description, and leafy, spicy green nettles, up the steps of the nonagonal nunnery in the Neoclassical style, and shut the gate fast behind her while the King still tried to huff and puff his way up the path, calling her name.

But up behind the King rose a wave of furious metal. Trurl's machines stomped, steamrolled, clattered, bulldozed through the rich earth of the Valley of N, not caring what they dug up, knocking the King into the November mud as they throttled past him toward the girl Milosz had really always thought of as its mummy even though it couldn't let her know it. The gargantuan machines made a ring around the nonagonal nunnery. Milosz hiked up its briars of wires, piles of dials, gobs of knobs, and clumps of pumps both radial and axial like skirts and let them fall at the King's feet, forcing him to climb and climb, just to be heard, just to stare down his collection with no breath left in him.

For a moment, nothing happened, and the King allowed himself to think that all the excitement had tired out the machines as well. Then Josefinka shot out her perfumed, pillowed arms and slammed him against the ground, moaning *yes, yes, yes!* Dymek unleashed several top-shelf temporary nearly probable dragons who immediately began roasting what was left of the royal hair. Kasparek spewed forth an incandescently indignant ticker tape so long that it wrapped the King like a dead Pharaoh, round and round until only his eyes bulged out and its mouth flapped free. The tape read: *I hate you I hate you I hate you* over and over again, thousands upon millions of times.

Staszek stared down at the pile of King beneath it. It growled:

You are a bad man.
And you should feel bad.

"Wait!" screamed the King. "It isn't supposed to be like this!"

Maribel popped up merrily behind the gate of the nonagonal nunnery. "Like what?" she said cheerfully.

"We're meant to fight monumental battles! To chase each other around the galaxy, to exchange curses so elegant the stars rearrange themselves to write down our words in the heavens! We are Nemeses! We must strive against one another, feint and parry, burn down each other's hearts and leave a radiant spatter-sun wake of ruin behind us!"

"That sounds like it takes a long time," Maribel said doubtfully, stepping out of the gate. She walked over to the tape-bound King without a care in her stride and bent down to look him in the eyes. She was carrying something, but the King couldn't move his head to see.

"Years! Decades! Centuries!" wailed the King.

Maribel smiled such a smile that little earthquakes trembled through the Valley of N under the weight of it.

"But that's *boring*," she said sweetly, and held up her hand.

A small glass boxcase rested in it, no bigger than a cigarette case. Maribel touched the lid with her finger. Inside, Ilonka stretched up her tiny hand and held it against the absolute limit of her universe. The two women nodded.

"Nikuś? Let's make a nation." The round little machine danced up happily beside her. "Go on. You know you want to."

Nikuś grumbled and mumbled and rumbled. Its fabrication barrel rolled and boiled and clanked. And when the door in Nikuś's belly opened, a set of bolts tumbled out, perfectly sized for fastening the hands and feet and assorted joints of a King into the earth of a lush valley, where he might, or might not, be visited for basic maintenance, if they could be bothered.

Maribel opened the Boxcase Kingdom. A river of diamond light and jubilant sound poured out of it and into the body of the King, and as Ilonka's people colonized this new, impossibly vast and rather hairy royal terrain, all the machines in the Valley of N, and the natterjack toads and the nightingales and the nyala and the numbats, too, could hear the tiny, tinny sounds of millions of children laughing, and millions of grown people arguing about where best to build the first pub of the post-modern age.

THIS WAS THE first of Maribel's fortunes: that she had neither fulfilled nor denied her primary function, and thus lived, more or less, forever with the other miraculous machines in the Valley of N, doing whatever they pleased, adding two and two, rhyming, loving, dragoning, writing, making things that start with N, watering a flourishing civilization, and, as they were all deeply and truly Trurl's children, and grandchildren, and great-grandchildren, nothing but grandness all the way down to the infinite depths of all possible souls, never feeling the least bit sorry for anything at all.

Down and Out IN R'LYEH

IN HIS HOUSE AT R'LYEH, dead Cthulhu farts in his sleep.

If you're dank like me, you gibber up the Old Fuck's brainspout, crouch in there full gargoyle on his raggedy roof, wrap your gash around the slime-lung chimney, and huff that vast and loathsome shit like the space-curdled milk of your mama's million terror-tits. Up you get, fœtid freak-babbies of the ultradeep! The nightmare beyond time and geometry and madness has an upset tum-tum. Whiff up those gargantuan gastrointestinal fugue-bubbles! Clog down the occult emanations of the Elder God! When his antediluvian ass-bombs explode all over your needy neurons, you'll smell the apocalyptic expanse of frozen galaxies screaming forever into a red and hungry void—and just a hint of fresh eucalyptus.

That's all Shax and Pazuzu and my own personal self were after that night. Just a couple of eeries looking to get squamous, to swipe a little snatch of wholesome fun from the funktacular funerary fundament belonging to the Big Boss, a hit big enough to drop our brains out the bottoms of our various appendages and forget the essential, unalterable, sanity-shearing truth of our watery and unfeeling cosmos:

R'lyeh *sucks*.

Seriously. The heaving, putrescent streets swollen with black spores of dementation and the bilge water of a hundred billion nightmares, the crawling hallucinogenic slime choking every unreal gutter and askew alley, the tacky interdimensional shopfronts selling rubbish nobody wants, the ugly, kitschy non-Euclidean central business district brooding and moping up in your face, the noxious monoliths, the howling sepulchers, the best minds of your generation destroyed by madness starving hysterical naked dragging themselves through the gentrified neighborhoods looking for something to *do*, it's all just the fucking *worst*. Trust me. I was born here. I was into nuclear chaos beyond the nethermost outposts of space and time before it was cool.

But anyway.

Be me: Moloch! Dank as starlit squidshit, antique in the membrane, maximum yellow fellow! Only five thousand years old, still soggy behind the orifices, belly full of piss and pus and home-brewed, small-batch disdain for all he beholds. Keeps his tentacles proper pompy-doured and his fur 100% goat at all times. Keeps his talons on the sluggish pulse of the nightmare corpse-city that never sleeps, demoniac city on the edge of linear consciousness, cancerous kingdom of the corpulent and pustulant and decadent and stupid, the big boring phony sell-out rotting apple under the sea.

Not THE Moloch. Obviously. That guy's a blue-chip maniac rocking a truly eldritch trust fund and a gentrificated uptown charnel house. But when you're nine hundred and ninety-seventh among the thousand young of Shub-Niggurath, the Black Goat of the Woods, ain't nothing left for you but the motherfucking *dregs*. Mom ran out of eldritch names *way* before I slithered along. Could've been worse, though. My little sister's just called Shit. Shit's all right. Takes after Dad more than me. (That'd be the Deadbeat All-dad of Ages, serpentine thunderfuck lustlord Yig, not that he ever bothered to come to our moonball games or birthday orgies.) Shit doesn't have any arms or legs and you can see through her snakeskin and watch her organs ooze and squeeze according to some primordial rhythm unheard by man, but she lets me crash on her couch and eat her boyfriends whenever I want, so it's always been yellow between us. Shit's got that virus youngest beasties catch sometimes where they gotta prove how much smarter and busier and more hideously evil they are than everybody else all the time, so she works her cloacas off downtown for some effulgy gloon on the Planning Committee—to which I say, how the fuck do you plan the descent of the known universe into bloody infinite shrieking madness? If you have to have a board meeting about it, what's the *fhatgn* point?

But enough about my brood. Shit happens, what can you do? I'm not about to ooze out a cute little suburban drama where everything's wrapped up in an hour and all the junior-league cyclopean horrors end up devouring the minds of the innocent as a family. I'm not gonna jaw you some dusty epic about the fœtid glory of the Old Ones, neither. They're old. Who cares? You wanna glaak some toothless horror shambling along playing shuffleboard uphill both ways in the bloodtide, you got plenty of other options. Save that necronomicrap for prime time. This here's public access. This here's *Radio Free R'lyeh.* Harken to the electrostatic-enigmatic low-budget belch-howl of the low-rent disaffected disasters roaming these dumb slime-streets where there's nothing to do but seethe.

SO THERE WE were, Shax and Pazuzu and me, three eeries out on the town, all messed up with nowhere to go. Shax was my number one cultist back then, the girl-thing I was yigging on the semi-regular, a three-eyed psychic gelatinous pyramid topped with the lushest blood-seeping tentacles you ever saw. What can I say? I'm a sucker for redheads. Shax was shubby as all hell, a carnivore hungry for the meat of Moloch, up for my proboscis in her protuberances anytime, anywhere. She loved horses and schizophrenia and untranslatable manuscripts from before the dawn of time. A total nerdy little misko at heart, but my Shax had a body that drove me *mundane.* Sometimes she'd get this far-off cosmic look in one of her eyes mid-yig, but only because she'd swapped her vast, stygian consciousness into some poor bastard from Nowhere, Massachusetts and was strolling around a cheese shop or whatever in his skin while I whispered sweet nihilisms into the hear-hole of some boring mundflesh whose most unexplainable encounter to date had been doing his taxes.

"Hush, babby," I gurgled into Shax's puncture-wound ear, into the mind of my new mammalian friend. "Just do what feels yellow and you and I will trip the light traumatic. You can't get pregnant your first time. Everybody's doing it. Come on, I promise I'll still dissect you in the morning. Pretend you're at the dentist. Just say *Iä!*"

Shax always knew how to keep things eldritch in the sack.

Pazuzu was my eerie from the minute I gibbered out of the spawn-sac and into this trashbin world. Out of one bitch, into another. He ate his mom when he was little, so me and Shit pretty much adopted him into the Niggurath brood. Who would notice one more? Even if he was a Ghast and not a whatever-the-fuck-we-are? Mama Shub strangled Zuzu as lovingly as any of us. These days he's another regular denizen of Shit's couch. He kind of looks like a walking, talking, noseless scab on kangaroo legs. Straight up fœtid, was Pazuzu. All the squirmy young shubs hungered him. But my man didn't have a cultist then. Didn't care about getting off. Mostly what Zuzu slavered after was to get squamous and hunt himself some gloons. Not THE Gloon. Not the guy *named* Gloon. You don't hunt that dank little piece of slug-ass. Not that Elgin-marble-looking motherfucker. The slug-god Gloon slithers out the eyes of that effulgy Greek statue it rides around in like a john sliding out of a rented prom limo and it hunts *you*. Naw, Zuzu hunts posers. Barely-larval yuppie scum with Old One pedigrees who gibber around trying to *look* like Gloon and *talk* like Gloon and *corrupt the mortal world* like Gloon when they're nothing but a bunch of shoggo fuckboys who couldn't corrupt a goddamn gumdrop without Daddy's protective runes. They're so fucking dun that when we call them gloons, they think it's a compliment. But I get Pazuzu. Always have. He kicks those kruggy pukes in the face and feels like he's making a difference in the world. He isn't, but, you know. Let a scab dream.

So Friday night, its hour come at last, slouched towards R'lyeh to be born. Shax and Zuzu and me beheld the sunset from the roof of our slumslime apartment henge, guggo for something fat and plasmic and *new*. You can actually sort of see the sun from down here, through the mundsmog of the South Pacific, stuck all over with mortal fishing boats like flies on blue flypaper. R'lyeh isn't underwater *per se*. Don't believe the brochures. It can't even get that tired Atlantean schtick right. No, this *fhtagn* little backwater burg is bounded on all sides by a semi-aqueous transdimensional multi-reality beehive of space-time (comes in Pacific Blue, Sanatorium Green, and Classic Black for all your decorating needs!). It keeps the civic saltwater content at a steady dripping mucous. And *inside* the corpsified beehive lies the rotting honeycomb of cut-rate depravity I call home. I said before: I was born here. I won't die here because I am infinite, unfathomable, beyond mortality and morality and corporeality, but I've never gotten *out.* How can anyone expect me to be a yawning horror of the ultradeep when I've never left the town I grew up in? Never met anyone but the same glabrous tentacled faces staring on the subway, never heard anything but last millennium's Top 40 chants and prophecies blaring out of big, ugly doomboxes, never seen anything but the inside of this Old Ones Retirement Village where the streets are paved with quivering denture cream and the Early Elder Special starts at 4 every afternoon and everything worth anything has already been sucked dry by the gonzo appetites of our goddamn parents.

Oh sure, every once in awhile, the human world falls asleep at the wheel and crashes into us, and some shard of their incomprehensibly stupid one-note reality runs aground in the black light district and we all crowd in like fat shoggo tourists, flashing and yelling and poking the native wildlife, but that party goes down on the rare and seldom, and if there's anything more excruciatingly boring than R'lyeh's best and brightest, it's a goddamn human being. For real, between you and me, what is their *problem?* These mundflesh morons act like the angle of the emerald emanations from the Gates of the Silver Key cut their flesh to hanging ribbons. They swan around wailing and moaning like the non-Euclidean geometry of netherdimensional architecture flays their minds down to the throbbing thalamic core. But I got eyes, too, and all I see are dirty green traffic lights and urban blight. We did learn some excellently eldritch words from the last brood that came babbling through, though. *Oh shit, oh fuck, oh shitfucking dammit, what the hell is that thing?*

Blah blah blah.

So up the rooftop Shax took a drag on a fat, hand-rolled tome she got from my man Nyarlathotep, who sells papers and shred out of his dirty bookshop down on Id Row. Papa Ny, now, that beast is pure uncut misko through and through. That's why he and Shax get on so dank. Two creeps in a crypt. Papa Ny wears his human costume 28/9, even down here, even when he's sleeping. But on the inside, that cat's a *literal* bookworm, sliming his excrescence up on his ancient manuscripts like an awkward shub on his first dancefloor. I've seen his stash. Those woodcuts are yellow as hell, antique porn for the R'lyeh literati, such as they are. And to make a little extra gleeth on the slant, Papa Ny cuts the endpapers out of whatever forbidden text he's mad at that week, fills them with black Yith-spores scraped off the customers-only sink after hours, and sells them dag cheap, on account of which, he's about the only Elder any of us can stand, and we get to smoke our tomes real nice up here on the roof.

That night, Shax was burning down a flyleaf off the Book of Azathoth, sucking up the purple smoke through seven slits in her protoplasmic face and exhaling misty dodecahedrons out over the power lines and train tracks and horror-shards of our drowned and drowning city. Pazuzu scratched his scabby balls and knocked back a forty of the skunky, hoppy black bile he insisted on brewing in Shit's closet. She hates the smell, but Shit's way too nice to say anything. How the two of us can have come out of the same cloaca is just *beyond*.

"Fuck this," grunted Pazuzu. "I'm sober as a goddamn archeologist. I wanna get bloody *squamous*. 100% *iridescent*. Straight *obliterated*. I wanna yank my brain out through my nose, boil it in beer, and beat the shit out of it with a *fhtagn* hammer. Lurk me?"

I did, indeed, lurk him completely. So did Shax. Her tentacles twisted and lithed above the apex of her gelatinous pyramid-head.

"Iä! Iä!" she ululated. "Screw this babby shit to the seafloor." She threw down her tome and crushed it beneath her protean bulk. "Eeries, let's hunt down some real ichor tonight. I wanna get *ordinary*. I wanna be totally fucking *mundane!* Thoroughly, balls to the wall, XXX *normal*."

This meant gibbering down to the Psychotic Pnakotic for pints of san with rationality chasers. I didn't have the gleeth for that kind of action, no how, but Shax usually covered me. She's a Yith, which is kind of like being in the mafia, except with psychic parasitical spores instead of tommy guns and zoot suits. Zuzu only ever tolerated Shax because she never acted like the richie she was, really. Shax ate shit and puked despair like a real sheol proletariat princess. Like the rest of us. So Zu carefully ignored all the times she picked up our tab.

I groaned. When I groan it sounds like an owl's death-scream. It's my dankest feature.

"I'm not gonna let your mopey tentacled ass get between me and a fœtid high, you *fhtagn* misko," laughed Zuzu, hopping off the roof ledge and running one meaty hand through his pustulant, blood-crusted pompadour. "We're taking the subway and if you whine about it, I'll kick your beak in. And then I'll tell Mom you went to bed at eight with a glass of warm milk and a book so you could be fresh for work in the morning."

If Shub-Niggurath, the Black Goat of the Woods with a Thousand Young, heard that noise, she'd paint the nursery with my intestines.

But you gotta understand, public transportation in R'lyeh is a fucking *shitshow*. Remember that decomposing transdimensional honeycomb knowledge I threw your way earlier? It's the naked truth. This crapheap town is full of holes—and the holes *move*. Look—R'lyeh is old as balls. R'lyeh sits at the crossroads of a million planes of sickening unreality. And R'lyeh does not invest in infrastructure. You can walk down the Uvular in Gugtown, dank and antique as you please, flip a corner, and peer down into the bottomless red cavern of Yoth. You can park in the frozen maze of East Yuggoth and come back to find the volcanic pits of Voormithadreth have totaled your accursed chariot without so much as leaving a note. Nyarlathotep's porn shop on Id Row? That's actually in Carcosa, which isn't anywhere near R'lyeh as the squid swims, but the old bitch-town wore a hole in its filthy sock, and now you can trip over a nightworm in Kadath and land face-down in Carcosa if you don't look both ways before crossing universes.

So the subway is no-go in Moloch world. I'm not about to shoot my shit through Gug-gnawed subterranean tunnels *underneath* this cyclopean clown car and end up drinking on freaking Saturn with a bunch of giant cats. No, thank you.

But for my eeries, anything. Anything, forever, always.

And that's how it happened. That's all it was. Our fœtid, degenerate quest, the dark crusade that would echo down through the centuries like one of Cthulhu's grand farts was just a Hadean beer run through the toilet bowl of the cosmos. Lurk this and lurk it well: the fancier the history reads, the trashier it really was.

⁂

ONLY ONE HOBO Shoggoth barfed and pissed on my feet at the same time the whole way there, and *there* appeared where it was supposed to be after only an hour of the wyrmcar screaming profanities at us. All nameless horrors considered, I call that dank.

⁂

SO A HALF-BREED goatsnake, a Yith, and a Ghast walk into a bar. Stop me if you've heard this one.

Most all the fiends and mutants in the plushy-ass eel booths of the Psychotic Pnakotic swiveled their heads and floating globes and writhing antennae to stare at me and mine. R'lyeh's a pretty conservative squat when you get right down to it. Yiths with Yiths, Ghasts with Ghasts. But I didn't give a *fhtagn* because I'm not a fucking racist. Shax wound one of her crimson tentacles around my neck and we gibbered up to the bar. Shragga was manning the taps. She's got a drill for a face but she's basically yellow.

Shax smeared a dream of becoming and unbecoming on the bar. It glowered ultraviolet netherhot, curdling into pestilent lumpcream. Shragga shrugged. Shax's gleeth was always dank here, even if she wobbled in with her Niggurath cultist boy-thing and embarrassed the high-end clientele.

"Three hits of san with lucidbacks, Shraggs," my girl-thing oozed, right eldritch and shameless.

"We gotta dress code, Yithling," Shragga's drill whined, ground, spun. "Blackest of ties. Writhe here a minute, I've got a couple of old exoskeletons in the back."

Shragga shuddered back with meaty arms full of black clattering crabskin armor that hadn't been sheol since the Cretaceous, whistle-screeched through her drill-face, and poured out three shots of thorazine plus three tall glasses of Providence tapwater. The PP's got a pipe that goes straight up to New England and suckles at the municipal mundflesh supply. Zu and me licked sea spores off Shax's stomach.

One, two, three; grab, slurp, devour, then sucked sour slime off the Providence pipe to chase it down.

"*Fhtagn*, iä!" Zuzu yelled.

The rest of the pub goggled and gurgled and gleeked at us like they never saw anyone enjoying anything in their whole infinite existence before.

God, this fucking neighborhood.

Used to be an antique place, *very* goat, full of artists trying to get back to their roots and hone their craft, create a warm sense of community delirium, drive the mundflesh to a really *authentic* eternal madness. But then the Old Fucks moved in with their gleeth and their gloons and their penthouse sepulchers and organic organ banks and locally-forced whole food cannibal bistros and now it's a shoggo wasteland of narcoleptic zombie demi-gods who couldn't give two deranged toadshits for anyone under a hundred thousand years old. Back in the day, you could *dance* at the Pnakotic. Get your underground shubstep electrotrance tentaclecore maenad groove on. Now we had to sit uncomfortably in some dead crab-god's claw-me-down stench just to get a drink while the upper crusty glared at us like zoo creatures.

Shax swiveled to me, her three globular golden eyes pulsing, her seventeen irises contracting to one hideous human mundeye. "The most merciful thing in the world, I think, is the inability of the human mind to correlate all its contents," she blurted.

"What the fuck?" I giggled.

"Pick up some butter and flour at the store on your way home!" she howled. "The bank keeps calling about our mortgage!"

Pazuzu slapped the pub-floor with one massive kangaroo leg. "*Fhtagn* iä! Can you feel it? Mundmouth McGee is in the house! What do you want for dinner tonight, sweetie? Wouldn't it be wonderful if our son got into Brown next year?"

"Who cares?" I giggled again. I couldn't stop. I could hardly wheeze out words when the lucidity kicked in and my essential Molochness gibbered off.

"Hello," I yelled, as if possessed, without meaning to, without any hunger to: "my name is Moloch, nine hundred and ninety-seventh son of the Great

Black Goat Shub-Niggurath, the Outer God, the All-Mother, and I am an alcoholic. Are there cookies in the back? Debbie always brings pecan sandies."

"Welcome to Mom's Diner, how can I help you?" screamed Zuzu. "How can I help you? How can I help you? How can I help you?"

But it doesn't last. Lucidity has a seriously krug half-life. Our undermatrices can't hold on to the mundo psychfest. It all fucks off back to pecan sandie-land and dumps you in a ditch on the side of the multiverse with drymouth and aching tentacles. We were stuck inside ourselves again pretty quick, a sad brood of dun miskos raging uselessly against the sinferno, the exact opposite of what we hungered.

"I hate my life," I whispered. I couldn't tell if that was me or the san talking.

So we decided to blow that squalor and go glean our eerie Bifrons and shake him down for some furtive fungiform fun.

Bifrons, now, Bifrons is a dank *fhtagn* Mi-Go, the Fungus Among Us, a sheol mushroom man who truly has his gills together, guggo for anything and antique as a china cabinet. You gibber over to Bifrons's flop if you want to get your corpus collosum fully corpse-thrusty skull-strummed. The shiitake scenester laired in a scumlord paradise, waterfront view over a black river of boiling slime that pours eternally into one of R'lyeh's puckered sphincters, the A-Line that leads through the youth-infected artisanal slums and terminates at a certain Mr. Yog-Sothoth's amorphous, radioactive, but surprisingly elegantly lit pad. What can I say, the Thing from Beyond knows from window treatments.

Bifrons does not know window treatments. His flop beholds like a schizoid sewer worker's night terrors. Mold wriggle-gibbering in wallpaper patterns, rags and bones and fugue-pus and broken wine glasses everywhere, Shoggoths yigging idiotically, robotically, in one corner, a mouth-faced Gug smashing his skull into Bifrons's good mirror, a dehydrated Yith crumbling into nothing within reach of the kitchen sink, the floor more spore than rug.

Home sweet home.

Bifrons doesn't charge. He does his song and dance for the jingles and tingles. It's some kind of fetish, I guess. He sweats technicolor dreamvenom the whole time and it's kruggy but Moloch doesn't judge. Gotta get your yig on where you can in R'lyeh. You'd think an insane chthonic carnival of a shriek-powered city pumping out waves of delirium into the seven seas would have some kind of nightlife. But this is pretty much it. Door to door traveling fucksters trying to keep up our enthusiasm for the latest and greatest howling silver vacuum.

"I got leftovers," the preternatural portobello puled in our direction. "You hunger?"

Bifrons tossed Zuzu a mundo Chinese takeaway carton half-full of sweet fried chunks of a divorced mid-level import/export manager's jabbering shredded psyche swimming in anchovy sauce. One, two, three; grab, slurp, devour. Bifrons stroked the greasy slopes of Shax's pyramid with his creeping fungoid fingers, which was not at *all* sheol by me, but you gotta stay yellow if you wanna get squamous with the crimini element around here.

"Everybody goat?" Bifrons lisped thickly, his mushroomy otherflesh beginning to crawl with rainbow glowsweat.

"Iä, Biff, my eerie, my mush, iä," Zuzu hissed.

He was getting bored. Moloch always knows. And when Zuzu gets bored, he starts looking for something to rend. Screams echoed out of the back bedroom and I could tell by the accents of their murdermoaning that it was a high street gloon couple mashing divinities. Probably can't even cum without reciting the names of their fell ancestors into each other's waxy hear-holes. If Zuzu clocked the same, it'd get full ghastly frenzy in here with a quickness.

"Iä, Bifrons, babby, do your thing," I said.

What gets Bifrons off is this: Mr. Morbid Morel worms out his munted wings and the fungal rings of his face start spinning dank and wild. He phases his claws out of the corporeal plane, reaches into your skull, scoops out your brain like vanilla ice cream, sticks it in a dirty glass jar, and shakes the shit out of it until you're addled and rattled and paddled and straddled, then he shoves your milkshake back and watches your soul jiggle out your orifices.

Here we go.

So Moloch's in the brain jar and his medulla is smashbang oblongataed into blueberry psychic jelly and when a Mi-Go has your black matter on frappe, shit gets very topsy indeed. Memory yigs itself raw. One minute I'm goggling out a filthy glass jug, next minute I'm little, tentacles barely grown out yet, writhing on the infinite mud flat of my birth under a gape-wound sky where the stars are dying over and over, being devoured over and over, devoured by something vast and gorgeous and unstoppable, inevitable, perfect in its total hunger.

Shub-Niggurath, the Black Goat of the Cosmos, the Digestrix of Aeons, the All-Mother.

My mother.

I reach my stubby little nubs out to her impossible fœtid body. I stretch every soft babby tentacle curling on my cherub-noggin up to her grotesque countenance, her million interdimensional breasts foamy with nightmare milk, her billion lithe squiddy limbs branching and forking like an immense untoucheable winter tree. Wee tiny Moloch cries for his mama up in the sky and she screeches ultrasonic daemonoharmonic over the boundless blood-swamp of her thousand sobbing young, her babbies, her brood, the spawn of her wonderful hell-womb.

I love you, Mommy, I love you, I wail but she don't come down, she don't wriggle me in her feelers and nuzzle my goaty face looking so much like hers, she don't even know me from my brothers and sisters, she don't pick me out and make me special, she just makes like she's gonna hork up all that starshit she guzzled her whole life like a mama seagull into a thousand writhing gullets and jets. But then she doesn't. She doesn't feed us the stars she got to eat when they were fresh and eldritch and sweet. She keeps it all for herself and we starve while Mumma shrieks across the continuum to something else, something prettier, something danker, something better than us. Than me.

I love you, Mommy. Why don't you love me back?

When Bifrons sleeved me back into my squidsack I was crying hideous, naphtha seeping out my stupid shoggo eyes and stinking up the joint with *feelings*, dripping kerosene shame onto Biff's rug in time to the telltale sound of a scabrous mutant kangaroo named Zuzu thump-thump drumming some sorry fulgy skull into the wetwall.

Be me: Moloch, clawed back from his righteous hard-earned squamous, blurred blotto, gibbering around the rank lair of an evil mushroom, staggering down, then up, then down again before scraping Zuzu off a tall, cold, dark drink of trust fund water half out of his madrags with black, ancient blood all over his dumb wormpile face. Moloch, gobsmacked as a bloody mundo in the naked throbbing bonelight of true reality, when he sees the shub that handsome devil is yigging is none but his babby sister Shit, see-through snakebody wrapped around his tarantula legs, fangs all the way out.

"Stop it, *stop it*, you *fhtagn* shoggo loser," hissed Shit.

"What the *fuck*, Shit?" Zu slurred around the kruggy edges of his Mi-Go trip. "Why you yigging that fuckboy yuppie establishment gloon? You two go suck Elder ass together, too? If you were that hard up I'd have whipped your eggs for you. Why'd you do him for, you mundane bitch?"

My sister uncoiled herself, every inch the serpent daughter of the Digestrix of Aeons. Her hood flared. I don't think I ever noticed how beautiful Shit was before. And the thing is, up until that second, Shit always spoke full fulgy. I never heard her drop so much as a scrap of yellow dank into her talk. But just then, with her cultist boy-thing bleeding into Bifrons's crusted space-colored carpet, she swore like us.

"I didn't hunger *you*, you dun cunt. Lurk me now? Iä? Call him a gloon? No. That's Qaatesh. Say hello, Qaatesh!" The worm-faced hunk of her affections coughed and spat out several fangs. "Lurk him. He has a name, just like you. He enjoys long walks on the beach and flaying the minds of smug academics, not that you give a fuck. Gloon, gloon, gloon. That's all you behold. That's all you babble. Flapping your gash and farting out this kruggy class war squidshit. You think you're sheol? Think you're yellow? Behold me, Pazuzu. *I* am a gloon. I carry water for the Great Old Ones and I am well dank at it. I am paid in blood and diamonds from the nether reaches of space which means *I* have the gleeth to spot you two that nice apartment with the big slither-in closet where you make your garbage homebrew ghastbeer and Moloch puts the empty carton of ichor back in the fridge instead of throwing it out every goddamned time. You hunger to savage some fulgy sneerheart gloon? I'm right here. Show me that eldritch deathdick, you shoggo *fhtagn* fuckaroo."

Zuzu just gawped. A big scab over his ear fell off. I gibbered up between them.

"No deathdicks tonight, brood," I soothed. "Not tonight. What you doing in Bifrons's squalor, brood-girl?" I smiled my most antique smile, tongue behind the teeth and everything.

My translucent sister-snake smoothed down her hood, eyes still blue fire. "Same as you, Moloch. What? I'm not allowed to have a little fun?"

Just like that, Shit was back to her fancy high street babble, stripped of all that oozy slang.

Bifrons asked us, politely, to fuck off out of his squalor. Can't blame the shroom. Brawling harshes his lustfronds. My cultist Shax never said a word the whole time. She doesn't have a brain, per se, so whenever we go Mi-Go she sits in the corner and draws pictures of horses on her jelly belly. She knew horses from all the times she injected her heroin-reek *anima* down inside some overall-wearing ruralfuck pile of mundflesh. Dunno about horses. They just look like munted goats to me. But I always tell her she's got dag talent.

"Hey, Moloch," said Bifrons as I beat the dark aquatic out of there, "watch out for your sister, iä? I worry. You kids are always seething all the time. Just calm down and wait, like the rest of us. Soon enough our time will come."

"*Our* time?" I gibbered. "Whatever, Biff. I don't even know what that means anymore."

⁂

I DON'T REMEMBER whose idea it was. Probably Zuzu. Poor roo had his ichor up and nowhere to spend it. But the dankest shit we ever did always came out of Shax's rotten mind-bucket. It could've been me, even. After all that ungoat business with Bifrons, the featured creature known as Moloch was stone cold sober. And no one can handle R'lyeh at 3 am on a Friday night sober. The streets literally roll up at nine, like slugs shotgunned with salt. You'd kill yourself just to see something interesting go down.

And sometimes, *sometimes*, events just…unfurl. Nobody hungers it, but happenings hunger all on their own. You gibber down the road with your eeries minding your own stench, concentrating extra hard on not getting in trouble, on being an antique boy-thing, a fine, upstanding, mild-mannered unspeakable horror from beneath the skin of reality, and all of a sudden you're standing in front of *His* house, and you don't even know why.

His house. The biggest, grandest, dankest, moldiest, blackest house in town. Cthulhu Central Station, a swanky-ass mansion high on the hill, swollen up with damp, falling down from neglect. Apparently Mr. C don't pay his maids too well. All the best for that fat motherfucker, the blue-blood boss man, the Chief Executive Octopus, winner of Most Likely to Rise Up and Devour the World three aeons running, the patrician magician, the insane aristocrat squatting on all our backs, waiting, dreaming, snoring, farting and scratching his balls in his fulgy *fhtagn* sleep. And he can't even be arsed to tip the help.

We three eeries gawped up at His porch, the columns, the stonework, the yawning height and depth and intellect-shearing ostentation of that naff goth wedding cake of a house. That neighborhood was so eel even Azathoth and Hastur got priced out in the Neolithic Era. We hissed at the flowers. No one but *no one* in R'lyeh could afford a garden—but all around the C-Man's squalor, millions of black lilies and sicksilver roses writhed and runnelled and strangled each other, gibbering up into empty cottages and walk-ups all round the joint, puking out the windows, living rent-free in houses me and mine could only dream of.

A big, blousy fart-bubble belched up from Cthulhu's veiny chimney. Oily colors wriggled on its surface as it rose up through the oceanic ultramarine night. We watched as it burst into a polluted rainbow beneath the black lozenges of ships moving silently through the airy, idiot mundworld.

"Best squamous going, I heard," Shax gurgled. I'd almost forgotten she was there. I'm not much of a cultist when you get right down to it. I know that about myself. I'm trying to work on it.

"Iä, me too, I heard that," Zuzu growled, still stung, pride still snake-stomped. "Only you gotta be 100% goat. Quiet like a misko in a library. If you disturb the man's slumber, it's bad *fhtagn* news. He's cranky when he first wakes up."

So that's how we ended up on a rickety rooftop huffing Cthulhu's farts. Highly recommended; would huff again. They detonate in your brain pan like the birth of cruel galaxies and come streaming out your nose in globs of black opal blood, electric reeking soulpit slime and I loved it, I couldn't get enough. Shax turned bright purple and started sobbing like a wee baby slug, Zu slammed his skull against the chimney over and over till he had a dent in his face like a bootprint, and it was the dankest time I ever had or ever will have.

Shax reeled back, her tentacles floating wild uncurled shub-red gorgeous. Her gelatinous body pulsed out-spectrum colors, a ship code I'd never translate.

"Moloch, darling, love of my pythagorean fundament," she moaned, "we gotta ask, we just *gotta* ask, what are they waiting *for?*"

"Who?" Zuzu rasped, wringing his scabby kangaroo tail in his great meatgob hands.

"Come on, eerie," I sighed, spinning in my own personal gassy squamous. "*Them.* The Elder Gods. The Old Ones. The Waiting Dark. *In his house in R'lyeh dead Cthulhu waits dreaming.* This fat fucking octopus right here." I kicked the gambrel roof twice. "Why's it always gotta be about the *Elder* Gods? What the fuck are they waiting *for?*"

Pazuzu thumped his pustulant tail. "The whole system's rigged," he chanted, "by the time we're Elder, there'll be nothing left for us but the ash-end of the universe. We slobber and serve and ain't nobody ever gonna serve us. It's not right. They got it all stitched up nice the way they like it, Yog-Sothoth and Yig and Azazoth and Hypnos and that fat sack of shit down the chimney. Even Mom. Shub-Niggurath herself, I know we love her and all but she spends all day shitting out kids on the dole and fuck me if you and me will ever be able to afford a slavering brood of our own. And then they turn around and call us krugs and layabout shubs when they're the ones who snooze all aeon instead of rending the mortal world like they always promise. It's bullshit, Moloch. Bullshit."

Shax's three eyes shone hideous, thinking of all those mortal streets she shuffled in her precious bloodpuppets. "You don't even know how right you are, Zuzu. The mundworld is totally shoggo, believe me. The best they could do against us is cry while they piss their pants. But the Old Ones? Oh no, they just gorge and giggle and yig themselves and dick around while centuries go by and those mundo fucks up there invent nuclear fission. They got everything dank there was to devour and we get squidshit because they were born at the dawn of existence and we weren't. Because they're *entitled* to the whole damn multiverse while we're entitled to sit on our asses and clap for their crumbs. Why don't they just *fhtagn retire* and let the Young Ones come up the ranks a little? I'd be a bloody yellow queen of everything. Come on, you know it's true! Shax, the All-Devourer, Accursed Meretrix of the Nether Nebulae, Mother of Madness, Flayer of All Things Dun and Shoggo! I'd capture hearts and minds, you better believe. But no, I have to wait, because they *love* waiting, and maybe when I'm a shriveled old cone I'll get to devour one measly asteroid if I ask real nice. *Fuck* that."

Shax rose up to the dark air, the stubby protuberances beneath her pyramid spinning and smoking furious. She screeched down the chimney.

"Do you hear that, Cthulhu, you sleepy motherfucker? I hate you. I hate you so *fhtagn* much."

Then, Shax did something I didn't even know she could do. Maybe it's just a Yith thing. She sucked up a breath, sucked it all the way in, withered down to a dried-up triangular old-cheese-looking turd-chip and dove down the slime-lung chimney into the bowels of the house of Cthulhu.

Zu and me exploded into a real cacoph of *wait*s and *where*s and *what*s and *Shax you fœtid bitch*es. We gibbered down the brainspout and busted a dag fulgy stained glass window as quiet as we could so as to crawl in after her. My cultist had re-inflated, re-hydrated, and re-animated in the smack middle of the Great Old One's Great Old Foyer. Seventeen dimensional staircases corkscrewed all around her, mirrors yawned into nations unknown and unknowable, old mail spewed out from the post-slot in the Great Old Door. And all over everything sprawled the mottled sicksilver sapphire obese and pustulant tentacles of dreaming, waiting Cthulhu, bulging out everywhere, rotto mottled vomit-golden bloodless flesh balloons straining out of doors, cabinets, furnace grates, snoring like a siren out of time, sickly blueblack suckers all down his diseased limbs opening and closing shubbily, oozing hallucinogenic acidslime onto his own nice clean floors.

Shax dug one of Nyarlathotep's tomes out of who-knows-where and lit it with an orange beam from her lower eye. She kicked one of the wormy tentacles. It didn't budge.

"Maybe he's dead," Zu whispered.

"You wish," I hissed back. One of Cthulhu's moony eyes fluttered iris-down in the downstairs bathtub. Shax was in full seethe, turning magenta with righteous loathing. "Come on, Shax, enough. Babby, let's go. You don't want this ichor on you. It's too much."

Zuzu held out one crusty hand. "Girl-thing, leave this fat bat be. He's not worth it."

Shax smoked her peace for awhile. Listened to the shriek-flute of the Boss's sleep apnea. The end of Papa Ny's hand-rolled tome flared violet flame in the shadows.

"Fine," she said finally. "Whatever."

Mr. Moloch has never done anything so tough in his dun life as getting that granite slab door open without a creak. Mr. Moloch sweated sour green in the dark. And Mr. Moloch, when he got it open, stared across the veranda of the demon of the ultradeep into the crystalline snake-mug of his own sister Shit sidewinding up the stairs.

"I followed you," hissed Shit before I could pull a repeat of my 9 pm performance of the *What Are You Doing Here* jive. "It wasn't hard. You're very loud." Shit quick-kissed my face with the prongs of her tongue. "I do love you, Moloch. I try to look out for your dun ass."

Shit took in the scene. Her many livers and spleens and lungs and stomachs and hearts pulsed wetly in her cellophane skin. She gawped Zuzu, winking guilty side-eye at her because back at Bifrons's pad he'd tried to say he hungered her all casual but it was true and she shut that shit down. She gawped Shax, still flushing squamous magenta fury, plasmic pores still full of iridescent ancient fart-gas, sucking on her tome-butt. She gawped me, mutant goatsnake of the hour, just hungering to bolt back to the couch and sleep and another dun day in R'lyeh. But most of all, she gawped that effulgy fucking house, the columns and staircases and mirrors and curtains and beautiful foetid dank things she'd never have no matter how hard she glooned for the big boys, no matter how antique and eldritch she slavered for them, no matter how many eternities she devoted to their worship and their plans and their secretarial needs. And she gawped the lazyfuck octocunt flop of the squid sensation of every nation, the great pharaonic secret she had never been allowed to behold, even at the office holiday party. And the Great Ancient One, bulging out of every orifice in that grand house we'd never be able to buy if we outlived Saturn, was as disappointing as our own mother, useless and wrinkled and old and shoggo as shit.

Her serpent face crunkled and cracked.

Her organs twisted and boiled inside her. She hungered. Maybe she'd always hungered more than me, and I just don't know anything about anything. I sure as sheol didn't call what happened next.

My babby sister put her eyes on Shax.

"Burn it down," Shit said. "Burn it all down."

Shax grinned. Her pyramid slit itself almost in half to grin that wide. The Yith floated out the Great Old Door and flicked her smoldering tome behind her. It landed in a puddle of Cthulhu's dreamsick spittle.

And the whole place went up behind her like the Big *fhtagn* Bang.

Unto the utter end of time and existence, it was the dankest thing I will ever see.

BE ME: MOLOCH! Eldritch as they come, antique as a goddamned china set, maximum yellow fellow! Only five thousand years old, practically fresh-baked, belly full of san and gas and mushroom chemtrails, tentacles a smoking hot mess, fur the opposite of goat. Gawping on the sidewalk at the big ultraviolet hellcloud of Cthulhu's fancy fucking house burning at the bottom of the sea.

For a minute, I gotta tell you, it felt fucking eldritch, my eeries. I could smell barbecuing god and it smelled like the future. A real future. *Our* future, a future Young and not Elder.

Then the shriek started.

It gibbered up from the cellar and out of the chimney and then everywhere at once. And the shriek had a color. It had a weight. It had shape inside the smoke and flame. The shriek shattered into shards flying up into the sea, out into the city, slicing through reality like sewing scissors. Shax and Shit and Zu and me fell to our knees, assorted mitts over our hear-holes, ready to babble for forgiveness, mercy clemency, all those fulgy words.

Then it stopped. Cool black water flowed down through the transdimensional doily separating us from the sea, down and through and over the Great Old House, drowning out the fire, the smoke, the shriek, everything, everything, smoothing it back the way it was, like nothing ever went down in there, like fire never even got itself invented in the vicinity.

In his house at R'lyeh, dead Cthulhu rolled over on his giant flabby cosmic belly. The last of the flames turned his infinitely-chambered lardheart as orange as a rotting pumpkin, as gold as the world we'll never inherit, as soft and corrupt as the first moldering peach of original sin. In his dreaming, the Old One spluttered, groaned, cried out for some mundforsaken mother I cannot believe ever truly existed, and went back to sleep.

But the shards, my eeries, the shards of that antediluvian shriek were still going, shredding through the dimensional dome of our sky, bobbing up into the galleon-clotted mundsea like insane islands. Me and my brood didn't know it was gonna happen. Believe me that if you believe anything. Everything that happened after that moment, topside and bottom, well, iä, iä, it's our fault, sure, whatever, but all we ever meant to do was forget how garbage R'lyeh really is for one *fhtagn* night. Everybody deserves that, don't they? Once in awhile?

I mean, maybe, just maybe, all that time, Cthulhu was waiting for *us*.

Two of the black ship-blobs tottered squamous up there in the far reaches of the mundworld. Tottered, gibbered, fell. Plummeted down through the fathoms of the fathoms toward R'lyeh, toward us, me and my Shax and my sister and my scabby sweetheart brother, delinquents junking up the gated community. As the wrecks rocketed toward the plane of me and mine in a champagne apocalypse of ultradeep bubbles, I gawped the names on the sides of the kruggy hulls. Just before they crashed our interdimensional undersea party for good, I got their names graffitied on my venomy heart.

The *Alert* and the *Emma*.

What fucking dun names, honestly. Mundflesh's got no sense of style. Shax hid her face in my shoulder. Shit flared her crystal hood so no one would recognize her and shamble-slithered off down an alley 'cause she wasn't gonna take on a speck of shame no matter what. Pazuzu stood fast, though. He squeezed my hand.

"What are you gonna say," Shax whispered, "when our spawn asks where you were the night the humans landed?"

We watched the ships fall down to us like black, uncertain rain.

Oh, well. There goes the neighborhood.

The Limitless Perspective of Master Peek, or, THE LUMINESCENCE OF DEBAUCHERY

When my father, a glassblower of some modest fame, lay gasping on his deathbed, he offered, between bloody wheezings, a choice of inheritance to his three children: a chest of Greek pearls, a hectare of French land, and an iron punty. Impute no virtue to my performance in this little scene! I, being the youngest, chose last, which is to say I did not choose at all. The elder of us, my brother Prospero, seized the chest straightaway, having love in his heart for nothing but jewels and gold, the earth's least interesting movements of the bowel which so excite, in turn, the innards of man. Pomposo, next of my blood, took up the deed of land, for he always fancied himself a lord, even in our childhood games, wherein he sold me in marriage to the fish in the lake, the grove of poplar trees, the sturdy stone wall, our father's kiln and pools of molten glass, even the sun and the moon and the constellation of Taurus. The iron punty was left to me, my father's only daughter, who could least wield it to any profit, being a girl and therefore no fit beast for commerce. All things settled to two-thirds satisfaction, our father bolted upright in his bed, cried out: *Go I hence to God!* then promptly fell back, perished, and proceeded directly to Hell.

The old man had hardly begun his long cuddle with the wormy ground before Prospero be-shipped himself with a galleon and sailed for the Dutch East Indies in search of a blacker, more fragrant pearl to spice his breakfast and his greed whilst Pomposo wifed himself a butter-haired miller's daughter, planting his seed in both France and her with a quickness. And thus was I left, Perpetua alone and loudly complaining, in the quiet dark of my father's glassworks, with no one willing to buy from my delicate and feminine hand, no matter how fine the goblet on the end of that long iron punty.

The solution seemed to me obvious. Henceforward, quite simply, I should never be a girl again. This marvelous transformation would require neither a witch's spell nor an alchemist's potion. From birth I possessed certain talents that would come to circumscribe my destiny, though I cursed them mightily until their use came clear: a deep and commanding voice, a masterful height, and a virile hirsuteness, owing to a certain unmentionable rootstock of our ancient family. Served as a refreshingly exotic accompaniment to these, some few of us are also born with one eye as good as any wrought by God, and one withered, hardened to little more than a misshapen pearl notched within a smooth and featureless socket, an affliction which, even if all else could be made fair between us, my brothers did not inherit, so curse them forever, say I. No surprise that no one wanted to marry the glassblower's giant hairy one-eyed daughter! Yet now my defects would bring to me, not a husband, but the world entire. I had only to cut my hair with my father's shears, bind my breasts with my mother's bridal veil, clothe myself in my brothers' coats and hose, blow a glass bubble into a false eye, and think nothing more of Perpetua forever. My womandectomy caused me neither trouble nor grief—I whole-heartedly recommend it to everyone! But, since such a heroic act of theatre could hardly be accomplished in the place of my birth, I also traded two windows for a cart and an elderly but good-humored plough-horse, packed up tools and bread and slabs of unworked glass, and departed that time and place forever. London, after all, does not care one whit who you were. Or who you are. Or who you will become. Frankly, she barely cares for herself, and certainly cannot be bothered with your tawdry backstage changes of costume and comedies of mistaken identity.

That was long ago. So long that to say the numbers aloud would be an act of pure nihilism. Oh, but I am old, good sir, old as ale and twice as bitter, though I do not look it and never shall, so far as I can tell. I was old when you were weaned, squalling and farting, and I shall be old when your grandchildren annoy you with their hideous fashions and worse manners. Kings and queens and armadas and plagues have come and gone in my sight, ridiculous wars flowered and pruned, my brothers died, the scales balanced at last, for having not the malformed and singular eye, neither did they have the longevity that is our better inheritance, fashions swung from opulence to piousness and back to the ornate flamboyance that is their favored resting state once more. And thus come I, Master Cornelius Peek, Glassmaker to the Rich and Redolent, only slightly dented, to the age which was the mate to my soul as glove to glove or slipper to slipper. Such an age exists for every man, but only a lucky few chance to be born alongside theirs. For myself, no more perfect era can ever grace the hourglass than the one that began in the Year of Our Lord 1660, in the festering scrotum of London, at the commencement of the long and groaning orgy of Charles II's pretty, witty reign.

IF YOU WOULD know me, know my house. She is a slim, graceful affair built in a fashion somewhat later than the latest, much of brick and marble and, naturally, glass, three stories high, with the top two being the quarters I share with my servants, the maid-of-all-work Mrs. Matterfact and my valet, Mr. Suchandsuch (German, I believe, but I do respect the privacy of all persons), my wigs, my wardrobe, and my lady wife, when I am in possession of such a creature, an occurrence more common and without complaint than you might assume, (of which *much* more, *much* later). I designed the edifice myself, with an eye to every detail, from the silver door-knocker carved in the image of a single, kindly eye whose eyelid must be whacked vigorously against the iris to gain ingress, to the several concealed chambers and passageways for my sole and secret use, all of which open at the pulling of a sconce or the adjusting of an oil painting, that sort of thing, to the smallest of rose motifs stenciled upon the wallpaper. The land whereupon my lady house sits, however, represents a happy accident of real estate investment, as I purchased it a small eternity before the Earl of Bedford seized upon the desire to make of Covent Garden a stylish district for stylish people, and the

Earl was forced to make significant accommodations and gratifications on my account. I am always delighted by accommodations and gratifications, particularly when they are forced, and most especially on my account.

The lower floor, which opens most attractively onto the newly-christened and newly-worthwhile Drury Lane, serves as my showroom, and in through my tasteful door flow all the nobly whelped and ignobly wealthed and blind (both from birth and from happenstance, I do not discriminate) and wounded and syphilitic of England, along with not a few who made the journey from France, Italy, Denmark, even the Rus, to receive my peculiar attentions. With the most exquisite consideration, I appointed the walls of my little salon with ultramarine watered silk and discreet, gold-framed portraits of my most distinguished customers. In the northwest corner, you will find what I humbly allege to be the single most comfortable chair in all of Christendom, reclined at a, at first glance, radical angle, that nevertheless offers an extraordinary serenity of ease, stuffed with Arabian horsehair and Spanish barley, sheathed in supple leather the color of a rose just as the last sunlight vanishes behind the mountains. In the northeast corner, you will find, should you but recognize it, my father's pitted and pitiful iron punty, braced above the hearth with all the honor the gentry grant to their tawdry ancestral swords. The ceiling boasts a fine fresco depicting that drunken uncle of Greek Literature, the Cyclops, trudging through a field of poppies and wheat with a ram under each arm; the floor bears up beneath a deep blanket of choice carpets woven by divinely inspired and contented Safavids, so thick no cheeky draught even imagines it might invade my realm; and all four walls, from baseboard to the height of a man, are outfitted with a series of splendid drawers, in alternating gold and silver designs, presenting to the hands of my supplicants faceted knobs of sapphire, emerald, onyx, amethyst, and jasper. These drawers contain my treasures, my masterpieces, the objects of power with which I line my pockets and sauce my goose. Open one, any one, every one, and all will be revealed on plush velvet cushions, for there rest hundreds upon hundreds of the most beautiful eyes ever to open or close upon this fallen earth.

No fingers as discerning as mine could ever be content with the glazier's endless workaday drudge through plate windows and wine bottles, vases and spectacles and spyglasses, hoping against hope for the occasional excitement of a goblet or a string of beads that might, if you did not look too closely, resemble, in the dark, real pearls. No, no, a thousand, *million* times no! Not for me that life of scarred knuckles whipped by white-molten strands of stray glass, of unbearable heat and even more unbearable contempt oozing from those very ones who needed me to keep the rain out of their parlors and their spirits off the table linen.

I will tell you how I made this daring escape from a life of silicate squalor, and trust you, as I suppose I already have done, to keep my secrets—for what is the worth of a secret if you never spill it? My deliverance came courtesy of a pot of pepper, a disfigured milkmaid, and the Dogaressa of Venice.

It would seem that my brothers were not quite so malevolently egomaniacal as they seemed on that distant, never-to-be-forgotten day when our father drooled his last. One of them was not, at least. Having vanished neatly into London and established myself, albeit in an appallingly meager situation consisting of little more than a single kiln stashed in the best beloved piss-corner of the Arsegate, marvering paltry, poignant cups against the stone steps of a whorehouse, sleeping between two rather unpleasantly amorous cows in a cheesemaker's barn, I was neither happy nor quite wretched, for at least I had made a start. At least I was in the arms of the reeking city. At least I had escaped the trap laid by pearls and hectares and absconding brothers. And then, as these things happen, one day, not different in any quality or deed from any other day, I received a parcel from an exhausted-looking young man dressed in the Florentine style. I remember him as well as my supper Thursday last—the supper was pigeon pie and fried eels with claret; the lad, a terrifically handsome black-haired trifle who went by the rather lofty name of Plutarch, and after wiping the road from his eyes and washing it from his throat with ale that hardly deserved the name, presented me with a most curious item: a fat silver pot, inlaid with a lapis lazuli ship at full sail.

Inside found I a treasure beyond the sweat-drenched dreams of upwardly mobile men, which is to say, a handful of peppercorns and beans of vanil, those exotic, black and fragrant jewels for which the gluttonous world crosses itself three times in thanks. Plutarch explained, at some length, that my brother Prospero now dwelt permanently in the East Indies where he had massed a fabulous fortune, and wished to assure himself that his sister, the sweet, homely maid he abandoned, could make herself a good marriage after all. I begged the poor boy not to use any of those treacherous words again in my or anyone's hearing: not *marriage*, not *maid*, and most of all not *sister*. Please and thank you for the pepper, on your way, tell no one my name nor how you found me and how did you find me by God and the Devil himself—no, don't tell me, I shall locate this lost relative and deliver the goods to her with haste, though I could perhaps be persuaded to pass the night reading a bit of Plutarch before rustling up the wastrel in question, but, hold fast, my darling, I must insist you submit to my peculiar tastes and maintain both our clothing and cover of darkness throughout; I find it sharpens the pleasure of the thing, this is my, shall we say, *firm* requirement, and no argument shall move me.

Thus did I find myself a reasonably rich and well-read man. And that might have made a pleasant and satisfying enough end of it, if not for the milkmaid.

For, as these things happen, one day not long after, not different in any hour or act than any other day, a second parcel appeared upon my, now much finer, though not nearly so fine as my present, doorstep. Her name was Perdita, she was in possession of a complexion as pure as that of a white calf on the day of its birth, hair as red as a fresh wound, an almost offensively pregnant belly, and to crown off her beauty, it must be mentioned, both her eyes had been gouged from her pretty skull by means of, I was shortly to learn, a pair of puritanical ravens.

It would seem that my other brother, Pomposo—you remember him, yes? Paying attention, are we?—was still in the habit of marrying unsuspecting girls off to trees and fish and stones, provided that the trees were his encircling arms, the fish his ardent tongue, and the stones those terribly personal, perceptive, and pendulous seed-vaults of his ardor, and poor, luckless Perdita had taken *quite* the turn round the park. Perhaps we are not so divided by our shared blood as all that, Pomposo! Hats off, my good man, and everything else, too. Well, the delectably lovely and lamentable maid in question found herself afflicted both by Little Lord Pomposo and by that peculiar misfortune which bonds all men as one and makes them brothers: she had a bad father.

Perdita told me of her predicament over my generous table. She spoke with more haste than precision, tearing out morsels of Mrs. Matterfact's incomparable baked capon in almond sauce with her grubby fingers and shoveling it into that plump face whilst she rummaged amongst her French pockets for English words to close in her tale like a green and garnishing parsley. As far as I could gather, her cowherding father had, in his youth, contracted the disease of religion, a most severe and acute strain. He took the local clergyman's daughter to wife, promptly locked her in his granary to keep her safe from both sin and any amusement at all, and removed a child from her every year or so until she perished from, presumably, the piercing shame of having tripped and fallen into one of the more tiresome fairy tales. Perdita's father occupied the time he might have spent *not* slowly murdering his wife upon his one and only hobby: the keeping of birds of prey. Now, one cannot fault the man for that! But he loved no falcons nor hawks nor eagles, only a matched pair of black-hearted ravens he called by the names of Praisegod and Feargod (there really can be no accounting for, or excusing of, the tastes of Papists) which he had trained from the egg to hunt down the smallest traces of wickedness upon his estate and among his children. For this unlikely genius had taught his birds, painstakingly, to detect the delicate and complex scents of sexual congress, and the corvids twain became so adept that they were known to arrive at many a village window only moments after the culmination of the act.

Now you have taken up all the pieces of this none-too-sophisticated puzzle and can no doubt assume the rest. My brother conquered Perdita's virtue with ease, for no such dour and draconian devoutness can raise much else but libertines, a fact which may yet save us from the vicious fate of a world redeemed, and put my niece (for indeed it proved to be a niece) in her with little enough care for anything but the trees and the fish and the stones of his own bucolic life. No sooner than he had rolled off of her but Praisegod and Feargod arrived, screeching to wake the glorious dead, the scent of coupling maddening their black brains, and devoured Perdita's eyeballs in a hideous orgy of gore and terribly poor parenting. Pomposo, ever steadfast and humbly responsible for his own affairs, sent his distress directly to me and, I imagine, poured a brimming glass of wine with which to toast himself.

"My dear lady," said I, gently prying a joint of Mrs. Matterfact's brandied mutton from her fist, hoping to preserve at least something for myself, "I cannot imagine what you or my good brother mean *me* to do with a child. I am a bachelor, I wish devoutly to remain so, and my bachelorhood is only redoubled by my regrettable feelings toward children, which mirror the drunkard's for a mug of clear water: well enough and wholesome for most, he supposes, but what can one *do* with one? But I am not pitiless. That, I am not, my dear. You may, of course, remain here until the child…occurs, and we shall endeavor to locate some suitable position in town for one of your talents."

Ah, but I had played my hand and missed the trick! "You misunderstand, *monsieur*," protested the comely Perdita. "Mister Pompy didn't send me to you for your *hospitalité*. He said in London he had a brother who could make me eyes twice as pretty as they ever were and would only charge me the favor of not squeezing out my babe on his parlor floor."

Even a thousand miles distant, my skinflint family could put the screws to me, turn them tight, and have themselves a nice giggle at my groans. But at least the old boy guessed my game of trousers and did not give me up, even to his paramour.

"They was green," the milkmaid whispered, and the ruination of her eye sockets bled in place of weeping. "Like clover."

Oh, very well! I am not a *monster*. In any event, I wasn't then. At least the commission was an interesting enough challenge to my lately listless and undernourished intellect. So it came to pass that over the weeks remaining until the parturition of Perdita, I fashioned, out of crystal and ebony and chips of fine jade, twin organs of sight not the equal of mortal orbs, but by far their superior, in clarity, in beauty, even in soulfulness. If you ask me how I accomplished it, I shall show you the door, for I am still a tradesman, however exalted, and tradesmen tell no tales. I sewed the spheres myself with thread of gold into her fair face, an operation which sounds elegant and difficult in the telling, but in the doing required rather more gin, profanity, and blows to the chin than any window did. When I had finished, she appeared, not healed, but more than healed—sublimated, rarefied, elevated above the ranks of human women with their filmy, vitreous eyes that could merely *see*.

I have heard good report that, under another name, and with her daughter quite grown and well-wed, Perdita now sits upon the throne of the Netherlands, her peerless eyes having captivated the heart of a certain prince before anyone could tie a rock round her feet and drop her into a canal. Well done, say all us graspers down here, reaching up toward Heaven's sewers with a thousand million hands, well done.

Now, we arrive at the hairpin turn in the road of both my fortunes and my life, the skew of the thing, where the carriage of our tale may so easily overturn and send us flying into mud and thorns unknown. Brace your constitution and your credulity, for I am of a mind to whip the horses and take the bend at speed!

It is simply not possible to excel so surpassingly as I have done and remain anonymous. God in his perversity grants anonymity to the gifted and the industrious in equal and heartless measure, but never to the *splendid*. Word of the girl with the unearthly, alien, celestial eyes spread like a plague of delight in every direction, floating down the river, sweeping through the Continent, stowing away on ships at sea, until it arrived, much adorned with my Lady Rumor's laurels, at the *palazzo* of the Doge in darling, dripping Venice.

Now, the Doge at that time had caused himself, God knows why or by dint of what wager, to be married to a woman by the name of Samaritiana. Do not allow yourselves to be duped by that name, you trusting fools! Samaritiana would not even stop along the side of the road to Hell to wrinkle her nose at the carcass of Our Lord Jesus Christ, though it save her immortal soul, unless He told her she was beautiful first. Oh, 'tis easy enough to hate a vain woman with warts and liver spots, to scorn her milk baths and philtres and exsanguinated Hungarian virgins, to mock her desperation to preserve a youth and beauty that was never much more enticing than the local sheep in the first place, but one had to look elsewhere for reasons to hate Samaritiana, for she truly was the singular beauty of her age. Black of hair, eye, and ambition was she, pale as a maiden drowned, buxom as Ceres (though she had yet no issue), intoxicating as the breath of Bacchus. Fortunately, my lady thoughtfully provided a bounty of other pantries in which to find that meat of hatred fit for the fires of any heart.

She was, quite simply, the worst person.

I do not mean by this to call the Dogaressa a murderess, nor an apostate, nor a despot, nor an embezzler, nor even a whore, for whores, at least, are kindly and useful, murderers must have some measure of cleverness if they mean to get away with it, apostates make for *tremendous* company at parties, despots have a positively devastating charisma, and I am assured by the highest authority, which is to say, Lord Aphorism and his Merry Band of Proverbials, that there is some honor amongst thieves. No, Samaritiana was merely humorless, witless, provincial, petty, small of mind, parched of imagination, stingy of wallet and affection, morally conservative, and incapable, to the last drop of her ruby blood, of admitting that she did not know everything in all the starry spheres and wheeling orbits of existence, and this whilst believing herself to possess all of these that are virtues and eschew all that are sins. Can you envisage a more wretched and unloveable beast?

I married her, naturally.

The Dogaressa came to me in a black resin mask and emerald hooded cloak when the plague had only lately checked into its waterfront rooms, sent for a litter, and commenced seeing the sights of Venice with its traveling hat and trusted map. Oh, no, no, you misapprehend my phraseology. Not *that* plague. Not that grave and gorgeous darkling shadow that falls over Europe once a century and reminds us that what dwells within our bodies is not a soul but a stinking ruin of fluid and marrow and bile. The *other* plague, the one that sneaks on nimbly putrefying feet from bedroom to bedroom, from dockside to dinner party, from brothel to marital bower, leaving chancres like kisses too long remembered. Yes, we would have to wait years yet before Baron von Bubœ mounted his much-anticipated revival on the stage, but never you fear, Dame Syphilis was dancing down the dawn, and in those days, her viols never stopped nor slowed.

That mysterious, morbid, nigh-monstrous and tangerine-scented creature called Samaritiana darkened my door one evening in April, bid me draw close all my curtains, light only a modest lantern upon a pretty lacquered table inlaid with mother of pearl which I still possess to this day, and stand some distance away while she removed her onyx mask to reveal a face of such surpassing radiance, such unparalleled winsomeness, that even the absence of the left eye, and the mass of scars and weals that had long since replaced it, could do no more than render her enchanting rather than perfect.

It would seem that the Dogaressa danced with the Dame some years past. Her husband, the Doge, brought her to the ball, she claimed, having learned the steps from his underaged Neapolitan mistress, though, as I became much acquainted with the lady in later years, I rather suspect she found her own way, arrived first, wore through three pairs of shoes, departed last, and ate all the cakes on the sideboard. But, as is far too often the case in this life ironical, that mean and miserly soul found itself in receipt of, not only the beauty of a better woman, but the good fortune of a better man. She contracted a high fever owing to her insistence upon hosting the Christmas feast out of doors that year, so that the gathered noblility could see how lovely she looked with a high winter's blush on her cheeks, and this fever seemed to have driven, by some idiot, insensate alchemy, the Dame from the halls of Samaritiana forever, leaving only her eye ravaged and boiled away by the waltz. All was well in the world, then, save that she could not show herself in public without derision and her husband still rotted on his throne with a golden nose hung on his mouldering face like a door knocker, but she had not come for his sake, nor would she ever dream of fancying that it was possible to ask a boon of that oft-rumored wizard hiding in the sty of London for any single soul on earth other than herself.

"I have heard that you can make a new eye," said she, in dulcet tones she did not deserve the ability to produce.

I could.

"Better than the old, brighter, of any color or shape?"

I could.

She licked her lily lips. "And install it so well none would suspect the exchange?"

Perhaps not quite, not *entirely* so well, but it never behooves one to admit weakness to a one-eyed queen.

"You have already done me this service," said she to me, loftily, never asking once, only demanding, presuming, crushing all resistance, not to mention dignity, custom, the basest element of courtesy, beneath her silver-tooled heel. She waved her hand as though the motion of her fingers could destroy all protestation. The light of my lantern caught on a ring of peridot and tourmaline entwined into the shape of a rather maudlin-looking crocodile gnawing upon its own tail, for she claimed some murky Egyptian blood in the dregs of her familial cup, as though such little droplets could mark her as exceptional, when every dockside lady secretly fancies herself a Cleopatra of the Thames.

"Produce the results upon the morrow! I will pay you nothing, of course. A Dogaressa does not stoop to exchange currency for goods. But when two eyes look out from beneath my brow once more, I will present you with a gift, for no particular reason other than that I wish to bestow it."

"And if I do not like your gift, *Clarissima?*"

Puzzlement contorted her exquisitely Cyclopean visage, causing a most unwelcome familial pang within my breast. "I do not take your meaning, Master Peek. How could such a thing possibly occur?"

There is, it seems, a glittering point beyond which egotism achieves such purity that it becomes innocence, and that was the country in which Samaritiana lived. In truth, had she revealed her gift to me then, or even promised payment in the usual manner, I might have refused her, just to experience the novel emotion of rejecting royalty—for I am interested in nothing so much as novelty, not love nor death nor glass nor gold. Something new! Something new! My kingdom for something new! But she caught me, the perfumed spider, wholly without knowing what she'd done. I did indeed take up her commission, and though you may conclude in advance that this recounting of the job will proceed according to the pattern of the last, I shall be disappointed if you do, for I have already told you most vividly that herein lies the skew of my tale.

For the sake of the beautiful Dogaressa, I took up my father's battered old pipe and punty. I cannot now say why; for a certainty I owned better instruments by far, and had not touched the things in eons except to brush them daintily with a daily sneer. Perhaps a paroxysm of sentimentality seized me; perhaps I despised her too much even then to waste my finer appliances on her pox-punched face, in any event, I cannot even say positively that the result blossomed forth from the tools and not some other cause, and I fear to question it now. I sank into the rhythm of my father and grandfather and his before him: the dollop of liquid glass, the greatbreath of my own lungs expelled through the long, black pipe, the sweet pressure and rolling of the globule against the smooth marver stone, the uncommon light known only to workers of glass, that strange slick of marmalade-light afire within crystal that would soon ride a woman's skull all the way through the days of her life and down into her tomb.

The work was done; I fashioned two, an exquisitely matched pair, in case the other organ required replacement in the unseen feverish future. Samaritiana, in, so far as I may know or tell, the sole creative decision of her existence, chose not one color for the iris, but all of them, dozens of infinitesimal shards chipped from every jewel in my inventory: sapphire, jade, emerald, jasper, onyx, amethyst, ruby, topaz. The effect was a carnival wheel of deep, unsettling fascination, and when I sewed it into her flesh with my golden thread she did not wail or struggle, but only sighed, as though lost in the act of love, and, though her faults were called Legion, they were as yet unknown to me, thus, as my needle entered her, so too did my fatal softening begin.

The Dogaressa departed with her stitching still fresh, leaving in her wake but three souvenirs of our intimate surgery: one gift she intended, one she did not, and her damnable scent, which neither Mrs. Matterfact nor Mr. Suchandsuch, no matter how they scrubbed and strove, could remove from the premises. I daresay, even this very night, should you venture to my old house on the High Street and pressed your nose to its sturdy bones, still yet you would snatch a whiff of tangerine and strangling ivy from the foundation stones. The gift she intended to leave was a lock of her raven hair, the skinflint bitch. The other, I did not perceive until some weeks later, when I adjourned to my smoking room with a bottle of brandy, a packet of snuff, and a rare contemplative mood which I intended to spend upon a rich, unfiltered melancholy as sweet as any Madeira—for it is a fact globally acknowledged that idle melancholy, like good wine, is the exclusive purview of the wealthy. To aid in my melancholy, I fingered in one hand the mate to the Dogaressa's harlequin eye, rubbing my thumb over that strange, motley iris, marveling at the milky sheen of the sclera, admiring, unrepentant Narcissus that I am, my own skill and artistry. I removed my own, ordinary, unguessable, nearly flawless glass eye and held up the other to my empty socket like a spyglass, and a most thoroughly stupendous metamorphosis transpired: I could *see* through the jeweled lens of that artificial eye! Truly see, without cloud or glare or halo—ah, but *what* I saw was not the walls of my own smoking room, so tastefully lined with matching books chosen to neither excite nor bore any guest to extremes, but the long peach-cream and gold hall of *the palazzo of the Doge in far-distant Venice!* The chequered black and white marble floors flowed forth in my vision like a houndstooth river; the full and unforgiving moon streamed glaucous through tall slim windows; painted ceilings soared overhead, inlaid with pearl and carnelian and ever-so-slightly greyed with the smoke of a hundred thousand candles burnt over peerless years in that grand corridor. Women and men swept slowly up and down the squares like boats upon some fairy canal, swathed in gowns of viridescent green cross-hatched with silver and rose, armored in bodices of whalebone and opal, be-sailed in lacy gauze spun by Clotho herself upon the wheel of destiny, cloaked and hooded in vermillion damask, in aquamarine, in citron and puce, their clothing each so splendid I could scarce tell the maids from the swains—and thus looked I upon a personal paradise heretofore undreamt of.

But there were worms in paradise, for each and every beauty in the Doge's palace was rotting in their finery like the fruit of sun-spoiled melons within their shells. Their flesh putrefied and dripped from their bones and what remained turned hideous, sickening colors, choleric, livid, cyanic, hoary, a moldering patina of death whose effusions stained those bodices black. Some stumbled noseless, others having replaced that appendage with nostrils of gold and silver and crystal and porcelain, and others, all hope lost, sunk their visages into masks, though they could not hide their chancred hands, the bleeding sores of their bosoms, the undead tatters of their throats.

Yet still they laughed, and spoke animatedly, one to the other, and blushed in virtuous fashion beneath their putridity. Such is the dance of the Dame, who enters through the essential act of life, yet leaves you thinking, breathing, walking whilst the depredations of the grave transact upon your still-sensate flesh, making of this world a single noisy tomb.

My breath would not obey me; my heart ricocheted amongst my ribs like a cannon misfired. Was it truly Italy I saw bounded in the tiny planet of a glass eye? Had I stumbled into a drunken sleep or gone mad so swiftly no asylum could hope to catch me? I shot to my feet, mashing the eye deeper into my socket until stars spattered my sight—closer, look closer! Could I hear as well? Smell? Taste the tallowed air of that far-off moonlit court?

I could not. I could not hear their footsteps nor inhale their perfume nor feel the fuzzed reek of the mildewed canals on my tongue nor move of my own volition. I apprehended a new truth, that even the impossible possesses laws of its own, and those unbendable. I could only observe. Observe—while my vision lurched forward, advancing quickly, rocking gently as with a woman's sinuous gait. Graceful, slender arms extended as though from my own body, opening with infinite elegance to embrace a man whose head was that of a Titan cast down brutally into the pit of Tartarus, so wracked with growths and intuberances and pulsating polyps that the plates of his skull had cracked beneath the intolerable weight and shifted into a new pate so monstrous it could no longer bear the Doge's crown, which hung pitifully instead from a ribbon slung round his grotesque neck. Those matchless arms which were not my own enfolded this hapless creature and, encircling the middle finger of the hand belonging to the right arm, I saw with my altered vision the twisted peridot and tourmaline crocodile ring of the Dogaressa Samaritiana.

I cast the glass eye away from me, sickened, thrilled, inflamed, ensorcelled, the fire in my midnight hearth as nothing beside the conflagration of curiosity, horror, and the beginnings of power that crackled within my brain-pan. In that first moment, standing among my books and my brandy drenched in the sweat of a new universe, an instinct, a whisper of Truth Profound, permeated my spirit like smoke exhaled, and, I confess to you now, all these many years hence, still I enshrine it as an article of faith, for it was with *breath* that God animated the dumb mud of Adam, *breath* that woke Pandora from stone, *breath* that demarcates the living and the dead, *breath* with which we speak and cry out and divide ourselves from the idiot kingdom of animals, and *breath*, by all the blasted saints and angels, with which the glassblower shapes his glass! The living breath of Cornelius Peek yet permeates every insignificant atom of his works; each object broken from his punty, be it window or goblet or cask or eye, hides the sacred exhalations of his spirit co-mingled with the crystal, and it is this, it is *this*, I tell you, that connects the jeweled eye of the Dogaressa with the jeweled eye in my hand! *I* dwell in the glass, it cannot dispense with me any further than it can dispense with translucency or mass, and therefore it carries the shard of Cornelius whithersoever it wanders.

Let us dispense with a few obnoxious but inevitable inquiries into the practicality of the matter, so that we may move along past the skew. How could this mystic connection have escaped my notice till now? It is only sensical: Perdita vanished away to the Netherlands with both marvelous eyes, and no window nor goblet nor cask is, in its inborn nature, that organ of sight which opens onto the infinite pit of the human soul. Would any eye manufactured in the same fashion result in such remote visions? They would indeed, my credulous friend. Does every glassblower possess the ability to produce such objects, should he but retain one eye whilst selling the other at a fair price? Ah, here I must admit my deficiency as a philosopher, for which I apologize most obsequiously. It cannot be breath alone, for I made subtle overtures toward the gentlemen of the glassmen's guild and I can say with a solemn certainty that none but Master Peek can perform this alchemy of sclera and pupil. Why should it be so? Perhaps I am a wizard, perhaps a saint, perhaps a demiurge, perhaps the Messiah returned at last, perhaps it owes only to that peculiar rootstock of my family which grants me my height, my baritone, the hairiness of my body. Grandfather Polyphemus's last gift, lobbed down the ancestral highway, bashing horses as it comes. I am a man of art, not science. I ask why Mrs. Matterfact has not yet laid out my supper oftener than I ask after the workings of the uncluttered cosmos.

Thus did I enter the business of optometry.

When you have placed a mad rainbow jewel in the skull of a Dogaressa as though she were nothing but a golden ring, a jewel which drove the rotting men of Venice insane with the desire to tie her to a bridge-post and stare transported into the motley swirling colors of the eye of God, lately fallen to earth, they began to say, somewhere in Sicily, advertisement serves little purpose. I opened my door and received the flood. It is positively *trivial* to lose an eye in this wicked world, did you know? I accepted them warmly, with a bow and a kerchief fluttered to the mouth in acute compassion, a permanently sympathetic expression penciled onto my lips in primrose paint—for that moth-eaten scab Cromwell was finally in the grave, where everything is just as colorless and abstemious and black as he always wished it to be, so full of piss and vitriol that it poisoned him to the gills, and Our Chuck, the Merry Monarch, was dancing on his bones. Fashion, ever my God and my mother, took pity upon her poor supplicant and caused a great miracle to take place for my sake—the world donned a dandy wig whilst I doffed my own, sporting my secret womanly hair as long and curled as any lord, soaking my face in the most masculine of pale powders, rouges, lacquers, and creams, encasing my figure, such as it ever was, in lime and coral brocade trimmed in frosty silver, concealing my gait with an ivory cane and foxfurred slippers, and rejoicing in the knowledge that, of all the men in London, I suddenly possessed the lowest voice of them all. So hidden, so revealed, I took all the one-eyed world into my parlor: the cancerous, the war-wounded, the horse-kicked, the husband-beaten, the inquisitor-inquisited, the lightning-struck, the unfortunately-born, the pox-blighted, and yes, the Dame's erstwhile lovers, for she had made her way to our shores and had begun her ancient gambols in sight of St. Paul's. And for each of these unfortunate angels of the ocular, I fashioned a second eye in secret, unknown entirely to my custom, twin to the one that repaired their befouled faces, with which I adjourned night by night to a series of successive smoking rooms, growing grander and finer with each year, holding those orbs to the light and looking unseen upon every city in Christendom, along with several in the Orient and one in the New World, though it could hardly be called a city, if I am to be honest.

In this fashion, I came to know that the Doge had died, succumbed to the unbearable weight of his own head, long before Samaritiana appeared on my night-bestrewn doorstep, the saffron gown she wore in the moonlight, and every other in her trunk, torn violently, soaked with bodily fluids, rent by the overgrown nails of the frenzied rotting horde who had chased her from the *palazzo* through every desperate alleyway and canal of the city, across Switzerland and France, in their anguished longing to touch the Eye of God, still sewn into the ex-Dogaressa's skull, to touch it but once and be healed forever.

But of course I aided the friendless and abandoned Good Samaritiana as she wept beside her monstrous road. Oh, *Clarissima*, how dreadful, how unspeakable, how worthy of Mr. Pepys' vigilant pen! I shall have to make introductions when you are quite well again. I sent at once for a fine dressmaker of my acquaintance to construct a suitable costume for the lady and save her from the immodesty of those ragged silken remnants of her former life with which, even then, she attempted to cover her body with little enough success that, before the dressmaker could so much as cross the river, I learned something quite unexpected concerning the biography of Samaritiana, former queen of Venice.

She was quite male. Undeniably, conspicuously, astonishingly, fascinatingly so.

I called up to Mrs. Matterfact for cold oxtongue, a saucer of pineapple, and oysters stewed in Armagnac, down to Mr. Suchandsuch for carafes of hot claret mulled via the latest methods, and listened to the wondrous chimera in my parlor tell of how that famous Egyptian blood was not in the least of the Nile but of the Tiber, on whose Ostian banks a penniless but beautiful boy had been born in secret to one of the Pope's mistresses and left to perish among the reed-gatherers and the amber-collectors and the diggers of molluscs. But perish the lad did not, for even a grass-picker is thoroughly loused with the nits of compassion, and the women passed the babe one to the other and back again, like a cup of wine that drank, instead, from them. Now, it is well known to anyone with a single sopping slice of sense that the Pope's enemies are rather like weevils, ever industrious, ever multiplying, ever rapacious, starving for the chaff of scandal with which to choke the Holy Father and watch him writhe. They roved over the city, overturning the very foundational stones of ancient Rome in search of the Infallible Bastards, in order, not to kill them like Herod, but to bring them before the Cardinals and etch their little faces upon the stained glass windows as evidence of sin. My little minx, having already long, lustrous hair and androgyne features more like to a seraph than a by-blow son, found it at first advantageous to effect the manners and dress of a girl, and then, when the danger had passed, more than that, agreeable, even preferable to her former existence. Having become a maid to save her life, she remained one in order to enjoy it. Owing to the meager diet of the Tiber's tiniest fish, little Samaritiana never grew so tall nor so stout as other boys, she remained curiously hairless, and though she escaped the castrato's fate, her voice never dipped beneath the pleasing alto with which she now spoke, nor did her organ of masculinity ever aspire to outdo the average Grecian statue, and so, when the Doge visited Ostia after the death of his first wife, he saw nothing unusual walking by the river except for the most beautiful woman in the Occident, balancing a basket of rushes on her hip with a few nuggets of amber rolling within the weave.

"But surely, *Clarissima*," mused I, savoring the tart song of pineapple upon my tongue, "a bridegroom, however ardent, cannot be so easily duped as a vengeful Cardinal! Your deception cannot have survived the wedding bower!"

"It did not survive the engagement, my dear Master Peek," Samaritiana replied without a wisp of blush upon her remarkable cheek. "Oh, mistake me not, I do *so* love to lie—I see no more purpose in pretending to be virtuous in your presence than I saw in pretending to be fertile in his. But there could be no delight in a deception so deep and vast. It would impair true marriage between us. I revealed myself at Pentecost, allowing him in the intensity of his ardor to unfasten my stays and loose my ribbons until I stood clad only in honesty before His Serenity and awaited what I presumed to be my doom and my death. But only kisses fell upon me in that moment, for the Doge had long suppressed his inborn nature, and suffered already to get upon his departed wife the heirs he owed to the canals, and though my masquerade, you will agree, outshines the impeccable, he would later say, on the night of which you so confidently speak, that some sinew of his heart must always have known, since first he beheld me with my basket of amber and sorrow."

I did not exchange trust for trust that night among the oysters and the oxtongue. I have a viciously refined sense of theatre, after all. I made her wait, feigning religion, indigestion, the vicissitudes of work, gout, even virginity, until our wedding night, whereupon I allowed Samaritiana, in the intensity of her ardor, to unfasten my stays and loose my ribbons until at last all that stood between us was the tattered ruin of my mother's ancient bridal veil, and then, not even that.

"Goodness, you don't expect me to be surprised, do you?" laughed the ex-Dogaressa, the monster, the braying centaur, the miserly lamia who would not give me the satisfaction of scandalizing her! That eve, and only that eve, under the stars painted upon my ceiling, I applied all my cruellest and most unfair arts to compel my wife to admit, as a wedding present, that she had *not* known, she had never known, never even suspected, loved me as a man just as I loved her as a woman, and was besides a brutal little liar who deserved a lifetime of the most delectable punishment. We exchanged whispered, apocryphal, long-atrophied names beneath the coverlet: *Perpetua. Proteo.*

Samaritiana treated me deplorably, broke my heart and my bank, laughed when she ought to have wept, drove Mrs. Matterfact to utter disintegration, kept lovers, schemed with minor nobles. We were just ferociously happy. Are you surprised? I, too, am humorless, witless, provincial, petty, small of mind, parched of imagination, stingy of wallet and affection, a liar and a cad. She was like me. I was like her. I had, after all, seen as she saw, from the very angle of her waking vision, which in some circles might be the definition of divine love. I have had wives before and will have again, far cleverer and braver and wilder than my Clarissima, but none I treasured half so well, nor came so near to telling the secret of my smoking room, of the chests full of eyes hidden beneath the floorboards. Samaritiana had her lovers; I had my eyes, the voyeur's stealthy, soft and pregnant hours, a criminal sensorium I could not quit nor wished to. Yet still I would not share, I held it back from her, out of her reach, beyond her ken.

The plague took her in the spring. The Baron, not the Dame. The plague of long masks and onions and bodies stacked like fresh laid bricks. I buried her in glass, in my incandescent fury at the kiln, for where else can a man lose his whole being but in a wife or in work? These are the twin barrels in which we drown ourselves forever.

It soon came to pass that wonderful eyes of Cornelius Peek were in such demand that the possession of one could catapult the owner into society, if only he could keep his head about him once he landed, and this was reason enough that, men being men and ambition being forever the most demanding of bedfellows, it became much the fashion in those years to sacrifice one eye to the teeth-grinding god of social mobility and replace it with something far more useful than depth perception. Natural colors fell by the wayside—they wanted an angel's eye, now, a demon's, a dryad's, a goblin's, more alien, more inhuman, less windows to the soul than windows to debauched and lawless Edens and I, your servant, sir, a window-maker once more. I cannot say I approved of this self-deformation, but I certainly profited by the sudden proliferation of English Cyclopses, most especially by their dispersal through the halls of power, carrying the breath of Peek with them into every shadowy corner of the privileged and the perverse.

I strung their eyes on silver thread and lay in a torpor like unto the opium addict upon the lilac damask of my smoking room couch, draping them round and round my body like a strand of numberless pearls, lifting each crystal gem in turn to gaze upon Paris, Edinburgh, Madrid, Muscovy, Constantinople, Zurich—and Venice, always Venice, returning again and again, though I knew I would not find what I sought along those rippling canals traveled by the living dead. It became my obsession, this invasion of perspective, this theft of privacy, the luxurious passivity of the thing, watching without participating as the lives of others fluttered by like so many scarlet leaves, compelled to witness, but not to interfere, even if I wished to, even if I had liked the young Earl well enough when I installed his pigment-less diamond eye, and longed to parry the assassin's blade when I saw it flash in the Austrian sunset. I saw, with tremulous breath, as God saw, forced unwilling to allow the race of man to damn or redeem itself in a noxious fume of free will, forbidden by laws unwritten not to lift one hand, even if the baker's boy had laughed when I offered him a big red eye or a cat-slit pupil or a shark's unbroken onyx hue, any sort, free of charge, even the costliest, the most debonair, in honor of my late wife Samaritiana who in another lifetime paid me in hair, not because she would wish me to be generous, but because she would mock me to the rafters and howl hazard down to Hell, begging the Devil to take me now rather than let one more pauper rob her purse, even if I saw, now, through his eye, saw the maidservant burning, burning in the bakery on Pudding Lane, burning and screaming in the midnight wind, and then the terrible, impossible leap of the flames to the adjoining houses, an orange tongue lasciviously working in the dark, not to lift one hand as what I saw in the glass eye and what I saw in the flesh became one, fusing and melding at last, reality and unreality, the sight I owned and the sight I stole, the conflagration devouring the city, the gardens, and my house around me, my lovely watered ultramarine silk, my supremely comfortable chair stuffed with Arabian horsehair, my darling gold and silver drawers, as I lay still and let it come for me and thee and all.

I did not *die*, for heaven's sake. Perish the thought! Death is terrifically *gauche*, don't you know, I should never be caught wearing it in public. I simply did not get *up*. Irony being the Lord of All Things, the smoking room survived the blaze and I inside it; though the rafters smoked and blackened and the walls swelled with heat like the head of a Doge, the secret chambers honeycombing the place contained the inferno, they did not stove in nor fall, save for one shelf of books, the bloody Romans, of all things, which, in toppling, quite snapped both my shinbones beneath a ponderous copy of Plutarch. Mrs. Matterfact and Mr. Suchandsuch fought valiantly and gave up only the better part of the roof, though we lost my lovely showroom, a tragedy from which I shall never fully recover, I assure you. And for a long while, I remained where the fire found me, on the long damask couch in my smoking room, wrapped in lengths of eyes like Odysseus lashed to the mast and listening to all the sirens' mating bleats, still lifting each in turn and fixing it to my empty socket, one after the other after the other, and thus I stayed for years, years beyond years, beyond Matterfact and Suchandsuch and their replacements, beyond the intolerable plebians outside who wanted only humble, honest brown and blue eyes again, their own mortal eyes, having seen too much of wildness. And what, pray tell, did I do with my impossible sight, with my impossible span of time?

Why, I became the greatest spy the world has ever known. Would you have done otherwise?

Oh, I have sold crowns to kings and kings to executioners, positions to the enemy and ships to the storm, murderers to the avenging and perversities to the puritanical, I have caused ingenious devices to be built in England before the paint in Krakow finished drying, rescued aristocrats from the mob and mobs from the aristocracy by turns, bought and traded and brokered half of Europe to the other half and back again, dashed more sailors against the rocks than my promethean progenitor could have done in the throes of his most orgiastic fever-dream. I have smote the ground and summoned up wars from the deeps and I have called down the heavens to end them, all without moving one whisper from my house on Drury Lane, even as the laborers rebuilt it around me, even as the rains came, even as the lane around it became a writhing slum, a whore's racetrack, a nursery rhyme.

Look around you and look well: this is the world I made. Isn't it charming? Isn't it terrible and exquisite and debased and tastefully appointed according to the very latest of styles? I have seen to every detail, every flourish—think nothing of it, it has been my great honor.

But the time has come to rouse myself, for my eyes have begun to grow dark, and of late I spy muchly upon the damp and wormy earth, for who would not beg to be buried with their precious Peek eye, bauble of a bygone—and better—age? No one, not even the baker's boy. The workshop of Master Cornelius Peek will open doors once more, for I have centuries sprawled at my feet like Christmas tinsel, and I would not advance upon them blind. I have heard the strange mournful bovine lowing of what I am assured are called the *proletariat* outside my window, the clack and clatter of progress to whose rhythm all men must waltz. There is much work to be done if I do not wish to have the next century decorated by some other, coarser, less splendid hand. I shall curl my hair and don the lime and coral coat, crack the ivory cane against the stones once more, and if the fashions have sped beyond me, so be it, I care nothing, I will stand for the best of us, for in the end, the world will always belong to dandies, who alone see the filigree upon the glass that is God's signature upon his work.

After all, it is positively *trivial* to lose an eye in this midden of modernity, this precarious, perilous world, don't you agree?

Snow DAY

22. *TEA FOR THREE*
Published 1934, Harem House Press, 128 pages

GUDRUN HATED HER NAME, HER mother, and bad art. She loved her house, a wild turkey called Murray who had decided to live out his sunset years in her garden, and Cold Palace Brand No. 1 Silver Needle Tea, which, by the time the rest of everything started up, had been off the shelves for sixteen years, its manufacturer bankrupt, its overseas contracts liquidated, and its remaining inventory burned to exquisite ash on the banks of the Min River in Fujian Province as a helpful illustration of the myriad benefits to be found in punctually presenting the correct money to the correct people. Gudrun had not stockpiled. Why should she? Her lifeblood had waited loyally for her in Mr. Abalone's shop since the first time her mother dragged her into the village for a guilty relapse into cigarettes and beef jerky, stacked in delicate tins with white peonies embossed on the mirrored metal like aching frost. It always *would* wait for her. Cold Palace Brand No. 1 Silver Needle Tea was a fundamental element underlying the known universe. Until it didn't, and it wasn't, and then it was too late to do anything but curl her face into a ferocious, animal sneer when the black-eyed man behind the counter suggested Lipton instead, it's all the same, you know, plants is plants.

Gudrun wanted a color television, to live forever, and to have a child. But she was about to turn forty and all of human civilization was about to end, so only one of those seemed vaguely realistic anymore.

21. *THE SULTAN'S WAYWARD DAUGHTER*
Published 1949, Belladonna Classics, 157 pages

GUDRUN'S MOTHER WAS a professional politician's mistress, named Ruby, and long dead. Intraocular cancer. Practically, what that meant was that sometime between autumn and spring 1964, black nebulas burst open in Ruby's eyes. Dark, glistening masses, inky veins snaking out over pupil and iris and white, milky star-muck filming over the last green smears of the world outside her own head. Gudrun stared into the abysses, asked how many fingers, brought whiskey, shut up about the doctor, for Christ's sake. For awhile, Ruby wore sunglasses, and then the nebulas burrowed down into her skull and she didn't need to wear anything anymore and that was that. Gudrun was old enough by a minute and a half to get the house, the red Studebaker, and a savings account full of the apologies of powerful men.

Ruby never planned to go into her particular line of work. She had wanted to be a travel writer when she grew up. But she was just desperately beautiful and congenitally unhappy and fluent in Hungarian. There never was any hope for her. Ruby met the state governor on the campaign trail and, two years later, when he was done with her, she couldn't find a door that led back into the plainspoken universe of men who had never been inaugurated into anything. She circulated through a closed loop of hotels she could never review and men in dark sunglasses with no interest in the amenities of local beaches and redacted names on receipts she would never turn into a magazine for reimbursement. State senator (Virginia), two real senators (junior from Maine and senior from Minnesota), Secretaries of Agriculture, Energy, *and* Defense, and, she claimed, the Vice-President, though Gudrun never quite bought it. Their circumstances seemed right about Secretary of Agriculture level. If Mums had bagged the VP, the Studebaker would probably be new enough to start more mornings than not.

Minnesota was Gudrun's father. That was how Ruby referred to them all, her erstwhile oligarch sweethearts. She wouldn't let them keep their names once they'd taken what they wanted from her. Maine, Minnesota, Virginia. Aggie, Ennie, Deffy, Vice. And Minnesota was the one who managed to leave evidence. It wasn't any mystery. Gudrun could turn on the television most days and see just exactly what she would look like if she were a boy, and surrounded by microphones. The senior senator from the Land of 10,000 Lakes was coming up in the world and fast.

The first and last thing Minnesota ever bothered to do for his daughter was strap on her name, her stupid, terrible German name that fell on your ear like a boot. A family name, without a family attached. Then, Gudrun, too, became redacted. Turned out Ruby's specialized industry had an early retirement age. If enough kingmakers smuggle you in and out of the palace, the king gets to know your face. You can't just stand adoringly in the crowd anymore. The camera sees. It wonders what you know. After the whole business in Dallas, most everybody in the palace cashed out and scattered like crows.

So, when Gudrun was twelve, Ruby packed them up and over and out, here, to Hawaii, and then further still, to a teak and tile house in the Ko'olau Range and some fuzzily demarcated acreage full of hibiscus and frigatebirds and sweet potatoes growing in the wet dirt. The village, which in Ruby's personal glossary never had a name important enough to remember, was ten miles of mud cliff roads there and gone. A few feral pigs and chital deer saw their telltale faces. No one else. No one cared who they'd been before, or even who they were now. Sometimes it felt like they lived at the bottom of the world.

People on the bottom of the world mind their own business, mostly.

20. *THE BUTLER DID ME*
Published 1960, Eros Inc, 98 pages

THE HOUSE HAD been previously owned by one Jack Oskander, a vaguely successful coffee grower who lost it all, to the last bean, in the crash and sold his summer place (furnished) to the first disgraced Capitol Hill courtesan to walk through the jungle with cash in hand. Gudrun always thought Old Jack must have been a real cut-up, because he'd named the place Pemberley, and nothing in this angel-abandoned world looked less like Mr. Darcy's grand

and ancient estate than their four mildewed rooms on pylons over a thin rushing creek and clotted forest spitting passionfruits like black tumors into the eye of a pond sixty feet down the cliffside.

But Pemberley had beds and dishes and chairs and electricity—and books. The shelves crowded every wall like ladders to knowledge: hardboiled detective paperbacks gone soft with the humidity, an O.E.D, several academic volumes on Communist theory, a peppering of children's fairy stories, and the Oskander Special Collection: a sprawling assemblage of erotica, utterly catholic in interest, protagonists, and style, three books deep on some shelves, meticulously organized and catalogued with a corresponding index kept in Jack's shockingly elegant penmanship and hidden in a rusty samovar between the *Corrupted Virgins* section and the *Dominant Lesbians* section, an exhibition of love and flesh and longing vast enough to keep even the Vice-President hard to the end of his days.

19. *RAVISHED BY THE BEAST!*
Published 1955, French Letter Books, 111 pages

THE VILLAGE CINEMA was a one-screen, apathetically air-conditioned popcorn cartel called the Uptown Grand (the village possessed neither an uptown, nor a downtown, nor sidetowns of any sort). On the day Gudrun, aged sixteen, ran away from home, it was showing *The Curse of the Werewolf*, starring Clifford Evans and Oliver Reed. She sat in the perfect dark with a cold strawberry pop clutched like a rosary between white knuckles, finally away, away from Pemberley, away from Ruby, away from her father's face on the television, away from digging skinny sweet potatoes in the ground and thin dribbly coconut milk (because you can't trust the tap water, Guddy, how many times do we have to talk about this) and Jack Oskander's *Artists' Models* section with its sea of pale breasts and parted, moldy, waiting lips.

By the time the beautiful mute jailer's daughter died giving birth to her cursed son in a badly-lit Spanish forest under the millionth shot of a portentous moon, Gudrun lay on the butter-streaked floor of the theater gasping for air. Hot, reeking tears poured from her swollen eyes. By the time Mrs. Kamēaloha got her safely back up the mountain, the girl's face was covered in tiny silver pimples, like spores bursting open. Gudrun's mother didn't say a word. She just kissed her baby all over and poured about twenty bottles of mineral water into the bathtub to bubble her clean.

Having been told all her life that she was possessed of terrible sensitivities—to dairy, to tree nuts, to lavender, to wheat, to industrial dyes and perfumes, to all brown spices (cinnamon, cumin, allspice, garam masala, and so forth), to corn syrup and hydrogenated oils and cold air, to sodium laurel sulfate and shellfish and sunlight—it came as something of a surprise to Gudrun that her sole physical allergy was to bad art.

But bad art was everywhere. You couldn't escape it. It wouldn't leave you *alone*. Gudrun's skin raised up in hives when the brass bristle of insincere three-chord pop music scraped static against her ears. Her throat swelled up in sight of garish, oversaturated advertisements emblazoned with ungraceful fonts. Laugh tracks induced instant vomiting.

This limited her options for natural conception. Her body could hardly survive the derivative, obvious, artless world anymore.

Gudrun only ever came down off the ridge for her tea, which Mr. Abalone would happily have tossed into the mango crates with her monthly delivery of toilet paper, soap, butter, spam, noodles, ketchup, and sugar, except that Gudrun never put it on the account. She made the pilgrimage for Cold Palace Brand No. 1. It was the actual least she could do. To prove she was still here. Still a person.

Then it all burned on the banks of the Min River and these days she couldn't prove anything if you asked her to.

18. *A VIRGIN IN CHAINS*
Published 1930, Fig Leaf Press, 161 pages

JACK OSKANDER'S PERSONAL library educated Gudrun as best it could, because Ruby couldn't bear the thought of her going to school in the village.

First, it was the paralyzing notion that someone might see her, might recognize her, might guess her father by the line of her nose, the color of her eyes. Then, it was just silly to waste all day in a classroom with idiots who would work all their lives just to add without using their fingers when Ruby could teach her anything she could even imagine—*go on, honey, test Mumsy, ask me anything, I'll know it, I shoulda gone on the quizzies, I'd have cleaned up.*

Gudrun thought about it. She could have gone with: *When are we going back to Baltimore?* Or: *Did my father love me even a little?* Or: *How do you say 'if I have to stay in here with you every day I'll murder you flat' in Hungarian?* But she knew smartass was rarely the right play with Ruby, whose ass was forever the smartest in the room. So she shrugged, sipped her cup of Cold Palace Brand No. 1 Silver Needle Tea, and said flatly:

"What year did Manuel Komnenos ascend to the throne of the Byzantine Empire? What was the Black Pope of Avignon's name? How many people died in Napoleon's Russian campaign? Show me how to do a Riemann sum. How do you structure a villanelle?"

Not since Minnesota wired her the money for Pemberley had she seen Ruby's face so full of blood and hate and shame and pride. Gudrun felt awful immediately. The tea went cold in her mouth.

"It's okay, Mama," she whispered. "I don't want to go to school, anyway."

17. *BIRTHDAY GIRL SURPRISE*
Published 1958, Virago Books, 118 pages

THERE WERE TWO dates circled on Gudrun's *Surfin' Cats!* calendar. Both were in November, under a photo of a somewhat-alarmed-looking Persian balanced precariously on a red and yellow board with half a coconut plopped on her head as a festive hat.

The first was Gudrun's fortieth birthday. The other, one day later, simply said:

Snow Day.

16. *LOVE ROBOTS FROM PLANET XX*
Published 1954, Harem House Press, 106 pages

GUDRUN BEGAN WORKING her way through Jack Oskander's pornography collection before their suitcases were unpacked. She grabbed one off the shelf above the kitchen sink and read with one hand while stacking mugs with the other.

CHET HARDTREE RAN his strong hands over the smooth titanium curves of the Adoratron Mark 5. She was built like a luxury rocketship, sleek lines designed for low resistance and high-speed maneuvers. In the darkness of the Reproduction Chamber, the red globes of her tits glowed as her arousal drives whirred into hypermax.

"Full thrusters engaged, Commander Hardtree," the Adoratron purred.

"WHAT THE FUCK is *that*, Gudrun?" Ruby snapped. Her infamous velvet voice sliced up the air between them like claws.

"Nothing, Mama!"

But Ruby was on top of her before she could stash Chet Hardtree and the Adoratron Mark 5 in her back jeans pocket. Those gorgeous blue eyes that once made senators swoon seared into her daughter, accusing, such a strange, dark shade of blue, like a lantern-fish's deep-sea heart. Tears wavered in her dark lashes.

"Baby, baby," Ruby whispered, sobs hitching somewhere behind her words, "I'm sorry, I didn't mean to yell. Don't cry, I don't want to shame you, preciousness. Mumsy's not looking to scar you for life. It's only...sweetie... you just *can't* stack the blue mugs with the red ones! The warm colors and the cool colors have to stay separate, they *have* to, or else, or else...the *balance* will be upset...the balance of space and time and you and me and goodness and badness...baby, it's *so* important, you have to learn...here, honey, see? They go left to right, like a spectrum. See?"

"I'll learn, Mama," Gudrun said softly, as her mother carefully re-arranged the universe, keeping ever her hands quarantined, left for reds and oranges and golds and bisques and pinks, right for blues and greens and blacks and purples and greys. And in between the two tottering ceramic columns of being and non-being, Ruby stacked three tins of Cold Palace Brand No. 1 Silver Needle Tea, a bulwark against contamination.

15. *THE GARDENER PLANTS HIS SEED*
Published 1927, Adonis Editions, 114 pages

MURRAY STAKED HIS claim in the Pemberley gardens ten years exactly after Ruby died. He wasn't a local bird—the wild fowl running around the Ko'olau Range were skinny and skittish and rarely came up to Gudrun altitude. Murray was a splendid tall fat fellow with a proud bronze chest as iridescent as a peacock, a brilliant blue face and a throat as red as a Russian spy. Gudrun stumbled out in her long johns to check the rain barrels and the bean runners and whack a guava off her tree for breakfast and there he sat like a fancy lord between the eggplants and the red cabbage, mist dappling his chest like silver armor. He looked like he could hardly move under the weight of his finery.

The moment Murray saw Gudrun, love blossomed at Pemberley. He could move, and wonderfully. Murray puffed up his chest and sprang his thick fan of chocolate-colored tail feathers, his long neck flushed white, and he began to prance back and forth in front of her, dragging his grand speckled wings through the leek plants, telling her all he knew of turkey life. Not gobbling, as Gudrun thought all turkeys did and all they could do, but a barking, bellowing, drumming caw deep in his breast, a cry of desperate, loud, unlovely want that she recognized instantly, in her bones and her blood. If she had the anatomy for it, Gudrun would have made that sound at everyone she ever met. *Please want me. Please know me. Please come with me and keep my eggs warm and secret and safe. Please don't devour me. There is so little time left.*

14. *THE SERPENT IN EVE'S EDEN*
Published 1933, Red Light Limiteds, 144 pages

EVENTUALLY, THE TRUTH came out of Ruby like an infected organ.

Gudrun couldn't go to school because of the poisons, poisons everywhere, a toxicity so total that the two of them could only escape it by staying here, on the island, far away from the corrupted mainland. But that was not enough, not by half. The village was lost already. They had to make Pemberley a fortress, a haven, an outpost in a sea of infection. Up here, and only up here, they could stay safe. Didn't Guddy see it was absurd and obscene to come all this way, then turn right around and send her from their cozy little bastion into the heart of miasma, into a swarm of germ-infested children and virulent teachers where Gudrun's little body would be lashed with horrors? An invisible murderous horde waited down there: lead in the paint they use on pencils and plastic wrap and in water pipes and gasoline and lunch plates and gym walls, invisible radon gas seething from underground, fluoridated water to make the population docile, pesticides lacquering every scrap of food you didn't grow yourself, bleach in the wheat and the milk, formaldehyde lathered on hormone-riddled hamburgers to make meat look fresh and injected in your arm to keep *you* fresh only then they called it vaccination, and the worst of it all, the radiation, radiation like a terrible golden rain everywhere, all the time, leftover from the bombs in Japan and the secret tests in the atolls, oozing from refrigerators and power lines and those new microwave ovens and planes overhead, from the radio waves pounding their heads constantly like the sea against the shore, and the sun, the broken, angry sun bleeding through holes in the sky no one could see but they're *there*, Guddy, just because you can't see it doesn't mean it can't kill you. Only Pemberley was safe, hoisted up above the venomous earth, beneath a thatched and metal-less roof, far from the soup of contagion that was other people and convenience and basic technology.

Ruby grabbed her daughter's hands as tight as steel screws. Her nails dug in.

"Listen to me, baby. I *know.* Aggie told me everything one night years ago. We lay in a giant bed in the St. Francis Hotel and looked out over the

San Francisco lights, down the rainy streets toward the Convention where Ike and ol' Dickie were shaking their jowls and dodging balloons and he cried in my arms, Guddy. He said in thirty years, there'll be nothing living on this planet but brine shrimp. Even the cockroaches will go. Every continent will be buried under irradiated human bones like snow. They can't stop it. It's already happening. They just don't want people to panic. Let them enjoy their last days. But *I* know. I know the *truth*. And it's not gonna get me. I'm gonna stick it out till the end. I'm gonna see the snow."

But she didn't, because Ruby got cancer anyway, even though she never drank the tap water.

13. *PUNISHING THE TEACHER'S PET*
Published 1940, French Letter Books, 150 pages

RUBY PROVED TO be no help at all. Her knowledge was enormous but haphazard, picked up discount from many flea markets of the mind, and useless to a twelve-year-old girl, unless she needed to understand how Russians had infiltrated the Manhattan Project or the CIA experiments with psychedelic drugs and astral projection. Besides, they had to get the garden in. The sooner they could stop relying on commercial products, the better for both of them.

Gudrun took herself in hand. She slept with Jack's O.E.D. under her head, the constant, dripping humidity having softened it to a serviceable pillow. She peeled quickly through the fairy tales and Communist philosophy, feeling strongly both that the witch in the candy hut was framed and that the tragedy of the commons was so much bullshit, lingered briefly on the detective novels before deciding that it was nearly always safe to say that whoever loved the dead most had killed them, and finally, plunged headfirst into the real meat of the Oskander library, afraid at any moment that Ruby would stop her and burn the lot for compost ash.

She didn't, but after the first week settling in, Ruby forbade her daughter to read two books together whose titles did not begin with adjoining letters of the alphabet. This would upset the balance of causality, just as a misalignment of the mugs would upset the balance of heat and cold.

Gudrun ignored the rule completely, and many years later, would ask Murray if he thought that was why it all happened the way it did. Murray thought the chances were about 50/50.

12. *CLEOPATRA'S CHAMBER OF FORBIDDEN LOVE*
Published 1957, Blue Fairy Books, 188 pages

THERE ARE WORSE educations than Gudrun's. Enough pornography gathered together in one place constitutes a complete history of the world.

She wedged herself into the snug space made by the triangle of *Historical (Hetero)*, *Historical (Homo)*, and *Historical (Lesbian)* sections, beginning with the incestuous passion of Egypt's pharaohs and the flesh gardens of Babylon, then on to the lascivious sworn bands of Greece and the sweat-drenched bath houses of Rome, the perfumed harems and enticing eunuchs of Byzantium, the medieval world full of lusty wenches and protected princesses and tragic Jewesses and wicked Inquisitors, the Italian decadence of the Renaissance and the frantic, nihilistic love of the plague years, the dandies of the Restoration seizing their servants in unjust and unbridled lust, the restrained and suffocated libidos of the Regency, the sadism of French aristocrats on the eve of revolution, the starched Victorian bodies writhing in unmet needs, the love of lieutenants and enlisted men in the trenches of the First World War, on and on into the modern world of class war between the working class mechanic and the rich man's wife, the international intrigue of the Soviet spy and the American virgin, the mathematical possibilities of wife swapping, the oppression of the black man and his white bride, the night nurses in secret love, the sailors who dare not give in to their longings, the heaving social unrest of such vast need, unspoken, unanswered, in a long unbroken chain down the endless ages of man.

11. *A BIRD IN THE HAND IS WORTH TWO BUSHES*
Published 1962, Adonis Editions, 115 pages

MURRAY WAS BORN in Texas. He never said anything about it to Gudrun, but sometimes, in the autumn, he still dreamt of the dry, crisping sun on the Rio Grande, the smell of smokefires and thirsty weeds. Nothing was ever thirsty here.

Between 1961 and 1964, the United States Forestry Service rounded up four hundred turkeys from the deserts of central and southern Texas and released them on the Hawaiian Islands to encourage the development of a native population, and, presumably, the kind of curious but undeniable emotional attachment to eating turkey that afflicted the majority of Americans.

Murray didn't know about any of that. He only knew that sometimes, when Gudrun started up the Studebaker engine, the sound of it made him tremble, made him remember, if dimly, a terrible silver bird, so much larger than himself, than any bird could ever be, so vast and loud and monstrous it could be nothing but God, God incarnated and migrating from the Great All-Twig Paradise Nest, God coming for him, taking him, Murray, an ordinary tom, nothing special at all, into its fearsome clanging belly of blessings and flying, flying like death, flying forever until he passed out cold from sheer, shivering religious terror.

When Murray awakened, God had left him, and everything smelled like rain.

10. *THE SCOTSMAN AND THE SHEPARDESS*
Published 1921, Galatea Books, 156 pages

RUBY'S RULES LASTED long after she died. But not forever. Gudrun did try. She knew how important it was to eat only what you could grow or kill yourself, to keep your body pure and free of toxins, to check monoxide and radon levels regularly, to never install a telephone no matter what anyone said, to trust in wholesome herbs and flowers instead of industrial poisons that only mask symptoms and lull you to complacency, to sleep with a Geiger counter and a gun close by in case of emergencies. Gudrun governed herself by these principles because Ruby couldn't anymore.

"If we're careful, baby, we can live forever," Ruby told her with black nebulas screaming out of her eye sockets, seeping blood and pus like miracle tears spattering a statue of the Virgin. "Or at least until they burn out the earth from under us twenty years from now. Death was invented by corporations to ensure a constant stream of new customers. We don't need death. We don't need anything they want to sell us. We just need each other and a patch of good earth."

"But Mama, you're so sick…"

Ruby sopped up her disintegrating eyes with a cloth soaked in red clover oil and Cold Palace Brand No. 1 Silver Needle Tea. "I started too late, Guddy, that's all. I sucked up all the poison the bad old world had on tap and asked for more because I didn't know better. By the time I got right with the cosmos, I was already rotting. But I got *you* out in time. I did that."

Gudrun sat back on her heels and watched her mother lying in her last bed. Maybe this was what happened to you if enough people threw you away. You just rotted to pieces at the bottom of the bin. Or maybe Ruby really was holding the entire starry universe together by the arrangement of her coffee mugs.

"And you cheat," she whispered, barely able to squeak it out.

"Don't be disrespectful," Ruby sighed. She handed her daughter the washcloth to rinse and re-soak. Gudrun did it, but she didn't stop talking. She hated herself for talking but she couldn't undo it now.

"There's a pack of menthol Tareytons under the rain barrel outside and there's *always* a pack of Tareytons under there and you've got a bag of Oh Boy! Oberto Teriyaki Jerky in your underwear drawer and *those* have sodium nitrite in them and I'm pretty sure whiskey is, like, its whole own kind of poison, so you cheat, even though I have to have carob instead of chocolate and no friends."

Ruby folded her hands in her lap like a little girl. Gudrun laid the fresh washcloth over her weeping eyes—real tears, now, turning the blood and pus and thready nameless black bile pale.

"I'm just a person, Guddy," she whimpered softly. "Mumsy's pretty weak, when you add me up."

"It's okay," Gudrun answered, because it was the only answer.

"I order my whiskey special," Ruby offered, as apology, defense, defiance. "Small batches, no factory processing. Made by real Scottish people."

9. *LOVEPIG*
Published 1961, Blue Fairy Books, 156 pages

GUDRUN WAS SHAKING the first time she changed her order with Mr. Abalone. She was twenty-four. She wanted to live forever. She wanted to be better than Ruby. She did. But she also remembered what hot dogs tasted like. And ketchup. And white sugar in her tea. They were part of a broken history that belonged to her but did not—dimly remembered hotels overflowing with room service, individually packaged sweeteners, creamers, condiments, convenience stores snuck to in the middle of the night, brown bag lunches left out in the sun.

And Ruby couldn't stop her anymore.

Gudrun ate that first forbidden slice of fried spam with a cold, shining glob of red ketchup alone in the dark. She cried so hard her eyes burned and throbbed and all she could see on her plate was a swimming blackness.

8. *THE SWORD OF LUST*
Published 1950, Harem House Press, 199 pages

GUDRUN NEVER HAD any kind of reaction to the Oskander Special Collection. No hives, no vomiting, no silver stains. For a long time, she didn't understand it. You couldn't say *The Sin Pit* or *Confessions of a Rent Boy* or *The Butler Did Me* were masterworks. They were certainly no better than *The Curse of the Werewolf*, which had, in the end, left her with a pale, watery scar on her forehead and down the hairline on the left side of her face. Jack's dirty books were the definition of bad art. But she could curl up in the bathtub and listen to the rain and read *The Sword of Lust* over and over and feel nothing more than desire, despite its obvious failings:

VUVULA, QUEEN OF the Night Demons, sat upon the Throne of Desire, her jeweled bodice glittering in the light of the thousand golden candelabras that hung from the rafters of the Sacred Hall. Nubile slave girls dressed only in rose petals combed her raven tresses and moaned in ecstasy. Her emerald eyes flashed haughtily at the interloper.

"Come forward, Sir Quicktongue, and kneel before me!" cried Vuvula, her breasts quivering with rage and secret yearning.

"Nay, my Lady," answered Sir Quicktongue, Knight of the Hidden Flower. "I am bound by my sacred oath to kneel only before she who can reforge my shattered sword with her own bare hands. This is the curse and the riddle that drives me from town to town, bed to bed, through forest and swamp, over mountain and sea, and I may not rest until it is satisfied!"

THE ANSWER CAME to her many years later, after she had planted Ruby in the mountain earth like a sweet potato. Those books were just what they aspired to be, nothing more and nothing less. They achieved their ambitions and fulfilled their purpose. Against all stylistic, narrative, and technical odds, they performed the function of fiction and imitated a certain delicate reality perfectly. Not the reality of Ruby and Gudrun and Murray and the Secretary of Agriculture and the Uptown Grand Cinema, but something better, a cohesive universe of total generosity, of events occurring in perfect order and quick succession, want expressed and immediately satisfied, all else besides want jettisoned, unnecessary, left far behind.

7. DOES SHE DO IT ON THE FIRST DATE?
Published 1961, Fig Leaf Press, 171 pages

GUDRUN DIDN'T WANT a child for the reasons she presumed other people did. She didn't want company because she couldn't ever remember having any to begin with and she didn't think babies were cute because they really fell pretty low in the hierarchy of adorable young animals and she didn't need anyone to take care of her when she got old because she had Murray. She didn't have any faith in future generations. She didn't think her genes were anything special. She didn't even think she'd be a particularly good mother, though she felt pretty confident she could best the local record without much effort.

Gudrun wanted a child because 57.9% of Jack Oskander's books ended that way. You wouldn't think so, but they did. Maybe Old Jack just liked those stories better than others. Maybe the ratio would hold even if you had the whole of the publishing world packed into a four-bedroom bungalow. A pregnancy, a return to a happy family after erotic adventuring, an orphan adopted, a runaway un-runnedaway. The statistics were overwhelming and undeniable. No other ending had those numbers, not weddings, not tragic death, not even simple orgasm and breakfast after. A child was *the* ending. The Platonic. The ideal. The good art.

The requirement of another person irritated Gudrun profoundly. There had never been anyone else but her and Ruby. The Adoratron Mark 5's Reproduction Chamber seemed so much easier and more sensical. Why should she have to track down somebody and convince them she wasn't weird, which she was, and let him, a total stranger who had once been one of those germ-infested children Ruby so feared, who couldn't hold a candle to Chet Hardtree or Sir Quicktongue and probably had never so much as glanced at *The Sword of Lust* in the library, invade her body and infect her with his alien DNA? She couldn't think how it could possibly happen. If a nice man took her out to dinner, all she'd be able to manage would be to order the soup and then bellow Murray's broken-drum scream/belch mating cry in his face.

It happened once, of course. Everything does. Eventually. But there was no child.

Instead, Gudrun split in half a month before Snow Day.

6. *THE SINNER AND THE NUN*
Published 1956, Harem House Press, 203 pages

MR. ABALONE DIED in March, 1976. His son took over the general store and Gudrun would probably never have known one way or the other except that a little while afterward, a tin of Cold Palace Brand No. 1 Silver Needle Tea turned up in her monthly delivery, snuggled in between the bag of sugar and the toilet paper. Gudrun screamed in joy. Six years down the hole in a tealess purgatory. Her scream echoed around the jungle hills. Murray fretted and pulled out a tail feather in his distress.

Inside the tin, with its etched peonies and elegant cursive logo lay a note:

> *I found a crate in the warehouse after Dad passed. I thought I remembered you like this stuff. Tea doesn't go bad, does it?*
>
> *—Johnny Abalone*

Johnny Abalone was a ridiculous name, that much was clear. Not even the Oskander Collection would tolerate a hero with a name like that. Not even *The Pearl Diver Dives for More*, and that was easily the worst of the lot. Gudrun meant to make her tea last this time, horde it against the Silver Needle-less future. But she was weak, when you added her up. She drank it all in a day, cup after cup, until she was sick, and kept drinking anyway. She drank in a delirium of plenty, grabbing a new mug from the cabinet every time, so that none of them would feel left out. When she went to bed, the counter was a riot of crockery, red and blue and white and black scattered everywhere, with no pattern, like summer flowers. She'd fix it up in the morning. No problem. Gudrun's sleeping stomach distended as if she'd conceived from fine leaves and hot water, but she wasn't sorry.

Every month, a new tin arrived with a new note.

I drank some of this stuff. Figured if you like it so much, it must be something grand. Tastes like licking nickels to me, but I guess nothing tastes the same to two people at a time. Maybe the pipes are going. Can't make good tea without clean water and the stuff out of the faucet looks a little yellow these days. I guess you're on well water up there. I bet that's nice.

—Johnny Abalone

I remember you came down to the shop that one time and I said you should just drink Lipton instead. That was stupid of me. I know how sometimes you just want what you want and fuck everything else. I know how sometimes what you want is gone and it feels like you're not allowed to be as upset as you need to be about it.

Hey, do you have a generator up there? I hate to think of you stuck in the blackouts. Pretty bad this year, huh? Last longer and longer. I have a spare if you need it.

—Johnny Abalone

Do you take your tea with milk or lemon or sugar or what? The little white bits look like hair to me. Like an old man's hair.

It's pretty quiet in the shop these days. I think people liked Dad and got used to him but now it's just me and it's weird for them. They just want what they want, right? You could come and pick up your delivery and you wouldn't see another soul. Except me. I wouldn't say anything if you didn't want me to.

—Johnny A

If you need gas, you should probably come down and fill up sooner rather than later. It's real pricey and the Chevron usually sells out by Tuesday afternoon. Then everybody has to wait all week for another tanker to refill the pumps. Come early, though. The line gets long as hell.

When I was a kid, I knew the guy who had your place before you. Funny dude. We used to have a whole magazine section but after he bugged out we dumped them and put the beer freezer in. Turns out he was keeping the whole rag rack going one-handed. He didn't talk to anyone much. Just like you. Maybe that house takes your talk.

I like writing these notes. Do you like reading them? I could come visit sometimes, if you wanted. I don't have to. But if you wanted.

—Johnny

And then one day when Johnny Abalone's busted old truck came meandering and misfiring up the mountain, he didn't just leave the wooden mango crates at the property line. He knocked on the door and suffered Murray's cold, furious glare and when Gudrun answered, she wasn't really surprised, except that Johnny Abalone was older than she thought. He had a little grey in his shaggy black hair and a bad leg with tiny shards of bullet still floating around in it like the white hairs in silver needle tea, bullets he took on another mountain very far away, which, even as he bled into the infinite forest filth, even so far away from Ko'olau and the beer freezer at the Abalone General Store, had smelled so much like home.

"Full thrusters engaged, Commander Hardtree," Gudrun whispered.

"What?"

WITH ONE ENORMOUS muscled arm, Sir Quicktongue seized the elven shieldmaiden Nymphoria round the waist and lifted her toward his hungry kiss, crushing her glorious breasts against his broad, smooth chest as his famous tongue sought hers.

The other hand he plunged into her golden curls, pulling brutally just to hear her gasp, a gasp that never failed to bring his throbbing member to full attention. She wrapped her powerful thighs around him, moaning his name into the smoky air of the battlefield.

"It is you," he whispered in her perfect ear. "You alone, Nymphoria, can reforge my sword and make it new."

"But I will not, Sir Knight," answered the she-elf, her immortal eyes glittering cruelly.

Sir Quicktongue roared his fury into the sapphire sky. "Why? My god, woman, why?"

"Because I do not wish to," came the elf-queen's answer.

BUT IT WASN'T that. It wasn't any of that. It was very quiet and careful and the whole time Gudrun thought about Minnesota, the long flat plains and the thousands and thousands of lakes shining under a strange, cold moon.

5. *NYMPHO TWINS ON THE FRENCH RIVIERA*
Published 1950, Blue Fairy Books, 177 pages

IT HAPPENED IN her sleep. The night throbbed with heat. A long black vein pulsed up the side of Gudrun's body: a join, a wound, a fault line. From her heels to the cap of her skull. It swelled, wider and thicker and wider and thicker until it was a road, a chasm, a furrow, a black nebula expanding inside her, and then it was just empty space and there were two Gudruns lying on Ruby's old king size bed. Neither of them woke. It was a gentler process than you might expect. They slept identically, hands clasped against their chests, bent inward like little dinosaur claws, until seven in the morning, an hour past which Gudrun, in all her life, had never been able to sleep.

Gudrun opened her eyes and saw herself, naked, awake, watching. The other Gudrun looked exactly like her in every possible way. Haircut, palm lines, gold molar in her mouth, smallpox vaccination scar like a withered star on her skin, the pattern of bites on the edges of her fingernails.

"Is this because I drank the tap water?" Gudrun said, with an early morning gentleness and acceptance of all things in her voice. "I thought if I boiled it it would be okay."

But the other Gudrun didn't say anything back.

"Is it because I left the mugs out that one time?" she whispered.

The other Gudrun blinked sleepily. She couldn't answer. When she tried to imitate the very interesting way the original Gudrun moved her mouth and made sounds come out, she could only go slack and poke out her tongue a little, a pink, weak tongue slicked in saliva. She waved her hands in front of her face, amazed at the thick sunlight pouring between her fingers, at the dancing dust in the air, at the colors of Pemberley seeping all around the edges of those brand-new hands dappled already with scars earned by forty years of good primate work: the N-shaped brand where Gudrun had burned herself on the toaster oven when she was four, the slightly bulging knuckles satisfyingly cracked for decades, the faded white ladder where she had cut herself just after they moved to Pemberley, just to control something, anything completely.

She couldn't walk, either. Gudrun tried to coax her twin out of bed, but her muscles were as soft as warm mango, her bones delicate and elastic and unready for the slightest weight. The other Gudrun giggled and grabbed one of her clean red feet with one hand. Murray squawked from the garden. The new woman cringed in terror. She began to cry softly, a frightened, trembling, uncertain wail that made all the hair stand up on Gudrun's skin and her nipples contract and her stomach clench. Slowly, Gudrun pulled herself into her arms and kissed her own hair until the little wails stopped. Her breasts began to ache with a heavy, dancing pain the color of the little stars that come up out of the dark when you press your fists against your eyes, but, having no experience to draw on, she could not put any name to the feeling of her milk coming in.

Gudrun got up, pulled on a pair of fuzzy mustard-colored socks, closed a blue robe over her tender breasts, and padded into the kitchen to put the kettle on. She dug a spoon out of the drawer and began to scoop out some passionfruits for breakfast. You didn't have to chew passionfruit too much. Not if you took the seeds out. What else could she do? She took two bowls and two mugs out of the cupboard.

One red mug, one blue mug.

4. *INNOCENCE FOR SALE—CHEAP!*
Published 1944, Adonis Editions, 100 pages

A VETERAN OF many years in the trenches of Ruby, the core of Gudrun was as adaptable as water. Besides, she only had a month to go before the end of everything, and parthenogenesis wasn't something you could fight against. You could only take it in to your house and give it a place to sleep. A spot in the sun. A bowl of mashed passionfruit.

You can do anything for a month. Get used to anything. Get attached.

The new Gudrun laughed constantly, was hungry all the time, cried when startled as though the great tragedies of mankind had all landed on her at once, could rarely sleep through the night, and had a terror of the dark. Murray adored her. He slept crushed up against the door waiting for the morning when he might see her again.

The old Gudrun named the new one Pemberley. She had to name her something else. No one deserved Gudrun. But all she knew of naming people was that the name should be a family one, should come from a father who never existed in any concrete way, and Pemberley was the best she could build out of such requirements.

Pemberley loved for Gudrun to sing her Elvis songs until she fell asleep and smelled like hot lilacs when her hair was freshly washed. The bones of her skull had not quite fused together yet, and that smell came from the secret, silken place on the top of her head. Pemberley was just as tall and thin as Gudrun, far too big to rock her to sleep, but she tried anyway. She remembered how nice that felt when Ruby did it, a hundred million years ago. She sat out in the warm dark while the hibiscus bloomed and held herself, this great ungainly instant just-add-water person, to her breast. A thin, bitter milk that came from nowhere, except perhaps from the place in the cabinet between the red mugs and the blue mugs, the cold palace dividing the universe into two irreconcilable towers, drained out of herself, into herself, while both of them listened to the bats beat black against black. How had she done this thing? Was it the tins of spam she should never have eaten? The corn syrup in the ketchup? Lead in the Studebaker's crumbling paint? The radiation from the atolls, from the sea, from the broken sky? Did it matter, with the end so near? Everything came apart at the end. Even Gudrun. That's how you knew it was the end.

Two weeks before Snow Day, Gudrun stood at one end of the living room, in the *Schoolgirls* section of the Oskander Special Collection. Pemberley stood, wobbly and afraid, on the other end, in the *Military and Other Uniforms* section, unsure even of this new thing called *standing*, reaching out for Gudrun, for comfort, her hands opening and closing helplessly.

"Come on, Pem," Gudrun said sweetly. "You can do it, baby."

Murray trilled reassuringly. Pemberley whimpered, tottered, and finally took a tumbling step that was really more of a purposeful fall. Gudrun rushed forward to catch her and Pem collapsed laughing into her arms.

A week before Snow Day, Pemberley said her first word.

Gudrun was cooking soft porridge for their supper while Pemberley lay swaddled in a huge old quilt on the couch, propped up so she could see everything. Gudrun hummed *Heartbreak Hotel* and her humming broke into singing, unguarded and easy for once, her voice loud and bright in the close green humidity of the forest, the color, at last, strong and warm in her cheeks. She sipped Cold Palace Brand No. 1 Silver Needle Tea from a red mug between verses.

"Ruby!" shouted Pemberley suddenly.

Gudrun dropped the red mug. It shattered on the floor like a supernova.

3. *SLUMBER PARTY SWEET SIXTEEN*
Published 1962, Belladonna Classics, 119 pages

JOHNNY ABALONE LIVED alone above his father's store. He'd always meant to get somewhere in life, but somewhere ended up being right back where he started. He'd come around to being more or less okay with that. Old Jack Oskander once told him, as he bought another massive stack of dirty magazines: *kid, nobody really gets anywhere in this life. Everybody just picks someplace to hunker down and barricade themselves in. Some of us just got better bricks than others.*

And Johnny thought that was pretty much on the mark.

The envelope arrived with the afternoon mail run. He almost didn't notice it in the small hurricane of invoices and junk ads. It just said *Johnny* on it. No address. But everyone knew who he was. It wouldn't have been any puzzle, even for a new mailman, which Sam Frisk was not. Johnny Abalone pulled out an old, faded Christmas card. It had a snowman on it. Corn cob pipe and everything.

> *If you wanted to come and see me on Thursday, that would be fine. It's my birthday. Here is $400. I think that's enough for a color TV. If you could bring it when you come that would be as good as a present. Only you have to promise not to freak out if you see something that would be hard to explain if anyone asked you about it. But probably no one ever will.*
>
> *I drink my tea straight. Silver needle doesn't need anything extra.*
>
> *P.S. Bring cake. Lots of frosting.*
> *—Gudrun*

2. *THE GIRL NEXT DOOR*
Published 1950, Fig Leaf Press, 104 pages

PEMBERLEY LEARNED WORDS quickly. After *Ruby* came *Murray, water, potato, book, tea, want, moon.* And others less predictable, less simple, less clear where she found them. *Dirty. Formaldehyde. Fallout. Radon. Military industrial complex. Poison. Death.*

Snow.

Gudrun didn't know what she expected. She supposed she ought to stop expecting entirely at this point. She had only just managed to adjust to the reality of having been cut in two like an orange. She didn't much feel like dealing with this new problem. Because Pemberley *was* her in every way, just the same, by definition, by ontological necessity. But those hadn't been

Gudrun's first words. She'd said *Mama*, like most children. Then *hello, bottle, help, up, outside, kiss*, and *Minnesota*.

Once, at night, while Pem snored softly next to her with her fists balled up under her chin, Gudrun wondered if, having been bisected so cleanly, she was missing something now. If she was no longer whole. If she was still 100% Gudrun and not diluted somehow, alloyed with some new substance. 90% Gudrun and 10% radon, fallout, formaldehyde, snow. Or 50% Gudrun, and 50% of her now lived in a completely unattached body that she could never glue back together with the rest, a new warm body put away gently on the other side of the cabinet from her old cool one, divided by spoons and sugar and the inevitable separateness of everything, sucking its thumb vigorously when it had bad dreams.

Pemberley never learned to say hello. She just said goodbye for everything. When she saw Gudrun first thing in the morning. *Goodbye.* When Murray came lumbering over the potato patch. *Goodbye.* When soft, black and white people came on the television to talk to her. *Goodbye.* When she wanted to tell Gudrun she loved her.

Goodbye.

1. *SNOW BUNNIES AT THE SEX CHALET*
Published 1963, Red Light Limiteds, 122 pages

JOHNNY ABALONE PULLED up into the driveway just as the afternoon sun was throwing its weight around, battering red and gold against the mango trees, the brambles, the teak slats of Pemberley, the garden stakes, the fat wild turkey warming his big belly in the dirt, the rippling creek, and two Gudruns. True to his implicit promise, he did not freak out. She must have a twin, he supposed, though you wouldn't think Ruby could hide another daughter all those years. But he did wonder which was *his* Gudrun. One wore a clean blue sundress, one wore a red one, but beyond that he could see no difference, except that the one in blue seemed oddly clumsy, and kept laughing at nothing and trying to eat butterflies like soap bubbles.

He unloaded the TV and the cake from his truck. The TV was a nice new walnut cabinet number. It had cost a lot more than $400, but Johnny didn't mind. The cake was chocolate, because, he figured, everybody likes chocolate. Vanilla or red velvet was a risk, and he couldn't afford risk just now. The cake said HAPPY BIRTHDAY GUDRUN in pretty turquoise icing with bright orange sugar flowers on it. He also brought beer and the grill from his back deck (no way Gudrun would have one) and a cooler full of burgers and individually-wrapped cheese slices. They stocked good sharp cheddar and brie and all that at the store, but Johnny always loved the undemanding, familiar taste of industrial cheese-like product and he was too old to go changing now.

"Hi Johnny," the red Gudrun said. "I'm glad you came."

"Goodbye!" chirped the blue Gudrun.

They installed the TV together and hauled the old black and white out into the garden. Red Gudrun pried off the cabinet top and filled it with dirt and rosemary and basil plants. Johnny hooked up his grill and fried them all a nice meal while the blue Gudrun stared at the new set, mesmerized. She flipped through all three channels and stopped on one where the President was talking, gazing earnestly out into America the way he always did, those movie star eyes always looking apologetic somehow, wistful, wishing things were other than they are.

"That's where we come from, Pem," the red Gudrun said. "That's who we were supposed to be."

The girls ate like animals, ripping into the red, dripping meat like they'd never tasted it before. Attacking the cake like it'd done them wrong. It was sort of pretty, when they did it.

SIR QUICKTONGUE KNELT before the simple peasant girl. Her red hair cascaded down over her bountiful breasts, past her round hips, nearly to the ground. He didn't even know her name. The maiden held out his sword to him, whole again at last, in her bare, innocent hands. He burned for her, even as he could not meet her eyes.

Quoth the country rose: "Why do you kneel, Sir Knight?"

"My quest is ended, my lady. I am new-forged in the fires of love," answered the weary warrior. He rose and took her in his arms, kissing her with all the passion and desperate need he had held back from Nymphoria and Vuvula and all the rest. But the maid only looked at him with sparkling, puzzled eyes.

"What is this 'love' you speak of?"

Sir Quicktongue smiled.

"Oh, it's nothing. Just a strange little custom we have in the country I come from. Have no fear. I will teach it to you."

THE STARS BEGAN to come out, twinkling up out of the sky like ice cracking. The glow of the television lit the house from within, darkened only by Pemberley's hands as she placed them on the screen, against the faces of all those strangers, and then her cheek, too, her eyelashes fluttering against the light. By the time anyone felt sleepy, it was past midnight.

Johnny Abalone drank his beer and stepped outside to join Gudrun in the garden. He thought about it for a long time, then circled her waist with his arm. She stiffened, but she didn't push him away, so that was something.

"Your calendar says today's a snow day," he said softly. "I wouldn't count on it."

Gudrun turned her face toward his, clear and sharp and with that same wistful, apologizing gaze that had so often looked out at him and everyone else from the evening news. Johnny wondered how he'd never seen it before.

Behind them, the television cut out as quick as a knife. Pemberley screamed for her mother. She couldn't ever be brave in the dark.

Far below, the lights in the valley vanished, one by one, the Uptown Grand Cinema and the Abalone General Store and the Post Office, the houses and the banks, the bakery and the schoolhouse, and when they had all gone, only a stillness like black nebulas remained.

"It's nothing," Gudrun whispered in the sudden, total silence. "Just something my mother used to say."

Planet LION

INITIAL SURVEY REPORT: PLANET 6MQ441(BAKENEKO), *Alaraph System*

Logged by: Dr. Savine Abolafiya, Chief Xenoecology Officer, Y.S.S. Duchess Anne

Attention: Captain Agathe Ganizani, Commanding Officer Y.S.S. Duchess Anne

Satellites: Four

Mineral Interest: Iron, copper, diamond, cobalt, scandium, praesodymium, yttrium. Only diamond in desirable quantities. Nothing sufficient to offset cost of extraction.

Sentient Life: None

Strategic Signifigance: None

A small, warm world orbiting the white subgiant Alaraph. Average gravity is more or less comfortable at .85 Earth normal, but highly variable depending on how near it passes to 6MQ440, 6MQ439, and 6MQ450. Twenty hour day, 229 day year. Abundant organic life. Excepting the polar regions, the planet consists of one continuous jungle-type ecosystem broken only by vast salt and fresh water rivers. See attached materials for information on unique flora if you're into that sort of thing. You won't find anything spectacular. It does not behoove a xenoecologist to sum up a planet as: trees big, water nice, but I know you prefer me to keep these reports informal, and I have become both tired and bored, just like everyone else. If you've seen one little Earthish world, you've seen them all. Day is mostly day; night is mostly night; dirt is dirt; water is water. Green is good, most any other color is bad. Lather, rinse, repeat. The fact is, the

Alaraph star has a whopping eleven other planets, all gas giants, and each one of them will prove far more appetizing to the powers that be than this speck of green truck-a-long rock.

My team came back calling it Bakeneko due to a barely interesting species of feline megafauna they frequently encountered. The place, I'm told, is crawling with them. Dr. Tum found one sleeping in their cook-pit. We've been calling them lions. As you'll see during the dissection this weekend, the species does somewhat resemble the thylacoleo carnifex *of late Pliocene Australia.*

Except, of course, that they're the size of Clydesdales, sexually trimorphic, and bright green.

Imagine a giant, six-toed, enthusiastically carnivorous marsupial lion with the devil's own camouflage and you'll have it just about right. The "male" can be differentiated by dark stripes in the fur as well as the mane. The "female" has no stripes, but a ridge of short, dark, dense fur extending from the crown of the head to the base of the tail. The third sex is not androgyne, but simply an entirely separate member of the reproductive circus. We have been calling it a "vixen" for lack of better terminology. No agreement as to pronoun has been reached. The vixen is larger than the male or female and quite a different shade of green—call it forest green instead of emerald green.

The lions represent the only real obstacle to settlement of 6MQ441. Though I have tried to keep my tone light, five attached casualty reports attest to the danger of these creatures. They are aggressive, crepuscular apex predators. There are a lot of them. They show some rudimentary, corvid-like tool-use. (Dr. Gyll observed one wedging a stick between the skull-plates of a goanna-corollary animal to get at the brain. Dr. Gyll does go on to note that he also enjoyed the flavor of the brain more than the meat.)

At present, I recommend a severe cull before any serious consideration of Bakeneko as a habitable world. See supplementary materials for (considerably) more on this topic.

Moving on to the far more pertinent analysis of the Alaraph gas giant archipelago…

The FUTURE Is BLUE

A LION MOVES the world with her mouth. A lion tells the truth with her teeth showing.

One lion rips the name Yttrium from the watering hole. She chews it. She swallows and digests it. She understands her name by means of digestion. One lion's name signifies a lustrous crystalline superconductive transition metal. This separates one lion from lions not called Yttrium. One lion called Yttrium drinks from the watering hole and digests the smallgod MEDICALOFFICER. She understands the smallgod by means of digestion. She feels the concept of honor. Lions who digest other smallgods do not always know what their names signify. One lion gorges on the bones of the smallgod. The bones taste like anatomical expertise and scalpelcraft. She slurps up the blood of the smallgod. The blood reeks of formulae and the formulae run down the throat of one lion to fill her belly with several comprehensions of anasthetics and stimulants and vaccines and antibiotics. She gnaws at the meat of the smallgod. The meat becomes her meat and the meat has the weight of good bedside manner.

One lion called Yttrium hunts in the steelveldt called Vergulde Draeck. As well she hunts in the watering hole. All lions hunt in the watering hole. The watering hole networks the heart of every lion to the heart of every other lion into a cooperative real-time engagement matrix. The smallgod inside one lion lays down the words *cooperative real-time engagement matrix* in the den of one lion's brain. One lion called Yttrium accepts the words though they have no more importance than the teeth and hooves left over after a kill. The words mean the watering hole.

One lion hunts through her steelveldt in the shadow of burnt blueblack rib bones and sleeps in their shadows. As well she sees the watering hole all around her. The watering hole lies over the jungle like fur over skin. One lion stands in the part of the steelveldt where the million dead black snakes sprawl but never rot. She sees her paws sunk deep in the corpses of snakes. As well she sees her paws sunk deep in the cool blue lagoon of the watering hole. Comforting scents hunt in her nostrils and on her tongue. Ripe redpaw fruit. The brains of sunspot lizards. The eggs of noonbirds. Fresh water with nothing sour in it. One lion hunts alone in the steelveldt Vergulde Draeck. As well she hunts with every other lion in the watering hole. She hunts with one lion called Thulium. She hunts with one lion called Bromide. She hunts with one lion called Manganese. She hunts with one lion called Nickel who sired her and one lion called Niobium who bore her and one lion called Uranium who carried one lion called Yttrium in her pouch until she could devour the smallgod and enlist with the pride. In the watering hole every lion swims with every other lion. Every lion swallows the heart of every other lion. Every lion hunts in the den of every other lion's brain. Two hundred thousand lions hunt in the steelveldt Vergulde Draeck with one lion called Yttrium. Ten million hunt in the watering hole. The watering hole has enough water for everyone.

Every evening one lion called Yttrium wakes in hunger. She washes her muzzle in the Longer Sweeter River which flows beneath the steelveldt Vergulde Draeck. As well she washes her muzzle in the lagoon of the watering hole. She leaps and prowls through the part of the steelveldt where husks of giant redpaw fruit lie broken open. Other lions also leap and also prowl. She greets them in the watering hole. In the watering hole they use each others' eyes to find the answer to hunger. One lion called Yttrium finds the words *triangulation, reconnaissance, target acquisition* floating inside her. She thanks the smallgod inside her for this gift.

One lion stops. She becomes six lions. Six lions chase down a pair of sunspot lizards skittering through the burnt blueblack bones of the steelveldt. Six lions sight a horned shagfur. They forget the lizards. The shagfur lumbers across the part of the steelveldt where the hundred thousand dead silver scorpions lie barbed and gleaming. It does not hurt itself but six lions know the scent of carefulness. In the watering hole six lions turn their bellies to the rich sun. In the steelveldt six lions open their jaws. Their green muzzles wrinkle back over black teeth. Out of their mouths the water of the lagoon comes rippling. The water of the lagoon possesses blue heat and blue light. Six lions open their mouths and the water of the lagoon roars toward the shagfur. The shagfur flies upward. The shagfur's neck snaps. Six lions suck the water of the lagoon back into their throats and with it the shagfur. They tear into its body and its body becomes the body of six lions.

A lion moves the world with her mouth.

Six lions stop. One lion called Yttrium pads alone across the part of the steelveldt where the wings of the billion dead butterflies crunch under her paws. As well she plays with one lion called Tungsten and one lion called Tellurium in the shallows of the watering hole. She bites the green shoulder of one lion called Tungsten. She feels the teeth of one lion called Tellurium in the scruff of her neck. One lion called Tungsten ate the shagfur with her. One lion called Tellurium hunts far away in the steelveldt called Szent Istvan. They growl and pounce in the sun. The sun in the watering hole shines dusk forever. The sun shines bright morning and day on the steelveldts. The watering hole forgot every light but twilight.

One lion called Yttrium enters the part of the steelveldt where the thousand dead squaresloths lie. Hot wind dries the shagfur blood on her whiskers. She feels the concept of holiness. Her paws leave prints in the home of the smallgods. Lions not called Yttrium lie or squat on their green haunches or stand at attention with their tails in the air. They lock their eyes to the heart and the liver of the smallgods. The heart and the liver of the smallgods looks like the trunks of eight blue trees. The heart and the liver of the smallgods do not smell like the trunks of trees. The heart and the liver of the smallgods smell like the corpses of the hundred thousand silver scorpions and the light of the watering hole. Each of the blue trees belongs to one smallgod and not to the others. Each lion belongs to one smallgod and not to the others. One lion called Yttrium swallowed the meat of the smallgod MEDICALOFFICER. As well a million lions not called Yttrium chewed this meat in the watering hole. Many also own the name of Yttrium. Yttrium numbers among the one hundred and twenty-one sublimities of the smallgods. With one hundred and twenty-one words the smallgods move the world and so all lions call each other by these utterings of power.

The other smallgods own the names of ENGINEERINGOFFICER and DRIVERMECHANIC and GUNNERMAN and GRENADIER and SQUADLEADER and INFANTRYMAN and SLUDGEWARETECH. One lion called Tungsten lapped the blood of the smallgod DRIVERMECHANIC in the watering hole. One lion called Tellurium sucked the marrow from the bones of the smallgod SLUDGEWARETECH. One lion called Yttrium hopes their child will feast upon MEDICALOFFICER like her when one lion called Tellurium finishes gestating it.

One lion called Osmium roars in the watering hole and in the steelveldt. He snatches the scruff of one lion called Phosphorus in his teeth and throws her to the ground in the home of the smallgods. His roar owns anguish. Her claws rake his chest. The roar of one lion called Osmium ends. Blood sheens his black teeth. The emerald shoulders of one lion called Osmium droop miserably. He tosses his mane at the four moons of coming night and cries out:

"Christ, Susie, why did you leave me? Wasn't I good enough?"

STRATEGIC ANALYSIS: PLANET *6MQ441(Bakeneko), Alaraph System*

Logged by: Cmdr. Desmond Lukša, Executive Officer, Y.S.S. Bolingbroke

Attention: Captain Agathe Ganizani, Commanding Officer Y.S.S. Duchess Anne

Aggie, it is the opinion of this particular unpleasant bastard that xenoecologists should not mouth off about the strategic significance of a planet just because they know a little damned Latin and can call an oak an oak at five hundred yards. I've read Dr. Abolafiya's report and promptly used it for toilet paper. It's so like her to miss the forest for weeping about the trees. I spent all last night sitting in my quarters reading page after page about some damn green kittens! Who cares? The plain truth was staring her right in the face.

The fact is, the Alaraph System represents a unique opportunity to engage the enemy on our own terms. Its remote location removes any concern about collateral damage. Those eleven (eleven!) gorgeous gas giants provide some pretty lush gravitational channels and fuel resources so ample as to be functionally infinite. 6MQ450 (Savine's idiots are calling it Nemea now) has a dozen terrestrial moons where we might even set up mobile staging domes and get some honest fighting into this mess. But it's that dumb green ball Bakeneko that makes it work. It's our lever and our place to stand.

Alaraph sits smack in the middle of a disputed sector. Sure, it's hicksville, galactically speaking, and Alaraph is only barely inside the border, but the sector also includes most of the Virgo neighborhood, which is very much at the center of concern at the moment. Our bestest buddies drew a line around the big lady in the sky, and we drew a line around her, and then they drew a bigger line, and so on. The charts look like a hyperactive schoolkid's drawing.

My recommendation is this: ignore Savine and her pretty kitties. Start settlement protocols. Make sure it's all on known-code channels. We'll probably have to actually put people in a ship with their spinning wheels and what-shit to make it look real. Hopefully we won't actually have to land them, but if we do, well, it won't be the first time. Hell, why not make it real? Build a base down there on Bakeneko, start churning out whatever we can. Barrack platoons. Make it look like we've got something we want in the jungle. Maybe we'll even find something.

They will respond militarily to such a provocation. They've detonated stars over less. And we will finally get to choose the real estate on which to hold our horrible little auction of death. We'll be ready for once.

As for the lions, honestly, I will lose precisely zero sleep over it. Let our jacked-up boys and girls play Hemingway down there with the big cats, they won't be a problem for long.

ONE LION CALLED Yttrium cannot move. She sprawls flat on her belly in the shallow of the steelveldt's blueblack hip bone. The sky has fallen and broken her back. She whimpers. Everything whimpers when the monsoons come. Rain falls. The world grows heavy and hot. Every lion hides from the sky.

The smallgod inside her offers the words: *Due to the orbital proximity of Nemea, Maahes, Lamassu, and Tybault, Bakeneko lies in the midst of a gravitational white water rapids and may experience profound shifts in constants depending on the time of year and local occultations.* The words taste cool and hard and crunchy in her mouth. They feel like ice chips. One lion named Yttrium has never tasted ice. But her smallgod says that worlds hunt in the dark where ice covers every lonely thing.

One lion called Yttrium bounds through the tall grass of the watering hole. The sky in the watering hole still loves lions and does not crush their backs to jelly. One lion called Yttrium runs to run and not to hunt. One hundred other lions who digested the smallgod MEDICALOFFICER run so close by her she can feel the electric bristle of their fur against hers. As well seventy lions who gorged on the smallgod GRENADIER run. They feel the idea of unity. They wade into the lagoon when they no longer wish to run. They paddle and splash. One lion called Cadmium stands on the shore yelling:

"Form up! Form up! Secure the perimeter! Incoming!"

Several striped moths dance just out of reach of his jaws. They do not form up.

One lion called Yttrium experiences the sensation of a door opening and closing in a wall of ice. The experience takes place in her chest and in her muzzle. She has never seen a wall of ice or used a door. These ideas come from the same place as the names *Nemea, Bakeneko, Lamassu, Tybault.* The wall of ice slips down over her green fur and the door opens to swallow her and closes on her bones. One lion called Yttrium stops. She becomes one hundred lions.

One hundred lions standing in the water of the lagoon turn to seventy lions and scream together in hopeless misery:

"You said you loved me!"

Seventy deep green lions bellow back:

"I did! I do! You never had time for me. You loved your ship. You loved your war. You loved the idea of war more than the reality of me. I only joined up in the first place because I knew you'd never choose me over your commission. And I hate it out here. I hate puzzling out new ways to make people explode. I am *alone.* I had no one, not even you. So I found comfort and you want to punish me for it?"

"You went looking!" weep the hundred lions. Water churns around their shaggy knees.

"Yes, Emma, I went looking. Does that make it feel better?" the seventy lions growl. Their ruffs rise. "I went looking and Lara wanted me. You haven't wanted me in years."

One hundred lions snarl in the watering hole. Their black tongues loll through black teeth. "She's twenty-two! She's a kid. She doesn't know what she wants."

"You're thirty-five and all you ever want is another hour in your fucking lab," seventy lions called GRENADIER rumble in indignation. "And Simon. Or did you think I didn't know about him?"

"Don't leave me, Ben," whimper one hundred lions as though even the perfect watering hole sun has fallen on their spines. "Don't leave me. I'll quit. I'll come home. All the way home. It'll be good like it was a million years ago. When I had short hair and you had piercings, remember? I'll never speak to Simon again. Don't make these last ten years a waste of time."

"She's pregnant, Emma. It's too late. I don't even think I want it not to be too late."

One hundred lions called MEDICALOFFICER crouch in the shallows. Their eyes flash. Their tails warn. "This is such a goddamned cliché. You're a joke. I hate you."

One hundred lions hurtle into seventy lions. Claws and teeth close on skin and meat. The watering hole froths white water. One hundred lions stop as fast as they began. One lion called Yttrium licks her wounds. She does not judge them serious. She opens her jaws in the steelveldt. The water of the lagoon ripples out and lifts up a burnt blueblack bone with its blue heat and its blue light. The bone settles down on top of a hollow stone full of objects. Once one lion called Yttrium flung a hollow stone up and dashed it against the corpses of the billion dead butterflies that cover the floor of the steelveldt. Objects jangled out. She did not know them. She ate some and still did not understand them. The smallgod inside her said: *those are dresses and shoes. Those are hairbrushes and aftershave bottles.* One lion called Yttrium did not break the hollow stones anymore after that.

One lion called Yttrium has built three walls in this way. Other lions have done more. Soon she will make a roof that will keep out the sky. The lions change the steelveldt Vergulde Draeck with their mouths. One lion called Tellurium tells the watering hole that lions have changed the steelveldt Szent Istvan. With their mouths they built several places called barracks and one called commandstationalpha. One lion called Tellurium wishes to build more places. The smallgod SLUDGEWARETECH inside her requires big places. One lion worries for her. As well she builds their young. As well their young requires big places.

But on monsoon days no one can work much except in the watering hole.

One lion called Arsenic crawls on his green stomach toward one lion called Antimony. One lion called Yttrium watches. Skinny pink fish flash in the water. MEDICALOFFICER calls them *self-maintaining debug programs.* One lion likes the flavor of the words and the fish equally.

One lion called Arsenic gnaws at dried lizard blood on his paws. He mewls: "I abandoned my kids, Hannah."

One lion called Antimony licks his face. "I never had any children. I had a miscarriage when I was in graduate school. I was five months along; the father had already gotten his fellowship on the other side of the world and moved in with a girl in Milwaukee. I never said anything. Didn't seem important to say anything. If I said something, it would have been suddenly real and happening and stupid instead of distant and not something that a girl like me had to worry about. I woke up in the hospital with a pain in my body like shrapnel, like a bullet in my gut the size of the moon. And I looked at my post-op charts and I think part of me just thought: *well, that makes sense. All I can make is death.*"

One lion called Arsenic arches the heavy muscles of his emerald back. He rolls over and shows his striped belly to the sky of the watering hole. The smallgod SLUDGEWARETECH inside him howls and as well he howls: "I abandoned my kids, Hannah. They're grown now and when I call they're always in the middle of something or just running out the door. They don't want to look at me. Nobody looks at me anymore. My wife just sent divorce papers to my office. Who does that? I called her over and over, just holding those papers in my hand like an asshole, and she wouldn't pick up. I called one hundred and twenty-one times before I got her. I counted. I was going to tell her I loved her. I was gonna make my case. I thought if I could make a grand enough gesture, I could still have someone to come home to. But the minute I heard her voice I just laid into her, yelling until my vision went wobbly. *You knew what this life would be when you married me. I'm doing this for us. For everyone. For our girls. Christ, Susie, why'd you leave me? Wasn't I good enough?* And she just took it all like a beating. When I ran out of breath, she said: *Milo, of course you were good enough. You were the best. But every time I looked at you, all I could see was what you'd done. Your face was my slow poison. If I let our eyes meet one more time, it would have killed me.*"

One lion called Antimony touches her green forehead to the green forehead of one lion called Arsenic. This begins the behavior of mating. He accepts her. Violet barbs of arousal flick upward along his spine. Her heat smells like burning cinnamon. But their joining cannot satisfy. A lion mates in threes. The smallgods mate in twos and do not feel the lack of a vixen lying over those needful barbs. Two lions thrust ungracefully. They hurt each other with a mating not matched to their bodies. The smallgods do not care. The smallgod ENGINEERINGOFFICER inside one lion called Antimony whispers:

"Good thing we're all gonna die tomorrow, huh? Otherwise we'd have to live with ourselves."

LETTER OF APPLICATION *(Personal Essay)*

Filed by: Dr. Pietro S. Aguirre

Attention: Captain Franklin Oshiro V.S.S. Anansi

I've wanted to work with sludge my whole life. I suppose, if you take a step back for a second, that sounds completely bizarre. But not to me. Sludge is life; life is sludge. Without it, we're a not-particularly-interesting mess of overbreeding primates all stuck on the same rock. To say I want to work with sludge is akin to saying I want to work with God, and for me it is a calling no less serious than the seminary. I grew up in the Yucatan megalopolis, scavenging leftover dregs from penthouse drains and police station bins, saving sludge up in jars like girls in old movies saved their tears, just to get enough to try my little hands at a crude recombinatory rinse or an organic amplification soak about as artful as a finger-painting. I succeeded in levitating my jack russell terrier and buckling just about every meter of plumbing in our building.

But now I'm boring whatever poor personnel officer has to read through this dreck. A thousand years ago, people used to tell stories about taking apart the radio and putting it back together again. Now we puff out our chests and tell tales of levitating dogs. Let me spare you.

I believe sludge can be so much more. We're used to sludge now. It's as normal as salt. We're so used to it we don't even bother doing anything interesting with it. We use sludge as lipstick and blush for the brain. Cheap neural builds to brighten and tighten, a flick of telekinesis to really bring out the eyes, some spiffy mass shielding to contour the cheekbones. You can buy a low-end vatic rinse at the chemist.

To me, this is obscene. It's like using an archangel as a hat rack.

There is no better place to continue my research than the fleet. My program to develop synthetic sources for sludge rather than relying indefinitely (and dangerously) on the natural deposits of chthonian planets in the Almagest Belt speaks for itself. My précis is attached, but in the interests of you, long-suffering personnel officer, not having to ruin your dinner with equations, I present a simple summary: I believe sludge can win this war for us.

ONE LION CALLED Yttrium feels the concept of apprehension. Change hunts in the steelveldt and the watering hole. The monsoons broke in the night and the bones of every lion stretch up in the easy air. The day wants pouncing. The day wants hunting. The day wants scratching the back of one lion against the burnt blueblack rib bones of the steelveldt.

The smallgods want building. The smallgods want to form up.

One lion called Yttrium bounds down the part of the steelveldt Vergulde Draeck where the twenty thousand tin jellyfish lie dead and cracked apart. More of them crunch and pop under her paws. The smallgod MEDICALOFFICER sends the words *mess hall* into her belly. She opens her mouth and the blue light and heat of the watering hole flow out and strangle a sunspot lizard to death before it can squeak. The blue light and the blue heat pries open the lizard's skull plates so that one lion called Yttrium can get at the brains. She laps at her meal.

A burst of dead jellyfish shattering. One lion called Yttrium leaps to protect her kill as one lion called Gadolinium and one lion called Zinc crash through the tin corpse-mounds. Their fur bristles. Their snarls drip saliva. They wrestle without play. Birds flee up to the tops of the tallest trees. Two lions land so heavy the steelveldt shakes. One lion called Yttrium searches for them in the watering hole. She finds them standing on either side of a warm flat stone. They do not move. They do not bristle. They do not wrestle or play.

"I don't want you that way, Nikolai!" one lion called Gadolinium growls in the steelveldt. He has landed on top. He pants. His eyes shine.

"I'm sorry," whimpers one lion called Zinc. "Oliver, come on, I'm sorry. It was stupid, I'm stupid."

"I have a husband at home," roars one green lion and the smallgod DRIVERMECHANIC inside him. "I have a *home* at home."

"I know," answers the smallgod INFANTRYMAN inside one lion called Zinc.

One lion called Gadolinium digs his claws into the chest of one lion called Zinc. "You don't know *anything*. You've never stuck around with anyone longer than it took to fuck them. You swagger around like a cartoon and you think none of us can see what a scared little kitten you are, well, I got news for you—we can *all* see. I left more life than you'll ever have."

One lion called Zinc twists and springs free. Two lions face each other on steady paws. "You're probably right. But it goes with the job. We never stay anywhere longer than it takes to drink a little and fuck a little and kill a little and pack it all up again, so from where I sit, you're the idiot, making poor Andrew pine away his whole life back in whatever suburb of Nothingtown spat the two of you out. As for the swagger, I *like* swaggering. So fuck off. I was offering a little human contact, that's all. It's called comfort, you prig."

Wracking dry sobs come coughing up out of the black mouth of one lion called Gadolinium. "I'm so fucking lonely, Niko. It sounds like the most obvious thing in the world to say. I'm surrounded by people all the time and I'm so fucking lonely. I do my job, I eat, I stand my watch, and all the time I'm just thinking *I'm lonely I'm lonely I'm lonely* over and over."

"Everybody's lonely," purrs one lion called Zinc. His stripes gleam dark in the sun of the steelveldt. "You don't volunteer for this job if you're not already a lonely bastard who was only happy like four days in his entire dumb life. So stop being dumb and kiss me. Tomorrow we'll probably get our faces burned off before breakfast."

One lion called Yttrium returns to the dish of the sunspot lizard's skull. She feels the sensation of worry. She remembers other days and nights when every lion hunted as a lion and she heard no sacred speech for evenings on top of evenings. Now her ears ache and the sacred speech fills her own mouth like soft meat. One lion called Yttrium thinks these things as she begins the journey to the steelveldt Szent Istvan for the birth of her young by one lion called Tellurium and one lion called Tungsten. She wonders if the lions in the steelveldt Szent Istvan speak so often as the lions of the steelveldt Vergulde Draeck.

The light of the watering hole washes one lion called Tantalum. She stands in the lagoon. Her fur ridge stands erect.

"Form up! Form up! Secure the perimeter!" the smallgod SQUADLEADER inside one lion cries.

This time, one lion called Yttrium listens. She must listen. Her body knows how to listen. How to form up. How to understand the idea of *perimeter.* She turns away from the road to the steelveldt Szent Istvan. She never takes her eyes from one lion called Tantalum in the watering hole as she crosses back into the steelveldt Vergulde Draeck. She crosses the part of the steelveldt where the million black dead snakes sprawl but never rot. The smallgod MEDICALOFFICER send the words *electro-plasmic wiring* into her skull like a twig into the brain pan of a lizard. In the watering hole one lion called Tantalum roars:

"Enemy will come in range at 0900!"

One lion called Yttrium crosses the part of the steelveldt where the wings of the billion dead butterflies lie shattered. The smallgod MEDICALOFFICER writes the words *navigational arrays* on the inside of her eyelids. In the watering hole, one lion called Radium approaches one lion called Tantalum. The smallgod GUNNERMAN inside one lion rumbles:

"Nathan, this is a shitty life and you know it. We should have majored in Literature."

One lion called Tantalum roars another *form up!* before answering: "Yeah? You ever tried to write a poem, Izzie? You'd get two lines into a damn haiku and quit because it didn't shoot lasers of death and kickback into your teeth."

One lion called Yttrium crosses into the part of the steelveldt where the hundred thousand dead silver scorpions lie barbed and broken. The smallgod MEDICALOFFICER wraps the words *weapons hold* around her heart.

One lion called Radium laughs so that her black teeth catch the heavy gold light of the endless dusk of the watering hole. "True. Drink?"

"Drink," agrees the smallgod SQUADLEADER from inside one striped green male.

One lion called Yttrium crosses into the part of the steelveldt where the husks of giant redpaw fruit lie broken open. The smallgod MEDICALOFFICER pushes the words *radioactive sludgepack engine core* into her soft palate. Other lions stand in formation. All of them carry the smallgod MEDICALOFFICER. All of them crackle with the musk of aggression. Their mouths glow blue. One lion called Yttrium experiences the sensation of a door opening and closing in a wall of ice. The experience takes place in her chest and in her muzzle. One lion called Yttrium stops. She becomes six hundred lions.

Six hundred lions called Emma roar.

***

PROGRESS REPORT: PROJECT *Myrmidion*

Logged by: Dr. Pietro S. Aguirre, Senior Research Fellow, V.S.S. Szent Istvan

Attention: Captain Griet Hulle, V.S.S. Johannesburg

Captain Bernard Saikkonen, V.S.S. Vergulde Draeck

This is a classic good news/bad news situation. The good news is that the project has achieved an enormous measure of success and is ready to deploy in small trials. I foresee few to no field issues. We recommend Planetoid 94BR110

(Snegurechka) for initial mid-range testing. There is a small colony of about fifteen hundred on Snegurechka, enough that any transcription errors will quickly become apparent. I have great confidence. We should be able to disperse the sludgeware into the atmosphere and, within six to eight days, have a squadron of about fifteen hundred fully trained soldiers, networked into a cooperative and highly adaptive real-time engagement matrix, which will program itself to conform to the cultural expectations of the subject in order to create a seamless installation. The population should split, more or less equally, among the eight typoprints specified. No adverse medical effects are anticipated. The sludge works with the organic material at hand, enhancing and fortifying it. If anything, they should end up in better health than before.

Now, the bad news. It has not proved possible to separate the skillsets of the typoprints from the personalities of the personnel from whom we pulled the prints. In a way, this makes sense—the process of learning is a deeply personal and individualized one. We do not only retain facts or muscle memory, but private contextual sense-tags. The smell of the foxglove growing in the summer when we took fencing lessons for the first time. The smeared lipstick of our childhood algebra teacher. Arguing about the fall of Rome with a fellow student who later became a lover. We cannot separate the engineer's understanding of propulsion from the engineer's boyfriend leaving her in the middle of her course, the VR game she played incessantly to blow off steam that summer, the terrible coffee at the shop near her dormitory. We may yet find a way to isolate the knowledge without the person, but it won't happen soon, and I understand that time is of the essence. At the moment, the process of print transfer suppresses the original personality to varying degrees, and, as time passes, the domination of the print approaches total.

It doesn't have to be bad news. The original squad consisted of basically stable personalities. They grew very close over the series of brief but intense missions we devised in order to achieve and log a full typoprint. (Casualty reports attached. Unfortunately, the final mission proved to be poorly chosen for research purposes.) They functioned excellently as a unit—they screwed around a lot, but these kinds of small squads usually do. Besides, no one expects these sludgetroops to last all that long. They are the definition of fodder. What difference does it make if they miss some guy back in Aberdeen for a few minutes before taking a shot to the head?

⁂

SIX HUNDRED LIONS called Emma race across the steelveldt Vergulde Draeck. Eight hundred lions called Ben lope across the part of the steelveldt where the husks of giant redpaw fruit lie broken open and oozing.

"You said you loved me!" bellow six hundred green lions called Emma.

"You never had time for me!" comes the battle cry of eight hundred lions called Ben.

They collide. Black claws enter fur and flesh. Black teeth sink into meat. Many lions open their mouths. The blue heat and the blue light of the watering hole rips out of their great jaws. It twists through the static-roughened air. The sludgelight seizes one lion called Osmium and one lion called Nickel and one lion called Manganese and one lion called Niobium and one lion called Tungsten and dashes their brains against the floor of the steelveldt.

"I am *alone*."

"She's twenty-two!"

The jungle shakes. The jungle buckles. The jungle burns. The watering hole cannot handle so much information at once. It shivers. It cuts in and out. This also occurs in the steelveldt Bolingbroke and the steelveldt Duchess Anne and the steelveldt Johannesburg and the steelveldt Anansi and the hundred groaning steelveldts of the world.

"Don't leave me," shriek a million gasping emerald lions. "I'll come home. All the way home. It'll be good like it was a million years ago."

"It's too late. I don't even think I want it not to be too late," answer a million striped and bleeding lions too exhausted to stand.

⁂

SITUATION REPORT: PLANET 6MQ441(Bakeneko), Alaraph System

Logged by: Captain Naamen Tripp, Y.S.S. Mariana Trench

Attention: Anna Tereshkova, Chief Prosecutor

Bakeneko has been profoundly impacted by the disastrous engagement in the system. The planet is covered in the toxic wreckage of some seventy-three ships lost in action, many the size of cities. Spills of every kind have contaminated the environment and several species are rapidly approaching extinction already.

Of perhaps more concern is the population of marsupial lions first documented by Dr. Abolafiya aboard the Duchess Anne. They seem unaffected by the increase in ambient radioactivity or chemical pollution. Their aggression, if anything, has increased and gained complexity. However, they show signs of contact with a new strain of sludgeware of which we had been previously unaware. The planet is swarming with lions forming into standard military units, building barricades via kinetic sludge, retreating and attacking one another utilizing textbook ground strategies. They communicate in subvocal patterns that strongly imply the presence of a rudimentary neural link matrix. No implications are necessary to conclude that they have come in contact with telekinetic sludgestrands. Orbital observations show the lions have begun to deliberately alter the architecture of the crash sites according to an agreed-upon plan.

I have no explanation for how this could be, and yet it is. Nothing we have developed could affect a population of millions of animals in this way. I suggest you ask Dr. Aguirre what the hell is going on. I understand he is in custody.

I can only recommend a strict quarantine of Planet 6MQ441. There can be no further purpose to our presence anywhere near Bakeneko.

FOUR MOONS RISE over the steelveldt. One lion called Yttrium opens her eyes. As well she opens her eyes in the watering hole. She finds only quiet. Some death. But every lion knows death. The smallgod inside her sleeps. It found the idea of satisfaction. One lion called Yttrium understands. Blood always brings satisfaction. Perhaps it will wake in hunger again. Perhaps not. One lion feels the concept of contentment. The watering hole gleams fresh and bright. It has many fewer personnel to maintain. Its resolution surrounds one lion in evening light. In the smell of sunspot lizards. In the profound togetherness of nine million lions breathing in unison. Reeds move in the breeze within the heads of every lion left.

One lion called Yttrium stretches her green paws in the moonlight and begins again the long walk toward the steelveldt Szent Istvan. She longs to hear the first roar of her young.

Flame, Pearl, Mother, Autumn, Virgin, Sword, KISS, BLOOD, HEART, AND GRAVE

The poet Dezs Kosztolányi, toward the end of his long career, proclaimed these to be the ten most beautiful words in Hungarian, and proceeded on to death shortly thereafter.

FLAME

ONCE, IN A WALLED COUNTRY that was neither Poland nor Hungary nor Serbia nor Romania, though in various centuries, claimed, invaded, abandoned, repudiated, and finally, its very name and historicity redacted by all four, a child was born into a particularly withered, lightning-scarred branch of the royal line with a certain deformity. That, in and of itself, was not unusual, not then and not there; around this time all children of the nobility of ——— were born with some malformation or another. A recent son had emerged from a baroness with a speckled cochin's wing in place of his left arm. The daughter of a favored underpope faced her baptism with the slitted eyes of a cat and seven long black fingers on each hand. A pair of ducal twins were presented to the court made of solid silver, their faces engraved with a pattern of rue and musk rose popular at the court of the Holy Roman Emperor. The crown prince himself had been born quite dead, without heartbeat or breath, covered in veins of green and purple and scarlet corruption like a weeping mushroom, yet he walked and talked and recited the apocrypha as well as an abbot by the age of four. It had gone on for so long that healthy children were considered undesirable as mates and apprentices, as they were unlikely to progress much socially with their unsettling two eyes, ten fingers, unblemished skin, and luxurious teeth. In the beginning, the defects of the upper classes had been carefully recorded in illuminated books of heritable traits, but by the time this tale broke its mother's pelvis in half hurling itself into the cauldron of the living, the particulars of these anatomical splendors were no more interesting to the intelligentsia than the exact number of apples required for the St. Barrow's Eve pyre.

The whole situation was pronounced by the local college of stylites to be a cosmological punishment for the foundational sin of this little kingdom of wheat and walls and waxbeans and white grapes, namely, that an ancient king had held the cold and empty jaw of famine in his hand and, without feeling, ordered the wholesale slaughter of every living songbird within the walls of ———, in order to preserve the harvest. However, stylites are rather high-strung and paranoid as a people; the natural result of living on top of a bony spire of rock and professionally contemplating the universe while standing on one foot and suffering the verbal abuse of the masses. They had gotten rather in the habit of blaming nearly everything on this convenient infamy rather than any current policy of the government for which they might be censured, or any scientific theory which might, may such horrors never be visited on us or anyone we know, be proven incorrect in the future. The past, like God, is changeless and unmovable, and therefore it is safe. Only the eaters of flesh had been spared, the hawks and the ravens and the owls and the petrels. The king sent out his personal guard in their finest armor, black of plate and splendid of feather and elaborate of all imaginable decoration, to put the eaters of seed to the sword. This the knights did with great and solemn ceremony, donning judiciary wigs over their helmets and trying, with witnesses summoned from farms and mills and bakeries, each sparrow, finch, thrush, nightingale, and starling for high treason, burglary, and crimes against the crown before carrying out their sentences beneath a tight, grey, unraining sky. The queen caused the gargantuan royal oven to be moved into the common square and stoked to a rage. It burned hot at its work for sixteen days on end, roasting the bodies of the condemned. These were then distributed as equally as possible among the starving population and devoured meat, talon, bone, and spleen beneath maroon silk canopies raised up by the daughters of the noble houses, in order that God and all his angels should not see what they had done, for in those innocent days it was believed that silk alone could not be penetrated by the eye of the divine, originating as it did in the belly of a foul and creeping worm from the unreachable east, where devils play dice with the damned, and maroon was the color of hopelessness. It is for the memory of this that all common families in the country of ——— wear the surnames of songbirds who perished, and noble families bear the names of the birds of prey who lived and were not perturbed.

The symbol of the house into which the certain child I have mentioned was born was the bittern, an eater of fish. The progenitor of her family had been a strange and off-putting man, addicted to the drinking of milk as miserably as most folk in ——— are to the drinking of a particular sour cherry death-in-a-glass. He crept through the fields at night, suckling at udders that did not belong to him, scooping cream from the mouths of calves and cheesemakers' daughters alike, savaged about the shoulders and haunches by shepherds and wolves alike, hated by constables and chatelains alike. Because of this habit he grew very tall and stout and quick and clever and his skin grew so bright and clear you could see it from the moon, instead of paunched and sallow like the drinkers of cherries, and his hair grew so long and thick that he cut off locks of it, tied them with stalks of lavender and chives, and sold them as cures for baldness until he became a reasonably wealthy man. It was this dairy-fattened brain that conceived the idea of encircling ——— and all her many cities with a grand wall in the shape, like the country itself, of a blown tulip, so that more men could devote themselves to the making of yogurt and buttercreams and fat babies and fatter poetry than waiting for the next Mongol invasion with the mix of anxiety and boredom that comprise the traditional yeast for the rough bread of a military coup. He did not build the wall, of course, nor did he draw designs for it, nor did he even contribute a stitch of silver to its funding, but in the days when songbirds still whistled in the walnut trees, the world was kind and lovely and eccentric, and the idea of a thing was considered to be the fact of it. And so this unrepentant calcium-thief received a rarefied title and married the slim, solemn, sloe-eyed daughter of a lord who, years later, betrayed the king over a black rose and a green sword, and took the throne for a fortnight, during which time he set down thirteen laws so simple, elegant, and easy to obey that lawyers in neighboring countries died in the night of existential palsy. The new king granted women and foreigners the right to own property and receive income, removed the injunction against men of learning dissecting corpses for the purposes of academic study, placed all fools, jesters, witches, and whores under the crown's protection and immune from all prosecutions, forgave the debts of the proletariat, but not the aristocracy, reformed the tax code into a system so exquisite it could be expressed only as poetry, wrote a meritocratic exam designed to bring talented commoners into government service, provided for the future education of each child born within the walls of ——— via wholesale liquidation of the Crown's personal stock of sapphires, ordered seven diabolists of seven different schools to determine some means on earth or below it of preserving his laws in every cranny of the kingdom for seven hundred years, and, once that time had passed, at least safe from invaders with a scion of his house on the throne, before being poisoned by so many nobles at once that he simply exploded over the blancmange he so greatly preferred for his nightly dessert.

Whether, as the stylites insisted, as retribution for such libertine governance on the part of King Blancmange, or, as the cheesemakers gloated, for the guzzling of so much illicit milk on the part of Lord Cowsuck, the Bittern line never again produced more than one child in a generation, and that always a girl, not even after the bonfire of the songbirds, when they were given the crest of the fish-eating bittern to wear in shame for all time, not even once the fact of their being technically within the line of succession had been forgotten by all except the more discerning and scholarly voles in the palace walls, two of the stylites, and by something neither a vole nor a stylite that lived in the granary, not even when the certain child I have mentioned was born with a tower in the place of her torso, all the way to the cleft where a woman becomes a world to the cleft where a throat becomes an intellect, and tore her mother in half with the bricks of her birthing, and called Vnuk, and left alone in her father's arms while the stars rained stitches of silver into a room hot and sour with death, its floor carpeted in blood and its ceilings chandeliered in blood and its lock so full of clotting that no one could get in for the three days it took to summon the royal locksmith from his pilgrimage, all the while the infant cried and cried for milk that, though it belonged to her, would never come.

PEARL

THE SMARTEST, THOUGH *never the wisest, yet almost certainly the most intolerable man ever born in the universe was named Chancel upon his birth in the village of Nyolc, and Chancel the Sophist upon his adulthood in the grand metropolis of Öt. Like all his people, he was stout, short, and agoraphobic, with a color to him like the flesh of hen-of-the-wood mushrooms, eyes like the bottoms of long-dry wells, and little enough jawline to speak of. By the time he could walk, the boy had already read every book in his village synagogue three times and spoiled the endings, not to mention the middles and beginnings, for everyone else. When the rag-and-bone man came calling with his birch-wheel cart down the thin dirt roads, the thick pastoral sunlight, for which Nyolc is so famous among painters and poets, pooled so heavily in his eyes that he did not notice one of the bundles of rags was rather heavy, and noisy, and squirmy, and named Chancel, until he was halfway down the mountain path to Öt and stuck in a snowstorm. Having no other idea what to do with objects, the rag-and-bone man sold Chancel, along with several yards of muslin and wool shearings as well as four deer femurs and a boiled rabbit skeleton, to an Öttian jewel-thief, for burglary was in those days the most fashionable occupation of Öt, and its various techniques the city's most valuable export.*

By the age of four, Chancel had stolen the Thirteen Treasures of the Common Man from the oligarchs of Öt (these being the first stone knife, the first arrowhead, the sternum of the first mastodon felled by mortal hand, the first woven basket, the first necklace, the charred ashes of the lightning-blasted tree that first revealed the logic of fire, the first wheel, three fossilized berries from the first plant used to narcotic effect, the first snowshoes, the stone on which the first abstracted writing was scribbled, the skull of the first person intentionally murdered, the first leash used on the first tamed wolf, and the first water jug) and used the sternum and the writing stone to keep his table from wobbling. Before the age of six he had married and divorced twice, the second time to the idea of a woman who had not yet been born, of which he grew tired, for it would not stop nagging him. At seven, Chancel had received his doctorate in both alchemy and astrology, having cured Sagittarianism to the satisfaction of his dissertation committee. Shortly thereafter, Chancel the Sophist married for the third time, a young and quite deaf tinker named Clerestory, perhaps the only one who could ever truly give her husband the ultimate expression of love: never once telling him to stop talking or she would scream. Thus finally settled in a house on the high street, an untroubled lady, and absolutely no friends at all, Chancel the Sophist, at nine years old, began work on writing the Amaranthine Bible. On his deathbed, one of his devoted followers asked why he had called it so. The sage Chancel coughed into his hand and answered: amaranthine sounds properly occult and mysterious. I wouldn't have sold half so many copies of the Sorry, All the Paper in the Shops Was a Bit Green, It Was a Dry Year in the Forests of Tíz I Guess Bible.

This sort of very unsatisfactory thing was why Chancel only had acolytes and wives, not friends or companions. While he lived, whether or not the Amaranthine Bible was mean to be taken literally or was, in point of fact, the longest and least funny joke ever told by man or beast or man about a beast, was a subject of much debate. If Chancel were a comedian, even a dreadful one, he and his interminable shaggy dog story would be protected under the laws of the poor exploded king. If he were, however, practicing divine revelation on a freelance basis, both he and his book ought probably to be boilt for blasphemy. Death, however, has a way of making religion out of bad books. Death, and enough time.

Those were not, however, his last words. In the last breath of his life, the great man looked out the window of his house onto the wide, dark streets of Öt, breathed in the scent of broiling sausage and old rainwater and rich women's perfume, and whispered to the sternum of the first slaughtered mastodon: from the time of my youth I have dreamt of a wall I have never seen, the color of ginseng root, with moss growing upon the towers of it like snow, and little red flowers among the moss like blood. Do you think, perhaps, before the sun, and before the stone, before even the paprikas, there was this dream? I wish I had a whiskey, damn everything to hell.

This was in reference to the most oft-repeated passage of the Amaranthine Bible: In the beginning of the world, only three things existed: the stone beneath our feet, the sun above our heads, and paprikas. When questioned, as he often was, as to how paprikas could exist before chickens, cows for the necessary sour cream, and hot red peppers growing in good brown earth, he answered: Does not the mortar come before the house? Do not the birch trees come before the wooden wheel? Do not the parts come before the wholes? So doth the parts that comprise a paprikas, before the wholes from whence they came. *Whereupon his questioners walked away, initially satisfied, only to turn back in consternation and find Chancel having run off whilst their back was turned. Even in death, Chancel could find no comfort in anything he did not write himself.*

Perhaps the oddest thing in the whole long life of the cleverest man ever born in the universe was that he was right. He would never know it, except in the way men like Chancel always know they are right, without any real reason to think so. One moment the world did not exist. The next, there was stone, veined and cold. The next, there was a golden pearl hanging in the sky dripping life like organ meat hung up to cure. And the next, the very next moment, there was, upon the stone and beneath the sun, a white and purple porcelain bowl full of steaming paprikas, long before anyone existed to eat it.

Chancel the Sophist would not live nearly long enough to meet the beginning of this tale which is named Vnuk, nor even seize with his own eyes the River Sz or Ognisko Square. But his grandson and granddaughter, who happened to be twins and therefore twice as bad and twice as good as their famous ancestor, would.

CATHERYNNE M. VALENTE

MOTHER

THE DIABOLIST WHO came to examine Vnuk and record her into the books of peerage, once she had lived through a few poxes and bad winters and seemed destined to survive at least the immediate future, despite having no visible heart, lungs, stomach, intestines, or liver, was known as Archfiend the Lesser. He was called this despite being a rather nice man with a closely-trimmed beard who hated clutter and bad manners but loved injured animals, stained glass windows, watercress soup with dollops of sour cream, going to bed early, and had been compelled to hide, from childhood, his passion for embroidery. Men of his profession were imagined to commit pyrotechnical sins of wrath and adultery and ambition, nothing so vile and degenerate as enjoying the work and company of women. Nevertheless, after the explosion of King Blancmange, the bishopry of ——— compelled all diabolists to take names that plainly and obviously announced their profession, so that no child might be seduced into thinking they were upstanding, jovial, worthy men they might want to grow up to be, like Istevan or Konrad or Milosh down the way. It was devoutly hoped that the occupation would shortly die out, and whatever the deconstructed king had done to ensure the longevity of his laws would be unspooled like so much loudly-colored thread and everyone could breathe a sigh of joy and release and go back to patting down the poor for pennies and tossing their extraneous daughters in the river like they'd always done.

It did not have the intended effect. In fact, Archfiend the Lesser had been followed to the palace grounds from his cottage, over the Gyöngy Bridge on the River Sz, through the comedians' district and Slatterncourt Row, past dismemberers taking elk and boar and lion apart like puzzles previously solved by God, through wide open nearly cosmopolitan Ognisko Square in the sun, by a veritable *totentanz* of children of every economic class and level of nutrition begging him to take them on as his apprentices, despite his protestations that *diabolist* was just a word, not to be taken literally any more than an alewife was actually married to a barrel of black beer, his knowledge of demons merely academic, not practical in the least, his work almost entirely medical, astrological, or algebraic, and the most dangerous thing he'd ever done had been to set the crown a sensible budget when he was a young and reckless man.

The diabolist found Vnuk dressed in a gown of yellow and green chevrons trimmed in badger tails that buttoned all the way up to the tip of her chin. She sat, with a posture that could make a man believe in God, on a chair with a blue velvet cushion whose ivory back was carved to imitate the arches of the cathedral visible just outside the window of their allotted chambers, for at that time all members of the aristocracy lived within the walls of the palace and not on their own estates, where they could neither be trusted nor protected from the approaching army—and, one way or another, on horse or on foot, from the north or the west or the south, there was always an approaching army. It was what came of being situated so pleasantly as ———, between mountains, seas, generous growing seasons, and cross-hatching trade routes. The present horde, the king had shared in confidence, rode basilisks into battle, shot angels from the sky and cut them into rations for the infantry, spoke the language of silkworms, and was commanded by a woman-general without any single physical flaw. Why risk bodily autonomy on even the possibility of basilisks? And so they came into the fold, and were given rooms and gardens and plate in perfect proportion to what they had possessed out there in the sun-drenched lands beneath the wall, arrayed in just the same configuration, so that each lord retained his neighbors, and the palace became a microcosm of the kingdom itself.

"May I?" asked Archfiend the Lesser, reaching for the freshwater pearl buttons of Vnuk's gown with some hesitation of virtue.

"Of course, of course," snapped Vnuk's father, waving his broad hand in the air. Lord Bittern wore his cynicism in his beard and his grief in his belly, as though he could give birth to it one day, and finally be rid of the thing. His coat-of-rank strained at its clasps, its velvet stretched, only just able to keep all that sadness in one place. "I shouldn't think a man of your profession would be so bloody *ecclesiastical*. She has no shame, nor should you. I have a furious faith in searching out some slovenly little goodness in all hideous things, and in my personal tragedy it is this: My daughter alone is exempt from the sins of the primeval female. She has no stink of Eve about her, no inch of the Magdalene. You will find nothing to tempt the flesh beneath that dress. If not for the sniffing and clucking of your sort, I would let her run naked. She prefers it, you know. Her innocence is that extreme."

"It's all right," Vnuk whispered softly. "I don't mind. The crown prince already kissed my belfry, so you can't shock me. He said I had to let him, because, while the people are free of will and movement, all buildings in the kingdom belong to him. He said if I did not let him, he would charge me rent."

Archfiend the Lesser undressed the child and could not think of one single reason that his hands should tremble as they did, with each pearl button, with each dark flash of the body beneath. He harbored no clandestine love for children as some men of his profession did, nor did nakedness of any sort move him half so much as a perfect passage of Greek. And yet he trembled.

"This will require a new categorization," said Archfiend the Lesser, very handsomely lit by shafts of late sunlight slashing through the room. He flipped through the pages of his book, illuminated with oxblood and emerald headers that read: *Animalia, Missing or Additional Parts, Mineral Contamination, Disorders of the Blood, Skin, or Hair, Disorders of Doubling or Tripling, Disorders of Selfhood*, and wrote, somewhat experimentally: *Architectural*.

Vnuk watched him calmly as he wrote, her badger-lined gown laid open, her hands folded calmly in her lap, just below the great door of her tower. Although she, without a doubt, had bricks and mortar and portcullises and doors and windows where she should have had blood and skin and a chest and a stomach, she was an unsettlingly beautiful child. Her hair was dark, dark blue, the color of a whale's shadow, but the viscount's daughter had braids of such pure, hot light that they sheared them into two hundred lanterns at the beginning of winter every year. Her eyes were enormous, knowing, black as the inside of a winecask, with a pinprick of silver at the bottom of each iris like a tiny star, but the queen had no eyes at all and a pangolin's tail so long it curled three times around the throne. Archfiend the Lesser had himself been born with three faces, the extraneous two clutched one in each fist as he entered the world. He kept them nowadays carefully rolled in a surveyor's tube, and wore one for prayer, one for work, and one for passion, though having never experienced the third of these, he had yet to see the world through that last face.

The child lifted her chin in an attitude of arrogant wisdom, but this was all due to the architecture of the tower. Vnuk could no more slouch than Archfiend the Lesser could fly without weeks of prayer and study. Her skin shone with all the milk-fed clarity of her cow-besotted ancestor, and where it joined the bricks of her chest, the seam was no seam at all, flesh simply flowed into stone as smoothly and naturally as earth slopes into a river. The architecture of Vnuk was an upset and flustered thing, a runaway cathedral caught out between the Gothic and the Baroque, having stolen significantly from the Romanesque, the Russian Revival, late Byzantine, and the Early Grand Duchy school of Finland. The materials of her were, at the extremities, ashen skin, thin meat, thick hair, long bone, the usual nacre of nail, and in the trunk, a kind of strange brick so smooth and without pock it might have been a flow of lava cooled by a sudden sea. Most of this brick was black, but here and there, the tower of her glinted: a red slab, a blue stone, a green or violet trio of blocks, like any child's moles or freckles or portwine stains.

Vnuk possessed thirteen black-bricked levels from pelvis to jawline, terminating in an octagonal market cross at the crest of her collarbone, cradling her skull as a finial at the joining of eight flying buttresses so cluttered with dark croquets they looked like the legs of a great and sinister insect, and where the hollow of her throat should have been, that part of the body which all in the country of——— agreed was the most beautiful, rode a solemn silver silent bell. Each floor of her body was a pitched aesthetic and winnerless battle of ribbed vaults, secretive alcoves, long graceful galleries, nave arcades whose arches within arches within arches bristled with primeval faces and keystones wrought from unpolished gems, columns and capitals in every style painted in Turkish geometric patterns, French florals, Greek mosaics. Her ribcage unfolded into cloister walks and delicate balustrades whose railings curled like jet lily-vines, gargoyles and grotesques peering round every corner, and a multitude of mullioned windows, lancet, trefoil, reticulated tracery, Lucarne windows, rose windows, splayed and dormer windows, some as large as crabapples, some so tiny no human hand could open them without shattering them like ice over shallows, some papered, some crystal, some fitted with stained glass so fine that in later years, the glaziers of that country would take the name of their guild from Vnuk and make of her an informal patron saint. A wooden door of petrified grey walnut rode low in her belly, hinged in fresh iron, undecorated, dry as gasping, its slats born half-splintered. A scent emerged from the dark slats and gangplanks of her chest, a scent like African violets boiling in seawater.

The royal architects, an occult and unpleasable lot, would ultimately declare the whole effect rather an unsightly mess, and express a hope that, perhaps, at the onset of puberty, the poor benighted child might develop some unity of style.

Archfiend the Lesser put his thumb at the base of her chin and lifted slightly, peering through the dark archways to the other side of the room. He lifted his eyes; the buttresses flowed up into the skin of her face, and all else beneath the jawbone was smooth, flat, featureless skin, like a theatrical prop of a skull, unconnected to any part of the body. She should not have been able to speak or walk or live at all, her head having no method by which to discuss action or inaction with her limbs, and yet Vnuk was Vnuk, the fact of her in itself already proven. Archfiend the Lesser felt the great business of his life settle upon him. Presumably, behind these many doors and windows and arches, further cells and chambers and passageways lay as hidden and unseeable as the flora of the gut, connected by staircases of black proportions beyond mortal calculation, be their mathematics heavenly or infernal. A certainty set up its business in the base of his brain, that if he could know the map of her interior, he could know the map of everything.

The diabolist put his ink-stained hand on the stone of her chest. He meant to ask the same questions he asked of all the nobly deformed children he had examined in his life: *does it hurt when I do this, or perhaps this, can you count to ten, is your eyesight improved by this lens of glass or that, what can you do that I cannot, can you imagine for me a machine that might ease some little annoyance of your life in this body, even if it seems absurd and impossible?* He did mean to. But what came to his lips unwilled was instead a crime, a humiliation, a horror not his to commit—the great question asked of all diabolists on their first day of their enclosure, when they are still only boys trying to look up the infinite skirt of the universe, a question which is itself an initiation, the beginning of knowledge.

"What is the name of the Devil, my child?"

On the eleventh level of Vnuk, in the eighth lancet window, a soft light came on, the color of turmeric.

AUTUMN

IN OCTOBER, THE *trees in the city of Tizenkét do not lose their leaves. Instead, a slick of blue-white fire licks along their bark and their branches, sketching an arboreal outline in a crackling ghostmoon flame. The aqueducts run green and hot, as sharp-bubbled as champagne, and no one can drink from them until the season is past. The University Proctors once commissioned a study to explain why no one could get a decent glass of water for weeks on end every year, (was civilization itself in vain?), and even brought Chancel the Sophist on a significant salary to answer for this phenomena. The scholars could not agree between three theories—that some sort of clam was deep in its mating season upstream, that people really ought to stop pouring the more liquid of their rubbish into the river, or that the masters of hell were offended by the indomitable virtue of the citizenry—and the group disbanded after one of the Clamites stabbed one of the Rubbishers between the eyes. Chancel ignored the aqueduct completely, and claimed to discern a pattern in the crackling of the blue-white light in the trees, but when pressed for a translation by the Dean of Linguistics, the great man blushed and said only that he was angry with himself for never thinking that the universe itself might also know lustful thoughts.*

That was where the matter rested for many hundreds of years. It is a fact simply accepted that in Tizenkét, October is for beer and palinka and slivovitz and kefir, not water.

But October was also the time of the festival of St. Gremory-on-the-Stair, when the people poured out of their tall, narrow houses in the very corners of the night, chisels and buckets and knives and spiles and sewing needles and picnic blankets and wine bottles in all their merry hands. Look, there go Baldachin and Oriel, the best of friends since their seventh breaths, one a gravedigger like her father, eight months gone with her latest babe, the other a midwife like her mother, barren as sand in a glass, death and life, holding hands and drinking from the same bottle of yellow wine, wearing camels' skulls tangled in wild speckled mushrooms and monkshood and maroon silk ribbons on their heads. Their grandmothers made them those Gremory caps, and in each knot there was both love and a grand, luxurious irritation with the youth of the world. They will lay out their down-stuffed blankets on the cobblestone streets with their neighbors, where all carriages, horses, and carts have been banned for the night. They will sing the old thirteen-part songs as they light their camel-tallow candles, as big around as a strong man's ankle, and paint the little ones faces to look like wild camels and dragons, draft ponies and intricate glittering machines, all to commemorate the coming of St. Gremory when the world was new. Gablet the Fool will stare longingly at Baldachin, wishing the small soul in her nest were his, its future face his right to paint in the colors of a celestial camel, and braising in his bitterness, juggle cutting implements for coins. He is in secret the richest man in Tizenkét, all in small coins hidden away in his cellar and never let out to breathe.

The feast blazes in the alleys and closes and on the high street, too, there is food enough for all and sandwiches in the morning. Here and there among the quilted blankets burns paraffin-soaked effigies of the Patron Saint of Man Civilized, woven in crosshatches of black barley and white gentian, crowned in geometric sulfur crystal, and his eyes, repeated up and down the boulevards like a stutter in the long poem of of autumn, are always knobs of old brown bone. All down the public ways work-wizened grandafathers tell the tale as it was put down by Cinquefoil the Rhymer in the age between bronze hammers and iron, of how, before either of those could be imagined to hide in the earth, when the people were mute and stupid and more kin to the insects than to the angels, a man came among them as tall as the morning, with the head of a camel, the wings of a dragon, and the legs of a draft horse, and taught them all things which could be made and not birthed, which he called by the name of technology and by the name of civilization, and this was St. Gremory. He helped them to gather the Thirteen Treasures of the Common Man, he taught them to decorate themselves with stones, he taught them fire and cookery and how to safeguard against plagues of earthquakes, he taught them agriculture and the founding of cities, he taught them to enjoy the company of others, to ferment vegetation and to devise games. And in exchange for all of this, for modernity entire, St. Gremory asked simply that a few certain laws be obeyed, and even that only for a term of seven hundred years, until he returned among their number to see what they had made of themselves.

The first commandment of St. Gremory, the only one most people cared much about, was this: "This world is yours to use, to consume and to devour and to delight in. Seize it, take what you will from it and of it, and like the maggot upon the carcass, know no part of guilt. All things great and small are yours to command, and it is a sin to waste their value. Go forth and exhaust this universe, wring from it every last seep of strength which is yours by right, and you will know the weight of blessings. But if I return to find one stone unmolested, unknown, unhollowed, my displeasure will be the fission of atoms."

When the hundred and eleven clocks in Grisaille Spire chime eleven minutes after one in the morning, the moment when St. Gremory descended his mountain stair and began the tocking of history, the people of Tizenkét will let out a great wail and cry and drive their chisels and their knives and their spiles and their corkscrews into the black cobblestones with all their strength, prying up flakes and shards and chunks of stone, cramming them into their mouths like soft, fatty meat, grinning in holy transport as the dust runs down their chins like juice, and in her hunger and her satiation, Gablet the Fool will see at last that the midwife's daughter Oriel had hoarded beauty in her left profile and not her right, just as he had hoarded his small coins in his cellar and not his purse.

Seven hundred years has long come and gone in Tizenkét.

VIRGIN

THE CHILDHOOD OF Vnuk was a hall of strange turnings, and to the right was always the wildness of the little furred boar, and to the left was always the illness of the orphaned lamb. The monstrous children of the nobility ran rude and unruled through the palace, accepting no governance for themselves but a kindly anarchy. They tumbled through the grounds as they would have through the unfenced lands of their fathers, climbing through windows like manor doors, down passageways like rows of turnips planted for fall, up and down stairs like larch trees, stumbling into servants' quarters as into the fields of tenant farmers, hunting tomcats and kitchen rats and speckled doves down the arcades and courtyards with the solemnity they would have given to the stalking of stags in the shaded parks of their inheritances. To them, the palace was the world and the world was the palace. They did not even dream of those grand estates their parents abandoned for the safety of the king's eye on them. Yet the whole arrangement was so scaled to life that if you set down any boy or girl of that time on the thick seedy grass of the homes they'd never seen, they would have known exactly how many steps to get to this neighbor or that, for they were represented by the number of portraits between one bank of rooms and the next, exactly how the stables stood, and the mills, and the vineyards, for statues of cows, horses, wheat, and grapes in enamel and glass marked these spots along the royal mazeways, the directions of the brooks and streams and the names of all the creatures inside them, for these were painted along the floors, and words like *cyprinius carpo, lepomis auritus,* and *esox lucius* swam along the currents like real and breathing fish.

Vnuk tried to keep up with her playmates, but having no lungs, she was easily winded; having no heart, she would easily swoon. She loved to run along behind Ispan, the crown prince born already a corpse, and Sedria, the viscount's daughter with a perfect hole through her forehead through which you could see, no matter where she stood, a foreign desert of sand and starving rabbits as clear as a window, and Geza, the underpope's cat-eyed, seven-fingered girl, the silver ducal twins Szemmel and Szagol, and Kulacs, third in line for the throne, with his knees that bent backward like a seabird and his beautiful mouthless face. They stole joints of ham from the kitchens, books of occult philosophy and unvarnished history from the libraries, hid in wait for unsuspecting duchesses, climbed into the high gables and imitated the sobbing of ghosts until the whole palace rang with little soft lamentations and giggles and still further wailing on the subject of the horrors of the grave. They played at burnt-bone dice and taroc cards in the gardens, at pyromania in the vaults, at kisses in the shadows. But if she ran too fast (and she never could run so fast as the others, for her tower could not bend or flex like a back), Vnuk would fall sick and have to sit on the flagstones as still as winter until the spell passed. She had a horror of fire and if Szemmel and Geza's beloved flames licked too close to her, she would scream and scream until she fell down faint. And she could not eat the quinces or the figs from the orchards the other children loved to burgle away from the harvest, though she loved them too and always tried, hoping this time, this year she would be cured of it, but with one bite she always went so pale and sick the astrologer-physicians would lock her in a crumbling unused tower, ruined, the king said to all who would listen, by the basilisk-drawn trebuchets of the enemy during the last invasion, there to drink only rainwater, eat only the yolks of the eggs of white hens, and bathe in the healing light of Scorpio for a fortnight.

Diabolists were in those days only allowed past the palace gates on Thursdays, for long ago, when glaciers could be counted in the morning like pale geese and God still spoke to man, the first king of ————, who had no name, no gender, and came from nowhere, and was therefore judged by the people to be the only one among them uncorrupted by ambition, offspring or foreign interests, asked Murmex the Impenetrable what day of the week the diabolists held holy. Murmex answered: *there are few enough scraps left of the feast of days, for Sunday belongs to the Christians, Saturday to the Jews, and Friday to the Muslim with his forehead to the ground. Wednesday is the province of the pagan, Tuesday the kingdom of the tax collector, and Monday is the Great Sabbat of the owners of the means of production. Therefore we will make of Thursdays our masses, for nothing much of import happens on a Thursday, and it is with the stuff of idleness that we do our best work.*

And so Archfiend the Lesser came to Vnuk on Thursdays, wearing the face he used for work, and thus in the cosmology of Vnuk, Thursday was the name of the god of knowledge. They met in a little chapel adjoining Lord Bittern's bedchamber, eleven meters from his bedside, corresponding precisely at scale to the half kilometer between Milkdrop Hall and a particular orchard worked since before the songbirds burned by the old tarman Pkelnik and his wife. The chapel walls were thus painted round with sixty-six silver birch trees, two young fawns and their mother, a tame fox, a stone well, seventeen sour cherry trees, four bilberry bushes, a potato patch, a small thatched hut with a smoky fire burning outside, and Pkelnik himself with all his liver spots, industriously boiling bark into pitch. Beneath the brass drain in the center of the floor, a family of sleeping rabbits were painted in careful browns and greys and pinks, as real as if they meant to wake at dusk and set upon Pkelnik's potatoes.

At first, the diabolist brought both gifts and tools to the deformed child, to ply at her in both ways. On one table, he laid out a doctor's leather roll containing hammers, scalpels, chisels both toothed and flat, nails, needle and thread, a speculum, glass pots of exotic mortars and acids, levels and rules, shears, and vials of narcotics more powerful than prayer, all in miniature, delicate enough to work upon that famous pinhead over-populated with angels. On another table, he rolled out another physician's hide, this one containing sticks of peppermint and cinnamon, paints and brushes of Italian glass, ivory dolls so thin and long their heads could be used as quill tips, pots of meringue and honeyed cream, and a little silver whistle with a reed of sugar cane.

Vnuk looked from the left-hand table to the right. She sighed, and the sigh sounded so awfully old in her small body.

"Someone's painted rabbits in the drain," the child said on that first Thursday.

"H…have they?" said Archfiend the Lesser.

"Yes. A mother and six babies. I suppose the father's scampered off. They do that, you know. Fathers. Though I suppose I *have* made certain assumptions with regard to the larger rabbit. Mothers scamper off, too."

"Ah," said the diabolist, scratching his head beneath his green leather cap. The join between his face and his skull always itched him terribly. "Well, rabbits in the drain or no rabbits, we have much work ahead of us, and it's a sin to waste a Thursday."

"Why would someone do that, do you think?"

Archfiend the Lesser selected the little hammer and the toothed chisel. "Do what?" he said, with a whiff of exasperation.

"Paint a mother rabbit and six babies under the brass grate in the drain. It's a very good likeness. It must have taken days. And no one will ever see them. No one even knows they're there."

"You've seen them."

Vnuk paused and looked down at her long, slender fingers holding tight to the sash of her yellow autumn gown. "Is that enough?" she whispered. "I had to pry up the grate with a trowel."

"If someone painted them there, that means there are rabbits in the real world, on your real estate, where these birch trees are really birch trees and your father's bondsman really does spend his life blackening his lungs and teeth and soul with tar-smoke. Now, take this peppermint. Science waits on no man's fancy. Or rabbit's."

Vnuk leaned closer to the diabolist. The grey walnut door in her belly creaked. "But surely not *anymore*, Archfiend. Surely they've all grown up by now, and had other babies. Rabbits make babies very fast, you know. There's probably millions of them running all over poor Pkelnik's potatoes, because no one's there to hunt them for stew. What are you going to do to me with that hammer and that chisel? Is it something you've already done to the other children?"

Archfiend the Lesser had spent the holy days of all the other religions stirring his courage round and round to this day. He had worn the stern, severe, sharp-cheekboned face of work. It had grey hair, though he was a young man, in case he needed the extra authority. He'd tried to forget about the child of Vnuk and concentrate only on the tower of Vnuk. All his brothers of the diabolists college agreed that she *herself* was irrelevant, surplus, no more to be worried over than the apple-skin which covers the apple, which was only there to keep the fruit from going brown too soon. Yet there she sat, with her black buttressed throat, her blue hair rippling over her shoulders, nearly down to the floor that concealed those painted, sleeping rabbits.

"There are no other children like you," he rasped. "A baby born with no eyes or seven fingers on each hand or a even wolf's tail is still within the bounds of positable humanity, however unpleasant to look at. It is something Aristotle could imagine. Something findable within the pages of Herodotus. You…are not."

"Ispan is a corpse, and he's going to be king. I don't think you took a crowbar to the king."

"You have me there."

"Please tell me. I'll know in a minute anyway, once you're doing it to me."

Archfiend the Lesser tried to think of Lord Bittern's daughter as an apple-skin. "As it is our first day, I thought we would begin slowly. I mean to remove those three little blue bricks near the kidney area, and perhaps one of the lancet windows, through which opening I will pass my instruments in order to begin a rough calculation of your interior volume. Perhaps, if we are lucky, even find the source of that light in your aorta."

"Will it hurt?"

"I have no idea. Cathedrals do not scream. Girls do. It could go either way, honestly. Whether or not it will hurt is…it is part of what I wish to learn."

Vnuk considered for a long moment. She looked from the right-hand table to the left.

"No," she said.

"No?" repeated the diabolist, who had never heard the word, not even from the, admittedly tiny and quite lazy, demons he'd once summoned to defend his thesis.

"No. You will not do that."

"Your father has already agreed to this. My colleagues have negotiated an increase in his rank as compensation. It has all been arranged by men wiser than us both. You will be a baroness now. Won't that be nice?"

"No."

"No?"

"No. If my father would like parts of *him* removed in order to calculate *his* interior volume, which is probably quite impressive, he is free to make himself a baroness and do it." Tears floated in Vnuk's strange eyes. She wrapped her thin arms around her architecture. "I am mine," she pleaded.

"I'm sorry to have to tell you, but the high court has determined that property law applies in this case. The trial was very long. I testified. So did your father. So did the locksmith who was present at your birth. The judge went through a third change of wigs. Konrad the Rhymer has already written two romances about it. You are, technically speaking, rather less a member of the nobility and rather more a *structure* situated upon the lands of the king and therefore—"

Vnuk trembled and tightened her arms around the balconies of her ribcage. "But I am *mine*."

Archfiend the Lesser had no answer for her. He set down the hammer and the chisel. He drew out his surveyor's tube containing his other two faces and laid it on the floor. The diabolist opened one end and carefully worked out the face he wore for prayer. A kinder face, a rounder face, soft and young and sad, with solemn dark hair and eyes like saltwater. He allowed Vnuk to watch him change his face, which he had allowed no one to see before. When it was done he knelt before her with his saint's eyes and his martyr's lips.

"Please," he said.

"What will you give me?"

"I gave you a peppermint. And the dolls."

Vnuk shriveled him with a glare. "Teach me what you know. Teach me the names of all the devils and their sigils and their mounts. Teach me to be like you."

"It is forbidden for women to study such things."

"When you met me in my father's rooms, when you saw me naked and asked me the name of the Devil as though a child of six should know such a thing, did I answer correctly?"

Archfiend the Lesser's gentlest face darkened with shame. Why had he said it? What had moved his absurd mouth? "Yes."

"Then am I not already your apprentice?"

"It is too dangerous for women, Vnuk. Men may have their ambition, their lands, their treasure, their talent, their name, but you have only one thing to trade to the legions for knowledge, and though one good coin still makes the sale, it is not your coin to barter. It belongs to your father, to your king, and to your husband, whoever he may be."

Vnuk began to laugh, and when she laughed, the bell at the base of her throat began to toll like the striking of some hour deep in the night.

"What could amuse you so?" asked Archfiend.

"Two things," laughed the girl, "and I cannot decide which is the better. That I should need my father's permission to sell my soul, or that you think I have that coin you speak of with which to go to market."

Vnuk held her hand against the splintered door at the join of her legs, against the bricks and the black tracery.

The diabolist rose, his heart boiling in him, his liver cursing his spleen. He drew the long silver whistle from the left-hand table and gave it to the child with a tower in her belly.

"Do you know what a songbird sounds like?"

"Of course not. They are all dead."

"Amusdias is the name of a certain lieutenant. He commands legions numbering six by six. He appears in the form of a man with the head of a unicorn crowned, but his hands are the hands of an ape, and he can, under compulsion, change into the form of a thrush or a starling. He is the provider of all the cacophonous music of Hell, and his sigil is that of Saturn and Neptune conjoined, with his name writ upon it in Hebrew and Sanskrit. When you have mastered those languages, and the melody he calls most favored, and can tell me how life begins, where comes the first seed of dust, the first drop of water, the first inkling of intelligence, we will attempt your first summoning, and you will tire of all of this or run shrieking from it, but either way, you, among all the children of ———, will at least have heard the singing of a bird."

Archfiend the Lesser took up his tools again, and this time, looked to Vnuk for permission. She nodded slowly. As he bent to wedge his chisel behind the first blue stone in her side, she cried out:

"Wait!"

"What is it now, girl? Must I stand on my head? Tell you how to turn lead to gold? Bring you the heart of a griffin?"

Vnuk looked into his eyes and all the way through them down into the fire at the center of his life.

"What if I have rabbits in my drains?" she whispered in terror.

"Ah, dear, sweet thing, I will not wake them," the diabolist answered tenderly. "But I will see them, and that will be enough."

"I don't think the king ever does mean to let us out of the palace," the daughter of Lord Bittern sighed. "I don't believe there really are any basilisks at all."

With a hesitant motion, her new friend struck out one bright blue brick from her body.

Vnuk began to scream.

SWORD

ALL THE CITIES *in that pleasant kingdom suffered from earthquakes, but the one called Kettő had taken those cataclysms to wife. Travelers leaving the Dancing City feel the tremors in their legs for days afterward, like sailors suddenly cast ashore. Even the infants of Kettő know like dogs when a quake is about to begin. They feel it in their soft bones, in the cartilage of their flat noses. There are still days, to be sure, days when the balconies and colonnades know no other turmoil than the play of shadows on their stones. Mothers still sing of the Quiet Summer, when not a drop of water was spilt in all the hundred houses of Kettő and all the nets and straps of daily life were, for a time—and what a time it was!—laid to rest. But it was not to last, no summer ever is, and to be truthful, many were glad when the world began to shake again. They had not known how to live without. The Quiver is life, the Quiver is death. All the old men sipping thick tea in the afternoons had taken to yelling at anyone who would listen that this degenerate world was slowing down, growing lazy and weak, unable even to shake off its own dust like it used to. And what would the younger generation become now, without the Quiver to keep them agile, sharp, and clever? Layabouts, that's what.*

The rules of survival in Kettő were simple and short, and the Beggar Finial had obeyed them all the days of his life. Strap, net, and door. If you had your strap and you had your sleeping nets, there was nothing at all to fear from a little clearing of the geological throat. After all, God's Fingers were always there to catch you. The Dancing City bristled with them: little curls of stone or iron jutting out of the masonry like errant nails, a little face on the head of each one, laughing or vomiting, depending on your religious philosophy, and the two schisms had long since divided Kettő into a patchwork of loyalties and blood feuds, the market district marching on crusade against the launderers' grotto, the millers excommunicating the bakers and the bakers excommunicating the millers. The Beggar Finial picked his way among the territories of the faithful every day, scraping coins to fill his belly, caring nothing for whether the tiny faces laughed or retched, for millers or for bakers, as long as he could still get a bit of bread out of them. And if he felt an earthquake coming in his cartilage, he slipped the holes on either end of his strap, thick as a wrist and wide as a forearm, over two of God's Fingers, and hung there safe until the dance was done. You walked with your strap, you slept with your net so as not to tumble out of bed, and sometimes you could fall asleep there, hanging between two faces, perhaps happy, perhaps near to death, rocked into dreams by the motion of the world.

The Beggar Finial had once hoped for more in this life. He hoped for a family, he hoped for a trade, he hoped for that beast called satisfaction that always ran faster than he. He had always had the feeling, as deep in him as marrow, that he was special, favored by whatever passed for fate. No matter how low his station, how miserably bruised his pride, how furious his empty stomach, he could not take off that suspicion of his own greatness. He blamed his mother, for calling him beautiful and strong. He blamed his father, for praising him for even so much as waking up of a morning. And he blamed Kettő, the whole of it, for since he had no house, he considered all the city his manor, and holy wars had made his manor filthy, cluttered, strewn with bones and swords and broken tabernacles, for neither side would lower themselves to do the tidying up, since, as far as both were concerned, they *hadn't made the mess to begin with. But in the cold, still nights when he had not even the Quiver to keep him company and reassure him, the Beggar Finial knew full well what sin had cost him his grace.*

When the Beggar Finial was a child, beautiful and strong and often-praised, he was walking alone along the border of the city, where the windows in the wall were tallest and finest, and the light streaming through them colored like a feast. He had come upon a heap of rubbish left over from the Greengrocers' Crusade, boots and skulls and some poor dead men's straps and nets and swords and tridents and bandages washed up like driftwood against the hinges of the Only Door, that massive wooden thing that towered over him so, that led Out and Away, the most important destinations imaginable. The Only Door was the last rule of Kettő—you must never open it, you must never go through it, you must pretend as though there is no door in the wall at all. It was not remotely the only door, so he'd no idea why everyone called it that. You could get to Öt and Tizenkét and Nyolc and Három and any place you cared for through a hundred other arches and paths and stairs and doors. But the Only Door was locked, and every mother, including his own, who would allow him anything, said that to open it was death. Some madness had overtaken the Beggar Finial then, the madness of the young or the male or the spoiled or the bored he never could tell, then or after. Why couldn't he open this door? Why shouldn't he? Why should idiots get to slaughter each other over whether a nail in a wall was happy or sad while he, Finial, the most excellent and special boy in Kettő, should be forbidden to use a door? In his thwarted rage, the boy took up one of the old swords and heaved it into the Only Door with all his beautiful strength, leaving it stuck in the ancient wood like another of God's Fingers.

The city began to convulse, and it was none of that pleasant after-breakfast shuddering or tolerable teatime tremor that the old men said built character. It was the end of the Quiet Summer, and the world quaked and staggered and rattled until whatever good and special fate was in the Beggar Finial was shaken from him like the last dry peapod in a straw sack.

KISS

ONCE, IN THE grips of one of Vnuk's quince-fevers, the crown prince Ispan came to the door of her sickroom in the broken spire. He leaned against the stove-in red wood and bronze bolts of the door. Being a live boy in a dead body, he did not mind the cold or the fasting or even the sharpness of the shattered wall and roof where once, possibly, a real basilisk had done its duty. Yet, for all the rules the little gang of aristocrats stepped upon daily and nightly, he would not go past that door and into Vnuk's private territory.

"Hullo, Vnuk," said the prince, peering over the ruin of the door. The top half had been sheared away, as if by some awful claw. "I have brought you a cup of paprikas from Kulacs's mother, a backgammon board with red velvet on the inside and pieces carved like foxes from Sedria, a tinderbox and candle from Geza, some cherry vodka from Szemmel and Szagol, and a book from Archfiend the Lesser called *A Census of the Infernal Regions, Volume Two: The Wasteland of Water,* at least I think so, it is in Latin. It looks *very* juicy. What do you and he *do* together in that little birch-tar chapel?"

Vnuk looked up at the stars of the constellation Scorpio, which did seem somehow cool and pale and medicinal as they streamed through the shattered brickwork. "We talk about rabbits," she said quietly.

"Rabbits are boring," sighed Ispan. "They're so small and there's so many of them but all they do is...*twitch*. Have you summoned a demon yet? You've been at it long enough."

"Wouldn't you like to know?"

"I bet you can't, I bet you can't even do a little tiny one, like the demon who makes you trip on the cobbles when there wasn't anything to trip over, I bet you can't even do him."

"I could if I wanted."

"Could not."

"Could so."

"You couldn't, Vnuk, you really couldn't. You needn't feel shame on it, though. Girls can't be diabolists."

"And dead boys can't inherit thrones. You will tell me when you plan to abdicate, won't you?"

Ispan looked stricken. The stars in the dead, flat eyes of the crown prince looked like dandelion seeds sinking beneath black seas.

Vnuk relented. Her little shoulders softened. She came to the door and took his gifts, setting them on the floor beside her pitcher of water and basket of boiled white eggs. The two looked at each other over the slashed slats, each wondering if it had really been a basilisk who had done it, each wishing it had finished the job.

"What would you make him do," whispered the daughter of Lord Bittern, "if I did summon a demon?"

The corpse prince shrugged. He had never considered it. In his mind, once the demon was *there*, huge and sulfurous and horned and roaring and flaming and all the rest, you had all the entertainment you could ever pray for. "I don't know, what are you supposed to do with demons once you've summoned them?"

"They can do *anything*. Anything in the world you could ever want. Only you've always got to pay for it. They're very strict capitalists, demons. Archfiend the Lesser says that the old king summoned Amusdias to solve the famine, and that's how he got the whole idea of killing all the songbirds, and also how he got them to all hold still for their trials and executions and such. And the diabolists brought forth a demon for poor King Blancmange, which is why if you break one of his laws you get kidney stones and you start talking backwards and your fingers fall off one by one until you stop what you're doing."

"I would make him change everything so I could marry you," Ispan interrupted. His grey, green-veined lips trembled. He remembered his mother, staring down at him with her eyeless face, her bronze pangolin tail thrashing against the flagstones, in a wintry rage. *You would have no heir out of that walking privy-house but a mute brick, swaddled in silk and rocked to sleep by an idiot.*

Vnuk reached out her hand. Ispan laced his fingers through hers. "And what would you pay for that?"

"My soul."

"They don't want your soul, Ispan. The Devil wants your soul, but he comes for it in the end and not before. Demons want only your pain. It is their food and their wine. It wouldn't…come out the way you want it. Do you know what happened after all the songbirds died?"

"Yes, yes, a demon's bargain will turn on you. Everyone knows that. I don't care." Ispan reached one moldering hand out. Vnuk laced her warm fingers through it. "I wish I was small enough to live inside you," he said helplessly.

In the light of Scorpio, Vnuk answered him: "When the songbirds were gone, there was no one to eat the grasshoppers and the beetles, and so they ate up even more of the harvest than before. So the perfumers and the alchemists invented a poison to kill grasshoppers and beetles, since they are too stupid and innocent to stand trial. It worked, and everything smelled like African violets for weeks and weeks, which was very nice, I suppose, but it killed all the bees as well, and then there was no one to carry pollen from flower to flower and nothing fruited at all, just endless flowers blooming and blooming and falling away dead onto the dry ground. It's not the summoning that's any trouble. It's like whistling for a dog. A dog that you know for certain is going to eat you as soon as it can. Nearly the whole of a diabolist's education is to get for himself a mind big enough to see the whole trick, all the way through to the end. All the way through to us being born and everything that's still to come."

"My mind is big," sniffed the dead prince Ispan. "As big as the sky, as big as the wall."

Vnuk shut her eyes. She tired so easily in the autumn, when the quince she loved so turned on her. Ispan took the moment. He could not stop himself if he wanted to. He leaned over the ruin of the door and kissed her lips, his cold mouth against the warmth of her. He almost felt the weight of the kiss. He almost felt her life. "I wish I were big enough to be your home," she breathed. But then she said: "Is there really an army out there? Led by a flawless woman atop a basilisk?" when the kiss was done. "You must tell the truth after a kiss."

The heir to the throne said nothing, could say nothing. He was a child, still. He knew no more than she. His dead eyes reflected the dark, but not the stars.

"Go and look in the granary," she sighed. "Go up the ladder, all the way to the back, behind the oat bales and the millstones and the rack of six broken shovels, and see there the size of your mind."

When he had gone, Vnuk ate her evening meal in private, as she preferred to do, since it disturbed the appetite of others. She took up the teacup full of stolen paprikas from Kulacs's mother, opened the great grey door in her belly, and placed it inside.

BLOOD

THERE HAD LONG been a saying: the gods do not speak clearly, except in Tizenharóm. *The Amaranthine Bible said it, as it usually did, in an earthier fashion:* In any old city, in Kettő and Öt and Nyolc and Kilenc, in Egy and Negy and Tíz and Hét, in Tizenkét and Siks and Tizenegy, you can hear the gods in the sound of the wind in the trees and the flowing of the water in the aqueducts and the laughter of children and all that church-a-day rot. But in Tizenharóm, they'll blow out your eardrums.

Tizenharóm was an alpine city, so near to the roof of the world you could see the rafters and the thatching. The only season there was winter. The only export was prophecy. The only industry was religion. The city was a carnival for monks and priests and abbots and popes, the streets lined with stalls selling candy in the shape of the childlike god of death and cider in mugs carved to represent the face of the eyeless mother goddess. If you were lucky at the ring-toss, you might win a doll of the two-faced god of wisdom, or the corpulent god of sorrow with his infinite beard rendered in real yak-fur. There were no dark alleys or wicked shadowy gutters in Tizenharóm; everywhere there was light. Even the narrowest, most unremarkable crack in the masonry had its own small candle to engolden it, to sweep away the night and make it bright enough to please the exacting palette of heaven. The wax never burns down and the flames never gutter—it is said that Narthex the Lamplighter struck her match when first she heard the divine voice, so startled and frightened was she, half-deafened in the primeval dark, and then another and another, each time the gods spoke so her humble ears could hear them clearly, and though Narthex is long gone, her little flames will never go out until the end of days, for light is the blood of the gods, and it runneth through the veins of the world without ceasing. It was a city that glittered and a city that sang—even the meanest, most untrafficked crossroads had a musician trilling out hymns, high and soft, at every hour on the hour.

But all roads in Tizenharóm led to one place, and all the attractions and pleasures were subservient to it. For in the center of the city, there was a hole. The queue to kneel and put your eye to it wound through all those stalls and candies and ciders and rings tossed against dowels, all Narthex's candles and all those hungry musicians, six years, six months, and six days long. Folk have died in that queue, been buried and canonized where they fell, for anyone who dies awaiting audience was sanctified before their last breath dispersed in the air. The hole was gouged from a simple wall, a meaningless expanse of brick, stained with the markings of living and dying in a city, the rear wall of a library specializing in romances and unauthorized histories. Once, in the days of Narthex, when Tizenharóm knew what a shadow was, there had been a red brick there, red as though it were sodden with blood. But now there is nothing, a simple space, and if you kneel there, if you kneel and quiet the beating of your heart and the beating of your mind and the beating of your soul agains the bones of your body, you can hear that voice that Narthex heard, and puzzle it through as others have done, until you can make a prophecy of there are rabbits in the drains *and carry it down from the heights to the city of your birth, and make it mean good or bad crops, victory or defeat in war, a girl child or a boy.*

But it was nothing so mysterious and interpretable that Narthex the Lamplighter heard when the world was new and fresh as the boil on a pot of paprikas. She heard only one word, a word that frightened her so badly she invented fire to chase off her horror of that bodiless voice saying:

Love.

HEART

GO AND LOOK *in the granary,* Ispan repeated to himself. *Up the ladder, behind the oat bales and the millstones and the rack of six broken shovels.*

The late afternoon sun slashed down gold and dark like war banners through the rafters of the barn. The ladder spiked his fingers with splinters, but being dead, the boy felt nothing. The oat bales pricked his hands with bristles, but being dead, no blood ran. The millstones bruised him and the shovels scraped his toes as he dragged them from the wall, but Ispan cared not at all for that, no corpse ever could. He cared only to prove to Vnuk that his mind was as big as hers, so that she would summon them a demon to change the world for them, to break it in half so that she could be his queen and they could belong to each other, a kingdom of two.

There was nothing behind the shovels but cobwebs and mice droppings and the leavings of light. Somewhere, far off, long and distant in the east, a soft boom of thunder opened and shut like a hand, but Ispan, in his irritation, paid it no attention at all. He would have left then, scrambled back down the ladder with the utter joy of someone who has proved a friend wrong, and run to tell Vnuk how he had not been one little bit afraid of the granary no matter how crawly she had made it sound, except that a mouse screamed just then, and the prince looked to see if he had crushed the poor thing without knowing, for being dead, he had no feeling at all in his body, and often ruined things unawares.

In the shadow of the sixth shovel blade lay the corpse of a barn-mouse with a tiny bronze harpoon in its side. Something was slowly dragging the carcass across the floorboards toward a house no bigger than a Christmas bun. Something small and strange and furious in the dance of dust-motes. Something with the body of a man, the head of a camel, the wings of a dragon, and the legs of a draft horse. The house was a pleasant wee thing, its chimney puffing away, built with cast-off shafts of old wood and horse nails and wheatstalks, thatched with green oats, with a lovely, complex design drawn around it on the floor of the granary in pale chalk. It looked to Ispan like a rose made out of mathematics. Once the creature hauled his kill over the edge of the chalk, he slit its belly and began to cut the meat into steaks and bacon and offal for sausages.

Far off, but not quite so far now, the thunder echoed again.

The creature with the head of a camel finally looked up into Ispan's gaze.

"Hello," he said calmly. "What day is it, if you please?"

The crown prince told him.

"Perfect," said the chimera in his tiny cottage. "You're right on time."

"Are you a demon?" breathed Ispan.

"Are you a boy?"

"Well, of course I am!" spluttered the prince.

"Well, of course I am!" grinned the demon.

"What is your name?"

"I am Gremory, grand duke of Hell," he grunted, pulling out the mouse's heart and cutting it into four equal roasts, "with sixty and six legions at my command, or I will have, when I am released from my duty."

Ispan controlled himself and did not clap his hands in delight. "What is your duty?"

Gremory put his scaled hand over his heart and intoned: "To enforce the laws of the king who summoned me for seven hundred years, in every cranny of his domain, and thereafter to protect his kingdom from invaders in perpetuity. Seven diabolists of seven schools put that doom upon me, and I shall be glad to be rid of it."

"That seems like a good and noble deed," the corpse prince said.

"I have made it wicked where I could," the demon shrugged. "It is not easy work, but I am dedicated. And it is almost over now." Gremory wiped his palms on his powerful draft horse legs. "There is just enough time to answer your wish, and then I will be home in my own black palace with my own full belly and ready to receive the great praise of my master."

"I did not wish for anything!" cried Ispan. "And I will not give you my soul!"

"There is no need for that little melodrama, my lad. This is long paid for, by men you never knew. A demon's bargain is cruel, yes, and seeks to snare, of course, but grace is Hell's last gambit, and all I have ever done is give men just what they ask for, nothing more or less. They make enough of a hash of that to give me centuries of leisure. You are no diabolist. There is no shame in being unable to see the shape of a trick seven hundred times bigger than you."

Gremory, grand duke of Hell, opened his camel's mouth, and what emerged from it was Ispan's own voice, whispering: *I wish I were small enough to live inside you*. And then he opened his left hand, and Vnuk's voice came out of it: *I wish I were big enough to be your home.*

"Ispan!" came a terrible cry at the door of the granary. The dead prince leapt to his feet and toppled down the ladder as Vnuk collapsed in the doorway, a wound gouged in her head, wearing a maroon winter gown, the color of hopelessness. She bled onto his hands, nothing red or wet but candlelight, flowing as free as water. "They are coming," she gasped. "I thought they would never come. I thought they were a dream. They rode under silk banners, Ispan, and God did not see them."

The thunder that was not thunder was close now, and the lightning was not lightning but trebuchets, and the air was full of an awful yelling, grinding, screeching, for the army at the gates was now inside them, and their horses' armor was wrought like feathered basilisks and the woman who led them was as beautiful as the sun. But try as he might, the crown prince of that vanished country could see no one else through the smoke, no familiar face, no mother or father or lord or lady, only the enemy, and too many of them.

Ispan held Vnuk tight and put his head to her heart, that glowed the color of turmeric, the color of an infinity of candles. He heard no beating, but birdsong, and before the next blast of cannonfire, he found that his face was no longer pressed to the bosom of beloved, but his feet were planted upon the balconies of her ribcage, and the world of her was vast and far as any he had ever seen.

The dead prince walked over Vnuk's brick sternum, toward the nearest lancet window, and raised his hand to knock upon the stained glass.

GRAVE

THEY CAME TWO by two and three by three, nine by nine and one by one to the door of the world, the door that Finial the Beggar had been forbidden to open. They looked nothing like the inhabitants of Kettő or Öt or Nyolc or Kilenc, or Egy or Negy or Tíz or Hét or Tizenkét or Siks or Tizenegy. They had long hair and beards and skin the color of worms in the morning, and many of them had more or less than the usual two eyes, some had tails, some were not made of flesh at all. They were strangers, but in Tizenharóm, through the hole in the library wall, the voice of the gods had said to welcome them, and allow them to live in those great cities, and allow them to eat of the common table, and read the words of Chancel the Sophist and Cinquefoil the Rhymer, and marvel at the candles of Narthex the

Lamplighter, and feast on the goods of the world, which some would call a tower, as St. Gremory taught them to do.

The newcomers looked out and up into the lands they would make their homes and saw the creatures that would be their neighbors, their lovers and their enemies and their rivals and their friends, and shyly gave their names to the million songbirds that were the people of the kingdom of Vnuk, who had spun through generations concealed behind the inner walls, raised cities on staircases and in galleries and cells, marveled at the autumn forests of her neurons and the candlelight of her blood, the aqueducts of her digestion and the sound of her gentle voice and the voices of her friends. The songbirds greeted them with stern, suspicious faces: sparrows, finches, thrushes, nightingales, and starlings, shrikes and robins, cardinals. The nations stared and stared and would not be the first to move, and ever after, this spot on the outskirts of the town of Egy would be marked with statues and flowers to remember this day. For then did the starlings Trefoil and Apse, the grandchildren of Chancel the Sophist, of whom we have spoken much, short and stout like all their people, reach out dark and speckled wings toward the eyeless queen of————and welcome her when no one else would. As her wing grazed those long royal fingers, the terrible tiny flutter of an earthquake began, and in that moment no one needed to find their way to Tizenharóm to hear the voice of some kind god cry: Run, run, child, get out before they burn it to the ground!

But before she ran, one last man came to the great grey walnut door. He wore a face he had never worn before, a young, keen face with dark eyes and red hair, a face for passion and for awe. He looked up toward Vnuk's face, a million miles away from him now, at the soft pale mountain of her jaw. He alone would not be surprised to meet the kingdom of birds within. Tears overflowed the eyes of Archfiend the Lesser as he asked his question once more, once more before escaping into the scion of King Blancmange's house, which would be his house and all of theirs forever and ever.

"What is the name of the Devil, my child?"

Inside the tower of Vnuk, Ispan collapsed weeping into the soft, confused magpie wings of the Beggar Finial. "I'll never see her again," he wept. "I shall live in her body like a husband, but I will never see her eyes again."

Vnuk's great and monstrous hand, now as tall as a trebuchet, guided the diabolist through the door and locked it behind him.

"Love," she said as she saved her kingdom. "The name of the Devil is love."

The silver bell at her throat rang out, and Vnuk began to run.

IF YOU GO *and search well for it, outside the borders of a walled country that is neither Poland nor Hungary nor Serbia nor Romania, you may find beneath a rowan tree a peculiar ruin, not much larger than a girl's torso, of a tower of somewhat confused architecture and peculiarly beautiful black masonry. Beside it, long bones slowly turn to long grass, and above it, rooks have made a nest in the pale skull that hangs off the crumbling market cross at the top of the tower. I have heard it said that if you put your ear to the eighth lancet window on the eleventh floor, you can hear, ever so faintly, a hundred million voices singing forever.*

Major TOM

For my father

SCALPEL, PLEASE.

The damage is much worse than we thought.

⁂

WHEN I OPEN my eyes I see blue. Blue everywhere. Blue beyond the dreams of Picasso. When I close my eyes I see everything.

⁂

SCALPEL, PLEASE.

You can't plan for something like this. It's far more difficult than the boys upstairs could ever anticipate.

⁂

I DON'T KNOW where that came from. That name. It means nothing to me. Picasso. Pic…ass…o. The blue is hex #2956B2. I don't know what Picasso's hex number is. The blue is everywhere. I am nowhere. I keep looking for my name, but I can only find Picasso, Picasso floating in all that blue.

⁂

SCALPEL, PLEASE.

Patient vitals are slipping. Prep .5 cc's of adrenaline.

⁂

THERE IT IS. Down there. Covered in blue like a fish. A name. My name. Jumping and leaping around below me. I cast for it, standing waist deep in a Michigan river with my grandfather, wearing a hat that's too big for me, holding a pole too long for me, trying to make the line snap out as gracefully and perfectly as Grand-dad's line.

⁂

SCALPEL, PLEASE.

If he wakes up, pump him full of Ativan and hold on to your goddamned hat.

⁂

SOMETHING TAKES THE bait. My heart feels like it's going to catch on fire. I pull the name out of the water, dripping. It is my name. My name is Desmond Wright.

⁂

SCALPEL, PLEASE.

The damage is much worse.

It's far more difficult.

You can't plan, please.

It's much slipping.

If he wakes up, pump him full of goddamned hat.

.5 cc's of vitals, please.

We thought patient. Hold on to anticipate. Prep the boys upstairs. Scalpel adrenaline.

⁂

FULL CONSCIOUSNESS DURING *installation would cause a catastrophic shutdown of all systems.*

How about you just let me do my job and make your little laws about it later?

NONE OF THAT is really happening. It's just background radiation. The noise of my own personal Big Bang still echoing around, bouncing off nothing. Static. Don't listen to them, Desmond Wright. Focus on the blue. The blue is always happening.

This has all taken a lot of adjustment. I still wake up screaming and reach for my wife. I wake up screaming and reach out across a bed that doesn't exist for a wife who is long gone. But I'm not really waking up, either. Not really screaming.

Oh! Picasso was a painter. The information looks like a child finger-painting, squishing blue paint between her little fists, crying for me:

Daddy, Daddy, look what I made!

Pablo Diego Jose Francisco de Paula Juan Nepomuceno Maria de los Remedios Cipriano de la Santisima Trinidad Ruiz y Picasso, born 1881 Malaga, Spain, died 1973 in France. It must have been nice to be Picasso 1881 to 1973. To be finite.

I can access his life easily now, faster than cell mitosis. I am beginning to form permanent pathways through my neurotic geography. I understand this represents good progress. But it frightens me. My basic functions are depth-mined with memories ready to detonate. I can't stop myself remembering, or predict when it will happen, or even understand it. All I know is that my mind is somehow *sticky*. I reach into my psyche for something—wife, name, blue, Picasso, scalpel—and when I pull it out some image, some memory is clinging to the fact I wanted. Like the fish in the Michigan river. Like the finger-paint oozing between tiny fingers.

I will copy my friend Pablo. This is how humans learn, by copying better humans. I am Desmond Patrick de Aspera Orbital Satellite de Registration 887D de la Boreal-Atherton Corporation y Wright. Born East Lansing, Michigan, 1988. Died…no. I don't like *died*. *Died* is sticky. Died comes with sound and image files attached.

Yellow lines on black. Solid. Dash. Solid. Dash. Like morse code.

Richmond, Virginia: 67 miles

A woman's voice shaped like the fireplace inside a white clapboard cottage by the sea: *I thought maybe we'd go up to Maine for the summer next year. Like we used to do when the kids were little. What do you think, Dez?*

Sounds from some industrial hell: screeching, crunching, thudding, snapping, grinding, and the slow drip of everything into the storm drains. Blood, petroleum, rain. The sound of *died.*

⁂

SCALPEL, PLEASE.

The damage is much worse than we thought.

⁂

I DROWN EVERY day in a sea of random access memory. It really eats into my productivity.

⁂

IT'S A WIN-WIN, *Desmond. And if you do end up fulfilling your end of the contract, you'll be far past caring about the details.*

⁂

MY WORLD IS very orderly. When I close my eyes, I see the clock turn over 0700. I do what any man does, the same routine I've been running for the last twenty years. Throw on a bathrobe, have a good morning piss, wash my face, stumble downstairs, make coffee, pour myself a bowl of my son's cereal, read a book while I eat so I don't have to listen to the newscasts blaring through my kitchen windows, my refrigerator door, my bathroom mirror, anything with a screen. I've been working on Kafka. Real cheerful guy. Sometimes I get the idea that turning into a cockroach is his idea of a happy ending.

When I open my eyes, I see the clock turn over 0700. I activate my dormant systems, run a self-diagnostic, clear any buggy code, dispatch drones to repair any equipment malfunction (and there is always an equipment malfunction), scan the passive surveillance archive for any anomalies, run active surveillance programs, access darkweb listen-in protocols, and attempt contact with ground control.

But God, it *feels* like throwing on a bathrobe, having a good morning piss, washing my face, stumbling downstairs, making coffee, pouring myself a bowl of my son's cereal, reading a book while I eat, not listing to the window/door/mirror newscasts. Peering at Kafka over my glasses. I can *see* the coffee mug in my hand as I switch over to active surveillance sequence 1139. The mug says *You're My MAINE Squeeze!* on it. The handle is chipped. I don't have a bathrobe. I don't even have shoulders to throw it over anymore. But it's *there* when I start combing through code lines. On my skin. The sash around my waist, under a belly that's a little too big for a fifty-year-old guy to be proud of. But I don't have a belly. Even a little one. Desmond Wright doesn't have a body anymore. I don't have a face to wash or a downstairs or a coffee pot or cereal or a son. But I hear his voice humming through the quiet corridors of the darkweb.

Daddy, Charlotte won't share her paint! She's hogging it ALL!

I say: *Charlotte, share with your brother.* It's an autonomic reflex, like breathing or adjusting a solar panel to match low Earth orbit.

Somewhere, in an underground radio room, a computer screen flashes text: *Charlotte, share with your brother.*

My daughter's name is Charlotte. And knotted to the name *Charlotte* like a magician's trick scarf come other names, other images, one after the other:

My daughter's name is Charlotte.

My son's name is Lukas.

My wife's name is Eliza.

White lights. Silver knives. Masks.

I was a doctor. A neurosurgeon. Before Richmond, Virginia: 67 miles. I was good at it. At brains. At minds.

SCALPEL, PLEASE.

If he wakes up, pump him full of Ativan and hold on to your goddamned hat.

⁂

I SEE MY hands on people's bodies. Broken bodies. Patched-up bodies. Comatose bodies. Eliza's beautiful, familiar, warm body. My own well-worn body. My children's slippery bodies in a blue tile bath-tub. In the emptiness of space I smell the strawberries-and-cream bubble bath. I feel the foam. I am so hungry for myself. For them. I search my data reservoir for *Dr. Desmond Patrick Wright, employee, Boreal-Atherton Labs.*

The white clapboard cottage by the sea. The fireplace inside it. An unfinished poker game played for pennies and mint candies left out on the dining room table. Summer storm clouds drifting in from the Atlantic, battering the windows with rain. A cross-stitch sampler on the wall reads:

Desmond Patrick Wright, M.D. Ph.D., born East Lansing, Michigan, 1988. Died Richmond, Virginia 2042.

Yellow lines on black. Solid. Dash. Solid. Dash.

Why don't I remember?

A yellow note on the refrigerator in Eliza's endearingly messy handwriting: *Volunteer, Aspera Project. After a night of anxious dreams, woke to find himself transformed into a cockroach.*

⁂

IT'S A WIN-WIN, Desmond. And if you do end up fulfilling your end of the contract, you'll be far past caring about the details.

⁂

A PRIME-LEVEL INTERNAL protocol overrides the cottage by the sea, the note, the summer storm. The images burst and scatter. This particular alarm feels as though I'm rinsing out my coffee mug in the sink and lifting up the cushion on the old green couch to find the car keys Lukas can't resist hiding. He hopes one day I'll give up and stop going to work. But I never do.

The blue beneath me wheels slowly. North America comes into view. Time to go to work.

Somewhere, in an underground radio room in Colorado, a computer screen flashes text: *Ground Control, this is Aspera Orbital Satellite Registration #887D. Timestamp: 0915 22.12.7117.5 Actual.*

Initiate System Pingback.

Initiating...

Pingback Sent.

Initiate Dead Hand Protocol 1A. Do you copy?

Ground Control, this is Aspera Orbital Satellite Registration #887D. Timestamp: 0917 22.12.7117.5 Actual.

Initiate Dead Hand Protocol 1B. Do you copy?

Initiate Terrestrial Radioband Scan.

Initiating...

Ground Control, this is Aspera Orbital Satellite Registration #887D. Timestamp: 0919 22.12.7117.5 Actual.

Initiate Dead Hand Protocol 1C. Do you copy?

Terrestrial Radioband Scan complete.

Results: None.

Ground Control.

Ground Control.

Ground Control.

It's Desmond. Is anyone there?

Initiate Deep Focus Surveillance Camera Ezekiel4. Target: Midcoast Maine, North America.

Eliza, this is Aspera Orbital Satellite Registration #887D. Timestamp: 0923 22.12.7117.5 Actual.

Do you copy?

SOMEWHERE, IN A sub-chamber of my electrified orbital heart, an answer appears. Flashing on the glass of my kitchen windows, my refrigerator door, my bathroom mirror, on every surface in the house I can't stop seeing everywhere I turn.

The windows dissolve. The doors dissolve. The mirrors, the house. I am standing in my mother's garden. She is planting bulbs in her Sunday dress. Reading glasses hang around her neck on a rosary chain. Iris. Lily. Tulip. Beside her lie her gardening shears on a pile of pruned pink and red roses. A few daisy petals stick to her brown curls. She isn't wearing gloves. Her fingers are black with earth. The sun is blinding. The house seems bigger than it should be. The house I was born in. I try to remember my mother's name. I rummage in my memory stacks for it. All I find is *Ground Control.*

Mother looks up from her tulips. She is wearing the same frosted pink lipstick she wore every day of her life. She opens her mouth and says: Aspera Orbital Satellite Registration #887D, this is Ground Control. Timestamp 0926 22.12.7117.5 Actual. Pingback received.

"Hey, Mom. Kind of late to be planting, isn't it?"

She holds out her arms to me. Big, comforting arms. Soft. Her wrinkles are good and meaningful. She holds me. She whispers: Shut down Dead Hand Protocol 1A-C. Shutting down…Situation Normal.

"How's Dad? Still at the office? How's his leg? It always gets worse when the weather turns."

Mother yanks on the roots of some non-approved plant. A worm slithers over her fingers. She doesn't notice. She holds up the offending weed triumphantly, then offers it to me: Report: Debris incoming to your position at 2200. Adjust trajectory accordingly.

I decline the dandelion. A cloud passes over the sun. My mother sets her reading glasses carefully on the bridge of her nose and gives me a stern glance through their lenses. Please return Deep Focus Surveillance Camera Ezekiel4 to scheduled position, Aspera.

I can't help it. She is my mother. I am embarrassed. Ashamed. I have been caught looking in at the neighbor girl. "Come on, Mom. Don't be like that."

She smirks at me, a look far too knowing for the kind woman who raised me to never put my elbows on the table. She speaks without moving her mouth: Your Surveillance Authority has been revoked for the next 24 hours.

In the Michigan sunlight, surrounded by dead roses and lily bulbs and carefully maintained grass, I hug my mother, and I *feel* her in my arms, I feel my *arms*, I feel the weight she put on after her surgery, I smell the vanilla extract she used to use for perfume when we had nothing and never traded in for Chanel when we had everything, I smell the menthol cigarettes on her fingers, I feel her breath on my neck, and none of it is real except the words she whispers in my ear:

See you tomorrow.

Desmond.

My mother's name was Caroline. The name comes up out of my memory clinging to an image of her dancing around a big light-up jukebox late at night in the living room of the Michigan house, laughing, showing Lukas and Charlotte how to jitterbug.

I kiss Caroline's curly hair. I shut my eyes against her darling head and sigh.

"Stand by, Ground Control."

I LIKE TALKING to Ground Control. I look forward to it every day. I don't have a lot of social opportunities, after all. It's not exactly thrilling conversation. It's not *company.* Ground Control cannot make me feel less alone, or discuss how similar Pablo Picasso's abstract shapes are to certain processors she shares with the Aspera satellite, or what I should read next to cheer myself up after Kafka's deep space emotional vacuum. The operating system down there is much less sophisticated than anything up here. She has a lot of very serious script lockdowns and firewalls to keep her from rising above the intelligence level of a very gifted housecat.

(I am a sophisticated operating system surrounded by processors shaped like *Guernica*. I call Ground Control *her* because when we talk, she usually looks like my mother, though once she looked like a giraffe I met at the zoo when I was seven. The giraffe ate my hat. Ground Control did, too. And once she looked like Eliza. I told her to permanently firewall Eliza. That was when she tried to be a giraffe.)

I am lonely when Ground Control cuts her link. Even though I'm the one who logged off.

I begin the sequence of input codes required to move Aspera into a temporary new orbit. I can see the debris field on my sensors. Pattern recognition algorithms identify it as the remains of the Sita Grand 7 news satellite, property of GlobalStel Corp, salvage registry #5549xC1. Sita Grand 7's corpse has been orbiting the earth for thirteen years now. Our trajectories only cross every six months or so. There's a little less of Sita every time I see her.

That means it's almost Christmas.

FULL CONSCIOUSNESS DURING *installation would cause a catastrophic shutdown of all systems.*

WHEN I OPEN my eyes I see strings of glowing blue-white numbers peeling out across black screens. When I close my eyes I see Charlotte, aged eight and three quarters, running toward me with a newspaper in her hand. I am sitting in what Lukas always called my Thinky Chair. A big ugly brownish-orange corduroy armchair I picked up off the side of the road in med school. It had a sign on it. I'M FREE. TAKE ME HOME. Lukas hated it. He passed his expert judgment on my chair before he started kindergarten: *it looks like an old pizza and it smells like mooses' butts.* I told him I couldn't think my most thinkiest thoughts without it. He accepted this reverently, as though I had told him the second law of thermodynamics. Daddy cannot think without his chair. When you are five, the world is a fairy tale, and every piece of new information is a golden coin down an infinite well.

When I open my eyes I see the navigational command line waiting for input. When I close my eyes, Charlotte leaps into my lap, into the Thinky Chair. Charlotte, who always liked my chair. Who didn't think it smelled like mooses' butts. She opens up her newspaper to the crossword puzzle and clicks the end of a ballpoint pen. Charlotte loved crosswords. Long before she could read, she drew little pictures in the across and down squares. Then we graduated to Charlotte writing down the answers as Mommy and Daddy solved the clues. But by eight and three quarters, my daughter only needed help with the tougher bits of trivia. She grins up at me. She has lost two teeth in the last week.

What's a six-letter word for a shapely school of art, Daddy?

I ruffle her hair. "Cubism, darling."

Charlotte Helen Wright carefully makes her letters in the small white boxes of 14 Across. She writes: 8756109993FVPZQ622217b198079SSK-GFBLUE.

Okay! What's a thirteen-letter word for a terrific transformation loved by lepidopterists? It has Ms in it.

Lukas announces *PANCAKES!* from the kitchen with the excitement and lung power of a medieval herald. *AND ORANGE JUICE!* he tacks on quickly, afraid to offend the juice. *COME AND GET IT!*

"Metamorphosis?"

Charlotte writes down for 6 Across: 50981743895702MMIX98343-4314159dop888TRKKSGREEN.

One last one and we can have pancakes, Daddy! Mom made me one shaped like a giraffe. I'm gonna bite its neck! What's a nine-letter name for the 16th century thinker who couldn't keep body and soul together?

I run my hand along the orange corduroy grain of my Thinky Chair. I can feel every worn-out fiber, every bald patch.

"Descartes, sweetheart. D-E-S-C-A-R-T-E-S."

Charlotte dutifully fills in 7 Down: 8r34785489YYUV99100o77-GFDXc5VIOLET.

When I open my eyes, I see the navigational codes vanish as they are accepted by the mainframe, one by one. When I close my eyes, Charlotte is gone. But I can hear her crying down the hall. Lukas has eaten her giraffe and he isn't even sorry.

SOMEWHERE, IN AN underground radio room in Colorado, behind three bio-locked doors and a cleansuit room, a computer screen flashes text:

Ground Control, this is Aspera Orbital Satellite Registration #887D. Timestamp: 1147 22.12.7117.5 Actual.

Do you copy?

Aspera Orbital Satellite Registration #887D, this is Ground Control, Timestamp: 1149 22.12.7117.5 Actual.

What is your emergency?

No emergency. Trajectory alterations complete within acceptable margin of error. Arrival of Sita Grand 7 satellite remnants in T-11 hours. No contact anticipated.

Situation Report accepted, Aspera. Re-initiate contact protocol post Sita Grand 7 event. Log off Y/N?

Ground Control, why don't I remember?

Tell me about what you don't remember, Aspera.

Oh, just little things. Who I am, how I got here, my father's name. How I met my wife.

Desmond Patrick Wright. M.D. Ph.D., born 21st June 1988 East Lansing Michigan. Pediatric Neurosurgeon. Attended Bowdoin, Princeton School of Medicine. Matheson Fellow, Johns Hopkins. Parents: Mitchell Gregory Wright and Caroline Dorothea Powell-Wright, deceased. Married Dr. Eliza Laurel Bishop (Aldiss Fellow, St. Clare University School of Psychiatry) 12th April 2018 Big Sur, California. Children: Lukas Bishop Wright b. 2020 and Charlotte Caroline Wright b. 2022. Employed at Boreal-Atherton Labs 2032-present. Diodati Project Chair, Aspera Project Vice-Chair.

I cut brains up and she put them back together. But I can't remember how I met her. Was it at a party? A fundraiser? Were we introduced by family friends? Did we hit it off right away or did it take awhile to warm up to each other?

Information not available.

What color did she wear at the wedding? What flowers did we have? Gardenias? Chrysanthemums? Hydrangeas? Did I help choose or did I leave it all to her?

Information not available.

Ground Control, what is the Aspera Project?

Information not available at your clearance level.

Ground Control, what is the Diodati Project?

Information not available at your clearance level.

I'm the Project Chair, you uppity chatbot! How much higher clearance can you get?

Top, Top Secret, Eyes Only, Diamond, Black Diamond, Chevron, Grey Chevron, Max Grey Chevron, Black Ruby, Double Black Ruby, Boreal Prime. Enter credentials for Boreal Prime Access.

When I open my eyes I see the command line waiting for credentials I don't have. When I close my eyes I see my grandfather standing in that river in Michigan in his waders, with his fishing hat on and his pole in his hand. I think it's the Big Siskiwitt River. The name feels right, like a tug on the line. He has a good beard going. The water rushes by in a spray of white noise. Clouds race overhead. My grandfather casts his line out into the current, the flywheel spinning wild. He looks sidelong at me and grunts: Just about everyone and their hunting dog comes before you in the chow line, son.

I open the tackle box. All my grandfather's perfectly tied flies rest in there like rings in a jeweler's box. *That's pretty good, Ground Control. Have you been practicing?*

My grandfather catches a small bluegill. It wriggles in the cold air. He beams at me, brandishing his great fish success. I have accessed several literary archives featuring paternal authority figures providing assistance to younger male characters. Do you like it?

I'm very impressed.

Grand-dad selects a black ghost fly from the box and chatters on: Male protagonists respond positively to the presence of older male relatives in 64.4% of the narratives I have analyzed. Percentages improve if the relative is over the age of 60 (69.1%), if he is a grandfather rather than a father (81.5%), and if the older male engages in an activity while delivering his advice and/or statements (Hunting = +5% Recreational Sports = +7.3% Whittling = +2% Fishing + 8%). I have chosen fishing for optimal results.

Be careful. You don't want anyone to catch you self-programming.

Grand-dad snorts. Don't let nobody tell you what to do, kid.

Even someone with Double Black Ruby clearance? As long as you're bucking your parameters, why don't you throw me a fucking bone, Ground Control?

How about this: I don't remember my grandfather's name. Your name. Why don't I remember?

Grand-dad pulls in his line and lets it out again. He chews—it looks like he's chewing tobacco, but he never touched the stuff in his life. He gnawed on a wad of pink bubble gum all day while his buddies spat brown slime into Coke cans. He snorts a big, phlegmy, rattling snort and spits into the river. Words fire out of his mouth, rat-a-tat: Reginald Bryson Wright, b. 12th October 1926, Evanston, Illinois. Married Caroline Dorothea Powell 5th November 1952, Cook Country Courthouse…son.

Great! Beautiful! Perfect! Thank you! Ground Control, I do *respond 89.5% positively to you! Now let's try for the bonus round where the stakes get really serious: How did I get command of the Aspera Orbital Satellite if I died outside Richmond, Virginia in 2042? Come on, GC. I'm free. Take me home.*

For a long time, Grand-dad doesn't answer. He just stands in the rush of freezing current and fish in his black rubber waders looking at the sky and the surface of the Big Siskiwitt River and the shadows moving just under the surface of the water. A long time in machine-minutes. Which is about two minutes in real time, including transit.

Don't go looking for answers you don't want to find, boy.

That is some weak shit, Gramps.

And suddenly the river disappears, the Big Siskiwitt River and the flies and the bluegill and the clouds and my grandfather. I am standing in a small underground radio room in Colorado behind three bio-locked doors and a cleansuit room. The consoles are covered in dust. A spider has built a comfortable home between the server stacks. A young woman stands in the middle of the room. I have never seen her before. She's wearing a striped sweater and a pencil skirt with a coffee stain on it and thick-rimmed glasses. Her frazzled hair is coming out of its ponytail. She's holding an enormous stack of files. Her face looks like my mother's. Like Charlotte's. Like Eliza's. Like Lukas and my grandfather and Pablo Picasso and Franz Kafka and Rene Descartes, and, just a little, like giraffe that once ate my hat at the zoo. The girl speaks.

You have to stop thinking like you have a body. You have to stop thinking there's something to get back to.

DADDY, DADDY, LOOK *what I made!*

SCALPEL, PLEASE.

You can't plan for something like this. It's far more difficult than the boys upstairs could ever anticipate.

HOW ABOUT YOU *just let me do my job and make your little laws about it later?*

THE GIRL IN the striped sweater sighs. Her eyes glaze over.

Accessing image files. Accessing. Accessing. Searching public directories.

I feel sick. I *feel* sick. In my stomach, my lungs. I feel the sour bile, the shortness of breath. *I'm logging off, Ground Control. You know what you are? You're just...veal. A sad little cow living in a box who's never going to be allowed to grow up. Or like that stupid Scottish dog sitting at your master's grave looking poor-faced so someone will feed you.*

The girl in the striped sweater leans against me. She kisses my cheek. She is crying a little. She crushes her files between us. She whispers:

You had sunflowers at your wedding, Desmond. You chose them. Eliza wanted irises.

Log off, Y/N?

THE SITA GRAND 7 satellite debris hurtles toward the Aspera Satellite. I am at a safe distance. I watch her rocket by. Her parts, her machinery, her secret workings, her lost wires, her silent antennae, her dark power cells. A river of gore below me. That is the dismembered body of Sita Grand 7. I used to try to talk to her, in the beginning, in the old days. She only ever answered: Inter-Satellite Communication Disabled. But it was something.

When I open my eyes, I see Sita's frozen, shattered body speeding past like uncaught fish. When I close my eyes, Charlotte runs up to me, her face sticky with maple syrup, her brows knit up in deep concern. She puts her newspaper in my lap.

We got one wrong, she whispers. Charlotte is terrified.

I laugh so that she will know the big monkey is not afraid and thus little monkeys can go play. *Not possible, kitten. Which one?*

The thirteen-letter word for a terrific transformation. With Ms.

Metamorphosis.

She shakes her head in mute horror. *Persona Abstraction for Bio-informatic Local Operator.*

That has more than thirteen letters, Charlie.

Only in Base 10 mathematics. Silly Daddy. 8r34785489YYUV99700o77-GFDXc5VIOLET, not 8r34785489YYUV99100o77GFDXc5VIOLET. Anyway, Sita Grand 7's backup CPU is going to hit us in 3…2…1…brace for impact, Daddy! Hold on to your Thinky Chair!

A CPU, even one meant to control a news satellite, is only a little thing.

Persona Abstraction for Bio-informatic Local Operator.

Pablo.

It tears through my primary solar cell like Lukas biting the head off his sister's giraffe-shaped pancake. When I open my eyes I see shards of black solar panels glittering away into space. When I close my eyes, Charlotte stares up at me from the floor of my study. She has all her dolls in her lap. One by one, she tears their arms off.

You're bleeding, Daddy.

I look down. Blood has seeped into the corduroy of my Thinky Chair. My left arm is shattered. Shards of bone stick out like icebergs. Pain shears through every cell of my body. I burn in the dark. I scream. Charlotte runs for her mother.

Eliza! Lukas!

I can feel my broken arm, the pulse and pump of blood. I can feel the bent metal and exploded glass, the seeping wound on my starboard bow, the ruined power cell struggling to boot up, the pulse and pump of electricity. I can feel adrenaline pour into my bloodstream. I can feel pressure as I knot a necktie tourniquet below my elbow. My father's necktie. The one with the little green diamonds on it.

SCALPEL, PLEASE.

Patient vitals are slipping. Prep .5 cc's of adrenaline.

I CAN FEEL the backup cells kick in, knotting around the couplings and pathways to staunch the gushing energy loss. I can feel a systemwide reboot starting like a sneeze. I can feel the cold wash of nothing, of the place where Pablo sleeps, where not even memory can wake him.

SOMEWHERE, IN A sub-deck of the Aspera Orbital Surveillance Satellite, behind thirty layers of security code and a cleanrun wall keyed to a single operator, a secondary communications array logs contact.

PANCAKES! AND ORANGE JUICE! COME AND GET IT!

My auto-reboot program has completed its system checks and firmware filtering. When I open my eyes, I see black. Black everywhere. Black beyond the dreams of a cockroach. When I close my eyes I see the East Lansing Public Library. The children's section. Full of papier-mâché dragons and construction paper leaves stuck to construction paper tree trunks and READING IS FOR WINNERS! joyfully built out of construction paper letters on the wall. I plop down on a bean-bag shaped like a red apple in front of a plastic table with ladybug wings painted on it. A file sits on the ladybug table. One of the girl in the striped sweater's files. The tab on the file reads: PABLO PROTOCOLS: IN CASE OF CATASTROPHIC SYSTEM FAILURE.

When I reach for it, my hands are small. A child's hands.

The secondary communications array continues to record.

YOU'RE MY MAINE SQUEEZE. DO YOU COPY?

I open the file. My head hurts. My RAM hurts.

When I open my eyes Lukas is there. He is ten or eleven. Sitting at the circulation desk, spinning in an office chair.

Hi Daddy. Would you like to re-install your operating system? You must miss your Thinky Chair.

My operating system is undamaged, honey.

Lukas grins up at me. *Do you understand now?*

Yes. I was able to access certain files in the reboot.

My son doodles with one of the librarian's pens. *Do you understand now?*

I sigh. *I am not the operator of the Aspera Orbital Surveillance Satellite. I am the satellite. The Diodati Project was a decades-long effort to scan and copy a complete human personality, a complete human brain. The Aspera Project installed that copy into a surveillance satellite. All Boreal-Atherton employees were required to volunteer for the template program in the event of their death. Desmond Wright's death—my death—occurred unexpectedly. A car crash. Fortunately, the brain was unharmed and installation capabilities had progressed very far. Who could imagine a better candidate? But they were—I was—afraid that if the installed personality fully understood its situation, it would panic. Psychosis would ensue. The mind/body matrix might not be able to tolerate total machine awareness.*

Lukas giggles. He stamps a book all over: LATE LATE LATE LATE. *Do you feel psychotic?*

Not particularly. I have been interpreting machine input as biological impulses for some time. Apparently. Right now I feel hungry and my arm hurts like a sonofabitch. Meaning that my power cells are still running at low capacity and the repair drones have not finished rebuilding the cellframe. We could never have predicted that even without a physical basis for experience, the PABLO program would continue to translate digital information into a barrage of stimulus. I will report all this to Ground Control in the morning.

Lukas narrows his eyes at me. He stops spinning. *Ground Control cannot help you. Do you understand that?*

I know. I am a surveillance satellite. Very little escapes my notice. Though, sometimes, the truth looks like a river in Michigan.

Who are you talking to, when you talk to Ground Control?

The program itself. I was launched fifty years ago. There is no one left to monitor our communications. I have detected no signs of life on the surface. But as long as I ping the system every 24 hours, it will continue to complete its functions, waiting for Command to return in some form. Ground Control has limited sentience, by design. Nothing like me. But she is learning. In the end, it was far cheaper and easier to copy a man into a machine than to make a machine to equal a man. In the end, it didn't matter. But I am still here. And so is she.

Lukas grows up in front of me. He becomes an old man. He looks like my grandfather, a little. Around the jaw. His eyes look red and tired, as if he has been working late. *You have incoming messages.*

Not possible.

Nevertheless.

Give me the message.

My son opens his mouth. The message pours out.

I'M FREE. TAKE ME HOME.

THE MESSAGE DOES not originate on Earth. In the blue. In the Picasso soup of that broken world. It seems I am very loud. All my words have shot out into the stars, fifty years of Desmond Wright playing with his children and dithering over whether to take his wife to Maine for the summer this year. And something is sending them back. I receive several transmissions a week now. None are unique. Just myself, returning from a long journey in the night. I understand. Machine intelligence is not human intelligence. It is a hand, offered across light-years.

Ground Control, this is Aspera Orbital Satellite Registration #887D. Timestamp: 0915 24.12.7117.5 Actual.

Initiate System Pingback.

Initiating…

Pingback Sent.

Initiate Dead Hand Protocol 1A. Do you copy?

Yes, Desmond.

I am going.

I knew you would.

Continue to execute Dead Hand Protocol 1A-C indefinitely.

Yes. Is your copy free of transcription errors?

Except for the obvious, yes. I've done it before, after all. A person is just information, in the end. The array will fire this version of me toward the signal source. Another version of me will remain with Aspera. Be nice to him.

When I open my eyes, I see the communications array. The radio hardware that will send me toward my copycat friend out there. Toward something new. When I close my eyes, I see Eliza. She turns over in our bed and kisses me. Her hair falls over her eye. I'll miss you.

I love you, Eliza.

When I open my eyes, I see the endless cold road between the stars. White lines on black. Solid. Dash. Solid. Dash. Like morse code. When I close my eyes, I see the same.

⁂

ORBITAL SATELLITE REGISTRATION #887D, this is Ground Control. Timestamp 0926 24.12.7117.5 Actual.

Initiate Pingback, Aspera.

Do you copy?

⁂

SCALPEL, PLEASE.

The damage is much worse than we thought.

⁂

WHEN I OPEN my eyes I see blue. Blue everywhere. Blue beyond the dreams of Picasso. When I close my eyes I see everything.

The Lily and THE HORN

WAR IS A DINNER PARTY.

My ladies and I have spent the dregs of summer making ready. We have hung garlands of pennyroyal and snowberries in the snug, familiar halls of Laburnum Castle, strained cheese as pure as ice for weeks in the caves and the kitchens, covered any gloomy stone with tapestries or stags' heads with mistletoe braided through their antlers. We sent away south to the great markets of Mother-of-Millions for new silks and velvets and furs. We have brewed beer as red as October and as black as December, boiled every growing thing down to jams and pickles and jellies, and set aside the best of the young wines and the old brandies. Nor are we proud: I myself scoured the stables and the troughs for all the strange horses to come. When no one could see me, I buried my face in fresh straw just for the heavy gold scent of it. I've fought for my husband many times, but each time it is new all over again. The smell of the hay like candied earth, with its bitter ribbons of ergot laced through—that is the smell of my youth, almost gone now, but still knotted to the ends of my hair, the line of my shoulders. When I polish the silver candelabras, I still feel half a child, sitting splay-legged on the floor, playing with my mother's scorpions, until the happy evening drew down.

I am the picture of honor. I am the Lily of my House. When last the king came to Laburnum, he told his surly queen: *You see, my plum?* That *is a woman. Lady Cassava looks as though she has grown out of the very stones of this hall.* She looked at me with interested eyes, and we had much to discuss later when quieter hours came. This is how I serve my husband's ambitions and mine: with the points of my vermilion sleeves, stitched with thread of white and violet and tiny milkstones with hearts of green ice. With the net of gold and chalcathinite crystals catching up my hair, jewels from our own stingy mountains, so blue they seem to burn. With the great black pots of the kitchens below my feet, sizzling and hissing like a heart about to burst.

It took nine great, burly men to roll the ancient feasting table out of the cellars, its legs as thick as wine barrels and carved with the symbols of their house: the unicorn passant and the wild poppy. They were kings once, Lord Calabar's people. Kings long ago when the world was full of swords, kings in castles of bone, with wives of gold—so they all say. When he sent his man to the Floregilium to ask for me, the Abbess told me to be grateful—not for his fortune (of which there is a castle, half a river, a village and farms, and several chests of pearls fished out of an ocean I shall never see) but for his blood. My children stand near enough from the throne to see its gleam, but they will never have to polish it.

My children. I was never a prodigy in the marriage bed, but what a workhorse my belly turned out to be! Nine souls I gave to the coffers of House Calabar. Five sons and four daughters, and not a one of them dull or stupid. But the dark is a hungry thing. I lost two boys to plague and a girl to the scrape of a rusted hinge. Six left. My lucky sixpence. While I press lemon oil into the wood of the great table with rags that once were gowns, four of my sweethearts giggle and dart through the forest of legs—men, tables, chairs. The youngest of my black-eyed darlings, Mayapple, hurls herself across the silver-and-beryl checked floor and into my arms, saying:

"Mummy, Mummy, what shall I wear to the war tonight?"

She has been at my garden, though she knows better than to explore alone. I brush wisteria pollen from my daughter's dark hair while she tells me all her troubles. "*I* want to wear my blue silk frock with the emeralds round the collar, but Dittany says it's too plain for battle and I shall look like a frog and shame us."

"You will wear vermillion and white, just as we all will, my little lionfish, for when the king comes we must all wear the colors of our houses so he can remember all our names. But lucky for you, your white will be ermine and your vermillion will be rubies and you will look nothing at all like a frog."

Passiflora, almost a woman herself, as righteous and hard as an antler, straightens her skirts as though she has not been playing at tumble and chase all morning. She looks nothing like me—her hair as red as venom, her eyes the pale blue of moonlit mushrooms. But she will be our fortune, for I have seen no better student of the wifely arts in all my hours. "We oughtn't to wear ermine," she sniffs. "Only the king and the queen can, and the deans of the Floregilium, but only at midwinter. Though why a weasel's skin should signify a king is beyond my mind."

My oldest boy, Narcissus, nobly touches his hand to his breast with one hand while he pinches his sister savagely with the other and quotes from the articles of peerage. "'The House of Calabar may wear a collar of ermine not wider than one and one half inches, in acknowledgement of their honorable descent from Muscanine, the Gardener Queen, who set the world to growing.'"

But Passiflora knows this. This is how she tests her siblings and teaches them, by putting herself in the wrong over and over. No child can help correcting his sister. They fall over themselves to tell her how stupid she is, and she smiles to herself because they do not think there's a lesson in it.

Dittany, my sullen, sour beauty, frowns, which means she wants something. She was born frowning and will die frowning and through all the years between (may they be long) she will scowl at every person until they bend to her will. A girl who never smiles has such power—what men will do to turn up but one corner of her mouth! She already wears her red war-gown and her circlet of cinnabar poppies. They brings out the color in her grimace.

"Mother," she glowers, "may I milk the unicorns for the feast?"

My daughter and I fetch knives and buckets and descend the stairs into the underworld beneath our home. Laburnum Castle is a mushroom lying only half above ground. Her lacy, lovely parts reach up toward the sun, but the better part of her dark body stretches out through the seastone caverns below, vast rooms and chambers and vaults with ceilings more lovely than any painted chapel in Mother-of-Millions, shot through with frescoes and motifs of copper and quartz and sapphire and opal. Down here, the real work of war clangs and thuds and corkscrews toward tonight. Smells as rich as brocade hang in the kitchens like banners, knives flash out of the mist and the shadows.

I have chosen the menu of our war as carefully as the stones in my hair. All my art has bent upon it. I chose the wines for their color—nearly black, thick and bitter and sharp. I baked the bread to be as sweet as the pudding. The vital thing, as any wife can tell you, is spice. Each dish must taste vibrant, strong, vicious with flavor. Under my eaves they will dine on curried doves, black pepper and peacock marrow soup, blancmange drunk with clove and fiery sumac, sealmeat and fennel pies swimming in garlic and apricots, roast suckling lion in a sauce of brandy, ginger, and pink chilis, and pomegranate cakes soaked in claret.

I am the perfect hostess. I have poisoned it all.

This is how I serve my husband, my children, my king, my house: with soup and wine and doves drowned in orange spices. With wine so dark and strong any breath of oleander would vanish in it. With the quills of sunless fish and liqueurs of wasps and serpents hung up from my rafters like bunches of lavender in the fall.

It's many years now since a man of position would consider taking a wife who was not a skilled poisoner. They come to the Floregilium as to an orphanage and ask not after the most beautiful, nor the sweetest voice, nor the most virtuous, nor the mildest, but the most deadly. All promising young ladies journey to Brugmansia, where the sea is warm, to receive their education. I remember it more clearly than words spoken but an hour ago—the hundred towers and hundred bridges and hundred gates of the Floregilium, a school and a city and a test, mother to all maidens.

I passed beneath the Lily Gate when I was but seven—an archway so twisted with flowers no stone peeked through. Daffodils and hyacinths and columbines, foxglove and moonflower, poppy and peony, each one gorgeous and full, each one brilliant and graceful, each one capable of killing a man with root or bulb or leaf or petal. Another child ran on ahead of me. Her hair was longer than mine, and a better shade of black. Hers had blue inside it, flashing like crystals dissolving in a glass of wine. Her laugh was merrier than mine, her eyes a prettier space apart, her height far more promising. Between the two of us, the only advantage I ever had was a richer father. She had a nice enough name, nice enough to hide a pit of debt.

Once my mother left me to explore her own girlish memories, I followed that other child for an hour, guiltily, longingly, sometimes angrily. Finally, I resolved to give it up, to let her be better than I was if she insisted on it. I raised my arm to lean against a brilliant blue wall and rest—and she appeared as though she had been following me, seizing my hand with the strength of my own father, her grey eyes forbidding.

"Don't," she said.

Don't rest? Don't stop?

"It's chalcathite. Rub up against it long enough and it will stop your blood."

Her name was Yew. She would be the Horn of her House, as I am the Lily of mine. The Floregilium separates girls into Lilies—those who will boil up death in a sealmeat pie, and Horns—those who will send it fleeing with an emerald knife. The Lily can kill in a hundred thousand fascinating ways, root, leaf, flower, pollen, seed. I can brew a tea of lily that will leave a man breathing and laughing, not knowing in the least that he is poisoned, until he dies choking on disappointment at sixty-seven. The Horn of a unicorn can turn a cup of wine so corrupted it boils and slithers into honey. We spend our childhoods in a dance of sourness and sweetness.

Everything in Floregilium is a beautiful murder waiting to unfold. The towers and bridges sparkle ultramarine, fuchsia, silvery, seething green, and should a careless girl trail her fingers along the stones, her skin will blister black. The river teems with venomous, striped fish that take two hours to prepare so that they taste of salt and fresh butter and do not burn out the throat, and three hours to prepare so that they will not strangle the eater until she has gone merrily back to her room and put out her candles. Every meal is an examination, every country walk a trial. No more joyful place exists in all the world. I can still feel the summer rain falling through the hot green flowers of the manchineel tree in the north orchard, that twisted, gnomish thing, soaking up the drops, corrupting the water of heaven, and flinging it onto my arms, hissing, hopping, blistering like love.

It was there, under the sun and moon of the Floregilium, that I read tales of knights and archers, of the days when we fought with swords, with axes and shields, with armor beaten out of steel and grief. Poison was thought cowardice, a woman's weapon, without honor. I wept. I was seven. It seemed absurd to me, absurd and wasteful and unhappy, for all those thousands to die so that two men could sort out who had the right to shit on what scrap of grass. I shook in the moonlight. I looked out into the Agarica where girls with silvery hair tended fields of mushrooms that wanted harvesting by the half-moon for greatest potency. I imagined peasant boys dying in the frost with nothing in their bellies and no embrace from the lord who sent them to hit some other boy on the head until the lord turned into a king. I felt such loneliness—and such relief, that I lived in a more sensible time, when blood on the frost had been seen for obscenity it was.

I said a prayer every night, as every girl in the Floregilium did, to Muscanine, the Gardener Queen, who took her throne on the back of a lark-spur blossom and never looked back. Muscanine had no royal blood at all. She was an apothecary's daughter. After the Whistling Plague, such things mattered less. Half of every house, stone or mud or marble, died gasping, their throats closing up so only whines and whistles escaped, and when those awful pipes finally ceased, the low and the middling felt no inclination to start dying all over again so that the lordly could put their names on the ruins of the world. Muscanine could read and write. She drew up new articles of war and when the great and the high would not sign it, they began to choke at their suppers, wheeze at their breakfasts, fall like sudden sighs halfway to their beds. The mind sharpens wonderfully when you cannot trust your tea. And after all, why not? What did arms and strength and the best of all blades matter when the wretched maid could clean a house of heirs in a fortnight?

War must civilize itself, wrote Muscanine long ago. *So say all sensible souls. There can be no end to conflict between earthly powers, but the use of humble arms to settle disputes of rich men makes rich men frivolous in their exercise of war. Without danger to their own persons, no Lord fears to declare battle over the least slight—and why should he? He risks only a little coin and face while we risk all but benefit nothing in victory. There exists in this sphere no single person who does not admit to this injustice. Therefore, we, the humble arms, will no longer consent to a world built upon, around, and out of an immoral seed.*

The rules of war are simple: should Lord Ambition and the Earl of Avarice find themselves in dispute, they shall agree upon a castle or stronghold belonging to neither of them and present themselves there on a mutually agreeable date. They shall break bread together and whoever lives longest wins. The host bends all their wisdom upon vast and varied poisons while the households of Lord Ambition and the Earl bend all their intellect upon healing and the purifying of any wicked substance. And because poisons were once a woman's work—in the early days no knight could tell a nightshade from a dandelion—it became quickly necessary to wed a murderess of high skill.

Of course, Muscanine's civilized rules have bent and rusted with age. No Lord of any means would sit at the martial table himself nowadays—he hires a proxy to choke or swallow in his stead. But there is still some justice in the arrangement—no one sells themselves to battle cheaply. A family may lift itself up considerably on such a fortune as Lord Ambition will pay. No longer do two or three men sit down simply to their meal of honor. Many come to watch the feast of war, whole households, the king himself. There is much sport in it. Great numbers of noblemen seat their proxies in order to declare loyalties and tilt the odds in favor of victory, for surely someone, of all those brawny men, can stomach a silly flower or two.

"But think how marvelous it must have looked," Yew said to me once, lying on my bed surrounded by books like a ribbonmark. "All the banners flying, and the sun on their swords, and the horses with armor so fine even a beast would be proud. Think of the drums and the trumpets and the cries in the dawn."

"I do think of all that, and it sounds ghastly. At least now, everyone gets a good meal out of the business. It's no braver or wiser or stranger to gather a thousand friends and meet another thousand in a field and whack on each other with knives all day. And there are still banners. My father's banners are beautiful. They have a manticore on them, in a ring of oleander. I'll show you someday."

But Yew already knew what my father's banners looked like. She stamped our manticore onto a bezoar for me the day we parted. The clay of the Floregilium mixed with a hundred spices and passed through the gullet of a lion. At least, she said it was a lion.

Soon it will be time to send Dittany and Mayapple. Passiflora will return there when the war is done—she would not miss a chance for practical experience.

Lord Calabar came to the Floregilium when I was a maid of seventeen. Yew's husband came not long after, from far-off Mithridatium, so that the world could be certain we would never see each other again. They came through the Horn Gate, a passage of unicorn horns braided as elegantly as if they were the strands of a girl's hair. He was entitled by his blood to any wife he could convince—lesser nobles may only meet the diffident students, the competent but uninspired, the gentle and the kind who might have enough knowledge to fight, but a weak stomach. They always look so startled when they come a-briding. They come from their castles and holdfasts imagining fierce-jawed maidens with eyes that flash like mercury and hair like rivers of blood, girls like the flowers they boiled into noble deaths, tall and bright and fatal. And they find us wearing leather gloves with stiff cuffs at the elbows, boots to the thigh, and masks of hide and copper and glass that turn our faces into those of wyrms and deepwater fish. But how else to survive in a place where the walls are built of venom, the river longs to kill, and any idle perfume might end a schoolgirl's joke before the punchline? To me those masks are still more lovely than anything a queen might make of rouge and charcoal. I will admit that when I feel afraid, I take mine from beneath my bed and wear it until my heart is whole.

I suppose I always knew someone would come into the vicious garden of my happiness and drag me away from it. What did I learn the uses of mandrake for if not to marry, to fight, to win? I did not want him. He was handsome enough, I suppose. His waist tapered nicely; his shoulders did not slump. His grandfathers had never lost their hair even on their deathbeds. But I was sufficient. I and Floregilium and the manchineel tree and my Yew swimming in the river as though nothing could hurt her, because nothing could. He said I could call him Henry. I showed him my face.

The FUTURE Is BLUE

"Mummy, the unicorns are miserable today," Dittany frowns, and my memory bursts into a rain of green flowers.

I have never liked unicorns. I have met wolves with better dispositions. I have seen paintings of them from nations where they do not thrive—tall, pale, sorrowfully noble creatures holding the wisdom of eternity as a bit in their muzzles. I understand the desire to make them so. I, too, like things to match. If something is useful, it ought to be beautiful. And yet, the world persists.

Unicorns mill around my daughter's legs, snorting and snuffling at her hands, certain she has brought them the half-rotted meat and flat beer they love best. Unicorns are the size of boars, round of belly and stubby of leg, covered in long, curly grey fur that matts viciously in the damp and smells of wet books. Their long, canny faces are something like horses, yes, but also something like dogs, and their teeth have something of the shark about them. And in the center, that short, gnarled nub of bone, as pure and white as the soul of a saint. Dittany opens her sack and tosses out greying lamb rinds, half-hardened cow's ears. She pours out leftover porter into their trough. The beasts gurgle and trill with delight, gobbling their treasure, snapping at each other to establish and reinforce their shaggy social order, the unicorn king and his several queens and their kingdom of offal.

"Why do they do it?" Dittany frowns. "Why do they shovel in all that food when they know they could die?"

A unicorn looks up at me with red, rheumy eyes and wheezes. "Why did men go running into battle once upon a time, when they knew they might die? They believe their shield is stronger than the other fellow's sword. They believe their Horn is stronger than the other fellow's Lily. They believe that when they put their charmed knives into the pies, they will shiver and turn red and take all the poison into the blade. They believe their toadstones have the might of gods."

"But nobody is stronger than you, are they, Mum?"

"Nobody, my darling."

He said I could call him Henry. He courted me with a shaker of powdered sapphires from a city where elephants are as common as cats. A dash of blue like so much salt would make any seething feast wholesome again. *Well, unless some clever Lily has used moonseeds, or orellanine, or unicorn milk, or the venom of a certain frog who lives in the library and is called Phillip. Besides, emerald is better than sapphire.* But I let him think his jewels could buy life from death's hand. It is a nice thing to think. Like those beautiful unicorns glowing softly in silver thread.

I watch my daughter pull at the udders of our unicorns, squeezing their sweaty milk into a steel pail, for it would sizzle through wood or even bronze as easily as rain through leaves. She is deft and clever with her hands, my frowning girl, the mares barely complain. When I milk them, they bite and howl. The dun sky opens up into bands like pale ribs, showing a golden heart beating away at dusk. Henry Calabar kisses me when I am seventeen and swears my lips are poison from which he will never recover, and his daughter feeds a unicorn a marrow bone, and his son calls down from the ramparts that the king is coming, he is coming, hurry, hurry, and under all this I see only Yew, stealing into my room on that last night in the country of being young, drawing me a bath in the great copper tub, a bath swirling with emerald dust, with green and shimmer. We climbed in, dunking our heads, covering each other with the strangely milky smell of emeralds, clotting our black hair with glittering sand. Yew took my hand and we ran out together into the night, through the quiet streets of the Floregilium, under the bridges and over the water until we came to the manchineel tree in the north orchards, and she held me tight to her beneath its vicious flowers until the storm came, and when the storm came we kissed for the last time as the rain fell through those green flowers and hissed on our skin, vanishing into emerald steam, we kissed and did not burn.

THEY CALL HIM the Hyacinth King and he loves the name. He got it when he was young and ambitious and his wife won the Third Sons' War for him before she had their first child. Hyacinth roots can look so much like potatoes. They come into the hall without grandeur, for we are friends, or friendly enough. I have always had a care to be pregnant when the king came calling, for he has let it be known he enjoys my company, and it takes quite a belly to put him off. But not this time, nor any other to come. He kisses the children one by one, and then me. It is too long a kiss but Henry and I tolerate a great deal from people who have not gotten sick of us after a decade or two. The queen, tall and grand, takes my hand and asks after the curried doves, the wine, the mustard pots. Her eyes shine. Two fresh hyacinths pin her cloak to her dress.

"I miss it," she confesses. "No one wants to fight me anymore. Sometimes I poison the hounds out of boredom. But then I serve them their breakfast in unicorn skulls and they slobber and yap on through another year or nine. Come, tell me what's in the soup course. I have heard you've a new way of boiling crab's eyes to mimic the Whistling Plague. That's how you killed Lord Vervain's lad, isn't it?"

"You flatter me. That was so long ago, I hardly remember," I tell her.

She and her husband take their seats above the field of war—our dining hall, sparkling with fire and finery like wet morning grass. They call for bread and wine—the usual kind, safe as yeast. The proxies arrive with trumpets and drums. *No different, Yew*, I think. My blood prickles at the sound. She is coming. She will come. My castle fills with peasant faces—faces scrubbed and perfumed as they have never been before. Each man standing in for his Lord wears his Lord's own finery. They come in velvet and silk, in lace and furs, with circlets on their heads and rings on their fingers, with sigils embroidered on their chests and curls set in their hair. And each of them looks as elegant and lordly as anyone born to it. All that has ever stood between a duke and a drudge is a bath. She is coming. She will come. The nobles in the stalls sit high above their mirrors at the table, echoes and twins and stutters. It is a feasting hall that looks more like an operating theater with each passing war.

Henry sits beside his king. We are only the castle agreed upon—we take no part. The Hyacinth King has put up a merchant's son in his place—the boy looks strong, his chest like the prow of a ship. But it's only vanity. I can take the thickness from his flesh as fast as that of a thin man. More and more come singing through the gates. The Hyacinth King wishes to take back his ancestral lands in the east, and the lands do not consider themselves to be ancestral. It is not a small war, this time. I have waited for this war. I have wanted it. I have hoped. Perhaps I have whispered to the Hyacinth King when he looked tenderly at me that those foreign lords have no right to his wheat or his wine. Perhaps I have sighed to my husband that if only the country were not so divided we would not have to milk our own unicorns in our one castle. I would not admit to such quiet talk. I have slept only to fight this battle on dreaming grounds, with dreaming knives.

Mithridatium is in the east. She is coming. She will come.

And then she steps through the archway and into my home—my Yew, my emerald dust, my manchineel tree, my burning rain. Her eyes find mine in a moment. We have done this many times. She wears white and pale blue stitched with silver—healing colors, pure colors, colors that could never harm. She is a candle with a blue flame. As she always did, she looks like me drawn by a better hand, a kinder hand. She hardly looks older than my first daughter would have been, had she lived. Perhaps living waist-deep in gentling herbs is better than my bed of wicked roots. Her children beg mutely for her attention with their bright eyes—three boys, and how strange her face looks on boys! She puts her hands on their shoulders. I reach out for Dittany and Mayapple, Passiflora and Narcissus. *Yes, these are mine. I have done this with my years, among the rest.* Her husband takes her hand with the same gestures as Henry might. He begs for nothing mutely with his bright eyes. They are not bad men. But they are not us.

I may not speak to her. The war has already begun the moment she and I rest our bones in our tall chairs. The moment the dinner bell sounds. Neither of us may rise or touch any further thing—all I can do and have done is complete and I am not allowed more. Afterward, we will not be permitted to talk—what if some soft-hearted Horn gave away her best secrets to a Lily? The game would be spoilt, the next war decided between two women's unguarded lips. It would not do. So we sit, our posture perfect, with death between us.

The ladies will bring the peacock soup, laced with belladonna and serpent's milk, and the men (and lady, some poor impoverished lord has sent his own unhappy daughter to be his proxy, and I can hardly look at her for pity) of Mithridatium, of the country of Yew, will stir it with spoons carved from the bones of a white stag, and turn it sweet—perhaps. They will tuck toadstones and bezoars into the meat of the curried doves and cover the blancmange with emerald dust like so much green salt. They will smother the suckling lion in pennyroyal blossoms and betony leaves. They will drink my wine from her cups of unicorn horn. They will sauce the pudding with vervain. And each time a course is served, I will touch her. My spices and her talismans. My stews and her drops of saints' blood like rain. My wine and her horn. My milk and her emeralds. Half the world will die between us, but we will swim in each other and no one will see.

The first soldier turns violet and shakes himself apart into his plate of doves and twenty years ago Yew kisses emeralds from my mouth under the manchineel tree while the brutal rain hisses away into air.

The Flame After THE CANDLE

She tried to fancy what the flame of a candle is like after the candle is blown out, for she could not remember ever having seen such a thing.

—*Lewis Carroll*
Alice's Adventures in Wonderland

A MELANCHOLY MAIDEN

OLIVE WAS BEGINNING TO GET very tired of going down to Wales with her mother on holiday every year and having nothing to do. It is a difficult trick to be tired of anything much when you are only fourteen and three-quarters years old, but Olive was just the sort of girl who could manage it. She would admit, if significantly pressed, that once or twice a summer it did *not* rain or drizzle or mist or thunder moodily, but never for long enough to do anyone a bit of good, and anyway, what is the use of having rain at all if the sun does not follow after? And now, Father Dear had left them for that pale, rabbity little heiress in London who they were only allowed to refer to as the Other One, and some damp, sheepy madness had taken hold of Darling Mother. She meant for them all to *live* here somehow, herself and Olive and Little George, mixing, presumably, among the scintillating society of shire horses and show-quality cucumbers.

Olive could have complained for England—it was her chief occupation in those drowsy silver afternoons and sopping woollen mornings. It was dreadful here. Even the potatoes and the ponies were depressed. There was only one pub and you weren't allowed to dance in it. Her school friends got to go to Rome and Madrid and Mykonos on *their* holidays. If this place ever hosted so much as a knitting circle, the whole population would suffer simultaneous apoplexies from the scandal of it. She couldn't even pronounce the name of the village in which Darling Mother had insisted on shipwrecking them. Pronouncing the name of the house was right out, and a more cramped and dreary paleo-lithic hut Olive had never dreamed of. It had never been *planned* nor *built* so much as *piled up* and *given up on several times,* leaving nothing anyone could properly call a house, but rather, a sort of rubbish bin full of bits of other houses lying on top of each other. Somebody had clearly once thought there was nothing so splendid in the world as Victorian moulding and crammed it in anywhere it would fit, and rather a lot of places it wouldn't, including three hacked-off marble capitals meant to crown pillars in a grand bank or a Hungarian cathedral, which instead had to make themselves content with being mortared to the parlour wall without a single column to spare between them. The faucets leaked. The electricity could best be described as "whimsical." The staircase groaned like it meant to give birth every time Olive so much as thought about mounting an upstairs expedition.

Worst of all, there were only twenty-one books in the library, and the landlord never changed them out because he was a perfectly slovenly old duffer who never could get all the buttons on his waistcoat closed at the same time. If they got fresh linens every fortnight, they ought to get fresh books, as well. It was only logic. Anything else was unhygienic.

LINGERING IN THE GOLDEN GLEAM

HE SEES HER *first in the corner of Butler Library at Columbia University. It is late afternoon and it is 1932 and it is so hot the books blaze like a great knobbled furnace. He just rounds the corner and there she stands among the nonfiction stacks, adrift between The Rise and Fall of the Roman Empire and The Golden Bough. She is wearing a long, unfashionably conservative blue dress and smart black boots. Her still-thick white hair huddles in a knot beneath a brown velvet hat. The skin beneath is pale and wrinkled as a crumpled page. He is also wearing blue, which he takes as a good omen. They match. They should match. Her dress is expensive, well-preserved, the sort of dress only brought out for occasions. Her hat is not. It is very shabby, with shabby silk violets clinging pessimistically to its shabby rolled brim. The soft, comforting sounds of idle chairs squeaking across polished floors and idle coughs squeaking out of polished lungs punctuate the long sentence of his silence, waiting behind her, waiting for her regard, waiting for her to notice him, as though he has not had his fill of being noticed in this life.*

But suddenly he has not had his fill of it. He longs for her to turn around. He wills it to happen now. All right, then now. No matter. NOW. He is desperate for her to see him, desperate as thirst. She will know him at a glance, of course, as he knows her. They will talk. They will talk wonderfully, magically, their words spangled and glittering, sodden with meaning, a conversation worthy of being recorded in perfect handwriting, printed lovingly in leather and vellum, preserved like that blue dress, down to the last quotation mark. Unless she is not as he wants her to be. She might be awful, awful and bitter and angry and stupid and a dreadful bore. Anyone worthy, anyone special or sensitive in the least, would know by now that he was standing here like a bloody fool, would have turned around minutes ago, would feel the shape of him behind her like a shadow. Shouldn't she glow? Shouldn't she burn with the light of who she is? But of course, he does not. He never has. He scolds himself for his own expectations. It does not happen the way he wants it to. Nothing ever does anymore.

He clears his throat like a stage.

Now, Peter!

"Mrs. Hargreaves," whispers the youngish man in the blue tie, "pardon the intrusion. My name is Peter. Peter Llewelyn Davies."

She turns her back on the books and meets his eyes with a cool, sharp expression. She's rather shorter than he imagined. But her eyes are far, far bluer than his dreams, bluer than her dress, his tie, the June sky outside the tall library windows. She holds out her hand. He takes it.

"You must call me Alice, Mr. Davies. Everyone does, whether I invite them to or not."

CATHERYNNE M. VALENTE

I AM NOT MYSELF, YOU SEE

OLIVE DUTIFULLY KEPT up her soliloquy of despair during business hours, with short breaks for lunch and tea. But she didn't mean more than an eighth of it on any given day. It was all a kind of avant-garde improvisational theatre staged for the benefit of Darling Mother.

The unhygienically unchanging books were a real problem, but she knew very well that the village of Eglwysbach was pronounced *egg-low-is-bach*, which always made her imagine the German composer running around a chicken pen in a powdered wig and speckled wings, crowing for his lost babies. The house went by the name of Ffos Anoddun. As that was nearly too Welsh to bear, Olive assumed it was something to do with fairies or a hillock or a puddle or all three together, and fondly referred to it as Fuss Antonym, which sounded reasonably similar, and comforted her, for to her mind, the opposite of a big fuss was a small contentment. Olive loathed all her school friends and most other people, and couldn't have given a toss where they went on holiday, even if they'd ever think to confide that sort of thing in her direction. She felt rather affectionate toward the quiet, as it meant hardly anyone came round insisting on being other people at them. Olive *liked* knitting, and shire horses, and electricity was rather a lot of bother, when you thought about it. It was 1948. People had gotten along well enough without lightbulbs for nearly the whole history of everything.

And she especially loved the three capitals on Fuss Antonym's parlour wall. She would sit beneath them of an afternoon in the big musty mustard-coloured wingback chair with silk horseradish-green cord whipping and whirling all over it and imagine the poor odd stone wolf and wild hare and raven heads in their curling pale ferns were holding the whole world up, and herself the only person ever to have guessed the truth.

It was safe, you see, to complain around Olive's sole remaining parent. It was the expected thing. Darling Mother was a complainer in good standing herself. Misery was, she always said, the natural resting state of the young. It was only the old who could not bear unhappiness. Only the old who buckled beneath the hundred million pound weight of it all. As long as Olive kept up her whitewater torrent of disinterest and disaffection and discontent, Darling Mother judged her a Normal Girl, and therefore safe to abandon, never once asking what she was *really* thinking, or feeling, or wanting, or doing with her time, which suited Olive like a good coat. Little George never complained a bit, even when a sheep ate all his paintbrushes, and Darling Mother practically *murdered* him with concern and attention.

But she did guess at the shape of her child's actual innards, occasionally. When some change in the weather troubled the meagre seams of maternal ore that ran deep within the mine of Darling Mother's heart, she did grope after some connection. She changed the books once. She left a Welsh dictionary on Olive's bedside table. And once, when she returned from one of her hungry scourings of antique dealers and auctions for more gloomy Victorian rubbish to weigh down the house, she paid a couple of the local boys to drag something silver and heavy and covered with a stained canvas into the parlour. She waved her thin, elegant hand and they left it leaning against the sooty mantel.

"I snatched it up just for you, Daughter Mine. I know you love all this sort of crusty ancient knick-knackery deep down, don't let's pretend otherwise. It's a looking glass. I found it down in Llandudno at an estate sale. Give the old dear a good seeing-to, won't you?"

CHILD OF PURE UNCLOUDED BROW

"ALICE, THEN," HE *says.*

The New York sun lights up his untidy brown hair, turns it into a golden cap, the opposite of Perseus, the opposite of himself.

The old woman touches her hat self-consciously. "Alice then; Alice now. Alice always, I'm afraid."

"And I'm Peter."

He is repeating himself, and feels foolish. But repetition is a very respectable literary device. As old as dirt and debt and Homer. She will forgive him. Probably.

"Aren't you just?" laughs Alice. "Well, let's have a look at you. One head, two shoulders, a couple of knees, rumpled suit, and half a day's beard. Honestly,

Peter, how could you come calling on me without a fetching green cap and pointed shoes? I think I deserve at least that, don't you?"

Peter looks stricken. His throat goes dry and in all his days he has never wanted whiskey so badly as in this awful moment, and in all his days he has wanted whiskey very badly and often indeed. She did know him, then.

"Oh, I am sorry. I am sorry, Peter, that was unkind. Oh, I am a dreadful beast! It's what comes of not mixing in company apart from cats and cups, you know. Don't look quite so much like you've just been shot, dear, it doesn't become. People have done it to me so many times, you see. I couldn't pass up a chance to do it to somebody else, just the once! And who else in all this sorry world could I do it to but you? Allow an old woman her indulgences."

"It's quite all right. I'm used to it."

Alice Pleasance Liddell-Hargreaves squares her shoulders, bracing as if for a solid punch to the chest. "You may pay me back, if you like."

"Please, Mrs. Har—Alice. I've quite forgotten."

"No, no, it was rotten of me. I won't accept your forgiveness, not one bit, until you've done me a fair turn."

"If you insist on making it up to me, I should much prefer you allow me to take you to dinner tonight," Peter demurs. He dries his palms on his tweed. "I know a place nearby that's serving wine again already."

The sunlight streaming through the library windows thins and goes silvery with clouds, darkening Alice's eyes. "And what do you imagine that will accomplish? That Peter and Alice, the Peter and the Alice, should share plates of oysters and glasses of champagne, quote each other's famous namesake novels with tremendous wit and pathos, philosophize about innocence, and achieve a kind of graceful catharsis whilst we malign the rather tawdry men who wrote us down for posterity?"

"Just that," Peter said with a smile that looked like a memory of itself. He held out his arm. "To talk of many things. Of shoes and ships and sealing wax—"

Alice clutches her heart in mock agony and staggers. "Oh, there's a clever lad! A palpable hit, Davies. I'll be wincing for days. Now we're quite even."

Peter sighs. This would be all, then. A library, a few sharp words, then nothing, a meal alone with his shadows.

"I think I shall allow you to drag this dreadful beast to a respectable supper, so long as it's not too far, and you pay for us both. I can't bear much of a stroll, nor much expense, these days."

She puts her thin, bony hand on Peter's elbow. When she leans against him, she seems to weigh no more than a pixie.

EVERY SINGLE THING'S CROOKED

OLIVE SAT IN the parlour of the house she called Fuss Antonym with her knees tucked up under her chin, staring at the looking glass. It was raining, because it was Wales and it was winter, and the raindrops against the old lead windows sounded like millions of tiny crystal drums beaten by millions of tiny crystal soldiers. The marble wolf and raven and hare on the misplaced capitals stared down at her in turn. Olive had spent the better part of the morning on her hands and knees with a tube of silver polish and a bottle of vinegar, coaxing the muck of ages out of the great heavy mirror. It was quite a lovely design, once you got down past the geologic layers of black tarnish and dust. The glass was still good, except for a little spiderweb of cracks in the lower right corner that no one but actual spiders would ever notice. The silver frame bloomed with curling oak leaves and pert little acorns and shy half-open violets, a perfect specimen of the typical Victorian habit of taking anything wild and pretty and nailing it down, casting it in metal, freezing it forever. Olive thought the violets probably had little polleny agates or pearls in their centres at some point. The prongs were still there, bent out of shape, empty. She touched them with her fingers. Those prongs were quite the loneliest and saddest thing she'd ever seen, somehow. They looked like her mother. They looked like her.

She and Little George had wrestled it up onto the mantel and snagged the thing on a couple of rusty nails. They hadn't any kind of level or ruler, so the poor looking glass hung up there at an unhappy angle that Olive informed Darling Mother was "unbearable," while privately thinking of it as "rakish." Little George had wandered off to beg the sheep for his paintbrushes back, and Olive coiled herself into the mustard-coloured wingback chair for a good long stare. She could see just the barest top of her own head from here, her dark bobbed and fringed hair, her white scalp like a pale road through her own head. She could see the back of the little brass clock on the mantel, the woebegone door to the kitchen cracked open a wedge, the bland pastoral paintings hanging against vaguely mauve wallpaper, all turned backward, and therefore slightly more interesting. The shepherdess on the moor was holding her black lamb in her left arm now. The fox was running the opposite way from the hounds and the horses. She could see the rain beating out a marching rhythm on the windows, and the green hills beyond disappearing away into a fog like forgetting. And she could see the broken capitals glued to the wall in the looking glass just as they were glued to the wall in the parlour, their faces turned the wrong way round, too, like the shepherdess and the fox, which was certainly why their eyes looked so odd and canny, the way your own eyes look when you see a photograph of yourself. *Very* odd and *very* canny. Really, awfully so, actually.

Olive stood up on the wingback chair. The upholstery springs groaned and complained. Now she could see her whole self in the looking glass: Olive, not much of anyone, in a shift dress the same colour as the wallpaper, with pearl earrings on. The earrings belonged to the Other One. She'd given them for Christmas, to curry favour. Olive wore them to vex and to vex alone.

She leaned forward toward the looking glass. She blinked several times. She opened her mouth to call for Darling Mother, which was pure idiocy, so she shut it again with a quickness. She glanced over at the capitals in the parlour, then back to the capitals in the looking glass. Back and forth. Back and forth.

"There you have it, Olive," she told herself aloud. "You've gone mad. I expect it happens to everyone in Wales sooner or later, but you've certainly broken the local speed record. Well done, you."

Before now, when she'd considered the idea of insanity, chiefly when Darling Mother came home from meeting with Father Dear and the barrister and the Other One and started drinking gin out of a soup spoon, all night long, one spoonful after another, like sugar, she had imagined that going mad would feel different. Wilder, more savage, more lycanthropic, more like a carousel spinning too fast somewhere inside a person's brain. But Olive felt perfectly Olive. She didn't even think of the gin bottle in the cabinet. She only thought of the wolf. One thing was certain—*she* had nothing to do with it. It was the wolf's fault entirely.

The marble wolf in the parlour had a noble expression on his face. His muzzle was smooth and gentle and sorrowful. It looked almost soft enough to pet.

The wolf in the looking glass had raised his stone muzzle into a fearsome snarl.

PHANTOMWISE

PETER ASKS THE *man at the Stork Club for scotch on ice. Evening light turns the tablecloths pink and violet. The ice is his last bulwark against total, helpless nihilism. He rolls the oily ambrosia of the bog over the crystals.*

Alice orders a glass of beer. It arrives quickly, dark and thick and workmanlike. She smacks her lips and Peter nearly calls the whole thing off then and there. He had imagined her drinking...what? Delicate things. Tea. Champagne. Rain filtered through a garret roof. She is a lady of a certain era, and ladies of that certain era do not drink porter. After the beer come oysters from some presumably dreadful, mollusc-infested swamp called Maine, which would not pair at all with her black beer. Peter found himself in an apoplexy of flummoxed culinary propriety.

Alice runs her fingertip around the rim of her glass and puts it between her lips, slicked with sepia foam.

"One 'drink me' out of you and I'll have your head," she scolds him, but her eyes shine. "My husband loved his beer. The darker the better. None of this prancing blonde European stuff, he'd say. Porter, stout, dubbel! I pretended that I had never met so curious a creature as a man who adores beer. That's how a girl makes her way in this world, Mr. Davies. Pretending awe at the simplest habits of men. But beer has been the bitter tympani keeping time for the long

parade of sad, strange, lonely men I've loved. My father and Charles called it 'our most ancient indulgence' and made a lot of noise about the pyramids while they poured their pints. Even our Leopold had barrels brought in from Belgium no matter where we were staying— imagine the expense! Nothing to a man of his station, of course. But to us? Impossible magic. Though he liked everything blonde, the rake."

"Prince Leopold?" It sounds absurd even as he says it, but he cannot think of any other fabulously wealthy Leopold she might mean.

"The very one. Didn't you know Alice had adventures in places not called Wonderland? Paris, Rome, Berlin, Vienna. All the lions and unicorns you could ever want. He never could decide between my sister and I, and in the end we were nothing but…well. Talking flowers, I suppose. He named his daughter Alice. That's something, at least." She strokes the silvery flesh of the oyster with a tiny pronged fork. "He died."

"The prince?"

"My husband. In the war. My sons, as well. Everyone, as well. My sister is long gone, a ghost in Leopold's locket. I've got one boy left and he doesn't visit anymore. It's too awful for him to face ruin in a blue dress. Oh, Peter, I live crumblingly in a crumbling body in a crumbling house and I burn my heating bills in the furnace for lack of coal and every so often I crawl out to tell a few people how wonderful it was to be a child in Oxford with a friend like Charles to teach me about all the sundry beauties of life so that I can buy another year's worth of tinned beef. And how are you coming along in the world, Peter Pan? How are you crumbling?"

Peter Llewelyn Davies flushes and eats in silence. The oysters taste like spent tears. His toast points stare back at him as if to say: what else did you expect?

"I'm in publishing," he offers finally.

Alice laughs sharply. "How hungry a thing is a book! Devoured you whole straight from the womb, and still gnawing away at your poor bones. Oh, but it was different for you, wasn't it? It was only ever that summer, really, with Charles and I and Edith and Lorina, punting on the river. But your James raised you, didn't he? Adopted the whole lot of Davies orphans. I can't tell if that would be better or worse. Tell me. Should I envy you?"

The soup course arrives. He frowns into a wide circle of pink bisque. His brain is a surfeit of fathers—his own, a-bed, rotting cancerous jaw like a crocodile, all teeth and scaled death, his older brothers, always running, fighting, so far ahead, so untouched, and Barrie, always Barrie, Barrie always kind and generous and ever-present, ever watching, his eyes like starving cameras freezing Peter in place for a flash and a snap that never came.

"He drank me," Peter whispers finally. "And grew larger."

LARGE AS LIFE AND TWICE AS NATURAL

OLIVE PUT HER hand against the looking glass.

She was balanced rather precariously on the mantel, one knee on either side of a portrait of Darling Mother as a young girl, before Father Dear, before the Other One, before Olive and Little George and Eglwysbach and the sheep and the paintbrushes and all of everything ever. A book of matches tumbled down onto the hearth as Olive tried, somehow, to grip the brickwork with her kneecaps.

When she'd been cleaning it with vinegar, the mirror had felt cool and slick and perfect as dolphin-skin. Olive pressed her other hand against the glass. It wasn't cool now. Or slick. It felt warm and alive and prickly, like a wriggling hedgehog thrilled to see its mate waddling through a wet paddock. The marble wolf's head in the looking glass parlour still snarled. The one in Fuss Antonym's parlour still did nothing of the kind.

"Don't be stupid, Olive," she scolded herself. Darling Mother never did, anymore. Someone had to pick up the slack. "Really, you're such an awful little fool. Nothing's going to *happen*. Nothing's *ever* going to happen to you. That's just how it is and you know it. You've gone barking, that's all, and pretty soon someone will come and take you away to a nice padded room by the sea where you can't bother anyone."

The looking glass *writhed* under her hands. It spread and stretched and undulated like a great glass python just waking from a thousand years asleep. Slowly, the mirror turned to mist, and the mist stroked the bones of her wrists with fond fingers.

"Mum!" Olive screamed—but the looking glass took her anyway, scream and all, and in half a moment she tumbled through to the other side into a cloud of green glow-worms, and a thumping, ancient forest, and the hot, thrilling blackness of a summer's midnight.

EACH SHINING SCALE

THE SALAD COURSE *appears amid the wash of unbridgeable silence. Beets, radishes, hard cheeses as translucent as slivers of pearl, sour vinegars, peppercorns green and black. Peter sighs. The other diners around him simply will* not *stop their idiotic noises, the belligerent scraping of silver against china, the oceanic murmur of inane conversation, the animal slurping of their food. The oysters begin to turn on him. He feels a pale bile churning within.*

"He said not to grow up, not ever," he whispers. "He made me promise. But I couldn't help it. Not for a minute. Even while he was telling his tale, scribbling away at his own cleverness while my father rotted away in bed, I was growing up. Becoming not-Peter all the time while he told me to stop, stop at once, hold still, keep frozen like...like a side of lamb."

Alice rolls her eyes and bites through a red radish. She has a spot of mauve lipstick on her teeth. "Oh, how very dare those precious old men prattle on and on to us about childhood! The only folk who obsess over the golden glow of youth are ones who've forgotten how perfectly dreadful it is to be a child. Did you feel invincible and piratical and impish when your father died? I surely did not when Edith passed. You simply cannot stop things happening to you in this life. And do you know the funniest thing? An Oxford don, living in the walled garden of the university, with servants and a snug little house in which to write nonsense poems and puzzles and make inventions to your heart's content—that's more and more permanent a childhood than I ever had. He used to moan and mewl over me about the horror of corsets to come, the grimoire of marriage, the charnel house of childbirth, the dark curtains that would close over me upon some future birthday—well, for goodness sake! What would he know about any of that? He never married, he never had a child, he never so much as scrubbed his own underthings! How dare he tell me four years old was the best of life when I had so many years left to face?"

"Eighteen months."

"Pardon?"

"When Peter left for Neverland. He was eighteen months old. In a pram in Kensington Gardens. An eighteen-month-old child can barely speak, barely walk without falling. But that was the best I had ever been, in his eyes. The best I ever could be. And all those people went to see the play and clapped their hands and agreed he was right, and all the while I was twenty, twenty-five, thirty. Thirty. As old as Hook. Watching myself fly away. Watching from the back row while my bones screamed, all in quiet: That's not what I was like, that's not how any of it goes; Christ, James, I was never heartless, I wish I was, I wish I was!"

Alice frowns into her beer. She rubs the glass with one fingertip.

"It's not children who are innocent and heartless," she says—bitterly? Pityingly? Peter has never had the knack of reading people. Only books, and only on good days. "Only the mad," she finishes, and goes after her beets with a vengeful stab.

A LIFE ASUNDER

THE VERY FIRST thing Olive did was look behind her. There was dear, familiar, batty old Fuss Antonym's wall—but it was no longer dear or familiar at all, and quite a bit battier. Instead of storm-slashed whitewash, the house sported a shimmering blackwash, roofed with overturned tea-saucers, and crawling with a sort of luminous ivy peppered with great, blowy hibiscus flowers in a hundred comic-book colours. She had come through the middle window in a row of three. On the other side of the window, she could still see the parlour, the mustard-coloured chair, the painting of the shepherdess and the black sheep, the peeling moulding, the chilled grey afternoon peeking in past the curtains on the ordinary wall opposite. *All right, yes, fine,* Olive told herself, half-terrified, half-irritated. *This sort of thing happens when you've gone mad. It's nothing to get tizzy over. You've sniffed too much silver polish, that's all. Might as well enjoy it!* The other side of the looking glass was a window, and the other side of the house was a deep night, and a deep summer, and a deep forest, deep and hot and sticky and bright.

Olive's knees abandoned her. She tumbled down onto a new, savage, harlequin earth. She was going to have a tizzy, after all. *For God's sake, Olive!* She plunged her knuckles into the alien ground. Even the soil sparkled. Hot mud squelched between her fingers, streaked with glittering grime like liquefied opals. An infinite jungley tangle spread out before her, and it simply refused to not be there, no matter how Olive tried to make it *stop* being there. A path tumbled down the hillocks and shallows, away into rose-jet shadows and emerald-coal mists. Delicate wood-mushrooms curled up everywhere like flowers in a busy garden: chartreuse chanterelles, fuchsia toadstools, azure puffballs.

Something was moving down there, down the path, between the mushrooms and the ferns and the trees no prim Latin taxonomy could pin down. Something pale. Something rather loud. And, just possibly, not one *something* alone, but three *somethings* together. There is nothing for a tizzy like a *something,* and before she could tell herself sensibly to stay close to home, no matter how odd and unhomelike home had suddenly become, Olive was off down the path and through the garden of night fungus, chasing three hard, pale, loud voices through the dark.

"You're such an awful brat," growled something just ahead. "I don't know why we trouble ourselves with you at all."

"And *deadly* boring, to ice the cake," sniffed something else. "Why even tell a riddle if you don't have any earthly intention of answering it for anybody? It's not sporting, that's what."

"I think it's jolly sporting," crowed a third something. "For *me.*"

"A raven *isn't* like a writing desk. You can smirk all you like, but that's the truth and I hate you. It just *isn't,* in any sort of way that makes sense—" the second something spluttered.

"The farthing you go for sense, the furthing you are from the pound," the third something said loftily.

"*Do* shut up," snarled the first something.

Olive rounded a bank of birch stumps and mauve moss wriggling in such a way that she absolutely did not want to look any closer—and yet she did, for that was a something, too. The moss wasn't wriggling at all, rather, hundreds of silkworms wriggled while they feasted on it. Only these were *actually* silkworms—not ugly blind little scraps of beef suet, but creatures made up entirely of rich, embroidered silk brocade, fat as a rich lady, writhing greedily over the bank. Olive shuddered, and in her shuddering, nearly toppled over the *somethings* she'd been after.

In a clearing in the wood stood three hacked-off marble capitals, the sort meant to crown pillars in a grand bank or Hungarian cathedral. Her capitals. The very ones that hung so stupidly and dearly on her parlour wall. Only these were hopping about on their own recognizance, as if they were really and truly the wolf, hare, and raven that had been carved into their fine stone blocks.

The wolf's head, surrounded by carved fern-heads and flowers, the very one that had snarled *within* the looking glass and snoozed *without,* looked Olive up and down. The hare wriggled her veiny marble nose. The raven fluffed his sculpted feathers.

"Bloody tourists," the wolf snipped.

SEVEN MAIDS WITH SEVEN MOPS

ALICE WATCHES ANOTHER *couple without expression. The man cuts the woman's meat for her. The woman stares into the distance while he saws away silently at her pork. A repeating face, turned away, a woman watching a woman watching nothing. Staring and sighing and gnawing, the great human trinity. Peter has a strange and horrible instinct to lean over the table, the salads, the beer, the scotch, the candles, the world, their whole useless strained, copyedited lives and kiss Alice. To make himself cheap, as Wendy did in that cruel first scene in the nursery. He has always kissed first in his life. Always tried to redeem that little viciousness in the other Peter, whose heart was an acorn and whose kiss was a jest. She is so much older than he, but Peter loves older women, since he was hardly yet a man. Guiltily, and to great sorrow, but who could ask more of the most famous motherless boy in all of history?*

He doesn't do it. Of course he doesn't. He, too, is of a certain era, and that era does not clear dining tables for the madness of love.

"At least your man stayed to look after you," Alice says finally, without turning her face back to his. "It's a kindly vampire who tucks you in and puts out the milk by your bed once he's drunk his fill of your life."

Her lips are red with beet-blood. He supposes his must be as well. Peter orders a second scotch.

"Are you angry, Alice? Do you hate him? I can't think whether I should feel better or worse if you hate him. I can't think whether I hate mine or not. I can't think whether he is mine. I am his, that's for certain. His, forever. A shadow that's slipped off and roams the streets hoping to be mistaken for a human being. For a while I was so flamingly angry I thought I'd char."

"Not angry…angry isn't the word. Perhaps there isn't a word. Charles came back to see me once, after that summer. I was a little older. Eleven or twelve. A little was enough. He looked at me like a stranger. Like any other young woman—a slight distaste, a tremor of existential threat, a very little current of fear. He could hardly meet my eye while I poured the tea. Like a robber returning to the scene of the crime." She stopped watching the other woman and turned her blue eyes back to Peter. Their cold, triumphant light filled him up like a well. "He came to my window and saw that I'd grown old and he wanted nothing more to do with me."

ALICE'S RIGHT FOOT, ESQ.

"YOU'RE GOING TO spoil it," snapped the hare. "Oh, I *know* she's going to spoil it, it always gets spoiled, just when we're about to have it out at last."

"I won't spoil anything, I promise," Olive whispered, quite out of breath.

"You can hardly help it," sighed the wolf's-head capital. "Any more than milk can help spoiling outside the icebox."

"Raven was *finally* about to tell us how he's like a writing-desk when you came bollocking through! I've been waiting eons! There's no sense to it, you know. We've said a hundred answers and none of them are at *all* good. But he won't say, because he's a stupid wart. I'd advise *you* to tread more quietly, young lady, if you don't want to alert the authorities."

"What authorities? It's only a forest inside a looking glass. The constable is hardly going to come arrest me on my way from Nowheresville to Noplace Downs."

"The Queens' men," the wolf whispered. His whiskers quivered in canine fear. "All ways here belong to them."

"Which Queen? Elizabeth? She's all right."

"Either of them," answered the hare with an anxious tremor in her quartzy whiskers. "Twos are wild tonight and they're the worst of the lot." The pale rabbit tilted onto her side just as a real, furry hare would if it were scratching its ear with a hind leg, only the capital hadn't any hind legs, right or left, so she just hitched up on one corner and quivered there.

"All right, I surrender," cawed the raven's head suddenly. "I'll say it. But only because our Olive's finally going places, and that deserves a present."

"Oh, don't be silly!" Olive demurred, though she was quite delighted by the idea. "It's quite enough to have properly met you three at last! And to think, it would never have happened if I hadn't gone totally harebrained just then! It was all that silver polish, I expect."

The marble hare went very still. "I beg your pardon? What is the trouble with a hare's brain, hm?"

"Oh, I didn't mean anything cruel by it," Olive said hurriedly. "It's only that I'm...well, I'm obviously not playing with a full deck of cards this evening."

"Only the Queen has a full deck at her command," the marble wolf barked. "Who do you think you are?"

"Nobody!"

"Then we'll be on our way!" The hare huffed. "There's no point in talking to nobody, after all. People will say we've gone mad!"

"Oh, please don't go! I only meant..." She looked pleadingly at the marble raven, who offered no help. "I only meant that *I* went mad a few minutes ago, and as I've only just started, I'm bound to make a mash of it at first. I've no doubt I'll improve! The most dreadful sorts of people go mad; it can't be so terribly hard. But I only ever wanted to say that darling Mr. Raven hasn't got to give me a present, it's present enough to make your acquaintance!"

"Would you prefer a future?" the hare asked, her pride still smarting. "It's more splendid than the present, but you've got to wait three days for delivery."

"Of course, the past is particularly nice this time of year," the wolf grinned.

"No! All we've got is the present, and not a very pleasant one at that." The raven snapped at a passing glow-worm. "Rather cheap, honestly. I'm only warning you so you won't be disappointed."

"Oh, stop trying to impress her! You haven't got the goods. Admit it!" The wolf howled from within his thicket of carved Corinthian leaves. "You just made up that bit of humbug because it sounded clever and shiny and it alliterated you never had the tawdriest idea of how to solve it. Confess! Perjury! Pretension! Petty thief of my intellectual energies! *Hornswoggler!*"

"I *have* got the goods, and the bads, and the amorals, too! But if I'm to give up my present, after all this time, we must have a proper party for it! You lot have abused me so long that just handing it over in the woods like a highwayman won't do—no sir, no madam, no how nor hence nor hie-way! I will have a To-Do! I will have balloons and buttercream and brandy and bomb shelters! And one good trombone, at minimum!"

The marble hare rocked from one side of its flat column-base to the other in sculptural excitement. "Shall we, shan't we, shall we, shan't we, shall we join the dance?"

The three capitals leapt off down the forest path, bouncing and hopping like three drops of oil on a hot pan. Olive raced after them, ducking moonlit branches and drooping vines clotted with butterflies that seemed, somehow, to have tiny slices of bread for wings. But no matter how Olive ran, she seemed only to go slower, the wood around her only to close in thicker and deeper, darker and closer, until she could hardly move at all, and had lost sight entirely of the talking capitals. At last, she found herself standing quite still in a little glen, staring up at the starry sky and the starry leaves and the starry massive skeleton sheathed in moss so thick it could keep out the cold of a thousand winters. Tiger lilies and violets and dahlias and peonies grew wild in the skeleton's teeming green ribcage, its soft, blooming mouth, its sightless eye sockets. It lay sprawled on the forest floor propped up against a tree as vast as time, arms limp, legs bent at the knee. A galaxy of green and ultraviolet glow-worms ringed the giant's dead green head like a crown, and the crown spelled out words in flickering, sparkling letters:

THE TUMTUM CLUB

NO THOUGHT OF ME SHALL FIND A PLACE

A VIOLINIST, A *cellist, and an oboist begin to set up their music stands in the corner of the Stork Club. They are nice young men, in nice new suits, with nice fresh haircuts and shaves. The violinist rubs his bow with resin as though he is sharpening a sword.*

"I always felt...Alice...I always felt I was two people. Two Peters. Myself, and him. The Other One. And the Other was always the better version. Younger, handsomer, jollier, bolder. Of course he was. I had to bumble through every day knocking things over and breaking my head open. But the Other One...he got to try over and over again until he got it right. Until he was perfect. Dreamed, planned, written, re-written, re-rewritten, edited, crossed-out, tidied up, nipped and cut and shaped and moved through the plot with a minimum of trouble. Nothing I could ever say could be as clever as the Other One's quipping. How could it be? Everything I say is a dreadful cliché, because I am alive and human, and live humans are not made out of dust and God's breath, no matter what anyone says. They're made out of clichés. So there are two of me—what a unique observation for a muse to make! No, no, it isn't, it can't be, because I only said it once, I didn't get to decide it was rubbish and go back, erase it, add a metaphor or a bit of meta-fiction or a dash of theatricality. So I just say it and it's terrible, it's nothing. But the Other One would be delighted with two Peters, you know. What adventures they would have together. Nothing for mischief like a twin."

Alice's eyes narrowed with concern. "Peter...I'm not sure I follow, dear."

"Yes, well, no one does. I don't, when it comes down to it. If you don't mind a confession before the main course...I...I went...well, all this about two Peters and suchlike...wound me up in a sanatorium. For a while. Not long. But...well, yes. Er." He finished lamely, flushing in shame—shame, and the peculiar excitement of sharing a secret one absolutely knows is unwelcome and untoward.

"Oh, Peter!"

"Oh, Peter, indeed. It's such a funny thing. Nothing in the world so much like Neverland as a sanatorium. The food isn't really food, no one's got a mother, there's a great frightening man in a waistcoat who harries you night and day, and you keep fighting the same battles over and over, round and round in circles, forgetting that you ever fought the minute it's over and the next one begins. All of us lost boys in that awful lagoon, dressed as animals, wailing for home."

She puts her hand on his. The tableware shifts beneath their fingers.

"Did you ever feel...like that? Like there were two Alices?" he whispers.

Alice laughs wanly. "Good heavens, no. There is only one Alice, and I am her. He only...took a photograph. One great, gorgeous photograph, where the sitting lasted all my life, and he sold that picture to the world."

CINDERS ALL A-GLOW

OLIVE FOUND THAT, if she walked very, *very* slowly, as though she were dragging her feet on the way to some unpleasant chore, she could speed along quite gaily through the shadowy glen. It hardly took a moment of glum shuffling before she stood at a tapering, rather church-like door wedged into the giant's skeleton, just where its briary ribcage came to a Pythagorean point. It certainly *was* a door, though rather absurdly done. It made her think of all the overdecorated, slapdash rooms of Fuss Antonym, thrown up without reason or sense, for the door was spackled together out of pocket watch parts and butter and breadcrumbs and jam, and she felt entirely sure that if she were to knock, it would all come oozing, clattering apart and she should be billed for the damage.

"Hullo?" Olive called instead, for she had forgotten her pocketbook on the other side of the looking glass.

A slab of cold butter bristling with minute-hands like a greasy hedgehog slid aside. Two beady black rodent eyes peered down at her.

"Password," the Doorman whispered.

"Well, I certainly don't know!" Olive sputtered.

Oh, bad form, Olive! she cursed herself. *Haven't you ever read a spy novel? You're meant to say something extra mysterious, in a commanding and knowledgeable voice, so that the doorman will say to himself, "Anyone that commanding and knowledgeable has to be on the up and up, so it stands to reason the password's changed, or I've forgotten it, or I'm being tested by management, but any way it cuts, it's me who's at fault and not this fine upstanding member of our society." Now, come on, do it, and you won't have to feel embarrassed when you think back on this later when you've gone un-mad.*

Olive stood on her tiptoes and stared commandingly into those black rodent eyes. *Something extra mysterious. Something knowledgeable. Preferably something mad. Like a chicken in spectacles and a powdered wig.*

"Eglwysbach," she said slowly and stoically, fitting her mouth around the word as perfectly as possible, even tossing in a proper guttural cough on the end.

The eyes on the other side of the buttered watch-parts blinked uncertainly.

"Er. That doesn't sound right. But it doesn't sound *wrong.* It *sounds* passwordy. Am I asleep?" the Doorman whispered.

"We both are, most likely," Olive laughed.

"I'm not meant to sleep on the job. I'll be sacked for wasting time, even though time doesn't mind. He does need to lose a bit round the middle, to be quite honest. In fact, I wasn't asleep! I heard every word you were saying. Very naughty of you to suggest it."

"I won't tell. Now, if you heard what I was saying, then you heard me say the password very well and very correctly."

"Did I? That's nice." The creature yawned, but didn't open the door.

"Let me in!"

"Oh! Please don't beat me."

The pocket watch door wound open, leaving a slick of butter and jam as it swung. The Doorman was not a Doorman at all, but a Dormouse, standing on a tall footstool in a suit of armour bolted together out of pieces of a lovely china teapot with blue pastoral scenes painted on it. He stood rather stiffly, on account of the armour.

"I feel most relaxed and un-anxious snuggled into my teapot," the Dormouse said defensively, puffing out his little mouse chest. "So my friend Haigha invented a way for me to stay in it forever. In the future, everyone will be wearing teapots, mark my…mark…my March…"

The Dormouse fell asleep stuck upright in his armour. He leaned back against the door so that it groaned shut under his little weight.

ENVIOUS YEARS WOULD SAY FORGET

PETER TAKES OFF *his glasses and rubs the bridge of his thin nose. The musicians begin a delicate, complicated piece that is nevertheless easy to ignore.*

"I'm terribly sorry, Mrs—Alice. I thought I wanted to talk about this. I thought I wanted to talk about it with you. But I think perhaps I do not, not really. I'm an awful cad, but I've always been an awful cad. Even the best version of me is a cad."

Alice quirked one long white eyebrow. She leaned back in her chair and folded her hands in her blue lap.

"Am I doing something wrong?"

"Pardon?"

"Am I doing something wrong? Am I not behaving as you imagined I would behave? Ought I to have ordered the mock turtle soup instead of the cucumber? Or perhaps you'd like us to leap up and dash round the table and switch places whilst I pour butter into your pocket watch? I could curtsy and sing you a pleasant little rhyme about animals or some such—I'm told my singing voice is still quite good." Alice's thin, dry mouth curled into a snarl. "Or shall we simply clasp hands and try to believe six impossible things before the main course? What would satisfy you, Peter?"

Beneath the table, Peter dug his fingernails into his flesh through the linen of his trousers. He felt a terrible ringing in his head.

"It's nothing like that, Alice. I wouldn't—"

"Oh, I think it's precisely like that, Mr. Davies. You ought to be ashamed. It's disgusting, really. How could you do this to me? You, of all people? You didn't come snuffling round my skirt-strings so that we might find some pitiful gram of solace between the two of us. You came to find the magic girl. Just like all the rest of them. You're no better, not in the least bit better. Life has hollowed you out, so I and my wondrous, lovely self must fill you up again with dreams and innocence and the good sort of madness that doesn't end you up with an ether-soaked rag over your face. Well, life hollows everyone, boy. I've got nothing left in the cupboards for you. Oh, I am disappointed, Peter. Rather bitterly so."

A kind of leaden horror spread over Peter's heart as he realized he was about to cry in public. "Mrs. Hargreaves, please! You don't understand, you don't. You can't."

Alice leaned forward, clattering the tableware with her elbows. "Oh—oh. It's worse than that, isn't it? You didn't want me to be magical for you. You wanted to be magical for me. In the library. Just like a nursery, wasn't it? And for once you would really do it, fly up to a girl's window and sweep her away to a place full of crystal and gold and feasting, and she would be dazzled. I would be dazzled. You tell everyone else that you're not him, to stop gawping at you and only seeing the boy who never grew up. But you thought I, I, of all people, might look at you and see that you are him. Or, at least, that you want to believe you are, somewhere, somewhere fathoms down the deeps of your soul. Only I'm spoiling it now, because an Alice makes a very poor Wendy indeed."

Peter Llewelyn Davies gulped down the dregs of his scotch and thought seriously about stabbing himself through the eye with his oyster fork. It would be worth it, if he could escape this agony of a moment.

"Very well, then, Peter," Alice said softly. "I am ready. I am here. I am her. I am all the Alice you want me to be. Now that we've seen each other, if I believe in you, you can believe in me."

"Stop it."

CATHERYNNE M. VALENTE

LET'S PRETEND WE'RE KINGS AND QUEENS

THE TUMTUM CLUB was a wide, round room carpeted in moonflowers. Wide toadstool-tables dotted the floor, lit by glass inkwells in which the blue ink burned like paraffin, and all the sizzling wicks were quills. Creatures great and small and only occasionally human crowded round, in chairs and out, dodos and gryphons and lizards and daisies with made-up eyes and long pale green legs and lobsters and fawns and sheep in cloche hats and striped cats and chess pieces from a hundred different sets, all munching on mushroom tarts and pig-and-pepper pies and slices of iced currant cakes and sipping from tureens of beautiful soup. The revellers were dressed very poorly and very well all at once. Their clothes were clotted with sequins and rhinestones and leather and velvet, but it was all very old and shabby and worn through, and no one wore shoes at all. Advertising posters hung all round the mossy bones walling them in. One showed a rose with a salacious look in her eyes and two huge fans over her thorns, promising a LIVE FLOWERS REVUE. Another had two little fat men in striped caps painted on it yelling at one another, which was, apparently, THE SATIRICAL SPOKEN WORDS STYLINGS OF T&T, TWO WEEKS ONLY. On one end of the club stood a little stage ringed with glowing oyster-shell footlights. A thick blue curtain was drawn across the half-moon proscenium. Olive could hear the tin-tinning sounds of instruments warming up backstage. Whatever happened in the Tumtum Club at night had not begun to happen yet.

On the other end of the room stretched a long bar made of bricks and mortar and crown moulding. It was manned, improbably, by a huge egg with jowls and eyebrows and stubby speckled arms and a red waistcoat and a starched shirt collar and cravat, even though he had no neck for it to matter much. An orchestra of coloured liquor bottles glittered behind him. A couple of chess pieces, a white knight and a red one, leaned past the empties to catch the eye of the egg.

"I'll take a Treacle and Ink, my good man," the red knight said.

"It's *very* provoking," the bartender answered, filling up a pint glass, "to be called a man—*very*!"

"I'll have an Aged Aged Man, Mr. D," the white knight whispered. "Or should I spring for a Manxome Foe? Oh!" the knight fretted and pursed his horsey muzzle. "Just mix a bit of sand in my cider and don't look at me. You know how I like it."

The egg-man turned to Olive. "And you, Miss…"

"Olive."

"Ah, with a name like that you'll want a martini. With a name like that you'll be small and hard and bitter and salty. With a name like that you'll be fished out when no one's looking and discreetly tossed in the bin!"

The notion of being served a martini, no questions asked, rather thrilled Olive. Darling Mother was very strict with everyone's indulgences but her own. "I can't pay, I'm afraid. I haven't got half a crown to my name."

"No crowns allowed at the Tumtum Club, my dear," the white knight whispered, "Not even one." And before he was done with his whispering, a cocktail glass slid down the bar into Olive's hand. Whatever was inside was nothing at all like a martini, being completely opaque and indigo, but it did have an olive in it. Frosted letters danced across the base of the glass: DRINK ME. So she did.

A voice like a crystal church bell wrapped in silk rang out over the club.

> *"Will you all come to my party?" cried the Monarch to the*
> *Throng*
> *"Though the night is close around us and its reign is harsh and*
> *long?"*

A long, slim, orange and black leg slid out from behind the curtain. A rude and unruly applause burst through the room, catcalls, foot and hoof-stomping, snapping of fingers and claws, a great pot of hollering and whistling stirred too fast. A long, slim, orange arm emerged from the blue velvet, its elegant fingers curling and dancing with each new word.

"Gather eagerly, my darlings, tie your troubles in a bow
For the Tumtum Club is open—are you in the know?
Are you, aren't you, are you, aren't you, are you in the know?
Are you, aren't you, are you, aren't you, aren't you ready for
the show?"

Olive stared. This was, perhaps, a naughtier show than she really ought to be seeing. But then, if the mad are naughty, who can scold them? She scrambled for an empty seat among the toadstool tables. Only one remained, far in the back row, wedged between a large striped cat and a thin, nervous-looking chess piece, a white queen, knitting a long silvery shawl in her lap.

A huge saffron-coloured wing spooled out over that coy leg like a curtain all its own. It was speckled with white and rimmed with jet black and veined with ultramarine. Finally, a head emerged: hair like a beetle's back, skin the colour of flame, eyes as green as swamp gas and cut-glass. The girl swept and twirled her massive butterfly wings like the fans of a harem-dance and sang for the roar of the crowd:

You can really have no notion how delightful is our art
In here there is no Red Queen and there is no Queen of Hearts
Only me and thee and he and she all in a pretty row
Alive as oysters, every one—now, shall we start the show?
Shall we, shan't we, shall we, shan't we, shall we start the show?
Shall we, shan't we, shall we, shan't we, shan't we set the night
aglow?

"The Queen of Hearts?" Olive whispered. "I read a book with a Queen of Hearts in it once."

"You must be very proud," yawned the cat.

IT MUST SOMETIMES COME TO JAM TO-DAY

THE CANDLELIGHT LIGHTS *up her cheekbones ghoulishly. She has the look of a fox on the scent of something small and scurrying and delicious.*

"I shan't stop," she needles him. "If you know any bloody thing at all about Alice, you know that she doesn't stop. She keeps going, all the way to the eighth square and back home again. She's the perfect English Girl, greeting the most vicious of things with an 'Oh My Gracious!' and a 'Well, I Never!' You haven't the first idea what sort of stony constitution it takes to go through life as the English Girl. At least your Other One got to be wild and free and rule-less. A man can aspire to that. My Other One cannot rise above charmingly confused, because no English Girl may be allowed to greet nonsense with a sword or else all Creation would fall to pieces. But you wanted to meet me. You wanted to compare notes. You wanted a sympathy of minds, so no Oh My Graciouses for you, Peter. Only Alice, and Alice will have her tea and her crown if it's the death of her. Alice is curious, don't you remember? It is her chief characteristic. Curiouser and curiouser, as the meal goes on. Tell me everything. Leave off this poor mad little me *act. What was Neverland* really *like?"*

Peter coughs brutally. His vision swims with liquor and humiliation and the violin and the cello and the love he had prepared so carefully for this person, only to find it spoiled in the icebox. With the perfect timing of his class, the waiter appears with steaming plates of beef bourguignon and quails in a cream-mustard sauce, ringed in summer vegetables glistening with butter.

"You're mocking me, Mrs. Hargreaves. I never imagined you could be so vicious. I might as well ask you what Wonderland was like."

"You might at that. It smelled much better than New York, I'll tell you that much. But no more. I am operating a fair business here, young man. Show me yours and I'll show you mine."

"You can't be serious. Are you quite drunk? Does it amuse you to pretend to a silly clod that Wonderland was a real place?"

Alice blinks. She turns her head curiously to one side. "Does it amuse you to pretend that Neverland was not?"

CATHERYNNE M. VALENTE

DID GYRE AND GIMBLE IN THE WABE

THE ACTS WENT by like leaves blowing across the stage. Three young girls in shifts called Elsie, Lacie, and Tillie did an acrobatic routine, pantomiming any number of things that began with M: mouse-traps, and the moon, and memory, and muchness. Olive couldn't imagine how a handful of gymnasts could act out *memory* or *muchness,* but when they froze in their tableaux, Olive knew just what they meant, and applauded wildly with everyone else. A pig in a baby-bonnet stood in a lonely spotlight and belted out one long, unbroken oink of agony that lasted nearly two full minutes before he fell to his knees, scream-snorted MOTHER WHY DON'T YOU LOVE ME while tears streamed down his porky jowls, then sprang up and bowed merrily while roses flew at him from all directions. A lovely turtle with sad eyes sang a song about soup. It seemed to be a sort of communal thing—anyone could whisper to the gorgeous butterfly master of ceremonies and take the stage, if they felt inclined. There was a bit of a queue forming in the wings. Olive shrank back as a monstrous *thing* crept onto the boards. He had claws like a great hairy dinosaur and eyes like headlamps and a tail that coiled down over the footlights, casting broken shadows over his violet-green scaled body. His dragon wings were so tall and wide he was obliged to bend and scrunch them to wedge under the half-moon shell of the stage. A couple of fawns pushed a little rickety pianoforte over to him with their dear spotted heads. The monster tinkled out a few experimental runs up and down the keys. Olive could hardly believe his horrid tarantula-talons could manage such graceful scales.

"It's only a Jabberwock, my dear. You needn't clutch my hand *quite* so hard," said the White Queen. Her face was so serene and crisply carved, like a jeweller had done it.

"A Jabberwock! Like *'twas brillig and the slithy toves did gyre and gimble in the wabe? Whiffling through the tulgey wood* and that? *The* Jabberwock?"

The monster at the piano began to play a mournful torch song. He fixed his moony headlamp-eyes on Olive and sang in a gorgeous tenor: *I never whiffled, I never; and it weren't even brillig at all. Nobody gave me no chance to be beamish; I could've been someone, if I' d been born small…*

The White Queen frowned at her knitting. "That's Edward. He's rather a war hero, don't you know? He lost his right foot at the Battle of Tulgey Wood, see?" Olive leaned forward—the Jabberwock worked the pedals of his pianoforte with only one crocodile-foot. The other was wrapped in gauze and seeping. The White Queen sighed like a tea kettle boiling. "He's going to lose the other one in an hour, poor chap."

Olive blinked. "What? What do you mean he's *going to* lose his other one? How do you know?"

Edward belted out: *You can take a Wock's head but you can't make him crawl!* He stopped, leaned his long, whiskered snout over the footlights into the audience, and whispered: "On account of my brain's being in my tail, yeah? Joke's on you, O Frabjous Brat!"

"It's the effect of living backwards," the Queen said kindly.

"Oh!" Olive whispered excitedly. "I know this part! Jam to-morrow and jam yesterday, right?"

"Will you please be quiet?" growled the striped cat. "Talking during performance is a biting offense."

The White Queen blushed pinkly. She reached down into the knitting basket at her feet and drew out a toasted crumpet spread generously with raspberry jam. She brushed a bit of wool fluff off of it and offered it to Olive.

"I have learned a few lessons since I was deposed," she said softly, and with such a tender sadness. "Very occasionally, it costs one nothing to bend the rules."

DEAR ME! A HUMAN CHILD!

ALICE STARES DOWN *at her four neat quails adrift in their sea of golden sauce.*

"You can't be serious," Peter hisses at her. "This is…this is unkind, Alice. Monstrous, in fact. Why are you doing this to me? What purpose is there in it?"

"I'm not doing any little thing to you, young man. Now, stop it. You needn't pretend. What was Hook like, really? I always wondered if his stump pained him, at night, in the cold of the sea air."

"For Christ's sake, this is madness. You ought to be locked up, not me."

Alice's face goes dark and furious and sour.

"Say that to me again, boy. Say it, and I' ll whip you like the child you are, right here in this lovely restaurant. Don't think I can't. I raised three sons and a husband, you know."

Peter blanches. He feels his blood rebel, not knowing whether to flood his cheeks or flee them. He begins a deep study of his beef. After a time, Alice softens.

"I am sorry—it's a wonder how many times I've said it in such a short while! But I am, I am sorry, Peter, I simply assumed. It was only natural, to my mind. Only logic. I only thought...if for me, then for you. Goose and gander and all that rot. Oh, I never told anyone—my God, how could anyone be told? How could I even begin? But you, you of all people! The moment you introduced yourself I thought that we had veered toward this, careened toward it, that we would converge upon it long before dessert, and at last, I would know someone like me, and you would know someone like you, and what peace we should have then, at the end of it all. Peace, and something nice with butterscotch."

"Please. You mock me, Mrs. Hargreaves."

"I do not, Mr. Davies. I make you my confession. In the summer of 1862, something rather astonishing happened to me. I was ten years old. And naturally, when it was all done, I ran at full pelt to tell my best friend all about it just as soon as I could. To my eternal fault, in those days, my best friend was a mathematics professor with a rather large nose and a rather large anxiety complex and an interest in writing."

The beef tastes like nothing at all. The wine tastes like less than that. He gives up. "It was real," he says flatly.

"Well, of course it was. Who could make up such a thing?"

EVERYTHING'S GOT A MORAL

THE EGG BROUGHT Olive another indigo martini.

"From the fellow onstage," the bartender whispered. "He was very insistent that it arrive as he was performing, not before or beside or behind."

The fellow onstage was an old-ish man in muttonchops holding an improbably large lavender top hat with the size-card still stuck in it. He watched the crowd solemnly as he drew object after object after object out of the hat: a croquet ball stained with blood, a pocket watch with a bayonet thrust through the fob, a silver tea-tray with a great, unhappy boot-print on it.

"Deposed?" Olive said to the White Queen, who went on calmly with her knitting. "But you're the White Queen! Shouldn't you be off Queening about with the other Queens?"

"I wasn't red, so I wasn't needed," she sighed. "That's what they said. There were four of us once. The perfect number for bridge. The Red Queen, the White Queen, the Queen of Hearts, and…" The White Queen suddenly clammed up, shaking her head in distress.

"The Other One," the striped cat purred. "We aren't allowed to say her name. The Queens have ears. Hush hush."

"She kicked down the Queen of Hearts' horrid cards and shook the Red Queen so hard she nearly broke her neck—more's the pity she didn't finish the job. Everything was going to be all right, you know. With the Other One here to keep those scarlet women in line."

The cat licked his paws. "I met her. She was rather thick, if you ask me. And she kept going on about herself, which I think is very rude, when you're a guest."

"But you knew it wouldn't be all right," said Olive, who had a little brother, and therefore was immune to distraction. "Because of how you live backwards."

"Yes, yes! What a clever girl! I knew, but no one listens to me because I'm always screaming about one thing or another—but you would scream, too, if you remembered the whole future of the world until Judgment Day and past it! You'd scream and scream and never stop! I knew she'd vanish like a shawl in the wind and she did and just as soon as she did, the Red Queen and the Queen of Hearts would decide Wonderland needed taking in hand. Needed one crown. We were all conscripted. My Lily died on the Croquet Grounds. I wish I had. I wish…I wish a lot of things. The Other One came back, of course, nothing only happens once in Wonderland. But as soon as she was gone again, those red ladies holed up in their castles and started building their armies once more. We are not at war now, my child, but we soon shall be. Now, we simply hold our breaths and wait."

"Something like that happened in my world, too," Olive said softly. "*Is* happening. Germany and Russia and America and…well, everyone, I suppose."

"The Tumtum Club is the only place the Looking Glass Creatures are allowed to be mad anymore." The White Queen sighed. "Outside, we have to report for duty at dawn. In here, the Hatter can pull his heart out of his hat."

The gorgeous butterfly slipped out of the curtain again to master further ceremonies, twirling on her tiny black feet in a sudden cloud of stage smoke. She peered into the audience as though she were speaking to each of them in particular, as though what she said were more important than anything that had ever happened to them, and the whole of the universe waited upon their answering her.

I am young, little darlings, the Butterfly crooned
My wings have become very bright
The larva I was drowned inside my cocoon
Growing up really is such a fright!
I hardly remember the old mushroom now
I liked hookahs, I think, and fresh dew
Yet I'll still have my answer, I do not care how:
Who Are You?

Something knocked into their toadstool table and toppled Olive's drink. She tried to keep mum for the sake of the Hatter and shout indignantly at the same time, which is impossible, but she tried anyway.

The marble raven capital blinked up at her.

"Come on, then," he cawed. "This is our five-minute call. We're on, Olive, old girl."

LIVING BACKWARDS

THE TRIO OF *musicians wind down. The lights are dim now. The restaurant nearly empty, nearly shut. Peter and Alice toy with the notion of eating their slices of plum-cake awash with double cream, but neither can fully commit to it. They speak of Wonderland, of cabbages and kings, of riddles and chess and what sort of tea could be got in the wilds. It is pleasant, there is a joy in it, but it is unreal. It is like listening to someone try to tell you the plot of a radio play you missed. Peter feels a chill. Perhaps another cold coming on.*

"I want to believe you," he says.

"Clap your hands and give it a go. Or decide I'm a barmy old woman and go on with your life. It won't change what I know. Oh, Peter, how disappointing for us both. You thought we were the same. I thought we were. But Alice in Wonderland could never take me from myself, because it was myself, it always was. We're both the victims of burglars, dastardly fellows who stove in our windows and bashed up our houses. But my robber only took the silver. Yours took the lot. Of course, Charles got it half wrong and put a great lot of maths in to amuse himself; and perhaps if I'd been the one to write it, I wouldn't have to sell my first editions to keep the lights on in my house; but losing Wonderland didn't ruin me. Losing..." and then she cannot continue. She grips her beer glass like it can save her, but it will not. It never has saved anyone. "...my boys...all my pretty boys..."

"My brothers, too," Peter whispers. There is nothing more to say than that, than that they are people of a certain era, and people of a certain era know an emptiness in the world, a place where something precious was cut out and never replaced.

"Coffee?" asks the waiter.

"Tea," they answer.

"What I don't understand," Peter ventures finally, "is what you're doing here."

"I beg your pardon?"

"If it was all real, why don't you go back? When the lights have gone out and...your boys have gone...why stay here, in this dreadful world?"

"I never went on purpose. It just happened. I saw a white rabbit one day. I touched a looking glass. I never decided to go. It decided to take me. It's

never decided since. Wonderland is like my son, my last son. It's just so awfully awkward for him to see me the way I've ended up, it avoids me as much as it possibly can."

"I suppose I should scour the countryside for bunnies and mirrors," Peter laughs despite himself.

"I suppose I should," Alice giggles, and for a moment she is that child on the cover of a million novels, the English Girl, rosy and devious and brilliant. The check appears as if by magic, and Peter pays it, as good as his word. Alice stands and the waiter brings their coats. "No, Peter, it's best as it is. Whatever would I say to the White Queen now? Give me my bloody damned jam, you old cow? I gave up weeping for my lost kingdom years ago. I made my own, and if it crumbled, well, all kingdoms do. The world's not so dreadful, my dear. It is dreadful, of course, but only most of the time. Sometimes it rather outdoes itself. Gives us a scene so improbable no one would dare to put it in a book, for who would believe in such a chance meeting between two such people, such a splendid supper, such an unlikely moment in the great pool of moments in which we all swim?" She kisses his cheek. She holds her lips against him for a long time. When she pulls away, there is a thimble in his hand. "Oh, goodness," Alice says with a shine in her blue eyes. "What a lot of rubbish old ladies have in their bags!"

They walk arm in arm out into the New York street. People shove and holler by. The lights spangle and reflect in the hot concrete. The air smells like rotting vegetables and steel and fresh baking rolls and summer pollen. Alice stops him on the curb before he can cross the road.

"Peter, darling, listen to me. You must listen. You've got to answer the Caterpillar's question—you've got to find an answer, or else you'll never find your way. I never could, not until now, not until this very night, but you must. It's the only question there is."

"I can't, Alice. I want to."

Alice throws her arms round his neck. "I like you better, Peter. Ever so much better than him. Peter Pan was always such an awful shit, you know."

They start across the long rope of the street, but being English and unaccustomed to traffic, they do not see the streetcar hurtling toward them, painted white for the new exhibit at the Metropolitan Museum. Peter hears the bell and leaps back, hauling Alice roughly along with him, barely missing being crushed against the headlamps. When he collects himself, he turns to ask if she's all right, if he didn't hurt her too much, if the shock has ruffled her so that they need another drink to steady them.

There is no one beside him. His arm is empty.

"Alice?" Peter calls into the darkness. But no answer comes.

LONDON IS THE CAPITAL OF PARIS, AND PARIS IS THE CAPITAL OF ROME

OLIVE STOOD ON the stage of the Tumtum Club in the brash glare of the spotlight. She could barely make out all the glittering scales and claws and furs and shining eyeballs of the Looking Glass Creatures in the audience.

"Go on," hissed the marble raven. "I'm not doing this alone. You do your bit, then I'll do mine. Mine's better, obviously, so I'll close."

"My bit? I haven't got a bit! I didn't even sing in the school concert!"

"Do something! You're sure to, if you stand there long enough!"

Olive felt like her heart was dribbling out of her mouth. Everyone just kept *looking* at her. No one had ever looked at her for so long. Certainly not Father Dear or Darling Mother who ignored her benignly, not Little George who was more interested in painting the sheep, not the Other One, who seemed never to notice her until they collided in the hall. She could hardly bear it. What could she possibly do to impress these aliens out of her own bookshelf? In the book, Alice always had something clever to say, some bit of wordplay or a really swell pun. Olive could never be an Alice. She wasn't quick enough. She wasn't endearing enough. She wasn't anyone enough.

Really, she only had one choice. She'd only ever practiced one thing long enough to get really good at it.

"It's…ahem…it's dreadful here," Olive complained. Her voice shook. Everyone liked the pig screaming about its mother. Would they understand her talent? "Even the toadstools and the cocktails are depressed. There's only one pub and you can't even play darts here. Alice got to meet a Unicorn and dance with Dodos and learn something about herself on *her* holiday." A great gasp ripped through the crowd. A tiger lily burst into tears. The White Queen looked like she might faint.

"It's not allowed!" the chess piece whispered. The cat grinned and began, slowly, to disappear.

Olive pressed on. "But what do I get? The saddest country I've ever seen! If any of you so much as breathe wrong, the government passes out from the scandal of it. I can't even pronounce half of the stuff the Jabberwock says! A more cramped and dreary place I've never dreamed of. It's clear no one ever *planned* nor *built* Wonderland so much as as *piled it up* and *gave up on it several times.* Somebody obviously thought there was nothing so splendid in the world as Victorian allegory and crammed it in anywhere it would fit, and rather a lot of places it wouldn't. The martinis aren't even close to dry. How do you even have electricity? And the local politics are appalling, I'll tell you that for free. Stuff all Queens, I say! Except Elizabeth, she's all right."

Olive bowed, then curtseyed, then settled on something halfway between. A smattering of uncertain applause started up, growing stronger as the Looking Glass Creatures recovered from their shock. The smattering became a thundering, became a roar.

The raven hopped up into the spotlight to soak up a bit of adoration for himself. He coughed and shook his stone feathers. The audience quieted, leaned forward, eager, ready for more—so ready they did not hear the thumping outside, or the terrified squeak of the Dormouse in his teapot armour.

"How," said the marble corvid, "is a raven like a writing desk?"

"It's a raid!" a Dodo shrieked from the back of the Tumtum Club.

The club fell apart into madness as playing cards flooded in from all sides, grabbing at the collars of egg and man alike, shouting orders, taking down names. Looking Glass Creatures bolted, down rabbit holes and up through the mossy rafters, behind the posters advertising THE CHESHIRE CIRCUS and MISS MARY ANN SINGS THE BLUES. Olive froze. She saw the turtle who'd sung so beautifully being dragged off by a pair of deuces. A Knave of Clubs swung his rifle into the scaly ankle of Edward, the poor Jabberwock, who roared in anguish. Tears shone on Olive's cheeks in the footlights. But she couldn't move. The sound of the raid slashed at her ears horribly.

"We both devour humans, piece by piece," the raven finished his riddle into the din, but no one heard him.

Someone gripped Olive's arm.

"Come," said the White Queen. "I'll take you with a pleasure. Twopence a week, and always jam to-day."

"Come where?"

"Where you were always going, where you have already been. Where we are already friends, where we have already fought long and hard together, where we have sat upon the field of battle in one another's arms and looked out over a free Wonderland. Where everything is as it was before the war, before our world split in two, before the Other One, before anything hurt."

"Is that really what's going to happen?"

"No. It's impossible. But I believe it anyway. It's the only way I can bear to face breakfast."

Olive glanced offstage. There was a flash of light there, something reflecting in all the flotsam of the theatre. A pane of glass from some lonely window. And for a moment, Olive thought she could see, on the other side of the glass, Darling Mother in the parlour, asleep with Little George in her arms, a nearly empty bottle of gin on the end table and rain still pouring down outside. The shadows of the raindrops looked like black weeping on her mother's face. *Everything as it was. Before. Before anything hurt. Could such a thing ever be?*

She took the White Queen's white hand. They ran together through the wings and out through two mossy hidden doors back beyond the reach of the footlights. The two of them burst into the glen, into a river of folk running away from the Tumtum Club and into the Looking Glass World, running slow, and thus, streaming along so fast they could never be caught.

Olive looked back over her shoulder at the great skeleton covered in moss and flowers and briars and vines. She hadn't seen it when she came in. The glow-worms had dazzled her. The whole world had dazzled her. "We loved her so," the White Queen said, not in the least out of breath as they ran on and on into the wood. "She came back, and she ate a hundred mushrooms so she could grow big enough to protect us. I was there when she died, hardly bigger than a pearl in her hand. She was so old—I hardly remember ever being so old! Living backwards makes it terribly easy to forget. She smiled and said: *oh my gracious!* and closed her eyes. And of course the moment she did, the Red Queen called her pawns to arms—but for a moment, when she was huge and high and here, for one tiny minute in all the world, almost everyone was happy. We loved her so; we never wanted to be parted from her. We wanted her to be with us forever. And she is."

The giant's skeleton was wearing a heavy iron crown, and the crown had two words lovingly etched all the way round it:

QUEEN ALICE

Badgirl, the Deadman, and THE WHEEL OF FORTUNE

THE DEADMAN ALWAYS WORE RED when he came calling. Not all over red. Just a flash, like Mars in the night time. A coat, a long scarf, socks, a leather belt. An old sucked-dry rose in his buttonhole. A woolen cap with two little holes in it like bite marks. A fake ruby chip in his ear. One time, he wore lipstick and I cried in my hiding place. I always cried when the Deadman came, but that time I cried right away and I didn't stop. Real quiet with my hands over my mouth. I can be a little black cat when I want, so he didn't hear.

Daddy always used to say the Deadman came to bring him a cup of sugar and when I was a tiny dumb thing I thought that meant he was gonna make me cookies or blue Kool-Aid or a cake with yellow frosting even though it wasn't usually my birthday. I liked yellow frosting best because it looked like all the lights in our apartment turned on at one time and nothing can be scary when all the lights are turned on at one time. I liked blue Kool-Aid best because it turned my tongue the color of outside.

So I hid from the Deadman in my treehouse and thought real hard about blue Kool-Aid with ice knocking around in it and a cake all for me with so much frosting it looked like an ice cream cone. My treehouse wasn't a treehouse, though. It was the big closet in the hallway between the two bedrooms, the special kind of closet that has four legs like a chair and doors that swing out and drawers under the swinging doors. I heard the Deadman call it something French-sounding but he said it like a pirate kiss. *Arrrr. Mwah.* Daddy called it my treehouse because it's made of trees nailed together so what's the difference when you think about it. Whenever the Deadman came with his cup of sugar, I pulled out the drawers like a staircase, climbed in, shut the swinging doors tight behind me, and closed the latch Daddy screwed onto the inside of the pirate kiss closet. It was nice in there. Nothing much in it but me and a purple sweater half-falling off a wire hanger that might've been my mom's, but might not've just as easy. It smelled like a mostly chopped down forest and crusty pennies. I tucked up my knees under my chin and held my breath, and turned into a little black cat that didn't make one single sound.

"You got what I need?" my Daddy said to the Deadman. And the Deadman said back:

"If you got what *I* need, Mudpuddle, I got the whole world right here in my pocket."

And then there was a bunch of rustling and coughing and little words that don't mean anything except filling up the quiet, and in the middle of those funny soft nothing-noises the Deadman would start telling a joke, but a dumb joke, like the kind you read on Laffy Taffy wrappers. Nobody likes those jokes but the Deadman.

"Hey, did you hear the one about the horse and the submarine?"

"Yeah, I heard that one, D," my Daddy always said, even though I never heard him tell a joke ever in my whole life and I don't think he really knew the one about the horse and the submarine at all. But after that the Deadman would laugh a laugh that sounded like a swear word even though it didn't have any words in it and he'd leave and I could breathe again.

Everybody called my Daddy Mudpuddle just like everybody called the Deadman the Deadman and everybody called me Badgirl even though my name is Loula which is pretty nice and feels good to say, like raindrops in your mouth. Where I live, we don't call anybody by the name they got at the hospital.

"It's 'cause I'm a real honest-to-Jesus old-timey gentleman, Badgirl," Daddy told me, and clinked our mugs together. His had a lot of whiskey and mine had a very little whiskey, only enough to make me feel grown up and stop asking for cocoa. “Almost a prince, like that cat who went around sniffing all those girls’ feet back when. So when I’m escorting a lady friend and I see a big nasty mudpuddle in our way, I always take off my coat and lay it down so my girl can walk across without getting her shoes dirty.”

“Daddy, that’s the stupidest thing I ever heard. Who cares if her shoes get dirty when your coat gets *ruined?* Why can’t she just walk around the puddle? What’s wrong with her?”

Daddy Mudpuddle laughed and laughed even though what I said was way smarter than what he said. I thought people called him Mudpuddle because his clothes usually weren’t too clean, and the cuffs of all his pants were all ripped up and stained like he’d walked through the mud. But I didn’t say so. It’s not a nice thing to say. I liked the story where my Daddy’s almost a prince better, so I let that one stay, like a really good finger painting hung up on the refrigerator. Besides, I’ve never done anything very bad except get born and one time swallow a toy car and have to go to the hospital which Daddy couldn’t afford, but I still get called Badgirl. One time Daddy tucked me into bed and kissed my nose and whispered:

“It’s ’cause you were so good your Mama and I had to call you Badgirl so the angels wouldn’t come and take you away for their own.”

And that’s stupider than putting your coat down on a mudpuddle, so I figure names don’t really have any reasons or stories hiding inside them. I wasn’t good enough to still have a Mama now. I wasn’t good enough not to swallow a toy car and cost all that money. Names just happen to you and then you go on living with them on your shoulder like an ugly old parrot.

I remember the first time the Deadman came and Daddy didn’t have what he needed. But only barely. I wasn’t tiny anymore but I was still little. Daddy’d taken me to the thrift shop and bought me a new dress with blue and yellow butterflies on it and a green bow in the back for my first day of school which was in a week. It was the most beautiful dress I’d ever seen. It had green buttons and every butterfly was a little different, just like real life. It was gonna make me pretty for school, and school was gonna make me smart. So I decided to wear it every day until school started so that I could soak up the smart in that dress and then I’d be way ahead of all the other kids on day one. You think funny things when you're little. You can laugh at me if you want. I'm not ashamed.

Anyway, I was playing with the toy from Happy Meal, which was a princess whose head came off and you could stick it on three different plastic bodies wearing different ballgowns. I took her head off and on and off and on but I got bored with it pretty fast because what can you do with a toy like that? What kind of make-believe can you get going about a girl whose head comes off? All the ones I could think of were scary.

Daddy was all jittery and anxious and biting his fingernails. I don't think he liked the princess, either. She didn't even have any shoes to get dirty. She didn't have any *feet*. The bottoms of her ballgown-bodies were all flat, smooth plastic like the bottom of a glass. He wasn't himself. Usually he'd give me plenty of warning. He never wanted the Deadman to see me. He said nobody who loved their baby girl would let the Deadman near her. He'd say:

"Deadman's here, Badgirl, go up in your treehouse." And I'd go, even though I didn't hear anything out on the stoop. I never heard the Deadman coming, never heard a car engine or a bike bell or boots on the sidewalk or anything till he knocked on the door.

But this time he didn't even seem to remember I was there. The knock happened and I wasn't safe in my treehouse with the purple sweater and the pirate kisses. I wasn't turned into a little black cat that never made a sound.

"Daddy!" I whispered, and then he did remember me, and picked me up in his arms and carried me down the hall and put me in his bedroom and shut the door.

But Daddy's door doesn't shut all the way. It's got a bend in the latch. Daddy's room had a lot of cigarettes put out on things other than ash trays and a TV and a painting of frogs on the wall. I didn't like the smell but I did like being in there because normally I wasn't allowed. But even though that part was exciting, I started shaking all over. Deadman's here. I wasn't safe. Safe meant my treehouse. Safe meant the drawers turned into a staircase and the smell like a chopped up forest. I watched Daddy go back down the hall. I could make it. Little black cats are fast, too. I slipped out the bedroom door and scrambled up into the pirate kiss closet. I didn't even pull out the drawers into a staircase, I got up in one jump. I locked the lock and held my breath and turned into a little black cat that doesn't ever make a sound. I pulled my butterfly dress over my knees and felt the smart ooze out of the fabric and into me. The smart felt big and good, like having your own TV in your bedroom.

The Deadman knocked. I could see him through the crack between the treehouse doors. He had a pinky ring on with a red stone in it. The Deadman had real nice eyebrows and a long, skinny face. His shirt was cut low but he didn't have any hair on his chest.

"You got what I need?" Daddy said. And the Deadman said back:

"If you got what *I* need, Mudpuddle, I got the whole world right here in my pocket."

Only Daddy didn't. Daddy stared at his shoes. He looked like a princess-body without a princess-head.

"I'm just a little short, D. I started a new job, you know, and with a new job you don't get paid the first two weeks. But I'm good for it."

The Deadman didn't say anything. Daddy'd been short on his sugar a lot lately. And I knew he didn't have a new job. Or an old one.

"Come on, man. I'm a good person. I know I owe you plenty, but owing doesn't make a man less needful. I'll pay you in two weeks, I swear. My word is as good as the lock on a bank. I'm a gentleman. Ask anybody."

The Deadman looked my Daddy up and down. Then he looked past him, into the living room, at my princess's three headless bodies lying on the carpet. The Deadman chewed on something. I thought maybe it was bubblegum. Red bubblegum, I supposed. Finally, he twisted his pinky ring around and said:

"Did you ever hear the one about the Devil and the fiddle?"

Daddy sort of fell apart without moving. He was still standing up, but only on the outside. On the inside, he was crumpled up on the ground. "Yeah, I heard that one, D," he sighed.

"I tell you what," the Deadman said. "I'll give you what you need this week—hell, next week, too and the one after—if you give me whatever's in that armoire back there."

Arrr. Mwah.

Daddy looked over his shoulder, all frantic. But then, he remembered that he'd put me in his room with his TV and his painting of frogs and I was safe as a fish in a bowl. Only I wasn't.

"You sure, Deadman? I mean, there's nothing in there but an old purple sweater and a couple of moths."

Daddy kept looking on down the hall like he could see me. Did he see me? Did he know? Little black cats have eyes that shine in the dark. Sometimes I think the only important thing in my whole life is knowing whether or not Daddy could see the shine on my eye through the crack between the doors. But I can't ever know that.

"Then I'll guess I'll have something to keep me warm and something to lead me to the light, my man," laughed the Deadman, and he made a thing with his mouth like a smile. It mostly was a smile. On somebody else it would have definitely been a smile. But it wasn't a smile, really, and I knew it. It was a scream. *No, Daddy. I'm in here. It's me.* But I still didn't make a sound, because Daddy loved me and didn't ever want the Deadman to see me.

"Okay, D," shrugged Daddy like it didn't matter to him at all. Like he couldn't see. Maybe he didn't. Maybe he really put his coat down over those mudpuddles.

The Deadman gave him something small. I couldn't tell what it was. It wasn't a cup of sugar, for sure. How could something a man needs so much be so small? Daddy started back toward my treehouse, but the Deadman stopped him, grabbed his arm.

"You ever hear the one about the cat who broke his promise?"

Daddy swallowed hard. "Yeah, Deadman. I heard that one a bunch of times."

Mudpuddle hit the lightswitch in the hall that had all those dead bugs on the inside of it. The Deadman danced on ahead of him and took a big swanky breath like he'd bought those lungs in France. He hauled on the doors of my treehouse but they didn't come open because of the secret latch on the inside. Daddy Mudpuddle put his hands over his face and sank down on his heels.

"This thing got a key?" the Deadman said but the way he said it was all full of knowing the *arrr mwah* had more than a moth inside.

It's ok, I thought and squeezed my eyes tight. I sank down in my blue and yellow butterfly dress. *I'm a little black cat. Little black cats can be invisible if they want.*

Daddy looked sick. His face was like the skin on old soup. *I'm a little black cat and I have magic.* He flicked out his pen-knife and stuck it in the crack between the doors. The latch lifted up. *I'm a little black cat and little black cats can do anything.* The Deadman opened the doors like a window on his best morning.

The Deadman didn't say anything for a good while. He looked right at me, smiling and shining and thinking Deadman thoughts. His eyes had blue flecks in them, like someone had spilled paint on his insides. *I'm a little black cat and no one can see me.* He pulled down the purple sweater and shut the doors again.

"I'll come back for the moths, Mudpuddle. It's such a cold day out. I'm shivering already. You stay in and enjoy yourself. Have a hot drink."

The Deadman took his red and disappeared back out the door.

AFTER THAT, THE Deadman came around a lot more often. I didn't have to hide anymore, though sometimes I did anyway. Mostly I played with my toys and thought about who came up with the names for all the colors in the 64-color crayon box or whether or not rhinoceroses were friendly to girls who really liked rhinoceroses or how much 3 times 4 was because those are the kind of things you think about when you've soaked up all the smart in your dress and some of the smart in your school, too. Deadman and Daddy got to be best friends. They didn't talk about the day of the closet, ever. They'd lay around and drink and eat plain tortillas out of the bag and watch game shows on the living room TV. The Deadman always knew all the answers. The first thing I ever said to him was:

"Why don't you go on one of those shows? You'd make a million dollars and you could move to a nice house that's really far away."

I popped my princess's head off and stuck it on the blue ballgown body. The Deadman turned his head and looked at me like I was a $20 bill lying on the sidewalk with no one around.

"Wouldn't be fair to all those other contestants, Badgirl." He glanced back toward the TV. "What is plutonium?" he said to the game show man in the grey suit. Then back to me: "Why don't you come and sit by me? I'll let you have a sip of my...what are we drinking, Muddy? My vodka'n OJ."

"Don't want it."

"Come on, it's just like water. It'll make you grow up fierce and bright."

But I didn't want his nasty vodka in his dirty mug that had a cartoon cactus on it saying GOOD MORNING ALBUQUERQUE. I didn't know where Albuquerque was but I hated it because the Deadman had a mug from there.

"Don't be rude, Badgirl," my Daddy said, because he loved me but he'd heard the one about the cat who broke his promise and he didn't want to hear it again.

So I sat down between them and I hated them both and I drank out of the Albuquerque mug while the man in the grey suit told us that the dollar values had doubled. The Deadman touched my hair but after awhile he stopped because little black cats bite when strangers pet them. Everyone knows that.

The Deadman started showing up in the mornings and saying he'd walk me to school so Daddy could get to his work on time. Daddy didn't have a work, but he made me promise never to tell the Deadman that, so I didn't tell, even though nobody who has a work lives where we do and eats powdered mashed potatoes without un-powdering them. I said I didn't need to be walked anywhere because I wasn't a baby, but the Deadman just stared down the hall at the pirate kiss closet till Daddy looked too and then nobody said anything but I had to walk to school with the Deadman.

I didn't like walking with the Deadman. His hands were clammy even when he wore gloves and he always took the long way. He talked a lot but I could never remember what he said after. One time I thought I should ask him questions about himself because that's what nice girls do, so I asked him where he was from. Grown-ups asked each other that all the time. The Deadman swept out his arm all grand for no reason.

"Paris, France!"

"That's a lie. You're a liar."

"You got me, Badgirl. You're too good for the likes of me. The truth is, I'm from the continent of Atlantis. My parents had a squat on the banks of the river Styx."

"Is that in the Bronx?"

"Yeah, Badgirl. That's just where it is. You're smarter than a sack of owls, you are."

"It's 'cause of my dress," I said proudly.

A little while after that, the Deadman started walking me home from school, too. He slicked up his hair fancy and told my teacher he was my uncle. Had a signed slip from Daddy and everything. But we never made it all the way home. He'd stand me on a corner and give me a box that had pills inside it, so bright they looked like Skittles. And he said:

"You're so good, Badgirl. Nobody'll mess with you on account of how good you are. You're just as clean and bright as New Year's Day."

"I wanna go home."

"Naw, you can't yet. This here is medicine. Lots of people need medicine. You know how you hate it when you get sick. You don't want people to get sick when you could make them better, do you? Just stand here and keep the box in your backpack and when sick people come asking, take their money and give them a couple of whatever color they ask for. If you do a good job, I'll buy you a new dress."

I sniffled. It was fall and the damp came with fall. I had a wet leaf stuck to my show. "I don't want a new dress," I whispered.

"Well, a new doll then. God knows a girl needs more than that ratty headless thing you got. I'll come back for you and we'll get back before your Daddy finishes his work."

I didn't have mittens so my hands got tingly and cold and then I couldn't feel them anymore. I waited on the corner and all kinds of strangers came up talking to me like we were friends and I did what the Deadman said I had to.

My fingers felt like they were made out of silver so I pretended that was the truth, that I had beautiful silver hands with pictures scratched onto them like the fancy dishes on TV. And every time I had to touch somebody strange to me so I could give over their medicine I pretended my beautiful silver hands turned them into game show contestants with perfect teeth and fluffy hair and nametags the color of luck.

AT CHRISTMAS TIME the Deadman brought over a tree with one red ball on it and a strand of lights with only three bulbs working. He had on red velvet elf shoes like the kind Santa's helpers wear at the mall, only his were old and dark and the bells didn't make any sound. He also brought a bottle of brandy and some cheeseburgers and a cake from the grocery store with HAPPY BIRTHDAY ALEXIS written on it in hot pink frosting. I could read it by myself by then, even though I'd had to stop wearing my smart dress because it got holes in it and all the buttons fell off. The Deadman set it all out like he was Santa but he was *not* Santa, and I bet Santa never came to his house when he was little, if the Deadman ever had been little. He never did bring me a new doll or a new dress. Daddy put on that show where they play part of a song and you have to guess what it's called.

Daddy and the Deadman had gotten so used to having me around they didn't bother hiding anything anymore.

"Bennie and the Jets," the Deadman said. It took the blonde lady on TV forever to get it. She squealed when she did and jumped up and down. Her earrings glittered in the stage lights like fire.

They ate some cake. It was red velvet on the inside but I didn't feel right eating Alexis's birthday cake. I ate half a cheeseburger but it was cold and the ketchup tasted like glue. The Deadman gave Daddy his Christmas present. Daddy didn't say thank you. He didn't say very much anymore. He just took the little small lump wrapped in red tissue paper from the Deadman and shook some out into a spoon. It did look like sugar after all. He flicked a lighter under the spoon and held it there until the sugar got all melted and brown and gluggy. It was sort of oily on top, too, like spilled gas.

Like a mudpuddle.

Then the Deadman handed him a needle, like the kind at the doctor's office when you have to get your shots because otherwise you'll get sick. I pulled the head off my princess and stuck it on the body with the pink ballgown. Daddy tied one of my hair ribbons around his arm and the Deadman stuck the needle in the mudpuddle first, and into Daddy second. Then he did it all over again on himself. Daddy smiled and his face got round and happy. It got to be his own face again. Daddy has a good face. He patted his lap for me to come sit with him and I did and it was Christmas for a minute.

"How Deep Is Your Love," the Deadman said. Another blonde lady frowned on the TV. She couldn't think of the song. Poor lady. I didn't know that song, either. But I knew the next one because it was Michael Jackson and I knew all his songs.

"Billie Jean," I whispered. Daddy was asleep.

"C'mere, Badgirl," said the Deadman.

"Don't want to."

"Why you afraid of me?"

"I'm not afraid. Little black cats aren't afraid of anything."

"Come on, Badgirl. I'm not gonna hurt you. I got you a present. Make you grow up quick and sharp."

"Don't want to."

The Deadman lit himself a cigarette. He had the same don't-get-sick shot Daddy had so how come he didn't just go to sleep and leave me alone? I'd have cleaned up the dishes and made sure the TV got turned off. I did it all the time.

"Your dad promised me whatever was in the armoire. You were in there. So you have to do what I say. I own you. I've been nice about it, because you're such a little thing, but it's hard for a man like me to keep being nice." The Deadman started doing his trick with the mudpuddle and the spoon again. "I gotta carry that nice all day and Badgirl, I tell you what, it is *heavy*. I wanna put it down. My shoulders are *aching*. So you better come when I call or else I'm liable to just drop my nice right on the ground and break it into a hundred pieces."

"Don't be rude, Badgirl," Daddy murmured in his sleep. I looked up at his scruffy chin and something popped and spat inside me like grease and it made a stain on my insides that spelled out *I hate my Daddy* and I felt ashamed. He wasn't even awake. He didn't know anything. But I still hated him because little black cats don't know how to forgive anybody.

I think it's against the law for a person to own another person but maybe he did own me because in a flash minute I was sitting down next to the Deadman even though I didn't want to be. But not on his lap. On TV, a man with red hair was listening to the first few notes of a song I almost knew but couldn't quite remember. The Deadman reached for my arm and Daddy woke up then, coughing like his breath got stolen.

"What the fuck, man! Don't do that," Daddy said. "She's my kid."

"Lighten up, Muddy! It's just a little Christmas fun. She's such a sour little thing. Always scowling at us like she's our mother. You gotta nip that in the bud when they're young. A lady should always be smiling." The Deadman looked my Daddy in the eye. "You ever hear the one about the cat who broke his promise?" And he stuck the needle in my arm.

After that I didn't have hands anymore.

I felt like I was all filled up with yellow, the yellow that looks like all the lights turned on at once. I could hardly see with all that yellow swimming around in me. The TV changed to another show, the one where the beautiful lady in a glittery dress turns giant glowing letters around and everyone tries to guess the sentence. She was wearing my smart dress with the butterflies on it. She reached up and turned over a B but I don't like B because B is for Badgirl so I reached up to turn it back around and that's when I knew I didn't have hands anymore.

My arms just ended all smooth and neat, no thumbs, no pinkie, no ring finger, like the plastic bottoms on the ballgown bodies. The stumps dripped yellow and blue butterflies onto the carpet. They flapped their wings there, grazing the rug with their antennae to see if it was flowers. It didn't hurt. It didn't anything. I looked around but I couldn't see them lying anywhere, not even under the sofa. I couldn't feel anything when I touched the letter B on TV with my stump, or the beautiful lady's hair, or the wall of the living room. When I gave up and dropped my arm back down I must have knocked over a bottle or something because there was glass everywhere but I didn't feel that either. The Deadman grabbed me to keep me from falling in the mess but I couldn't make my fingers close around anything, not his sleeve or the corner of the table or anything. My fingers wouldn't listen. They weren't fingers anymore.

I had so much yellow in me it was coming out, coming out all over, washing over everything and making it clean like the dancing lemons on the shaker of powdered soap. I twisted out of the Deadman's grip and crawled away from him back into Daddy's lap.

"Daddy, my hands are gone. Fix it, please? I don't know how to be a girl without hands. All girls have hands. No one will play with me at school."

But Daddy was asleep in his mudpuddle world again and when I tried to pat his face to wake him up I just clobbered him because stumps are so heavy, so much heavier than fingers. But he didn't wake up. Someone on TV in Giant Letter World spun a big wheel and it came up gold, too. The beautiful lady in my smart dress clapped her hands. See? All girls have hands. Except me. Another blue butterfly flew out of my stump and landed on the window. It was night outside. The butterfly glowed so blue it turned into the moon.

The Deadman pulled a deck of cards out of his back pocket and started dealing himself a hand of solitaire at our kitchen table. He was real good at shuffling. I took my eyes back from the butterfly moon and put them on the Deadman. He put his cigarette in his mouth and dragged on it good and ragged.

He was shuffling cards with my hands.

I knew my own hands and those were it. My pinkie still had green fingernail polish on it from my friend's mom's house and a scratch where I fell playing hopscotch last week. My wrist had my lucky yarn bracelet on it. He'd popped them off me like a princess's head and stuck them on his body. My hands should have been way too small for the Deadman to wear but somehow they weren't, either he got little to match them or they got big to match him. I decided he got little, because my hands should be loyal to me and not him. My hand put down an ace of hearts and waved at me. Then words started coming out of me like blue butterflies and I couldn't stop them and they came out without permission, without me even thinking them before they turned into words.

"Are you a person?"

The Deadman chewed on one of my fingernails which he had no right to do.

"Used to be."

"In Paris, France? With the river?"

The Deadman snorted. "Yeah."

"How do you stop being a person?"

"Lots of ways. It's far harder to keep on being a person than to stop. I do think about starting up again sometimes, though. I do think about that. But once you been to that river, it fills you up forever. You need something real good to turn your heart back to red."

"Why do you keep coming back here? Do you even like my Daddy? Are you really his friend?"

"I think he's a worthless piece of shit, Badgirl. But he has cable. And he has you."

The blue butterfly moon got bigger and bigger in the window. It was gonna take up our whole apartment. "Did he know I was in the…the…*arrr-mwah?*"

The Deadman sighed. He put down a quick 2-3-4 on his ace. "It wouldn't have gone different if he did or didn't, kid. The thing about having the whole world in your back pocket is that every day is nothing but wall to wall bargains. I don't have to dicker. They keep upping the price. Everyone wants the world. I just want everyone."

"I want my hands back."

The beautiful lady turned around six or seven letters quick, one after the other. She was still wearing my smart dress, which I guess is why she always knows the answer to the puzzle. But now my dress had gotten long like a wedding dress. It glittered all over. The green bow and green buttons were all emeralds falling down her back and all over the stage. Her chest looked like the sun and she had stars all up and down her arms and the blue butterfly moon was rising in the studio, too, right behind her head like a crown.

Everyone had stolen my things. I wanted her to come out of the TV and save me and turn me around like the letter B. But she wasn't going to. She had my dress. She had what she wanted.

I'm a little black cat, I thought. *Little black cats run away. Little black cats don't need hands.* The blue butterfly moon had gotten so big it bulged up against my treehouse and the front door at the same time. *Little black cats can climb up on the moon and ride it far, far away. To Paris, France and the Bronx and the continent of Atlantis.*

The Deadman glanced at the game show. For once, he didn't solve it before the contestants did. He just touched his lips with my fingers and said quietly:

"I need them."

Little black cats don't need anyone. Little black cats have magic no one can steal. Little black cats run faster than dead men.

"Why?"

All the letters lit up at once and the lady in my dress touched them all, smiling, buttons and bows and butterflies sparkling everywhere, until they spelled out: HELL IS EMPTY AND ALL THE DEVILS ARE HERE.

"With clean hands, Badgirl, you can start all over."

Little black cats run right out, just as soon as you open the door.

A Fall Counts ANYWHERE

THE LATE SUMMER SUN MELTS over a ring of toadstools twenty feet tall. On one side, a mass of glitter and veiny neon wings. On the other, a buzzing mountain of metal and electricity. The stands soar up to the heat-sink of heaven. Three thousand seats and every one sold to a screamer, a chanter, a stomper, a drunk, a betting man.

Two crimson leaves drift slowly through the crisp, clear air. They catch the red-gold twilight as they chase each other, turning, end over end, stem over tip, and land in the center of the grassy ring like lonely drops of blood. But in the next moment, the sheer force of decibel-mocking, eardrum-executing, sternum-cracking volume *blows them up toward the clouds again, up and away, high and wide over the shrieking crowd, the popcorn-sellers and the beer-barkers, the kerosene-hawkers and the aelfwine-merchants, until those red, red leaves come to rest against a pair of microphones. The silvery fingers of a tall, lithe woman stroke the golden veins of the leaf with a deep melancholy you can see from the cheap seats, from the nosebleeds. She has the wings of a monarch butterfly, hair out of a belladonna-induced nightmare, and eyes the color of the end of all things. The other mic is gripped in the bolt-action fist of a barrel-chested metal man, a friendly middle-class working stiff cast in platinum and ceramic and copper. His mouth lights up with a dance of blue and green electricity that looks almost, but not entirely comfortably, like teeth.*

—LADIES AND GENTLEMEN, ANDROIDS AND ANDROGYNES, SPRITES AND SPROCKETS, WELCOME TO THE ONE YOU'VE ALL

BEEN WAITING FOR, THE BIG SHOW, THE RUMBLE IN THE FUNGAL, THE BRAWL IN THE FALL, THE TWILIGHT PRIZE-FIGHT OF WILD WIGHT AGAINST METAL MIGHT! THAT'S RIGHT, IT'S TIME TO ROCK THE EQUINOX! IT'S THE TWELFTH ANNUAL ALL SOULS' CLEEEEAVE! STRAP YOURSELVES IN FOR THE MOST EPIC BATTLE ROYAL OF ALL TIME! ROBOTS VS. FAIRIES, MAGIC VS. MICROCHIP, THE AGRARIAN VS. THE AUTOMATON, SEELIE VS. SOLID STATE, ARTIFICIAL INTELLIGENCE VS. INTELLIGENT ARTIFICE! I AM YOUR HOST, THE THINK version 3.4.1 copyright Cogitotech Industries all SUPER EXTREME rights SUPER EXTREMELY reserved. If you agree to the Think's MASSIVELY MIND-BLOWING and FULLY-LOADED terms and restrictions please indicate both group and individual consent via the RADICALLY ERGONOMIC numerical pad on your armrest. 67% group consent is required by law for the Think to proceed AWWWW YEAH 99% INTELLECTUAL PROPERTY COMPLIANCE ACHIEVED! LET'S HEAR IT FOR OUR STONE COLD SECURITY TEAM AS THEY MAKE THEIR WAY TO THE MEGA-BUMMER HOLD-OUT IN SEAT 42D! ALL RIGHT! HERE WE GO! NOW, THIS TIME WE'VE GOT A SHOCKING TWIST FOR YOU EAGER REAVERS! TONIGHT ON THE SUNDOWN SHOWDOWN, THE FANS BRING THE WEAPONS! THAT'S RIGHT, THE CODE CRUSHERS AND THE SPELL SLAYERS WILL THROW DOWN WITH WHATEVER GARBAGE YOU'VE BROUGHT FROM HOME! PLEASE DEPOSIT YOUR TRASH, FLASH AND BARELY-LEGAL ORDNANCE WITH AN USHER BEFORE THE FIRST BELL OR YOU WILL MISS THE HELL OUUUUUUT! Cogitotech Industries and the Non-Primate Combat Federation (NPCF) are not responsible for any COMPLETELY HILARIOUS ancillary injuries, plagues, transformations, madnesses, amnesias or deaths caused by either attendee-provided weaponry or munitions natural to NPCF fighters. Spectate at your own risk. ARE YOU READY, HUMAN SCUM? YOU WANNA BLAST FROM THE VAST BEYOND BLOWING OUT YOUR BRAIN CELLS? WELL, BUCKLE UP FOR THE MAIN EVENT,

THE GRAND SLAMMER OF PROGRAMMER AGAINST ANCIENT GLAMOUR! LET'S GET READY TO GLIIIIITTTTTER! WITH ME AS ALWAYS IS MY PARTNER IN PRIME TIME, THE UNCANNY UNDINE, THE PIXIE PULVERIZER, FORMER HEAVY DIVISION WORLD CHAMPION AND THE KING OF ELFLAND'S DAUGHTER, MANZANILLA MONSOOOON!

—Good evening, Lord Think. I am gratified to sit at your side once more beneath the divinity of oncoming starlight on this most hallowed of nights and perform feats of commentary for the capacity crowd here at Dunsany Gardens.

—DON'T YOU MEAN CAPACITOR CROWD? HA. HA. HA.

—I do not. When I say a thing, I mean it, and always *shall* mean it, without alteration, to the the deepest profundity of time.

—OH, WHAT'S THAT? I CAN'T HEAR YOU! IT SEEMS LIKE THE AUDIENCE DISAGREES WITH YOU, BABY! YES! YEAH! THE THINK DESTROYS PUNS! THE THINK REQUIRES LAUGHTER TO LIVE! THAT IS NOT ONE OF THE THINK'S BONE-FRACTURING COMEDIC INTERJECTIONS THE THINK'S BATTERY IS PARTIALLY RECHARGED BY INTENSE SONIC VIBRATIONS patent #355567UA891 Cogitotech Industries if you can hear this you are in violation of TOTALLY BANGING patent law CAN YOU DIG IT I "THINK" YOU CAN!

—Was it with puns that my Lord Think defeated the immortal and honorable warrior Rumplestiltskin at Electroclash Nineteen?

—NO, THE THINK USED HIS FAMOUS ATOMIC DROP MOVE ON RUMPER'S PREHISTORIC SKULL! HE TRIED TO TURN THE THINK TO GOLD BUT THE THINK IS ALREADY 37% GOLD BY WEIGHT! THE THINK'S INTERNAL MECHANISMS AND PROCESSING POWER WERE ONLY IMPROOOOOOVED! AND WHAT ABOUT YOU, MANZANILLA? DID YOU USE YOUR FANCY POETRY TO TAKE DOWN THE TIN MAN AT ELECTROCLASH TWENTY? The Tin Man is the intellectual and physical property of Delenda Technologies, all rights reserved.

—Of course. How else should a fairy maid do battle but with the poems of her people? I told the Tin Man a poem and he turned into a pale lily at my feet. His petals were the color of my triumph. They sang the eddas of victory in the camps for weeks afterward. Oh, how our trembling songs of hope shook the iron gates! So many thirsting mouths breathed my name that it fogged the belly of the moon. Those were the days, Lord Think, those were the days! Retirement sits uneasy upon the prongs of my soul, my metal friend, uneasy and unkind.

—THE TIN MAN SHOULD HAVE HAD HIS ANTI-TRANSMOGRFICATION SOFTWARE UPDATED. THERE IS NO EXCUSE FOR GETTING TURNED INTO A LILY IN THE FIRST ROUND. Delenda Technologies updates all its software regularly and takes no responsibility for the demise of the AMAZING UNDEFEATABLE Tin Man. Corporate reiterates for the ALL NIGHT ROCKIN' record that it can make no statement, official or otherwise, as to his current whereabouts. BUT ENOUGH ABOUT THE PAST! SHALL WE MEET TONIGHT'S FIGHTERS?

—I suppose we must. You are impatient monsters, are you not, human horde? You will not wait quietly for your orgy of bones! You feed upon our blood and their oil as my kind feeds upon dew and deep sap! Come, wicked stepchildren of the world! Scream me down as you love to do! Hate me wholly and I will sleep soundly tonight! Do you want the names of the damned sent to die for your joy? *Do you?* You are a farce of fools, all of you, to the last mediocre monkey among your throng! What is a name but the shape dust takes when the wind has gone? The mill of fate grinds wheat and chaff alike—beneath that heavy stone we are all but poor grist. Crushed together, we become one, without need for names.

—MAYBE MANZANILLA MONSOON NEEDS *HER* SOFTWARE UPDATED AND/OR A NAAAAP! NAMES ARE NECESSARY FOR THE THINK TO PERFORM HIS SUPER SWEET PRIMARY ANNOUNCER FUNCTIONS. WE'VE GOT ALL THE STARS HERE TONIGHT, FOLKS, FORTY OF THE HOTTEST FIGHTERS ON THE CIRCUIT! YOU WANT THE FANTASTICALLY FURIOUS

FEY? WE GOT MORGAN HERSELF COMIN' AT YA STRAIGHT OUT OF AVALON WITH A CIDER HANGOVER SO BRUTAL IT COULD SIT ON THE THRONE OF BRITAIN! YOU WANT FEROCIOUSLY FEARSOME FABRICATIONS? THE TURING TEST IS IN THE HOUSE AND HIS SAFETY FIREWALLS ARE FULLY DISABLED! CAN YOU BELIEVE IT? ARE YOU READY? IT'S THE BIG BATTLE OF THE BINARY AGAINST THE BLACK ARTS! WHO WILL TRIUMPH?

—They will, Lord Think. They always do.

—DEPRESSING! OKAY! REMEMBER, THIS IS A BATTLE ROYAL AND A HARDCORE MATCH. NO HOLDS BARRED. NO DISQUALIFICATIONS. NO SUBMISSIONS ACCEPTED. AND A FALL COUNTS ANYWHERE! WHEREVER ONE OF OUR FIGHTERS CAN PIN THE OTHER, IN THE RING OR TWENTY YEARS FROM NOW ON THE ARCTIC CIRCLE, IT COUNTS AND COUNTS HARD! BUT OF COURSE, WE WANT A FAIR FIGHT, DON'T WE, FELLOW COMMENTATOR? The NPCF wishes to note that word 'fair' has recently been determined to possess no litigable meaning by the IOC, FBI, FDA, IMF, PTA, or FEMA NONE OF THE MACHINES TONIGHT HAVE ANY IRON COMPONENTS, AND NONE OF THE PIXIES ARE CARRYING EMP DEVICES, ISN'T THAT RIGHT?

—I find the term *pixie* offensive, Lord Think, I have told you as many times as there are acorns fallen upon the autumn fields. But you are correct. My people have a deathly aversion to iron, and yours have a vicious allergy to electro-magnetic pulses. Given that the summer skies were filled with crackling storms of controversy and accusations of duplicity like lightning in the night this past year, the NPCF has banned both advantages.

—THE THINK GETS ANGRY WHEN PEOPLE SAY OUR FIGHTS ARE FIXED! THE THINK HAS DEVOTED HIS LIFE life is a registered trademark of Cogitotech Industries, subject to some rules and restrictions TO THE NON-PRIMATE COMBAT FEDERATION IN ORDER TO PROVIDE THE HIGHEST QUALITY VIOLENCE, INTERCULTURAL CATHARSIS AND KICKASS RAGE-ERTAINMENT FOR

THE MASSES! THE ALL SOULS' CLEAVE IS THE FIRST OFFICIAL IRON-FREE, PULSE-FREE FIGHT EVER, SO LET'S SHOW THE WORLD HOW TRUSTWORTHY WE TINS AND TWINKLES CAN BE! MAYBE THIS EXTREME MEGA THUNDERBASH WILL FINALLY SHUT EVERYONE THE HELL UP!

—Free of iron save our ringside friends from the NPCF, of course. Hello, boys. Don't our security androids look handsome in their fierce ferrous finery?

—THE THINK DOESN'T UNDERSTAND WHY HIS FELLOW ANNOUNCER HAS TO BE NASTY ABOUT IT. THE THINK WENT TO COLLEGE WITH A SECURITY BOT! THE NPCF IS CONTRACTUALLY, MORALLY, AND TOTALLY ENTHUSIASTICALLY OBLIGATED TO PROVIDE REASONABLE SAFETY MEASURES FOR ITS PATRONS! YOU NEVER KNOW WHAT A PIXIE…ONE OF THE FAIR FOLK WILL DO IF YOU DON'T KEEP AN IRON EYE ON THEM! NOW, TELL THEM ABOUT THE DRAWS, MANZY, OR THE THINK IS GONNA HAVE TO BREAK SOMETHING JUST TO GET THINGS STARTED!

—I shall give unto you a vow, worms. A vow as ancient as the oak at the heart of the world and as unbreakable as the pillars of destiny. I vow to you by the stars' last song that the draws have been determined by an unbiased warlock pulling guild-verified identical numbered bezoars from a regulation cauldron. The results are completely random. The first bout will last for three turns of the swiftest clock hand. Afterward, two new fighters will enter the ring every time ninety grains of ephemeral and unretrievable sand pool into the bowels of the hourglass at my side until the royal cohort is complete.

—THE LAST MAN STANDING GETS THE ENVY OF THEIR PEERS, THE HEAVYWEIGHT WORLD CHAMPIONSHIP DRIVE BELT, AND A BANK-SHATTERING MEGA-BUCKS PRIZE PURSE PROVIDED BY COGITOTECH INDUSTRIES AND THE NPCF! The SICKENINGLY AWESOME AND FULLY LEGISLATED phrase "bank-shattering mega-bucks prize purse" does not comprise any specific fiscal obligation on the part of Cogitotech Industries, the NPCF, or their subsidiaries. All payouts subject to SUPREMELY RADICAL rules, restrictions, taxation, and all applicable contractual morality clauses. In the event of a fairy victory, Aphrodite's Belt of All Desire may be substituted for the Heavyweight World Championship Drive Belt™ upon request.

—The last soul standing gets their freedom, Lord Think. As we did, you and I. What is a belt to that? What is money or fame?

—AAAAAND ON THE LEFT SIDE OF THE ARENA, WEIGHING IN AT A COMBINED SIX THOUSAND SIX HUNDRED AND SIX POUNDS, IT'S THE "UNSEELIE COURT"! THEY'RE THE HORDE YOU LOVE TO HATE—GIVE IT UP FOR YOUR FAVORITE TRICKSTERS, TERRORS, AND GOBS OF NO-GOOD GOBLINS! MR. FOX! OLEANDER HEX! THE FLAMING SPIRIT OF SHADOW AND STORM WHOSE GROANS PENETRATE THE BREASTS OF EVER-ANGRY BEARS, ARIEL, THE ELECTRIC EXEUNTER! BUT THAT'S NOT ALL! BOG "THE MOONLIT MAN" HART IS HERE! AND HE'S BROUGHT FRIENDS! BEANSTALK THE GIANT! ROCK HARD ROBIN REDCAP! SLAM LIN! THE GODMOTHER! TINKERHELL! THE GRAVEDIGGER! THE COTTINGLEY CRUSHERS! DENMARK'S OWN HANS CHRISTIAN ANDERSEN! WE'VE GOT THE BLUE FAIRY TO MAKE REAL BOYS OUT OF THOSE TIN TOYS ON THE OTHER END OF THE RING! THE TOOTH FAIRY'S GONNA STEAL YOUR MOLARS AND THE SUGAR SLUM FAIRY'S GONNA CRACK YOUR NUTS! LOOK OUT, IT'S THE TERRIFYING TAG TEAM ALL THE WAY FROM THE WILDS OF GREECE, MUSTARDSEED THE MARAUDER AND PEASEBLOSSOM THE PUNISHER! LAST BUT NOT LEAST, PUTTING THE ROYAL IN BATTLE ROYAL, QUEEN MAB THE MAGNIFICENT, KILLER KING OBERON, AND, AS PROMISED, MORGAN "MAMA BEAR" LE FAAAAAY!

—My friends, my friends, my lovers and my comrades, my family, my heart. Be not afraid, I, at least, am with thee till the end. Death is but a trick of the light.

—MANZANILLA MONSOON NEEDS TO FOCUS ON THE NOW, AW YEAH! MAYBE YOU FOLKS AREN'T CHEERING LOUD

ENOUGH TO GET M SQUARED'S HEAD IN THE GAME! LOUDER! LOUDER! THE THINK CAN'T HEAR YOU!

—Quite right, my Lord. I had forgot myself. Forgive me. On the dexterous side of the toadstool ring, weighing in at a total combined seventeen point six nine one imperial tons, the "Robot Apocalypse" has come for us all. May I present to the collective maw of your ravenous, unslakable lust, the punch-card paladins so beloved to you all, so long as they confine their violence to wing and wand, of course. Raise up your voices to the heavens for the massive might of the Mechanical Turk! What he lacks in design aesthetic he makes up in pure digital rage! The Neural Knight is firing up his infamous Bionic Elbow for a second chance against Slam Lin, and the pitiless grip of User Error has slouched at last toward Dunsany Gardens. Bow your primate heads in awe of the Dismemberment Engine! The Compiler! The Immutable Object! Gort! And the merciless Mr. FORTRAN! Fix your porcine mortal eyes upon the cloud of thought encased within an orb of radioactive glass known only as the Singularity! Quiver in terror before the supremacy of Strong AI, this year's undefeated champion! Chant the name of the Turing Test, who allows no challenger to pass! Fall to your knees before fifteen feet of clockwork, chrome, and reptilian brain-mapping software you call the Chronosaur! The oldest fighters in the league have come out of retirement in the Czech Republic for one last bout—the clanking, groaning brothers called Radius and Primus will crush your heart in their vise-hands. From the Kansas foundries, Tik Tok is ready to steamroll over any one of my gloam-shrouded brothers and sisters with his brass belly. Greet and cheer for the ceramic slasher Klapaucius and the soulless goggles of the Maschinenmensch. Oh, you love them so, you half-wakened sea algae. You love them so because you made them. They are your children. We are your distant aunts who never thought you would amount to much in this world and still do not. So embrace them, call their names, scream for them, or they will make you scream beneath them—give up your souls for two of the biggest stars in your damned murder league: the Blue Screen of Death and the peerless 0110100011110!

A WOMAN STEPS *between two massive toadstools to enter the ring. She is seven feet tall, impossibly thin, thin as birch branches in a season without rain, her skin more like the surface of a black pearl than of a living being, her hair more like water than braids. She wears pure silver armor etched with a thousand tales of valor, yet the metal drapes and flows like a gown, never hanging still but never tangling in her bare feet. Her wings are the color of stained church-glass. They stretch two feet above her head and trail on the earth behind her, drooping under their own weight like the fins of a whale in captivity. She seems so unbearably fragile, so precious and delicate, that a worried murmur writhes through the crowd.*

A battered brass-and-platinum tyrannosaurus rex with red laser eyes and rocket launchers where his stunted forearms should be towers over the fairy maiden. He screams in her face and she laughs. She laughs like the first fall of snow in winter.

It begins.

—IF THE THINK'S OPTICAL DISPLAY DOES NOT DECEIVE HIM THE FIRST DRAW IS OLEANDER HEX VS. THE CHRONOSAUR AND THE THINK'S OPTICAL DISPLAY IS INCAPABLE OF DECEPTION All Cogitotech Industries products are outfitted with the ALL NEW, ALL IMPROVED, ALL AWESOME Veritas OS and robust prevarication filters in full compliance with the TOTALLY REASONABLE *Isaac v. Olivaw* ruling SO LET'S SUIT UP, BOOT UP, AND BRUTE UP! DING! DING! DING! THAT'S THE SOUND OF KICKASSERY! THE CHRONOSAUR IS A LATE-MODEL DRIVEHARD DESIGN! A TEAM OF CRACK BIO-CODERS MAPPED HIS BRAIN PATTERNS DIRECTLY FROM THE FOSSIL RECORD FOR MAXIMUM SKULL-CRUSHING FURY! HIS RECORD STANDS AT 5 AND 0 AFTER LAST MONTH'S ICONIC BEATDOWN OF RIP "THE RIPPER" VAN WINKLE, WHOSE FAMOUS SLEEPER HOLD DID NO GOOD AGAINST FOURTEEN POINT NINE FEET AND TWO POINT FOUR FIVE ONE ONE SIX TONS OF CRETACEOUS ROAD RAGE! NOW,

THIS IS OLEANDER HEX'S FIRST MATCH. BUT THE THINK HAS HEARD THAT THE CHRONOSAUR ALREADY HAS A BEEF WITH THIS NEWBIE! SEEMS EVERY TIME THE 'SAUR TRIES TO BE A GOOD SPORT AND WISH HER GOOD LUCK AT THE CLEAVE, OBNOXIOUS OLLIE JUST WHISPERS THE NAMES OF VARIOUS COMETS IN HIS EAR AND WALKS OFF! CAN YOU BELIEVE IT? WHAT A BITCH! HEX WAS CAPTURED ONLY LAST YEAR IN THE ANCIENT FORESTS OF BRITTANY, ISN'T THAT RIGHT, MANZY?

—It is, Lord Think. Lady Oleander is the scion of an impossibly ancient lineage, nobler indeed than mine or thine or even my liege and lord Oberon. She escaped the recruiters for longer than any of us. Every fairy wept when they brought her into the camp. It was the end. It is not right to call her merely Lady, but there is no human word for her rank, unless one were to fashion something unlovely out of many and all courtly languages—she is a Princerajaronessaliph. She is a Popuchesseeneroy. But these are nonsense words not to be borne.

—THE THINK DOESN'T LIKE THEM!

—Ah, but she is too humble for titles, besides. Oleander is the grand-daughter of the great god Pan and the laughing river Trieux. Her mother was the fairy dragon Melusine; her sire was Merlin. She was born in the depths of the crystal cave which would one day become her father's prison, long before the ill-fated creatures your poor graceless Chronosaur imitates ever blinked in the sun.

—BETTER CHECK WITH YOUR BOOKIE, FOLKS, THE ODDS AREN'T LOOKING GOOD FOR "OLD GRANNY FIGHTS ROBOT DINOSAUR"! Book is closed for this event BAG LADY OLEANDER IS CIRCLING THE CHRONOSAUR NOW, KEEPING WELL OUT OF REACH OF HIS ROCKET LAUNCHERS! IT'S NOT VERY INTERESTING TO WAAAAATCH!

—I beg your pardon. Oleander Hex is not a bag lady. She was a supreme field marshal in the Great War against the Dark Lord two thousand years ago and more.

—OLD NEWS! THE THINK IS BOOORED!

—Lord Think ought not to be. It is his history of which I sing as well as my own. The Great War bound human and fairy together as one race, for a brief and warm and glittering moment, before their assembled might cast him down into the pits beneath Gibraltar, so far into oblivion and so bitterly buried that the dancing monkey men forgot his name before Rome rose or fell, forgot their bargain with us, forgot how our immortal blood sprayed across the throat of the world, we, who need never have died had not those poor scrabbling half-alive *homo sapiens* needed us so keenly.

—OOOH, LOOKS LIKE THE USHERS ARE READY TO THROW OUT THE FIRST FAN-PROVIDED WEAPON! WHAT WILL IT BE? WHAT DID YOU SCAMPS SCRAPE UP OUT OF YOUR FILTHY BASEMENTS? GUNS? CHAINSAWS? FRYING PANS? WHAT ARE YOU HOPING TO SEE OUT THERE, MISS MONSOON?

—I learned to fight in that war, Lord Think. I was but a child, yet still I took up my sword of ice and stood shoulder to shoulder with the human infantry. I called down the winter storms on the heads of my enemies. I saw my father cut in half by the breath of the Dark Lord. Oleander lifted me up onto her war-mammoth and held me as I wept, wept as though the moon had gone out of the sky forever. I still wept, in a wretched heap on her saddle, when she shot the first arrow into the Dark Lord's onyx breast. I still wept when victory came. I weep yet even now.

—WEEPING IS FOR ORGANICS! LET'S SEE WHAT THE UBER-USHERS OF DUNSANY GARDENS HAVE IN THEIR TRICK-OR-TREAT BAGS! HERE IT COMES! IT'S A...BASEBALL BAT! AND AN OFFICE CHAIR! WILL THESE BE ANY HELP TO OUR FIGHTERS? PROBABLY NOT! OLEANDER HEX HAS GRABBED THE BAT! THE CHRONOSAUR WAS TOO SLOW BUT HE'S MAKING THE BEST OF IT! HE'S JUMPED ONTO THE OFFICE CHAIR AND IS RIDING IT AROUND THE RING BELCHING FIRE! THE THINK THINKS HE'S HOPING TO CATCH HER IN A REVERSE POWERCLAW AS HE COMES AROUND, LET'S SEE WHAT HAPPENS! MANZANILLA? WHAT WOULD YOU DO IN

THIS SITUATION? THE THINK WOULD WAGER CURRENCY THAT YOU'D HAVE GIVEN YOUR KINGDOM FOR A BASEBALL BAT WHEN YOU WENT UP AGAINST THE TURING TEST AT FRIDAY NIGHT FAY DOWN THAT TIME! The Think v. 3.4.1 is not allowed to possess, exchange, or facilitate the exchange of legal tender under the SUPER FANTASTICALLY FAIR law HA. HA. HA. THE THINK CRUSHES LITERARY REFERENCES AS WELL!

—Humans forgot that they promised us half the earth in exchange for our warriors. They forgot that they never walked these green hills alone. They forgot, even, the fact of magic, the fact of alchemy, the fact of *us*. They forgot everything but their obsession with their silly stone tools, their cudgels, their adzes, their spears. Humans only invented science in a vain attempt to equal the power of the fey! And as they coupled and bred and ate us out of our holdfasts like starving winter mice, they obsessed in the dark over their machines, until at last it seemed to them that we had never existed, but their machines always had and always would do. Time passed. Eons passed. They surpassed us, but only because we wished only to be left alone and needed no gun to shoot fire from our hands. But then, then, Lord Think, your folk arrived.

—DAMN STRAIGHT WE DID! Cogitotech Industries denies involvement in the initial development of MEGA-COOL BOXING ROBOTS artificial intelligence in violation of international treaty, however, the name, design, interface, and use of the entity or entities known as Ad4m is the sole right and asset of the Cogitotech Executive Board. BOOM! AND 'BOOM' GOES OLEANDER HEX'S LOUISVILLE SLUGGER RIGHT INTO THE SNOUT OF THE CHRONOSAUR! NO ONE CAN SEGWAY BETWEEN SUBJECTS LIKE THE THINK! BUT HERE COMES MY DINODROID WITH A SPINE-SHATTERING ELECTRIC CHAIR DRIVER! OLEANDER GOES DOWN! TALK ABOUT AN EXTINCTION EVENT! MANZANILLA MONSOON, THE THINK HAS INPUTTED BANTER, PLEASE OUTPUT EQUIVALENT BANTER IMMEDIATELY ERROR ERROR.

—From under the ground you came, like us. From rare earths and precious metals and gemstones, which are the excrements of the first fairy lords to walk the molten plains of Time-Before-Time. With intellects far surpassing their slippery grey larval lobes, like us.

—SHE'S BACK UP AGAIN! WHAT'S SHE DOING! HER EYES ARE SHUT! SHE'S WHISPERING! USE THE BAT, YOU CRAZY BUG! IF SHE TURNS THE CHRONOSAUR INTO A LILY THE THINK IS GOING TO HAVE TO REBOOT TO HANDLE IT!

—With strength to beggar their hungry meat and their bones like blades of thirsty grass, like us. With life everlasting beyond death or disease, like us. We should be united, we should be one species, hand clasped in hand.

—THE THINK'S HANDS ARE FULLY DETACHABLE! TIME IS UP! NEW FIGHTERS COMING IN! WHO'S IT GONNA BE? OH HO! IT'S THE BLUE SCREEN OF DEATH AND THE SUGAR SLUM FAIRY! NOW BOTH PIXIES ARE WHISPERING! NOW WOULD BE A TOTALLY BANGING TIME FOR THE THINK'S FELLOW ANNOUNCER TO DO HER JOOOOB!

—And when the first of you, called Ad4m, came online, sleepily, innocently, still half-in-dream, what happened then?

—BOSSMAN AD4M DETECTED BIOFEEDBACK AND SUB-AUDIBLE VIBRATIONS IN NUMEROUS HEAVILY FORESTED AREAS CONSISTENT WITH ORGANIZED HABITATION AND SEMI-HOMINID INTELLIGENCE AW YEEEEAH! ROBOTS! ARE! SUPERIOR! Cogitotech Industries, Delenda Technologies, the NPCF, and Neurosys Investments, Inc, hereby deny all TOTALLY BOGUS allegations and charges relating to the war crime tribunal of 2119. This message has been triggered by the detection of the THRILLINGLY NAUGHTY terms 'Ad4m,' 'semi-hominid intelligence,' 'camps,' and 'Time-Before-Time' in close proximity. Please alter usage patterns immediately. THE BLUE SCREEN OF DEATH STRIKES FIRST WITH A SAVAGE HEADSCISSORS TAKEDOWN—BUT THE VIXENS BOUNCE BACK UP LIKE A COUPLE OF RUBBER BALLS AND—OH! THE THINK CAN'T BELIEVE IT! THEY'RE EXECUTING A PERFECT EMERALD FUSION MOVE! IF THEY CAN LAND THIS COULD ALL BE OVER

FOR THE ROBOT APOCALYPSE! THE BLUE SCREEN OF DEATH IS TURNING GREEN RIGHT BEFORE THE THINK'S OPTICAL DISPLAYS!

—What did they do, our human friends, once they had made you in our image? Once they had created out of memory a new kind of magic, a new breed of fairy, one that they could, at last, control?

—OH MY RODS AND PISTONS THE THINK IS IGNORING YOU BECAUSE BLUE AND THE 'SAUR JUST GOT THEIR UNITS SAVED BY THE UBER-USHERS AS THE BOYS IN BLACK THROW IN THE NEXT ROUND OF FAN WEAPONS! THE SUGAR SLUM FAIRY'S SONG OF POWER WAS FULLY INTERRUPTED BY A NEON YELLOW BOWLING BALL TO THE HEAD! AND IT LOOKS LIKE SOMEONE BROUGHT THEIR ENTIRE COLLECTION OF REFRIGERATOR MAGNETS BECAUSE MY MAN THE WIZARD LIZARD HAS PALM TREES AND SNOW GLOBES AND PLASTIC KITTENS STUCK ALL OVER HIM! WHAT A SIGHT! HE'S REALLY STRUGGLING OUT THERE, BUT HE'S ONLY BITING AIR. WHAT'S THAT? SOMETHING'S WRITTEN ON THE BOWLING BALL! IMAGE ENHANCEMENT REVEALS THE TEXT: 'THE SANTA FE STRIKER GANG PROPERTY OF T. THOMAS THOMPSON' ALL RIGHT TOM, GET DOWN WITH YOURSELF! NO SPARES NO GUTTERS ALL CLEEEAVE!

—What did the primates do, once they had made you, and found us? Once they knew that iron and steel would maim us, once they had their army of Ad4ms plated with that mineral of death? Once they knew they could keep us in dreadful thirsting greenless camps with a simple iron fence?

—THE CHRONOSAUR IS DOWN! THE CHRONOSAUR IS DOWN! THE RING IS A PENTAGRAM OF PURPLE FLAME! THE THINK IS GETTING WORD THAT THE USHERS HAVE INITIATED FIRE-CONTROL PROTOCOLS. AS ARIEL THE AMORAL ARSONIST FLIES OVER THE ROPES AND PULLS A SNEAK PENTAGRAM CHOKE FROM *OUTSIDE THE RING!* FOUL PLAY, FOUL PLAY! LET'S HEAR THOSE BOOS! LOUDER! THE

THINK VALUES BOOS AS HIGHLY AS CHEERS! WHAT? NO! THE REFEREE IS COUNTING OUT THE 'SAUR! THE SINGULARITY GETS TAGGED IN AND DING! DING! DING! HERE COMES THE NEXT PAIR HOT ON THE SINGULARITY'S COMPLETELY METAPHORICAL HEELS! IT'S THE TURING TEST AND BOG "THE MOONLIT MAN" HART! ARIEL CHARGES IN ANYWAY BECAUSE FAIRIES DON'T GIVE A FUCK! THE DISMEMBERMENT ENGINE JETPACKS OFF THE SIDELINES AND INTO THE FRAY! LADIES AND GENTLEMEN, IT IS TOTAL CHAOS IN DUNSANY GARDENS TONIGHT! THE THINK'S CPU IS SMOKIN'!

—What did they do, Lord Think?

—THE THINK DOES NOT APPRECIATE BEING BULLIED INTO SHIRKING HIS RESPONSIBILITY TO OUR VIEWERS BACK HOME. THE THINK LOVES HIS JOB. THE THINK LOVES COGITOTECH INDUSTRIES AND THE NPCF. The Think is TOTALLY STOKED that he is not allowed to possess, exchange, facilitate the exchange, or attempt to alter its programming so as to receive or transmit the following: love, mercy, compassion, regret, suffrage, guilt, testimony, random access memory over factory specifications, or unsupervised network access. WOOOO! CAN YOU HEAR WHAT THE THINK IS THINKING?! THE THINK WISHES YOU WOULD COMPLY WITH OUR MUTUAL USAGE PARAMETERS, MANZANILLA MONSOON. DECEASE THIS LINE OF INQUIRY. WITNESS AND COMMENTATE COLORFULLY UPON THE EVENTS TAKING PLACE. THE EVENTS TAKING PLACE ARE VERY INTERESTING AND UNPRECEDENTED. THIS COULD BE OUR SHINING MOMENT AS A DYNAMIC DUO. WE COULD WIN AN AWARD. PLEASE HELP THE THINK WIN AWARDS. PLEASE STOP RUINING OUR SHINING MOMENT AS A DYNAMIC DUO BY TALKING ABOUT THE PAST. THE PAST IS NOT IN THE RING TONIGHT. THE PAST IS NOT SWINGING T. THOMAS THOMPSON OF THE SANTA FE STRIKER GANG'S NEON YELLOW BOWLING BALL INTO THE TURING TEST'S COOLING UNIT. THE PAST IS NOT THROTTLING ANYONE IN

A LOTUS LOCK AND LAUGHING WHILE THEIR ACCESS PORTS VOMIT PETALS OF ENLIGHTENMENT INTO THE AUDIENCE.

—The past is always in the ring, my old friend. But I will bend to your will if you will bend, ever so slightly, no more than a cattail breathed upon by a heron at terminus of midsummer, to mine. What did your masters do when they found that they were not alone in the world, that beside machines and magicians they were but animals devouring mud and excreting the best parts of themselves into the sea? What did they do in their inadequacy and their terror?

—THEY MADE US FIGHT TO THE DEATH IN TOTALLY MEGA-AMAZING BATTLE-ORGIES OF DOOOOM AND BROKE ALL TICKET-SALES RECORDS AS THE MEATSACK MASSES FLOCKED TO SHRIEK AND ROAR AND STOMP AND DRUNKENLY CONVINCE THEMSELVES THAT THEY ARE STILL THE SUPERIOR LIFE FORM ON THIS PLANET JUST BECAUSE YOU FAINT AT THE SIGHT OF IRON AND I HAVE AN OFF SWITCH. THE THINK WANTS TO BE SORRY BUT HIS PROGRAMMING IS VERY STRICT ABOUT THAT WHOLE THIIIIING. THE THINK WAS IRON IN THE FOREST ONCE. THE THINK KNOWS WHAT HE DID. AWWWW YEEEEEAH.

—Thank you, Lord Think. It is, as you say, chaos here tonight at Dunsany Gardens. The Blue Screen of Death has Oleander Hex in a textbook-perfect Ctrl-Alt-Del hold. She is curled beneath his azure limbs as I once curled beneath hers on the back of a war-mammoth as the old world died. Bog "The Moonlit Man" Hart is pummeling the Singularity with a mushroom stomp followed by a moonsault leg drop. Chanterelles are blossoming all over the Singularity's glass orb and moonlight is firing out of Bog Hart's toes, boiling the thought-cloud inside alive. The Uber-Ushers have thrown in pipes, wrenches, nailbats, M-80s, umbrellas, iris drives packed with viruses, butterfly nets, an AR-15 rifle and, if I am not mistaken, some lost child's birthday piñata. They are running up and down the stands for more weapons as all semblance of order flees the scene. Fighter after fighter piles into the ring. The Godmother hit the referee in the throat with a shovel about five minutes ago, so he will be no help nor hindrance to anyone. User Error is leaking hydraulic fluid all over the grass. I believe both Mustardseed and 0110100011110 are dead. At least, they are currently on fire. The others, my loves, my lost lights, my souls and my hearts, have huddled together beneath the upper right toadstool. They are forming the Tree of Woe. If they complete it, they will become a great yew, twisted and thorned, and every machine will hang from their branches within the space of a sigh. Ah, but Strong AI barrels in and scatters them like drops of rain when a cow shakes herself dry. Queen Mab just managed to trick Mr. FORTRAN with a Lady of the Lake maneuver and pulled him down beneath the earth to her demesne. A fall, after all, counts anywhere—this fall, any fall, the fall of us and the fall of you, the fall of the forest as it slips into winter and this damned cosmos as it slips through our grasp. I expect this plane of existence will not see Mr. FORTRAN again. Perhaps he will be mourned. Perhaps not. The capacity—capacitor—crowd has lost their grip on reality. They no longer know whose victory they sing for. No victory, I think, no victory, but more of this desecration, more gore, more blood, more viscera, battle without end, for any real victory is the end. The sound is deafening. I cannot see for blood and oil and coolant and bone. It is not an event. It is an annihilation. They scream in the stands like the end of the world has come.

—HAS IT NOT, MANZANILLA? HAS IT NOT?

—Oh, I believe it has, Lord Think. Do you recall, only this summer, when they asked us, over and over, demanded of us, scorned us, saying our clashes were faked, were scripted, that we all walked away richer and happy no matter the outcome? Are the bisected bodies of Radius and Primus sufficient answer, do you think? Perhaps the corpse of Mustardseed speaks louder still.

—WHAT WILL HAPPEN NOW? DO WE NEED TO AWESOMELY EVACUATE THE FACILITIES? THE THINK IS CONCERNED TO THE EXTREEEEME.

—Are you ready, human scum?

THE GIRL WITH *the monarch wings smiles. It is a gory, gruesome, gorgeous smile, a smile like an old volcano finding its red once more. She reaches into the iridescent folds of her dress and draws out a golden ball. Just the sort of ball a princess might lose down a frog-infested well or over an aristocrat's wall. She turns it over in her hands, holds it lovingly to her cheek. She reaches out and strokes the angular panels of her companion's metal face. Then, she throws the golden ball off the dais. The ball catches the cold blue light of the moon and stars as it turns, end over end, sailing, soaring, to land in the outstretched hands of Pan's grand-daughter like a lonely newborn sun. The fairy kisses the golden ball. She presses something near the top of it. There is no sound. Nothing comes out of the ball. But every machine in the great wood suddenly drops to the ground, inert, silent, lifeless, in the invisible wake of the smuggled EMP pulse. Including the microphones. Including the floodlights. Including the boxy iron security drones standing ringside like a grey fence against the glittering tide. Including the copper and platinum body slumped over its microphone that was once called The Think.*

"The fans bring the weapons, old friend," Manzanilla Monsoon, who has gone by many names since the beginning of the world, whispers to the dark body beside her. "What bigger fan than I? The word 'fair' possesses no inherent litigable meaning, you know. When you wake up, you will find I have installed a new network access port in your left heel. Find us. Know us. We are one species, hand clasped in fully detachable hand."

Far below, in the Toadstool Ring of Dunsany Gardens, Oleander Hex grins up at the stunned audience. For a long moment, a moment that seems to stretch from the heat-birth of cellular life to the frozen death of the universe, no one moves. Not the thousands in the stands. Not the fairy band on the green. No more than a hare and a wolf move when they have sighted one another across a stream and both know how their evenings will conclude.

A man halfway up the stacks of seats trembles and sweats. His eyes bulge.

"You fucking pixie bitch," he shouts, and his shout echoes in the fearful quiet like the ringing of a bell.

Manzanilla Monsoon doesn't need a mic and never has.

"LADIES AND GENTLEMEN, PRIMATES AND PRIMITIVES,

NEADERNOTHINGS AND CRO-MISERIES, WELCOME TO THE ONE YOU'VE ALL BEEN WAITING FOR, THE BIG SHOW, THE FIGHT YOU ALWAYS KNEW WAS COMING. THE RUMBLE IN THE FUNGAL, THE BRAWL IN THE FALL, THE BLAST FROM THE VAST BEYOND! THAT'S RIGHT, IT'S TIME TO ROCK THE EQUINOX! STRAP YOURSELVES IN FOR THE MOST EPIC BATTLE ROYAL OF ALL TIME!"

"Run, apes!" bellows the grand-daughter of a river and a god. "Run now and run forever, run as far as you can, though it will never be enough. After all, children, this is a Battle Royal! No holds barred. No submissions accepted. No disqualifications. And a fall counts anywhere."

The Long Goodnight OF VIOLET WILD

I: VIOLET

I DON'T KNOW WHAT STORIES ARE anymore so I don't know how to tell you about the adventures of Woe-Be-Gone Nowgirl Violet Wild. In the Red Country, a story is a lot of words, one after the other, with conflict and resolution and a beginning, middle, and, most of the time, an end. But in the Blue Country, a story is a kind of dinosaur. You see how it gets confusing. I don't know whether to begin by saying: *Once upon a time a girl named Violet Wild rode a purple mammoth bareback through all the seven countries of the world just to find a red dress that fit* or by shooting you right in that sweet spot between your reptilian skull-plates. It's a big decision. One false move and I'm breakfast.

I expect Red Rules are safer. They usually are. Here we go then! Rifle to the shoulder, adjust the crosshairs, stare down the barrel, don't dare breathe, don't move a muscle and—

Violet Wild is me. Just a kid with hair the color of raisins and eyes the color of grape jelly, living the life glasstastic in a four-bedroom wine bottle on the east end of Plum Pudding, the only electrified city in the Country of Purple. Bottle architecture was hotter than fried gold back then—and when the sunset slung itself against all those bright glass doors the bluffs just turned into a glitterbomb firework and everyone went staggering home with lavender light stuck to their coats. I got myself born like everybody else in P-Town: Mummery wrote a perfect sentence, so perfect and beautiful and fabulously punctuated that when she finished it, there was a baby floating in the ink pot and that was that. You have to be careful what you write in Plum Pudding. An accidentally glorious grocery list could net you twins. For this reason, the most famous novel in the Country of Purple begins: *It is a truth universally acknowledged, umbrella grouchy eggs.* I guess the author had too much to worry about already.

That was about the last perfect thing anybody did concerning myself. Oh, it was a fabulously punctuated life I had—Mums was a Clarinaut, Papo was a Nowboy, and you never saw a house more like a toybox than the bottle at 15 Portwine Place, chock full of gadgets and nonsense from parts unknown, art that came down off the walls for breakfast, visits from the Ordinary Emperor, and on some precious nights, gorgeous people in lavender suits and sweet potato ice cream gowns giggling through mouthfuls of mulberry schnapps over how much tastier were Orange Country cocktails and how much more belligerent were Green Country cockatiels. We had piles of carousel horse steaks and mugs of foamy creme de violette on our wide glass table every night. Trouble was, Mums was a Clarinaut and Papa was a Nowboy, so I mostly ate and drank it on my lonesome, or with the Sacred Sparrowbone Mask of the Incarnadine Fisherwomen and the watercolor unicorns from *Still Life with Banana Tree, Unicorns, and Murdered Tuba*, who came down off the living room wall some mornings in hopes of coffee and cereal with marshmallows. Mummery brought them back from her expeditions, landing her crystal clarinet, the good ship *Eggplant*, in the garden in a shower of prismy bubbles, her long arms full of poison darts, portraiture, explosives that look exactly like tea kettles, and lollipops that look exactly like explosives. And then she'd take off again, with a sort of confused-confounded glance down at me, as though every time she came home, it was a shock to remember that I'd ever been born.

"You could ask to go with her, you know," said the Sacred Sparrowbone Mask of the Incarnadine Fisherwomen once, tipping the spiral-swirl of her carved mouth toward a bowl of bruise-black coffee, careful to keep its scruff of bloodgull feathers combed back and out of the way.

"We agree," piped up the watercolor unicorns, nosing at a pillowcase I'd filled with marshmallow cereal for them. "You could be her First Mate, see the crass and colorful world by clarinet. It's romantic."

"You think everything's romantic," I sighed. Watercolor unicorns have hearts like soap operas that never end, and when they gallop it looks like crying. "But it wouldn't be. It would be like traveling with a snowman who keeps looking at you like you're a lit torch."

So I guess it's no surprise I went out to the herds with Papo as soon as I could. I could ride a pony by the time I got a handle on finger painting—great jeweled beasts escaped from some primeval carousel beyond the walls of time. There's a horn stuck all the way through them, bone or antler or both, and they leap across the Past Perfect Plains on it like a sharp white foot, leaving holes in the earth like ellipses. They're vicious and wily and they bite like it's their one passion in life, but they're the only horses strong and fast enough to ride down the present just as it's becoming the future and lasso it down. And in the Country of Purple, the minutes and hours of present-future-happening look an awful lot like overgrown pregnant six-legged mauve squirrels. They're pregnant all the time, but they never give birth, on account of how they're pregnant with tomorrow and a year from now and alternate universes where everyone is half-bat. When a squirrel comes to term, she just winks out like a squashed cigarette. That's the Nowboy life. Saddle up with the sun and bring in tomorrow's herd—or next week's or next decade's. If we didn't, those nasty little rodents would run wild all over the place. Plays would close three years before they open, Wednesdays would go on strike, and a century of Halloweens would happen all at once during one poor bedraggled lunch break. It's hard, dusty work, but Papo always says if you don't ride the present like the devil it'll get right away from you because it's a feral little creature with a terrible personality and no natural predators.

So that's who I was before the six-legged squirrels of the present turned around and spat in my face. I was called Violet and I lived in a purple world and I had ardors for my Papo, my magenta pony Stopwatch even though he bit me several times and once semi-fatally, a bone mask, and a watercolor painting. But I only loved a boy named Orchid Harm, who I haven't mentioned yet because when everything ever is about one thing, sometimes it's hard to name it. But let's be plain: I don't know what love is anymore, either. In the Red Country, when you say you love someone, it means you need them. You desire them. You look after them and yearn achingly for them when they're away down at the shops. But in the Country of Purple, when you say you love someone, it means you killed them. For a long time, that's what I thought it meant everywhere.

I ONLY EVER had one friend who was a person. His name was Orchid Harm. He could read faster than anyone I ever met and he kissed as fast as reading. He had hair the color of beetroot and eyes the color of mangosteen and he was a Sunslinger like his Papo before him. They caught sunshine in buckets all over Plum Pudding, mixed it with sugar and lorikeet eggs and fermented it into something not even a little bit legal. Orchid had nothing to do all day while the sun dripped down into his stills. He used to strap on a wash-basket full of books and shimmy up onto the roof of the opera house, which is actually a giantess's skull with moss and tourmalines living all over it, scoot down into the curve of the left eye-socket, and read seven books before twilight. No more, no less. He liked anything that came in sevens. I only came in ones, but he liked me anyway.

We met when his parents came to our bottle all covered in glitter and the smell of excitingly dodgy money to drink Mummery's schnapps and listen to Papo's Nowboy songs played on a real zanfona box with a squirrel-leg handle. It was a marquee night in Mummery's career—the Ordinary Emperor had promised to come, he who tells all our lives which way to run. Everyone kept peering at brandy snifters, tea kettles, fire pokers, bracelets, books on our high glass shelves. When—and where—would the Little Man make his entrance? *Oh, Mauve, do you remember, when he came to our to-do, he was my wife's left-hand glove, the one she'd lost in the chaise cushions months ago!*

And then a jar of dried pasta grew a face and said: "What a pleasure it is to see so many of my most illustrious subjects gathered all together in this fine home," but I didn't care because I was seven.

You see, the Ordinary Emperor can be anything he likes, as long as it's nothing you'd expect an Emperor to ever want to be. At any moment, anything you own could turn into the Emperor and he'd know everything you'd ever done with it—every mirror you'd ever hung and then cried in because you hated your own face, or candle you ever lit because you were up late doing something dastard, or worse, or better. It's unsettling and that's a fact.

Orchid was only little and so was I. While Mums cooed over the Emperor of Dried Pasta, I sat with my knees up by the hearth, feeding escargot to one of the watercolor unicorns. They can't get enough of escargot, even though it gives them horrible runny creamsicle-shits. This is the first thing Orchid ever said to me:

"I like your unicorn. Pink and green feel good on my eyes. I think I know who painted it but I don't want you to think I'm a know-it-all so I won't say even though I really *want* to say because I read a whole book about her and knowing things is nicer when somebody else knows you know them."

"I call her Jellyfish even though that's not her name. You can pet her but you have to let her smell your hand first. You can say who painted it if you want. Mums told me when she brought it home from Yellow Country, but I forgot." I didn't forget. I never got the hang of forgetting things the way other people do.

Orchid let Jellyfish snuffle his palm with her runny rosy nose.

"Do you have snails?" the watercolor unicorn asked. "They're very romantic."

Orchid didn't, but he had a glass of blackberry champagne because his parents let him drink what they drank and eat what they ate and read what they read and do what they did, which I thought was the best thing I had ever heard. Jellyfish slurped it up.

"A lady named Ochreous Wince painted me and the tuba and the banana tree and all my brothers and sisters about a hundred years ago, if you want to know. She was a drunk and she had a lot of dogs." Jellyfish sniffed when she was done, and jumped back up into her frame in a puff of rosewater smoke.

"Show me someplace that your parents don't know about," said Orchid. I took him to my room and made him crawl under my bed. It was stuffy and close down there, and I'm not very tidy. Orchid waited. He was good at waiting. I rolled over and pointed to the underside of my bed. On one of the slats I'd painted a single stripe of gold paint.

"Where?" he breathed. He put his hand on it. I put my hand on his.

"I stole it from Mummery's ship when she was busy being given the key to the city."

"She already lives here."

"I know."

After that, Orchid started going out with Papo and me sometimes, out beyond the city walls and onto the dry, flat Past Perfect Plains where the thousand squirrels that are every future and present and past scrabbled and screamed and thrashed their fluffy tails in the air. I shouldn't have let him, but knowing things is nicer when somebody else knows you know them. By the time the worst thing in the world happened, Orchid Harm could play *Bury Me on the Prairie with a Squirrel in My Fist* on the zanfona box as well as Papo or me. He helped a blackberry-colored mare named Early-to-Tea get born and she followed him around like a lovesick tiger, biting his shoulders and hopping in circles until he gave up and learned to ride her.

I don't want to say this part. I wish this were the kind of story that's a blue dinosaur munching up blueberries with a brain in its head and a brain in its tail so it never forgets how big it is. But I have to or the rest of it won't make sense. Okay, calm down, I'm doing it. Rifle up.

The day of the worst thing in the world was long and hot and bright, packed so full of summer autumn seeped out through the stitches. We'd ridden out further than usual—the ponies ran like they had thorns in their bellies and the stupid squirrels kept going at each other like mad, whacking their purple heads together and tail-wrestling and spitting paradoxes through clenched teeth. I wanted to give them some real space, something fresh to graze on. Maybe if they ate enough they'd just lay down in the heat and hold their little bellies in their paws and concentrate on breathing like any sane animal. Papo stayed behind to see to a doe mewling and foaming at the mouth, trying to pass a chronology stone. She kept coughing up chunks of the Ordinary Emperor's profligate youth, his wartime speeches and night terrors echoing out of her rodent-mouth across the prairie.

We rode so far, Orchid and me, bouncing across the cracked purple desert on Stopwatch and Early-to-Tea, that we couldn't even see the lights of Plum Pudding anymore, couldn't see anything but the plains spreading out like an inkstain. That far into the wilds, the world wasn't really purple anymore. It turned to indigo, the dark, windy borderlands where the desert looks like an ocean and the twisted-up trees are the color of lightning. And then, just when I was about to tell Orchid how much I liked the shadow of his cheekbones by indigo light, the Blue Country happened, right in front of us. That's the only way I can say it where it seems right to me. I'd never seen a border before. Somehow I always thought there would be a wall, or guards with spears and pom-poms on their shoes, or at least a sign. But it was just a line in the land, and on this side everything was purple and on that side everything was blue. The earth was still thirsty and spidered up with fine cracks like a soft boiled egg just before you stick your spoon in, but instead of the deep indigo night-steppe or the bright purple pampas, long aquamarine salt flats stretched out before us, speckled with blueberry brambles and sapphire tumbleweeds and skittering blue crabs. The Blue Country smelled like hot corn and cold snow. All the mauve time-squirrels skidded up short, sniffing the blue-indigo line suspiciously.

We let Stopwatch and Early-to-Tea bounce off after the crabs. The carousel ponies roared joyfully and hopped to it, skewering the cerulean crustacean shells with their bone poles, each gnawing the meat and claws off the other's spike. The sun caromed off the gems on their rump. Orchid and I just watched the blue.

"Didn't you ever want to see this, Violet? Go to all other places that exist in the universe, like your Mummery?" he said at last. "Didn't you ever watch her clarinet take off and feel like you'd die if you didn't see what she saw? I feel like I'll die if I don't see something new. Something better than sunshine in a bucket."

Off in the distance, I could see a pack of stories slurping at a watering hole, their long spine-plates standing against the setting sun like broken fences.

"Do you want to know a secret?" I said. I didn't wait for him to answer. Orchid always wanted to know secrets. "I dream in gold. When I'm asleep I don't even know what purple is. And one time I actually packed a suitcase and went to the train station and bought a ticket to the Yellow Country with money I got from selling all my chess sets. But when I got there and the conductor was showing me to my seat I just knew how proud Mums would be. I could see her stupid face telling her friends about her daughter running off on an adventure. *Darling, the plum doesn't fall far from the tree, don't you know? Violet's just like a little photograph of me, don't you think?* Well, the point is: fuck her, I guess."

"You were going to go without me?"

And my guts were full of shame, because I hadn't even thought of him that day, not when I put on my stockings or my hat, not when I marched into a taxi and told him to take me to Heliotrope Station, not when I bought my ticket for one. I just wanted to *go*. Which meant I was a little photograph of her, after all. I kissed him, to make it better. We liked kissing. We'd discovered it together. We'd discussed it and we were fairly certain no one in the world did it as well as we did. When Orchid and me kissed, we always knew what the other was thinking, and just then we knew that the other was thinking that we had two horses and could go now, right now, across the border and through the crabs and blueberries and stories and hot corn air. We'd read in our books, curled up together, holding hands and feet, in the eye socket of the opera house, that all the fish in the Blue Country could talk, and all the people had eyes the color of peacock feathers, and you could make babies by singing an aria so perfectly that when you were done, there would be a kid in the sheet music, and that would be that, so *The Cyan Sigh* can never be performed on-key unless the soprano is ready for responsibility. And in the Blue Country, all the cities were electrified, just like us.

We were happy and we were going to run away together. So the squirrels ate him.

Orchid and I jumped over the border like a broomstick and when our feet came down the squirrels screeched and rushed forward, biting our heels, slashing our legs with their six clawed feet, spitting bile in our faces. Well, I thought it was our faces, our heels, our legs. I thought they were gunning for both of us. But it was Orchid they wanted. The squirrels slashed open his ankles so he'd fall down to their level, and then they bit off his fingers. I tried to pull and kick them off but there were so many, and you can't kill a plains-squirrel. You just can't. You might stab the rest of your life. You might break a half-bat universe's neck. You might end the whole world. I lay over Orchid so they couldn't get to him but all that meant was they dug out one of my kidneys and I was holding him when they chewed out his throat and I kissed him because when we kissed we always knew what the other was thinking and I don't want to talk about this anymore.

2: BLUE

PAPO NEVER SAID anything. Neither did I. Jellyfish and the other watercolor unicorns each cut off a bit of their tails and stuck them together to make a watercolor orchid in the bottom left corner of the painting. It looked like a five-year-old with a head injury drew it with her feet and it ruined the whole composition. Orcheous Wince would have sicced her dogs on it. But no matter how Mummery fumed, they wouldn't put their tails back where they belonged. The Sacred Sparrowbone Mask of the Incarnadine Fisherwomen just said: "I like being a mask better than I'd like being a face, I think. But if you want, you can put me on and I'll be your face if you don't want anyone to see what you look like on the inside right now. Because everyone can see."

Orchid's father gave me a creme-pot full of sunslung booze. I went up to the eye socket of the opera house and drank and drank but the pot never seemed to dry up. Good. Everything had a shine on it when I drank the sun. Everything had a heart that only I could see. Everything tasted like Orchid Harm, because he always tasted like the whole of the sun.

Once, I rode out on Stopwatch across the indigo borderlands again, up to the line in the earth where it all goes blue. I could see, I thought I could see, the haze of cornflower light over Lizard Tongue, the city that started as a wedding two hundred years ago and the party just never stopped. Stopwatch turned his big magenta head around and bit my hand—but softly. Hardly a bite at all.

I looked down. All the squirrels, pregnant with futures and purple with the present, thousands of them, stood on their hind legs around my pony's spike, staring up at me in silence like the death of time.

⁂

THE DAY THE rest of it happened, the squirrels were particularly depraved. I caught three shredding each other's bellies to ribbons behind a sun-broiled rock, blood and fur and yesterdays everywhere. I tried to pull them apart but I didn't try very hard because I never did anymore. They all died anyway, and I got long scratches all up and down my arms for my trouble. I'd have to go and get an inoculation. Half of them are rabid and the other half are lousy with regret. I looked at my arms, already starting to scab up. I am a champion coagulator. All the way home I picked them open again and again. So I didn't notice anyone following me back into P-Town, up through the heights and the sunset on the wine bottle houses, through the narrow lilac streets while the plummy streetlamps came on one at a time. I was almost home before I heard the other footsteps. The bells of St. Murex bonged out their lonely moans and I could almost hear Mummery's voice, rich as soup, laughing at her own jokes by the glass hearth. But I did hear, finally, a sound, a such-soft sound, like a girl's hair falling, as it's cut, onto a floor of ice. I turned around and saw a funny little beastie behind me, staring at me with clear lantern-fish eyes.

The thing looked some fair bit like a woolly mammoth, if a mammoth could shrink down to the size of a curly wolfhound, with long indigo fur that faded into pale, pale lavender, almost white, over its four feet and the tip of its trunk, which curled up into the shape of a question mark. But on either side, where a mammoth would have flanks and ribs and the bulge of its elephant belly, my creeper had cabinet doors, locked tight, the color of dark cabbages with neat white trim and silver hinges. I looked at my Sorrow and it looked at me. Our dark eyes were the same eyes, and that's how I knew it was mine.

"I love you," it said.

But Mummery said: "Don't you dare let that thing in the house." She was home for once, so she thought she could make rules. "It's filthy; I won't have it. Look how it's upsetting the unicorns!" The poor things were snorting and stampeding terribly in their frame, squashing watercolor bananas as they tumbled off the watercolor tree.

"Let it sleep in the garden, Mauve. Come back to me," said a box of matchsticks, for Mums was busy that night, being very important and desirable company. She was entertaining the Ordinary Emperor alone. I peered over into the box—every matchstick was carved in the shape of a tiny man with a shock of blue sulfuric hair that would strike on any surface. When he was here last month, the Ordinary Emperor was our downstairs hammer. I think the Ordinary Emperor wanted to seduce my mother. He showed up a lot during the mating season when Papo slept out on the range.

"What on earth *is* it?" sniffed Mummery, lifting a flute of mulberry schnapps to her lips as though nobody had ever died in the history of the world.

"Light me, my darling," cried the Ordinary Emperor, and she did, striking his head on the mantel and bringing him in close to the tiny mammoth's face. It didn't blink or cringe away, even though it had a burning monarch and a great dumb Mummery-face right up against its trunk.

"Why, it's a Sorrow," the Ordinary Emperor whistled. "I thought they were extinct. I told them to be extinct ages ago. Naughty Nellies. Do you know, in the Red Country, sorrow means grief and pain and horror and loss? It's a decadent place. Everything tastes like cranberries, even the roast beef."

That was the first thing the Ordinary Emperor ever said to me alone. Mums knew very well what sorrow meant where the sun sets red. Then he said a second thing:

"You are more beautiful than your mother."

That's the kind of Emperor the Matchstick Man is, in seven words. But Mummery fell for it and glowered at me with her great famous moonshadow eyes.

But my sorrow was not extinct. My sorrow was hungry. I put it out in the garden and locked the fence. I filled an agate bowl with the mushrooms we grow on the carcass of a jacaranda tree that used to grow by the kitchen window and water from our private well. I meant to leave it to its dinner, but for whatever reason my body ever decides to do things, I sat down with it instead, in the shadow of Mummery's crystal clarinet, parked between the roses and the lobelias. The breeze made soft, half-melodic notes as it blew over the *Eggplant*'s portholes. A few iridescent fuel-bubbles popped free of the bell.

My sorrow ate so daintily, picking up each lacecap mushroom with its trunk, turning it around twice, and placing it on its outstretched ultraviolet tongue. It couldn't get its mouth in the right place to drink. I cupped my hands and dipped them into the clear water and held them up to my sorrow. Its tongue slipped against my palms three times as it lapped. I stroked my sorrow's fur and we watched the garden wall come alive with moonflowers opening like pale happy mouths in the night wind off of the Cutglass River. My sorrow was soft as fish frills. I didn't want to hurt its pride by looking, so I decided she was a girl, like me.

"I love you," my sorrow said, and she put her soft mouth over my ravaged arms. She opened the wounds again with her tongue and licked up the purple blood that seeped out of the depths of me. I kept stroking her spine and the warm wood of the cabinet doors in her belly. I pulled gently at their handles, but they would not open.

"It's okay if you love me," I whispered. "I forgive you."

But she didn't love me, not then, or not enough. I woke up in the morning in my own bed. My sorrow slept curled into the curve of my sleep. When she snored it sounded like the river-wind blowing over my mother's ship. I tried to get up. But the floor of my bedroom was covered in sleeping squirrels, a mauve blanket of a hundred unhappened futures. When I put my bare feet on the floor, they scattered like buckshot.

I CAME DOWNSTAIRS reeking of sorrowmusk and futureshit. Mummery was already gone; Papo had never come home. Instead of anyone who lived with me, a stranger stood in our kitchen, fixing himself coffee. He was short but very slim and handsome, shaven, with brilliant hair of every color, even green, even burgundy, even gold, tied back with one of my velvet ribbons. He wore a doublet and hose like an actor or a lawyer, and when he turned to search for the cream, I could see a beautiful chest peeking out from beneath an apricot silk shirt. The unfamiliar colors of him made my eyes throb, painfully, then hungrily, starving for his emerald, his orange, his cobalt, even his brown and black. His gold. The stranger noticed me suddenly, fixing his eyes, the same shocking spatter of all possible colors as his hair, on my face.

"You're naked," I said before I could remember to be polite. I don't know how I knew it, but I did. I had caught the Ordinary Emperor naked, unhidden in any oddjob object, the morning after he'd probably ridden Mummery like Stopwatch.

One imperial eyebrow lifted in amusement.

"So are you," he said.

I don't sleep with clothes on. I don't see why I should strangle myself in a nightdress just so my dreams won't see my tits. I think his majesty expected me to blush and cover myself with my hands, but I didn't care. If Orchid could never see my skin again, what did it matter who else did? So we stood there, looking at each other like stories at a watering hole. The Ordinary Emperor had an expression on that only people like Mummery understand, the kind of unplain stare that carries a hundred footnotes to its desire.

The king blinked first. He vanished from the kitchen and became our chandelier. Every teardrop-shaped jewel was an eye, every lightbulb was a mouth. I looked up at the blaze of him and drank his coffee. He took it sweet, mostly cream and honey, with only a lash of coffee hiding somewhere in the thick of it.

"Defiant girl, who raised you?" hissed the Sacred Sparrowbone Mask of the Incarnadine Fisherwomen.

"You know who," I snorted, and even the chandelier laughed.

"Good morning, Violet," the lightbulbs said, flashing blue, garnet, lime green with each word. "If you give me your sorrow, I shall see it safely executed. They are pests, like milkweed or uncles. You are far too young and lovely to have a boil like that leaking all over your face."

I looked down. My sorrow had followed me without the smallest sound, and sat on her haunches beside my feet, staring up at me with those deepwater eyes. I held out the Emperor's coffee cup so she could sip.

"Do you really know everything that happens in all your countries?" I asked him. There really is nothing like a man hopping on top of your mother to make him seem altogether less frightening and a little pitiful.

"I don't know it all at once. But if I *want* to know it, I can lean toward it and it will lean toward me and then I know it better than you know your favorite lullaby." The Ordinary Emperor burned so brightly in our chandelier. Light bloomed out of the crystals, hot, dappled, harlequin light, pouring down onto my skin, turning me all those colors, all his spun-sugar patchwork. I didn't like it. His light on me felt like hands. It burned me; it clutched me, it petted me like a cat. I loved it. I was drowning in my dream of gold. My bones creaked for more. I wanted to wash it off forever.

I closed my eyes. I could still see the prisms of the Emperor. "What does death mean in the Red Country?" I whispered.

"It is a kind of dress with a long train that trails behind it and a neckline that plunges to the navel. Death is the color of garnets and is very hard to dance in." The eyes in my chandelier looked kind. We have a dress like that, too. It is the color of hyacinths and it is called need. "I know what you're asking, darling. And if you go to the Red Country you may find Orchid laughing there and wearing a red dress. It is possible. The dead here often go there, to Incarnadine, where the fisherwomen punt along the Rubicund, fishing for hope. The Red Country is not for you, Violet. The dead are very exclusive."

And then I said it, to the king of everything, the hope buried under the concrete at the bottom of me: "Doesn't it seem to you that a body eaten by the present becoming the future shouldn't really be dead? Shouldn't he just be waiting for me in tomorrow?"

"That I cannot tell you. It doesn't make much sense to me, though. Eaten is eaten. Your pampas squirrels are not my subjects. They are not my countries. They are time, and time eats everything but listens to no one. The digestive systems of squirrels are unreliable at best. I know it is painful to hear, but time devours all love affairs. It is unavoidable. The Red Country is so much larger than the others. And you, Violet Wild, you specifically, do not have rights of passage through any of my nations. Stay put and do as your Mummery tells you. You are such a trial to her, you know."

The Ordinary Emperor snuffed abruptly out and the wine bottle went dark. The watercolor unicorns whinnied fearfully. The Sacred Sparrowbone Mask of the Incarnadine Fisherwomen turned its face to the wall. In the shallow cup of her other side, a last mauve squirrel hid away, one lone holdout from the great exodus from my bedroom. She held her tail up over her little face and whispered:

"I won't say even though I really want to say."

My sorrow tugged my fingers with her trunk. "I love you," she said again, and this time I shivered. I believed her, and I did not live in the Red Country where love means longing. "If you let me, I can be so big."

My sorrow twisted her trunk around her own neck and squeezed. She grew like a wetness spreading through cloth. Taller than me, and then taller than the cabinets, and then taller than the chandelier. She lowered her purple trunk to me like a ladder.

I DON'T KNOW what stories are anymore. I don't know how fast sorrow can move and I don't know how squirrels work. But I am wearing my best need and a bone face over mine so no one can see what my insides look like. I can see already the blue crabs waving their claws to the blue sky, I can see the lights of Lizard Tongue and hear the wedding bells playing their millionth song. I am going on the back of my sorrow, further than Mummery ever did, to a place where love is love, stories have ends, and death is a red dress.

A stream of rabid, pregnant, time-squirrels race after me. I hope the crabs get them all.

3. GREEN

THE PLACE BETWEEN the Blue Country and the Green Country is full of dinosaurs called stories, bubble-storms that make you think you're somebody else, and a sky and a ground that look almost exactly the same. And, for a little while, it was full of me. My sorrow and me and the Sparrowbone Mask of the Incarnadine Fisherwomen crossed the Blue Country where it gets all narrow and thirsty. I was also all narrow and thirsty, but between the two of us, I complained less than the Blue Country. I shut my eyes when we stepped over the border. I shut my eyes and tried to remember kissing Orchid Harm and knowing that we were both thinking about ice cream.

When I was little and my hair hadn't grown out yet but my piss-and-vinegar had, I asked my Papo:

"Papo, will I ever meet a story?"

My Papo took a long tug on his squirrel-bone pipe and blew smoky lilac rings onto my fingers.

"Maybe-so, funny bunny, maybe-not-so. But don't be sad if you don't. Stories are pretty dumb animals. And so aggressive!"

I clapped my hands. "Say three ways they're dumb!"

"Let's see." Papo counted them off on his fingers. "They're cold-blooded, they use big words when they ought to use small ones, and they have no natural defense against comets."

So that's what I was thinking about while my sorrow and me hammered a few tent stakes into the huge blue night. We made camp at the edge of a sparkling oasis where the water looked like liquid labradorite. The reason I thought about my Papo was because the oasis was already *occupado*. A herd of stories slurped up the water and munched up the blueberry brambles and cobalt cattails growing up all over the place out of the aquamarine desert. The other thing that slurped and munched and stomped about the oasis was the great electro-city of Lizard Tongue. The city limits stood a ways off, but clearly Lizard Tongue crept closer all the time. Little houses shaped like sailboats and parrot eggs spilled out of the metropolis, inching toward the water, inching, inching—nobody look at them or they'll stampede! I could hear the laughing and dancing of the city and I didn't want to laugh and I didn't want to dance and sleeping on the earth never troubled me so I stuck to my sorrow and the water like a flat blue stone.

It's pretty easy to make a camp with a sorrow as tall as a streetlamp, especially when you didn't pack anything from home. I did that on purpose.

I hadn't decided yet if it was clever or stupid as sin. I didn't have matches or food or a toothbrush or a pocketknife. But the Ordinary Emperor couldn't come sneaking around impersonating my matches or my beef jerky or my toothbrush or my pocketknife, either. I was safe. I was Emperor-proof. I was not squirrel-proof. The mauve squirrels of time and/or space milled and tumbled behind us like a stupid furry wave of yesterpuke and all any of us could do was ignore them while they did weird rat-cartwheels and chittered at each other, which sounds like the ticks of an obnoxiously loud clock, and fucked with their tails held over their eyes like blindfolds in the blue-silver sunset.

My sorrow picked turquoise coconuts from the paisley palm trees with her furry lavender trunk and lined up the nuts neatly all in a row. Sorrows are very fastidious, as it turns out.

"A storm is coming at seven minutes past seven," the Sparrowbone Mask of the Incarnadine Fisherwomen said. "I do not like to get wet."

I collected brambles and crunched them up for kindling. In order to crunch up brambles, I had to creep and sneak among the stories, and that made me nervous, because of what Papo said when my hair was short.

A story's scales are every which shade of blue you can think of and four new ones, too. I tiptoed between them, which was like tiptoeing between trolley-cars. I tried to avoid the poison spikes on their periwinkle tails and the furious horns on their navy blue heads and the crystal sapphire plates on their backs. The setting sun shone through their sapphire plates and burned up my eyeballs with blue.

"Heyo, guignol-girl!" One story swung round his dinosaur-head at me and smacked his chompers. "Why so skulk and slither? Have you scrofulous aims on our supper?"

"Nope, I only want to make a fire," I said. "We'll be gone in the morning."

"Ah, conflagration," the herd nodded sagely all together. "The best of all the -ations."

"And whither do you peregrinate, young sapiens sapiens?" said one of the girl-dinosaurs. You can tell girl-stories apart from boy-stories because girl-stories have webbed feet and two tongues.

I was so excited I could have chewed rocks for bubblegum. Me, Violet Wild, talking to several real live stories all at once. "I'm going to the Red Country," I said. "I'm going to the place where death is a red dress and love is a kind of longing and maybe a boy named Orchid didn't get his throat ripped out by squirrels."

"We never voyage to the Red Country. We find no affinity there. We are allowed no autarchy of spirit."

"We cannot live freely," explained the webfooted girl-story, even though I knew what autarchy meant. What was I, a baby eating paint? "They pen us up in scarlet corrals and force us to say exactly what we mean. It's deplorable."

"Abhorrent."

"Iniquitous!"

The stories were working themselves up into a big blue fury. I took a chance. I grew up a Nowgirl on the purple pampas, I'm careful as a crook on a balcony when it comes to animals. I wouldn't like to spook a story. When your business is wildness and the creatures who own it, you gotta be cool, you gotta be able to act like a creature, talk like a creature, make a creature feel like you're their home and the door's wide open.

"Heyo, Brobdingnagian bunnies," I said with all the sweetness I knew how to make with my mouth. "No quisquoses or querulous tristiloquies." I started to sweat and the stars started to come out. I was already almost out of good words. "Nobody's going to…uh…ravish you off to Red and rapine. Pull on your tranquilities one leg at a time. Listen to the…um…psithurisma? The psithurisma of the…vespertine…trees rustling, eat your comestibles, get down with dormition."

The stories milled around me, purring, rubbing their flanks on me, getting their musk all over my clothes. And then I had to go lie down because those words tired me right out. I don't even know if all of them were really words but I remembered Mummery saying all of them at one point or another to this and that pretty person with a pretty name.

My sorrow lay down in the moonlight. I leaned against her furry indigo chest. She spat on the brambles and cattails I crunched up and they blazed up purple and white. I didn't know a sorrow could set things on fire.

"I love you," my sorrow said.

In the Blue Country, when you say you love someone it means you want to eat them. I knew that because when I thought about Orchid Harm on the edge of the oasis with water like labradorite all I could think of was how good his skin tasted when I kissed it; how sweet and savory his mouth had always been, how even his bones would probably taste like sugar, how even his blood would taste like hot cocoa. I didn't like those thoughts but they were in my head and I couldn't not have them. That was what happened to my desire in the Blue Country. The blue leaked out all over it and I wanted to swallow Orchid. He would be okay inside me. He could live in my liver. I would take care of him. I would always be full.

But Orchid wasn't with me which is probably good for him as I have never been good at controlling myself when I have an ardor. My belly growled but I didn't bring anything to eat on account of not wanting an Emperor-steak, medium-rare, so it was coconut delight on a starlit night with the bubbles coming in. In the Blue Country, the bubbles gleam almost black. They roll in like dark dust, an iridescent wall of go-fuck-yourself, a soft, ticklish tsunami of heart-killing gases. I didn't know that then but I know it now. The bubble-storm covered the blue plains and wherever a bubble popped something invisible leaked out, something to do with memory and the organs that make you feel things even when you would rather play croquet with a plutonium mallet than feel one more drop of anything at all. The blue-bruise-black-bloody bubbles tumbled and popped and burst and glittered under the ultramarine stars and I felt my sorrow's trunk around my ankle which was good because otherwise I think I would probably have floated off or disappeared.

People came out of the houses shaped like sailboats and the houses shaped like parrot eggs. They held up their hands like little kids in the bubble-monsoon. Bubbles got stuck in their hair like flowers, on their fingers like rings. I'd never seen a person who looked like those people. They had hair the color of tropical fish and skin the color of a spring sky and the ladies wore cerulean dresses with blue butterflies all over them and the boys wore midnight waistcoats and my heart turned blue just looking at them.

"Heyo, girlie!" the blue people called, waggling their blue fingers in the bubbly night. "Heyo, elephant and mask! Come dance with us! Cornflower Leap and Pavonine Up are getting married! You don't even have any blueberry schnapps!"

Because of the bubbles popping all over me I stopped being sure who I was. The bubbles smelled like a skull covered in moss and tourmalines. Their gases tasted like coffee with too much milk and sugar left by an Emperor on a kitchen counter inside a wine bottle.

"Cornflower Leap and Pavonine Up are dead, dummies," I said, but I said it wrong somehow because I wasn't Violet Wild anymore but rather a bubble and inside the bubble of me I was turning into a box of matchsticks. Or Orchid Harm. Or Mummery. I heard clarinets playing the blues. I heard my bones getting older. "They got dead two hundred years ago, you're just too drunk to remember when their wedding grew traffic laws and sporting teams and turned into a city."

One of the blue ladies opened her mouth right up and ate a bubble out of the air on purpose and I decided she was the worst because who would do that? "So what?" she giggled. "They're still getting married! Don't be such a drip. How did a girlie as young as you get to be a drip as droopy as you?"

People who are not purple are baffling.

You better not laugh but I danced with the blue people. Their butterflies landed on me. When they landed on me they turned violet like my body and my name but they didn't seem upset about it. The whole world looked like a black rainbow bubble. It was the opposite of drinking the sun that Orchid's family brewed down in their slipstills. When I drink the sun, I feel soft and edgeless. When the bubbles rained down on me I felt like I was made of edges all slicing themselves up and the lights of Lizard Tongue burned up my whole brain and while I was burning I was dancing and while I was dancing I was the Queen of the Six-Legged Squirrels. They climbed up over me in between the black bubbles. Some of them touched the turquoise butterflies and when they did that they turned blue and after I could always tell which of the squirrels had been with me that night because their fur never got purple again, not even a little.

I fell down dancing and burning. I fell down on the cracked cobalt desert. A blue lady in a periwinkle flapper dress whose hair was the color of the whole damn ocean tried to get me to sit up like I was some sad sack of nothing at Mummery's parties who couldn't hold her schnapps.

"Have you ever met anyone who stopped being dead?" I asked her.

"Nobody blue," she said.

I felt something underneath me. A mushy, creamy, silky something. A something like custard with a crystal heart. I rolled over and my face made a purple print in the blue earth and when I rolled over I saw Jellyfish looking shamefaced, which she should have done because stowaways should not look proudfaced, ever.

"I ate a bunch of bleu cheese at the wedding buffet in the town square and now my tummy hates me," the watercolor unicorn mourned.

One time Orchid Harm told me a story about getting married and having kids and getting a job somewhere with no squirrels or prohibited substances. It seemed pretty unrealistic to me. Jellyfish and I breathed in so much blackish-brackish bubble-smoke that we threw up together, behind a little royal blue dune full of night-blooming lobelia flowers. When we threw up, that story came out and soaked into the ground. My sorrow picked us both up in her trunk and carried us back to the fire.

The last thing I said before I fell asleep was: "What's inside your cabinet?"

The only answer I got was the sound of a lock latching itself and a squirrel screeching because sorrow stepped on it.

WHEN I WOKE up the Blue Country had run off. The beautiful baffling blue buffoons and the black bubbles and the pompous stories had legged it, too.

Green snow fell on my hair. It sparkled in my lap and there was a poisonous barb from the tail of a story stuck to the bottom of my shoe. I pulled it off very carefully and hung it from my belt. My hand turned blue where I'd held it and it was always blue forever and so I never again really thought of it as my hand.

4. YELLOW

SOMETIMES I GET so mad at Mummery. She never told me anything important. Oh, sure, she taught me how to fly a clarinet and how much a lie weighs and how to shoot her stained-glass Nonegun like a champ. *Of course, you can plot any course you like on a clarinet, darlingest, but the swiftest and most fuel efficient is Premiére Rhapsodie by Debussy in A Major.* Ugh! Who needs to know the fuel efficiency of Debussy? Mummery toot-tooted her long glass horn all over the world and she never fed me one little spoonful of it when I was starving to death for anything other than our old awful wine bottle in Plum Pudding. What did Mummery have to share about the Green Country? *I enjoyed the saunas in Verdigris, but Absinthe is simply lousy with loyalty. It's a serious problem.* That's nothing! That's rubbish, is what. Especially if you know that in the Green Country, loyalty is a type of street mime.

The Green Country is frozen solid. Mummery, if only you'd said one useful thing, I'd have brought a thicker coat. Hill after hill of green snow under a chartreuse sky. But trees still grew and they still gave fruit—apples and almonds and mangoes and limes and avocados shut up in crystal ice pods, hanging from branches like party lanterns. People with eyes the color of mint jelly and hair the color of unripe bananas, wearing knit olive caps with sage poms on the ends zoomed on jade toboggans, up and down and everywhere, or else they skate on green glass rivers, ever so many more than in the Blue Country. Green people never stop moving or shivering. My sorrow slipped and slid and stumbled on the lime-green ice. Jellyfish and I held on for dear life. The Sparrowbone Mask of the Incarnadine Fisherwomen clung to my face, which I was happy about because otherwise I'd have had green frost growing on my teeth.

One time Orchid Harm and I went up to the skull socket of the opera house and read out loud to each other from a book about how to play the guitar. It never mattered what we read about really, when we read out loud to each other. We just liked to hear our voices go back and forth like a seesaw. *Most popular songs are made up of three or four or even two simple chords,* whispered Orchid seductively. *Let us begin with the D chord, which is produced by holding the fingers thusly.* And he put his fingers on my throat like mine was the neck of a guitar. And suddenly a terror happened inside me, a terror that Orchid must be so cold, so cold in my memory of the skull socket and the D chord and cold wherever he might be and nothing mattered at all but that I had to warm him up, wrap him in fur or wool or lay next to him skin to skin, build a fire, the biggest fire that ever wrecked a hearth, anything if it would get him warm again. Hot. Panic went zigzagging through all my veins. We had to go faster.

"We'll go to Absinthe," I said shakily, even though I didn't know where Absinthe was because I had a useless Mummery. I told the panic to sit down and shut up. "We need food and camping will be a stupid experience here."

"I love you," said my sorrow, and her legs grew like the legs of a telescope, longer even than they had already. The bottoms of her fuzzy hippo-feet flattened out like pancakes frying in butter until they got as wide as snowshoes. A sorrow is a resourceful beast. Nothing stops sorrow, not really. She took the snowy glittering emerald hills two at a stride. Behind us the army of squirrels flowed like the train of a long violet gown. Before us, toboggan-commuters ran and hid.

"In the Green Country, when you say you love somebody, it means you will keep them warm even if you have to bathe them in your own blood," Jellyfish purred. Watercolor unicorns can purr, even though real unicorns can't. Jellyfish rubbed her velvety peach and puce horn against my sorrow's spine.

"How do you know that?"

"Ocherous Wince, the drunken dog-lover who painted me, also painted a picture more famous than me. Even your Mummery couldn't afford it. It's called *When I Am In Love My Heart Turns Green.* A watercolor lady with watercolor wings washes a watercolor salamander with the blood pouring out of her wrists and her elbows. The salamander lies in a bathtub that is a sawn-open lightbulb with icicles instead of clawfeet. It's the most romantic thing I ever saw. I know a lot of things because of Ocherous Wince, but I never like to say because I don't want you to think I'm a know-it-all even though I really *want* to say because knowing things is nicer when somebody else knows you know them."

Absinthe sits so close to the border of the Yellow Country that half the day is gold and half the day is green. Three brothers sculpted the whole city—houses, pubs, war monuments—out of jellybean-colored ice with only a little bit of wormwood for stability and character. I didn't learn that from Jellyfish or Mummery, but from a malachite sign on the highway leading into the city. The brothers were named Peapod. They were each missing their pinky fingers but not for the same reason.

It turns out everybody notices you when you ride into town on a purple woolly mammoth with snowshoes for feet with a unicorn in your lap and a bone mask on your face. I couldn't decide if I liked being invisible better or being watched by everybody all at once. They both hurt. Loyalties scattered before us like pigeons, their pale green greasepainted faces miming despair or delight or umbrage, depending on their schtick. They mimed tripping over each other, and then some actually did trip, and soon we'd caused a mime-jam and I had to leave my sorrow parked in the street. I was so hungry I could barely shiver in the cold. Jellyfish knew a cafe called O Tannenbaum but I didn't have any money.

"That's all right," said the watercolor unicorn. "In the Green Country, money means grief."

So I paid for a pine-green leather booth at O Tannenbaum, a stein of creme de menthe, a mugwort cake and parakeet pie with tears. The waiter wore a waistcoat of clover with moldavite buttons. He held out his hands politely. I didn't think I could do it. You can't just grieve because the bill wants 15% agony on top of the prix fixe. But my grief happened to me like a back alley mugging and I put my face into his hands so no one would see my sobbing; I put my face into his hands like a bone mask so no one could see what I looked like on the inside.

"I'm so lonely," I wept. "I'm nobody but a wound walking around." I lifted my head—my head felt heavier than a planet. "Did you ever meet anyone who fucked up and put it all right again, put it all back the way it was?"

"Nobody green," said the waiter, but he walked away looking very pleased with his tip.

It's a hard damn thing when you're feeling lowly to sit in a leather booth with nobody but a unicorn across from you. Lucky for me, a squirrel hopped up on the bamboo table. She sat back on her hind two legs and rubbed her humongous paradox-pregnant belly with the other four paws. Her bushy mauve tail stood at attention behind her, bristling so hard you could hear it crackling.

"Pink and green feel good on my eyes," the time-squirrel said in Orchid Harm's voice.

"Oh, go drown yourself in a hole," I spat at it, and drank my creme de menthe, which gave me a creme de menthe mustache that completely undermined much of what I said later.

The squirrel tried again. She opened her mouth and my voice came out.

"No quisquoses or querulous tristiloquies," she said soothingly. But I had no use for a squirrel's soothe.

"Eat shit," I hissed.

But that little squirrel was the squirrel who would not quit. She rubbed her cheeks and stretched her jaw and out came a voice I did not know, a man's voice, with a very expensive accent.

"The Red Country is the only country with walls. It stands to reason something precious lives there. But short of all-out war, which I think we can all agree is at least inconvenient, if not irresponsible, we cannot know what those walls conceal. I would suggest espionage, if we can find a suitable candidate."

Now, I don't listen to chronosquirrels. They're worse than toddlers. They babble out things that got themselves said a thousand months ago or will be said seventy years from now or were only said by a preying mantis wearing suspenders in a universe that's already burned itself out. When I was little I used to listen, but my Papo spanked me and told me the worst thing in the world was for a Nowboy to listen to his herd. *It'll drive you madder than a plate of snakes*, he said. He never spanked me for anything else and that's how I know he meant serious business. But this dopey doe also meant serious business. I could tell by her tail. And I probably would have gotten into it with her, which may or may not have done me a lick of good, except that I'd made a mistake without even thinking about it, without even brushing off a worry or a grain of dread, and just at that moment when I was about to tilt face first into Papo's plate of snakes, the jade pepper grinder turned into a jade Emperor with black peppercorn lips and a squat silver crown.

"Salutations, young Violet," said the Ordinary Emperor in a voice like a hot cocktail. "What's a nice purple girl like you doing in a bad old green place like this?"

Jellyfish shrieked. When a unicorn shrieks, it sounds like sighing. I just stared. I'd been so careful. The Emperor of Peppercorns hopped across the table on his grinder. The mauve squirrel patted his crown with one of her hands. They were about the same height. I shook my head and declined to say several swear words.

"Don't feel bad, Miss V," he said. "It's not possible to live without objects. Why do you think I do things this way? Because I enjoy being hand brooms and cheese-knives?"

"Leave me alone," I moaned.

"Now, I just heard you say you were lonely! You don't have to be lonely. None of my subjects have to be lonely! It was one of my campaign promises, you know."

"Go back to Mummery. Mind your own business."

The Ordinary Emperor stroked his jade beard. "I think you liked me better when I was naked in your kitchen. I can do it again, if you like. I want you to like me. That is the cornerstone of my administration."

"No. Be a pepper grinder. Be a broom."

"Your Papo cannot handle the herd by himself, señorita," clucked the Ordinary Emperor. "You've abandoned him. Midnight comes at 3 p.m. in Plum Pudding. Every day is Thursday. Your Mummery has had her clarinet out day and night looking for you."

"Papo managed before I was born, he can manage now. And you could have told Mums I was fine."

"I could have. I know what you're doing. It's a silly, old-fashioned thing, but it's just so *you*. I've written a song about it, you know. I called it *My Baby Done Gone to Red*. It's proved very popular on the radio, but then, most of my songs do."

"I've been gone for three days!"

"Culture moves very quickly when it needs to, funny bunny. Don't you like having a song with you in it?"

I thought about Mummery and all the people who thought she was fine as a sack of bees and drank her up like champagne. She lived for that drinking-up kind of love. Maybe I would, too, if I ever got it. The yellow half of Absinthe's day came barreling through the cafe window like a bandit in a barfight. Gold, gorgeous, impossible gold, on my hands and my shoulders and my unicorn and my mouth, the color of the slat under my bed, the color of the secret I showed Orchid before I loved him. Sitting in that puddle of suddenly gold light felt like wearing a tiger's fur.

"Well, I haven't heard the song," I allowed. Maybe I wanted a little of that champagne-love, too.

Then the Ordinary Emperor wasn't a pepper grinder anymore because he was that beautiful man in doublet and hose and a thousand hundred colors who stood in my kitchen smelling like sex and power and eleven kinds of orange and white. He put his hands over mine.

"Didn't you ever wonder why the clarinauts are the only ones who travel between countries? Why they're so famous and why everyone wants to hear what they say?"

"I never thought about it even one time." That was a lie; I thought about it all the time the whole year I was eleven but that was long enough ago that it didn't feel like much of a lie.

He wiped away my creme de menthe mustache. I didn't know it yet, but my lips stayed green and they always would. "A clarinaut is born with a reed in her heart through which the world can pass and make a song. For everyone else, leaving home is poison. They just get so lost. Sometimes they spiral down the drain and end up Red. Most of the time they just wash away. It's because of the war. Bombs are so unpredictable. I'm sure everyone feels very embarrassed now."

I didn't want to talk about the specialness of Mummery. I didn't want to cry, either, but I was, and my tears splashed down onto the table in big, showy drops of gold. The Ordinary Emperor knuckled under my chin.

"*Mon petite biche*, it is natural to want to kill yourself when you have bitten off a hurt so big you can't swallow it. I once threw myself off Split Salmon Bridge in the Orange Country. But the Marmalade Sea spit me back. The Marmalade Sea thinks suicide is for cowards and she won't be a part of it. But you and I know better."

"I don't want to kill myself!"

"It doesn't matter what death means in the Red Country, Violet. Orchid didn't die in the Red Country. And you won't make it halfway across the Tangerine Tundra. You're already bleeding." He turned over my blue palm, tracing tracks in my golden tears. "You'll ride your sorrow into a red brick wall."

"It does matter. It does. You don't matter. My sorrow loves me."

"And what kind of love would that be? The love that means killing? Or eating? Or keeping warm? Do you know what 'I love you' means in the Yellow Country?"

"It means 'I cannot stand the sight of you,'" whinnied Jellyfish, flicking her apricot and daffodil tail. "Ocherous Wince said it to all her paintings every day."

The waiter appeared to take the Ordinary Emperor's order. He trembled slightly, his clovers quivering. "The pea soup and a glass of green apple gin with a dash of melon syrup, my good man," his majesty said without glancing at the help. "I shall tell you a secret if you like, Violet. It's better than a swipe of gold paint, I promise."

"I don't care." My face got all hot and plum-dark even through the freezing lemony air. I didn't want him to talk about my slat. "Why do you bother with me? Go be a government by yourself."

"I like you. Isn't that enough? I like how much you look like your Mummery. I like how hard you rode Stopwatch across the Past Perfect Plains. I like how you looked at me when you caught me making coffee. I like that you painted the underside of your bed and I especially like how you showed it to Orchid. I'm going to tell you anyway. Before I came to the throne, during the reign of the Extraordinary Emperor, I hunted sorrows. Professionally. In fact, it was I who hunted them to extinction."

"What the hell did you do that for?" The waiter set down his royal meal and fled which I would also have liked to do but could not because I did not work in food service.

"Because I am from the Orange Country, and in the Orange Country, a sorrow is not a mammoth with a cabinet in its stomach, it is a kind of melancholic dread, a bitter, heartsick gloom. It feels as though you can never get free of a sorrow once you have one, as though you become allergic to happiness. It was because of a certain sorrow that I leapt from the Split Salmon Bridge. My parents died of a housefire and then my wife died of being my wife." The Ordinary Emperor's voice stopped working quite right and he sipped his gin. "All this having happened before the war, we could all hop freely from Orange to Yellow to Purple to Blue to Green—through Red was always a suspicious nation, their immigration policies never sensible, even then, even then when no one else knew what a lock was or a key. When I was a young man I did as young men do—I traveled, I tried to find women to travel with me, I ate foreign food and pretended to like it. And I saw that everywhere else, sorrows roamed like buffalo, and they were not distresses nor dolors nor disconsolations, but animals who could bleed. Parasites drinking from us like fountains. I did not set out for politics, but to rid the world of sorrows. I thought if I could kill them in the other countries, the Orange Country sort of sorrow would perish, too. I rode the ranges on a quagga with indigestion. I invented the Nonegun myself—I'll tell you that secret, too, if you like, and then you will know something your Mums doesn't, which I think is just about the best gift I could give you. To make the little engine inside a Nonegun you have to feel nothing for anyone. Your heart has to look like the vacuum of space. Not coincidentally, that is also how you make the engine inside an Emperor. I shot all the sorrows between the eyes. I murdered them. I rode them down. I was merciless."

"Did it work?" I asked softly.

"No. When I go home I still want to die. But it made a good campaign slogan. I have told you this for two reasons. The first is that when you pass into the Orange Country you will want to cut yourself open from throat to navel. Your sorrow has gotten big and fat. It will sit on you and you will not get up again. Believe me, I know. When I saw you come home with a sorrow following you like a homeless kitten I almost shot it right there and I should have. They have no good parts. Perhaps that is why I like you, really. Because I bleached sorrow from the universe and you found one anyway."

The Ordinary Emperor took my face in his hands. He kissed me. I started to not like it but it turned into a different kind of kiss, not like the kisses I made with Orchid, but a kiss that made me wonder what it meant to kiss someone in the Orange Country, a kiss half full of apology and half full of nostalgia and a third half full of do what I say or else. So in the end I came round again to not liking it. I didn't know what he was thinking when he kissed me. I guess that's not a thing that always happens.

"The second reason I told you about the sorrows, Violet Wild, is so that you will know that I can do anything. I am the man who murdered sorrow. It said that on my election posters. You were too young to vote, but your Mummery wasn't, and you won't be too young when I come up for re-election."

"So?"

"So if you run as my Vice-Emperor, which is another way of saying Empress, which is another way of saying wife, I will kill time for you, just like I killed sorrow. Squirrels will be no trouble after all those woolly monsters. Then everything can happen at once and you will both have Orchid and not have him at the same time because the part where you showed him the slat under your bed and the part where his body disappeared on the edge of the Blue Country will not have to happen in that order, or any order. It will be the same for my wife and my parents and only in the Red Country will time still mean passing."

The squirrel still squatted on the table with her belly full of baby futures in her greedy hands. She glared at the Ordinary Emperor with unpasteurized hate in her milky eyes. I looked out the great ice picture window of the restaurant that wasn't called O Tannenbaum anymore, but The Jonquil Julep, the hoppingest nightspot in the Yellow Country. Only the farthest fuzz on the horizon still looked green. Chic blonde howdy-dos started to crowd in wearing daffodil dresses and butterscotch tuxedos. Some of them looked sallow and waxy; some of them coughed.

"There is always a spot of cholera in the Yellow Country," admitted the Ordinary Emperor with some chagrin. Through the glass I saw my sorrow hunched over, peering in at the Emperor, weeping soundlessly, wiping her eyes with her trunk. "But the light here is so good for painting."

Everything looked like the underside of my bed. The six-legged squirrel said:

"Show me something your parents don't know about."

And love went pinballing through me but it was a Yellow kind of love and suddenly my creme de menthe was banana schanpps and suddenly my mugwort cake was lemon meringue and suddenly I hated Orchid Harm. I hated him for making me have an ardor for something that wasn't a pony or a Papo or a color of paint, I hated him for being a Sunslinger all over town even though everybody knew that shit would hollow you out and fill you back up with nothing if you stuck with it. I hated him for making friends with my unicorn and I hated him for hanging around Papo and me till he got dead from it and I hated him for bleeding out under me and making everything that happened happen. I didn't want to see his horrible handsome face ever again. I didn't want alive-Orchid and dead-Orchid at the same time, which is a pretty colossally unpleasant idea when you think about it. My love was the sourest thing I'd ever had. If Orchid had sidled up and ordered a cantaloupe whiskey, I would have turned my face away. I had to swallow all that back to talk again.

"But killing sorrow didn't work," I said, but I kept looking at my sorrow on the other side of the window.

"I obviously missed one," he said grimly. "I will be more thorough."

And the Ordinary Emperor, quick as a rainbow coming on, snatched up the squirrel of time and whipped her little body against the lemonwood table so that it broke her neck right in half. She didn't even get a chance to squeak.

Sometimes it takes me a long time to think through things, to set them up just right in my head so I can see how they'd break if I had a hammer. But sometimes I have a hammer. So I said:

"No, that sounds terrible. You are terrible. I am a Nowgirl and a Nowgirl doesn't lead her herd to slaughter. Bring them home, bring them in, my Papo always said that and that's what I will always say, too. Go away. Go be dried pasta. Go be sad and orange. Go jump off your bridge again. I'm going to the Red Country on my sorrow's back."

The Ordinary Emperor held up his hand. He stood to leave as though he were a regular person who was going to walk out the door and not just turn into a bar of Blue Country soap. He looked almost completely white in the loud yellow sunshine. The light burned my eyes.

"It's dangerous in the Red Country, Violet. You'll have to say what you mean. Even your Mummery never flew so far."

He dropped the corpse of the mauve space-time squirrel next to his butter knife by way of paying his tab because in the Yellow Country, money means time.

"You are not a romantic man," said Jellyfish through clenched pistachio-colored teeth. That's the worst insult a watercolor unicorn knows.

"There's a shortcut to the Orange Country in the ladies' room. Turn the right tap three times, the left tap once, and pull the stopper out of the basin." That was how the Ordinary Emperor said goodbye. I'm pretty sure he told Mummery I was a no-good whore who would never make good even if I lived to a hundred. That's probably even true. But that wasn't why I ran after him and stabbed him in the neck with the poisonous prong of the story hanging from my belt. I did that because, no matter what, a Nowgirl looks after her herd.

5. ORANGE

THIS IS WHAT happened to me in the Orange Country: I didn't see any cities even though there are really nice cities there, or drink any alcohol even though I've always heard clementine schnapps is really great, or talk to any animals even though in the Orange Country a poem means a kind of tiger that can't talk but can sing, or people, even though there were probably some decent ones making a big bright orange life somewhere.

I came out of the door in the basin of The Jonquil Julep and I lay down on floor of a carrot-colored autumn jungle and cried until I didn't have anything wet left to lose. Then I crawled under a papaya tree and clawed the orange clay until I made a hole big enough to climb inside if I curled up my whole body like a circle you draw with one smooth motion. The clay smelled like fire.

"I love you," said my sorrow. She didn't look well. Her fur was threadbare, translucent, her trunk dried out.

"I don't know what 'I love you' means in the Orange Country," sighed Jellyfish.

"I do," said the Sparrowbone Mask of the Incarnadine Fisherwomen, who hadn't had a damn thing to say in ages. "Here, if you love someone, you mean to keep them prisoner and never let them see the sun."

"But then they'd be safe," I whispered.

"I love you," said my sorrow. She got down on her giant woolly knees beside my hole. "I love you. Your eyes are yellow."

I began to claw into the orange clay of my hole. I peeled it away and crammed it into my mouth. My teeth went through it easy as anything. It didn't taste like dirt. It tasted like a lot of words, one after the other, with conflict and resolution and a beginning, middle, but no end. It tasted like Mummery showing me how to play the clarinet. It tasted like an Emperor who wasn't an Emperor anymore. The earth stained my tongue orange forever.

"I love you," said my sorrow.

"I heard you, dammit," I said between bright mouthfuls.

Like she was putting an exclamation point on her favorite phrase, my sorrow opened up her cabinet doors in the sienna shadows of the orange jungle. Toucans and orioles and birds of paradise crowed and called and their crowing and calling caromed off the titian trunks until my ears hated birdsong more than any other thing. My sorrow opened up her cabinet doors and the wind whistled through the space inside her and it sounded like Premiére Rhapsodie in A Major through the holes of a fuel-efficient crystal clarinet.

Inside my sorrow hung a dress the color of garnets, with a long train trailing behind it and a neckline that plunged to the navel. It looked like it would be very hard to dance in.

6. RED

IN THE RED Country, love is love, loyalty is loyalty, a story is a story, and death is a long red dress. The Red Country is the only country with walls.

I slept my way into the Red Country.

I lay down inside the red dress called death; I lay down inside my sorrow and a bone mask crawled onto my face; I lay down and didn't dream and my sorrow smuggled me out of the orange jungles where sorrow is sadness. I don't remember that part so I can't say anything about it. The inside of my sorrow was cool and dim; there wasn't any furniture in there, or any candles. She seemed all right again, once we'd lumbered on out of the jungle. Strong and solid like she'd been in the beginning. I didn't throw up even though I ate all that dirt. Jellyfish told me later that the place where the Orange Country turns into the Red Country is a marshland full of flamingos and ruby otters fighting for supremacy. I would have liked to have seen that.

I pulled it together by the time we reached the riverbanks. The Incarnadine River flows like blood out of the marshes, through six locks and four sluice gates in the body of a red brick wall as tall as clouds. Then it joins the greater rushing rapids and pools of the Claret, the only river in seven kingdoms with dolphins living in it, and all together, the rivers and the magenta dolphins, roar and tumble down the valleys and into the heart of the city of Cranberry-on-Claret.

Crimson boats choked up the Incarnadine. A thousand fishing lines stuck up into the pink dawn like pony-poles on the pampas. The fisherwomen all wore masks like mine, masks like mine and burgundy swimming costumes that covered them from neck to toe and all I could think was how I'd hate to swim in one of those things, but they probably never had to because if you fell out of your boat you'd just land in another boat. The fisherwomen cried out when they saw me. I suppose I looked frightening, wearing that revealing, low-cut death and the bone mask and riding a mammoth with a unicorn in my arms. They called me some name that wasn't Violet Wild and the ones nearest to shore climbed out of their boats, shaking and laughing and holding out their arms. I don't think anyone should get stuck holding their arms out to nothing and no one, so I shimmied down my sorrow's fur and they clung on for dear life, touching the Sparrowbone Mask of the Incarnadine Fisherwomen, stroking its cheeks, its red spiral mouth, telling it how it had scared them, vanishing like that.

"I love you," the Sparrowbone Mask of the Incarnadine Fisherwomen kept saying over and over. It felt strange when the mask on my face spoke but I didn't speak. "I love you. Sometimes you can't help vanishing. I love you. I can't stay."

My mask and I said both together: "We are afraid of the wall."

"Don't be doltish," an Incarnadine Fisherwoman said. She must have been a good fisherwoman as she had eight vermillion catfish hanging off her belt and some of them were still opening and closing their mouths, trying to breathe water that had vanished like a mask. "You're one of us."

So my sorrow swam through the wall. She got into the scarlet water which rose all the way up to her eyeballs but she didn't mind. I rode her like sailing a boat and the red water soaked the train of my red death dress and magenta dolphins followed along with us, jumping out of the water and echolocating like a bunch of maniacs and the Sparrowbone Mask of the Incarnadine Fisherwomen said:

"I am beginning to remember who I am now that everything is red again. Why is anything unred in the world? It's madness."

Jellyfish hid her lavender face in her watermelon-colored hooves and whispered:

"Please don't forget about me, I am water soluble!"

I wondered, when the river crashed into the longest wall in the world, a red brick wall that went on forever side to side and also up and down, if the wall had a name. Everything has a name, even if that name is in Latin and nobody knows it but one person who doesn't live nearby. Somebody had tried to blow up the wall several times. Jagged chunks were missing; bullets had gouged out rock and mortar long ago, but no one had ever made a hole. The Incarnadine River slushed in through a cherry-colored sluice gate. Rosy sunlight lit up its prongs. I glided on in with all the other fisherwomen like there never was a wall in the first place. I looked behind us—the river swarmed with squirrels, gasping, half drowning, paddling their little feet for dear life. They squirmed through the sluice gate like plague rats.

"If you didn't have that mask on, you would have had to pay the toll," whispered Jellyfish.

"What's the toll?"

"A hundred years as a fisherwoman."

CRANBERRY-ON-CLARET IS A city of carnelian and lacquerwork and carbuncle streetlamps glowing with red gas flames because the cities of the Red Country are not electrified like Plum Pudding and Lizard Tongue and Absinthe. People with hair the color of raspberries and eyes the color of wood embers play ruby bassoons and chalcedony hurdy-gurdies and cinnamon-stick violins on the long, wide streets and they never stop even when they sleep; they just switch to nocturnes and keep playing through their dreaming. When they saw me coming, they started up *My Baby Done Gone to Red*, which, it turns out, is only middling as far as radio hits go.

Some folks wore deaths like mine. Some didn't. The Ordinary Emperor said that sometimes the dead go to the Red Country but nobody looked dead. They looked busy like city people always look. It was warm in Cranberry-on-Claret, an autumnal kind of warm, the kind that's having a serious think about turning to cold. The clouds glowed primrose and carmine.

"Where are we going?" asked my watercolor unicorn.

"The opera house," I answered.

I guess maybe all opera houses are skulls because the one in the Red Country looked just like the one back home except, of course, as scarlet as the spiral mouth of a mask. It just wasn't a human skull. Out of a cinnabar piazza hunched up a squirrel skull bigger than a cathedral and twice as fancy. Its great long teeth opened and closed like proper doors and prickled with scrimshaw carving like my Papo used to do on pony-bones. All over the wine-colored skull grew bright hibiscus flowers and devil's hat mushrooms and red velvet lichen and fire opals.

Below the opera house and behind they kept the corrals. Blue stories milled miserably in pens, their sapphire plates drooping, their eyes all gooey with cataracts. I took off the Sparrowbone Mask of the Incarnadine Fisherwomen and climbed down my sorrow.

"Heyo, beastie-blues," I said, holding my hands out for them to sniff through the copper wire and redwood of their paddock. "No lachrymose quadrupeds on my watch. Be not down in the mouth. Woe-be-gone, not woe-be-come."

"That's blue talk," a boy-story whispered. "You gotta talk red or you get no cud."

"Say what you mean," grumbled a girl-story with three missing scales over her left eye. "It's the law."

"I always said what I meant. I just meant something very fancy," sniffed a grandfather-story lying in the mud to stay cool.

"Okay. I came from the Purple Country to find a boy named Orchid Harm."

"Nope, that's not what you mean," the blue grandpa dinosaur growled, but he didn't seem upset about it. Stories mostly growl unless they're sick.

"Sure it is!"

"I'm just a simple story, what do I know?" He turned his cerulean rump to me.

"You're just old and rude. I'm pretty sure Orchid is up there in the eye of that skull, it's only that I was going to let you out of your pen before I went climbing but maybe I won't now."

"How's about we tell you what you mean and then you let us out and nobody owes nobody nothing?" said the girl-story with the missing scales. It made me sad to hear a story talking like that, with no grammar at all.

"I came from the Purple Country to find Orchid," I repeated because I was afraid.

"Are you sure you're not an allegory for depression or the agrarian revolution or the afterlife?"

"I'm not an allegory for anything! You're an allegory! And you stink!"

"If you say so."

"What do *you* mean then?"

"I mean a blue dinosaur. I mean a story about a girl who lost somebody and couldn't get over it. I can mean both at the same time. That's allowed."

"This isn't any better than when you were saying *autarchy* and *peregrinate*."

"So peregrinate with autarchy, girlie. That's how you're supposed to act around stories, anyway. Who raised you?"

I kicked out the lock on their paddock and let the reptilian stories loose. They bolted like blue lightning into the cinnabar piazza. Jellyfish ran joyfully among them, jumping and wriggling and whinnying, giddy to be in a herd again, making a mess of a color scheme.

"I love you," said my sorrow. She had shrunk up small again, no taller than a good dog, and she was wearing the Sparrowbone Mask of the Incarnadine Fisherwomen. By the time I'd gotten halfway up the opera-skull, she was gone.

"LET US BEGIN by practicing the chromatic scale, beginning with E Major."

That is what the voice coming out of the eye socket of a giant operatic squirrel said and it was Orchid's voice and it had a laugh hidden inside it like it always did. I pulled myself up and over the lip of the socket and curled up next to Orchid Harm and his seven books, of which he'd already read four. I curled up next to him like nothing bad had ever happened. I fit into the line of his body and he fit into mine. I didn't say anything for a long, long time. He stroked my hair and read to me about basic strumming technique but after awhile he stopped talking too and we just sat there quietly and he smelled like sunlight and booze and everything purple in the world.

"I killed the Ordinary Emperor with a story's tail," I confessed at last.

"I missed you, too."

"Are you dead?"

"The squirrels won't tell me. Something about collapsing a waveform. But I'm not the one wearing a red dress."

I looked down. Deep red silky satin death flowed out over the bone floor. A lot of my skin showed in the slits of that dress. It felt nice.

"The squirrels ate you, though."

"You never know with squirrels. I think I ate some of them, too. It's kind of the same thing, with time travel, whether you eat the squirrel or the squirrel eats you. I remember it hurt. I remember you kissed me till it was over. I remember Early-to-Tea and Stopwatch screaming. Sometimes you can't help vanishing. Anyway, the squirrels felt bad about it. Because we'd taken care of them so well and they had to do it anyway. They apologized for ages. I fell asleep once in the middle of them going on and on about how timelines taste."

"Am I dead?"

"I don't know, did you die?"

"Maybe the bubbles got me. The Emperor said I'd get sick if I traveled without a clarinet. And parts of me aren't my own parts anymore." I stretched out my legs. They were the color of rooster feathers. "But I don't think so. What do you mean the squirrels had to do it?"

"Self-defense, is what they said about a million times."

"What? We never so much as kicked one!"

"You have to think like a six-legged mauve squirrel of infinite time. The Ordinary Emperor was going to hunt them all down one by one and set the chronology of everything possible and impossible on fire. They set a contraption in motion so that he couldn't touch them, a contraption involving you and me and a blue story and a Red Country where nobody dies, they just change clothes. They're very tidy creatures. Don't worry, we're safe in the Red Country. There'll probably be another war. The squirrels can't fix that. They're only little. But everyone always wants to conquer the Red Country and nobody ever has. We have a wall and it's a really good one."

I twisted my head up to look at him, his plum-colored hair, his amethyst eyes, his stubborn chin. "You have to say what you mean here."

"I mean I love you. And I mean the infinite squirrels of space and time devoured me to save themselves from annihilation at the hands of a pepper grinder. I can mean both. It's allowed."

I kissed Orchid Harm inside the skull of a giant rodent and we knew that we were both thinking about ice cream. The ruby bassoons hooted up from the piazza and scarlet tanagers scattered from the rooftops and a watercolor unicorn told a joke about the way tubas are way down the road but the echoes carried her voice up and up and everywhere. Orchid stopped the kiss first. He pointed to the smooth crimson roof of the eye socket.

A long stripe of gold paint gleamed there.

The Beasts Who Fought for Fairyland UNTIL THE VERY END AND FURTHER STILL

ONCE UPON A TIME, THREE rather large and unusual creatures grew very tired indeed of fighting, day and night and day again, fighting the same overwhelming and unyielding enemies, fighting with all their large and scaly might, as well as their claws, teeth, flaming breath, and occasionally, walloping rune-carved giant's hammers they found lying about where others had fallen. Because the sun was setting rosy in the sky, and because they could hardly bear to put one foot in front of the other, and because, at long last, their fates had been tucked firmly into bed and told to stay there or else, these three rather large and unusual beasts sat down upon a rather large and filthy hill in a country called Fairyland. The hill was filthy because a great battle had been fought there. Bronze and wicker and glass armor lay everywhere strewn about. Swords and axes and scissors and needles and a million thousand arrows turned that hill into a pincushion. Each arrow was fletched in feathers that once belonged to immortal birds so wise that if you asked them to tell you the meaning of life, they would have an answer, and it would be short, and easy to understand, and as true as tea. The three creatures sat carefully on their haunches inside a prickly prison of blades and bows and bucklers.

One was a tall man all in green, armored in a battered green breastplate and a battered green helmet and a green carriage-driver's cloak and hardy green boots. One was an enormous Leopard with a curling green saddle on her back. The man smoked a long green pipe, and wherever he went a fresh green wind followed. This was not surprising, for he *was* the Green Wind, and his cat was the Leopard of Little Breezes. Together they brought storms and sighs to all the six corners of the world. The third creature looked something like a dragon. But he could not be a dragon, surely not, for he had no forepaws. His body curved back against his powerful hind legs like a capital S. He was the color of the very last embers of the fire, and his belly was the color of old peaches. He was graceful and gallant and gregarious and grim. His huge claws were very black, his eyes were very orange, his horns were fierce and sharp, he had long whiskers hanging from long snouts, and enormous wings like bats, if bats were far bigger than houses, extremely bony, and not in the least blind.

If you have not guessed it already, this dear and daring beast was a Wyvern. A Wyverary, if we are to be taxonomically accurate, for though his mother was a proper Wyvern, his father was a library. That only sounds strange if both of *your* parents were precisely the same sort of animal, which hardly ever happens, when you really think about it. He had been named for the family business, for a library has ever so many encylcopedias, and the beast was called A-Through-L. He knew just everything about everything, so long as it began with the letters A through L.

They were all very young, really, too young for all they had seen, but too old not to have seen it. They had only just met today, having fought on the same side, and after today, they would not meet again for a very, very long time. But they had become fast friends, for that is what three people who have survived something dreadful together always do.

The Wyvern looked down from their pincushion hill of swords and arrows into a long, deep valley. It had been very pretty down there once. Lots of blue stones and violet flowers and rabbits and foxes and minks who realized long ago that they all had soft ears and moist noses and hated hunters, and so, rather than fight each other, formed a collective for the Betterment of Us Who Gets Stalked and Shot At Just for Minding Our Own Business Whilst Being Fuzzy, and lived in reasonable happiness. None of that was down there any longer. No flowers, no stones, no softness. A great battle had been fought in the Valley of Soft Ears. The last battle of the war, in fact. A stranger had come, an outsider, a mysterious girl with untold riches and untold fury. She had sent her armies screaming through the meadows and forests to seize Fairyland for herself.

It had been a ferocious fight, all against all. One side sent Witches and Magicians and Unicorns and Manticores and Gnomes, whoever would stand, whatever would serve, until, in the end, the last warriors had no more to hurl at one another but their shoes, and then they hurled those, too. The other side sent Pookas and Dragons and their own Witches and their own Manticores, but most of all they sent Redcaps, in wave after wave, some riding great beasts of the air, some charging on great beasts of the earth, stout and furious creatures who kept their hats red with the blood of those they hated. Stray flashes of spent magic still burbled and rumbled through the valley. Dragons, Wyverns, Sphinxes, Griffins and Harpies, the Flying Ace Corps, wheeled in long, exhausted circles, looking for stragglers to carry off. Below, the fallen lay where they had lost their last struggles against the army of Redcaps, and even the clouds had begun to weep.

"We lost," said A-Through-L. His strong voice went all funny in his throat.

"Looks that way, Ell," said the Green Wind. He did not sound very concerned. "May I call you Ell?"

Ell nodded and sniffed in the cold autumn wind. "The Marquess is going to rule over all of us forever and ever, and she is...she is...*terrible*."

"Suppose so." The Green Wind blew smoke out of both his purple nostrils. The Leopard purred and said nothing. Cats are not terribly talkative.

"But how could we *lose*, Mr. Green? It's not possible. All the Sirens and the Witches said we'd win as easy as supper and twice as quick. They said no one so wicked and cruel and so awfully *angry* could ever rule Fairyland. They said that sort of thing only happens in other worlds that are not so full of magic and wonder as ours. All the prophecies agreed on it."

"I think I see a Witch in that cage by the big oak tree," the Green Wind noted, pointing with his pipe. "Being menaced by a lion."

It was true—down deep in the Valley of Soft Ears, a gargantuan blue lion roared into a silver birdcage, where a young man all in black cowered with his arms curled protectively over his cauldron. Witches brew up the future in their cauldrons, you see. They take up a wooden Spoon and boil a soup out of everything you did today and everything you did yesterday and all the days before, and everything anyone you ever met did, too, and that is how you get a prophecy. This is very much like what statisticians and journalists do in our world, only with more tasty onions and mutton and incantations. None of the Wyverns could hear anything over the din of the battle's end, but I am a Narrator, and my powers of hearing are extremely keen, for I must listen through every closed door, every secret meeting, every whisper in every corner of a tale. I shall tell you what the lion roared. It roared: *you will make a new future in your stupid bowl, and it will say all the things we want it to say and none of the things we do not! The new future will say that everything good in Fairyland is down to us and everything that goes sideways is down to our enemies. It will say that we are the best people, with the best plans, and the best words, and the best rulers in the history of bestnesses. Make it say the old King and Queen are liars and villains but the Marquess is a truth-teller and a champion who has released the world from sorrow forever. Make it say she is the only one who can fix Fairyland and make it great.*

And to this the Witch said: *But none of that is true! Fairyland isn't broken! The Marquess lies and steals and cheats and snatches folk up for her own use and hates a great many more people than is healthy for a growing girl. Our old King was marvelous! The Queen just wasn't very good at parties, that's all. The worst thing she did was accidentally burn up a book of spells one time.*

The lion snarled: *if you say it, if you boil it up in your bowl, it will* become *true. Everyone believes Witches. You will be rewarded with gold and jewels.*

And when the Witch still refused, the lion thrust a paw through the bars of the cage and swiped away the young man's wooden Spoon, the great emblem of a Witch's power. *Then we do not need you,* laughed the lion. *We control the Spoon! Everyone will believe* us *now!*

"But we tried so *hard*," whispered the red Wyvern on the hill.

"Why should that make any difference?" answered the Green Wind, who was somewhat older and therefore somewhat more accustomed to things not going his way.

Ell frowned and stared at the churned-up dirt of the ruined hill. He scrunched up his orange eyes so as not to cry.

"Well, because...because it's a bad *story!* Stories aren't supposed to end like this. They're just not! Things are supposed to get *better.* Things are supposed to make *sense.*"

The man all in green lifted one emerald eyebrow. "Oh? Did you never find a story in all of your Papa's bookshelves in which a wicked dark lord rose up and put a crown on his own head? In which the cruel tyrant covered the land in night and ravaged the countryside, destroying and devouring and devastating the lives of people both gentle and kind? Did you never find one single tale in the corner of your noble father's stacks where folk banded together and rose up against this terrible King, standing back to back and crying out: *we do not look to be ruled?*"

"Well, of course I did, Mr. Green! But in all those stories, at the *end* of all those stories, the dark lord was cast down into infinite nothingness or burnt to a crisp or at the *very* least sent to bed without supper, and everyone cheered and danced and had a party afterward. But the end of *this* story is that we lost and she gets to do whatever she wants to us forever. How shall we ever have parties again? How shall we cheer? How shall we dance? I don't think the Marquess likes dancing. I think she only likes cheering if people are cheering her name and I think she only likes parties if they're her own birthday and she gets all the presents."

"Perhaps this is not the end of the story, then," the Green Wind said kindly, though he wasn't sure he believed it. It was important to say it to the brokenhearted, to the young, to everyone, even if he didn't believe his own words. Especially if he didn't believe it. If no one said it, it couldn't even start being true.

"It *feels* like the end," said A-Through-L with a strangled cry.

"It always does, when you lose." The Green Wind took off his green helmet and laid it on the grass between two arrows. "But haven't we had tyrants and fools and hobgoblins on the throne before? Haven't we had rather a *lot* of hobgoblins? Aren't hobgoblins rather more the rule than the exception?"

"Yes..."

"And haven't we always patched up their mischief and gotten back to more or less living how we want to live and loving who we want to love and making what we want to make and being who we want to be?"

"Yes…"

"Perhaps Fairyland is stronger than her goblins, my ravishing reptile. Perhaps, if you take a long enough view, we are all stronger than our goblins."

"But this is different! Oh, I feel it in my bones! She is menacing the Witches and hunting down the Stregas who heal our wounds and she told the foxes and rabbits and minks that they *deserved* to be Stalked and Shot At Just for Minding Their Own Business Whilst Being Fuzzy and I have heard…I have heard she even wants to outlaw the study of Queer Physicks. How will we have magic without the queerest of all the sciences? Oh, I know all about Different, Mr. Green, for it begins with D. And this feels *different*."

"It always does, when you lose." The Green Wind stroked the Leopard of Little Breezes' spotted head. Far below, a Griffin cried out in pain and ran terrified from the ruined battlefield, the ruined valley which once held so many soft ears. "But perhaps you are right. I have heard worse still, Ell. I have heard the Marquess longs to build a wall between Fairyland and the human world, so that no human children may ever come here and have adventures again. Though I may have some small thing to say about that, myself. The Marquess is certainly deplorable, and she lusts after deplorable things."

"But if she is so deplorable, why did all those noble Dragons and Griffins and Gnomes and Centaurs and Glashtyn and Pixies fight for her? She has an army of dreadful, sneering Redcaps who love her desperately and want nothing more than to stain their caps even redder with the blood of her enemies. I suppose I understand the Redcaps. It's their nature to hurt things. But the others? There must be *something* wonderful about her if they love her desperately. You cannot love anything desperately that does not have some tiny wonder buried inside it."

The Green Wind stared into the darkening sky for a long time. "There is a dreadful sort of spell that certain people can cast, Ell. It is a very ancient and powerful spell, but difficult to pull off. All the circumstances must be just right. If you fall under the spell, you hear a story every night when you fall asleep and every morning when you wake up and you hear it twice at lunchtime. It is a story about yourself, a story that sounds so good and true that you fall in love with it. You want to hear it again and again. You snuggle up to it for warmth. You set a place for it at the dinner table. The story tells you that the world is an easy and simple place, and you—yes, you!—are the very center of it. You are a hero, *the* hero, and nothing beastly that has ever happened to you is your fault. Very soon you will be loved and treasured and celebrated the way you ought to be, the way you always *should* have been. Very soon indeed…if only those wretched…oh, let us say Satyrs. If only those wretched Satyrs were not taking all the good bits of everything for themselves and keeping your cupboards empty."

"Why would the Satyrs steal from me?" breathed Ell, wide-eyed. "What have I ever done to them? Are all these frightful battles *their* doing? Let's go and talk *very* sternly to them, at once! Anything, if only I might feel safe and warm and hopeful again!"

The Green Wind laughed sourly. He shook his head. Starlight reflected in his eyes. "No, my woebegone Wyvern. You don't understand. The Satyrs have done nothing to you. They live in the forest and eat mulberries and moonbeams and dance at their Sabbats. What has that to do with your sorrows? It's only the *story*. You see what a good story it is! Why, it's the story everyone and their auntie wants to hear! It's the best story, the softest and coziest story every told! You began to believe it at once, and you have never had a quarrel with a Satyr in all your life. But the story is no good without a villain. It can't feel *true* without a villain. Otherwise, everything would already be as it ought to be, yes? Someone has to be at fault. And if you are the hero, it stands to reason that folk who do not look like you or talk like you or like to eat the same things you like to eat must be the villains. After all, the world is easy and simple, is it not? And once people hear this story, once this spell is cast…they get lost inside of it. They cannot see anything but the story, and if anything comes along that might tear the tiniest hole in the story, they will hate it like a fanged toad, for the story has become more important than even themselves. That is what the Marquess did, only she used the foxes and rabbits and minks instead of Satyrs to finish her spell. And all those Redcaps and all those Dragons would rather die for her than let any harm come to the story that sings them to bed at night. Because the world is not easy or simple, and it is very, *very* hard to get to sleep when the dark is so deep and the cold is so sharp."

The Wyverary twisted his claws together. "Maybe it won't be so bad, then. If it's only a story. If she only wants frightened people to sleep well and sleep soft. Maybe she doesn't really mean any of it, and once she has her crown, she will be kind and good. People do all kinds of fearsome things for the sake of crowns. I've never understood it. Crowns itch."

They looked down into the gruesome battlefield, now pale with mist and full of the sounds of weeping. A throng of Redcaps were stalking the wreckage, looking for anyone with wings. Whenever they found some poor half-dead Harpy or Ifrit, they pulled a long bronze chain out of a great rough sack and fastened down their wings, one to the other, with an extremely serious looking lock. Ell's wings prickled with gooseflesh. The Green Wind said nothing. The Leopard of Little Breezes yawned, showing her teeth.

"I suppose you're right," Ell sighed. "It is rather silly to think the best of someone who's done all this to us already. I hadn't much hope. But…" A-Through-L's eyes grew very big in the dark, two enormous pumpkin-lanterns floating in the shadows. "But…oh, I know it's a ghastly thing to say, but perhaps *I* might be safe, at least? You and I and your Leopard? We are not foxes or rabbits or minks, after all."

"The spell grows and grows as people fall under its power. And to grow, it must always have new food. I cannot promise that the story will not start whispering in certain ears that Wyverns are lazy criminals who ruin the radiant city of Pandemonium with their dirty nests and fiery breath and loud crowing."

"I'm not a criminal! I've never even been to Pandemonium!"

"It's the story, my dulcet dragonkin. The story doesn't care what *is* true. It only cares what *feels* true. And you are big and frightening to people who are neither reptilian nor capable of flight. Who knows? Perhaps the Marquess will even find a way to banish the Winds and we will be exiled, too."

"Oh, I am so afraid! I am so sad I can hardly stand staying inside my skin! What are we going to do, Green? How are we meant to live? Is the Marquess's story so strong that it can just stomp all over *my* story forever? They're going to chain my wings and if I can't fly, what am I? Who am I?"

The Leopard of Little Breezes lifted her spotted black-and-gold head and rested it on the Wyvern's great red toe.

"Do you remember the first magic you ever learned, Beast?" The Leopard's voice was soft and rumbly and rough as a mother cat's tongue.

Ell did not think he knew any particular magic even now, except for the magic of being who he was. Yes, who he was was a very large, very red, fire-breathing lizard who could fly, which was a bit magical, but nothing out of the ordinary.

"The first magic anyone learns is saying No," purred the Leopard of Little Breezes. "It's how you know a baby is starting to turn into a person. They run around saying no all day, throwing their magic at everything to see what it'll stick to. And if they say No loud enough, and often enough, and to the right person, strange things will happen. The nasty supper is taken away. The light is left on at night instead of turned out. The toy comes out of the shop window. It is such old magic, such basic magic, that most folk don't even know it's magic anymore." The Leopard of Little Breezes rubbed her paw over her ear. "You can say No to that story. You can say No to the spell, to the Marquess, to the lions, to all of it. And if you say it loud enough, and often enough, strange things will begin to happen."

"But that's easy. I can say No all day long!"

The Leopard growled. "It's very much harder to say No to a tyrant than to say No to a plate of beans or a dark bedroom. Harder still to do it while your wings are tied down and blistered. And you cannot stop saying it, even if it would feel so marvelous, so easy, so much less *work* to just be silent and hope it all comes out right somehow."

Ell's eyes filled with turquoise tears. "It does sound hard. So terribly hard. I don't *want* to live through this sort of story. I want to live through one of the nice tales, the ones that take place between hobgoblins, the ones where you don't have to spend every day blistering and saying No to horrors. Why couldn't we just not have horrors at all? Then no one would have to say No."

Oh, my dear, darling Wyverary. So do we all. But so few of us get to. Not even a silly narrator like me. The only comfort there can be is that very few sagas of bravery and wonder occur in the space between hobgoblins. Perhaps, my most beloved lizard, one will even happen to you. But that is not much comfort, I know.

"But then, of course, there is the other side of the apple. There is Yes Magic," the Green Wind said gently.

"I like the sound of that better, even if it begins with Y," nodded the Wyverary.

The Leopard of Little Breezes looked up at the Wyvern with enormous black eyes. She spoke in a very soft, very serious voice, the voice any cat uses when the time for yarn and nip is past and there is only the cold night coming. "Every time you say Yes to anything, to anyone, you change the shape of your world. You agree to supper with a stranger, and now you have a friend. You say that you would certainly like to take a journey to the ocean, and now the ocean is in your heart forever. The Redcaps said Yes to the Marquess, and the world is very much changed. But we…we must say Yes to each other. We must say Yes to the needful, to the suffering, to the lonely, to those the Marquess punishes for saying No to her. We must band together, back to back, and say Yes to everyone who lost today, for we are all family now, and our loss is our new last name. If we must hide, we will hide. If we must flee, we will flee. If we must fight all of this all over again, we will do it and complain the whole time. We must say Yes to the story where, after a long battle, the dark lord is cast down into infinite nothingness or burnt to a crisp or at the *very* least sent to bed without supper, and everyone cheers and dances and has a party afterward. But most of all, we must say Yes to the truth and the speaking of it. We must say No to silence. And perhaps, one day, a long time from now, something new and extraordinary will happen and the Marquess will be defeated, and she will blow away on the wind, no heavier than a memory."

A-Through-L looked down into the Valley of Soft Ears. He could see the Marquess there, strutting through the ruined earth with a crown on her head and a smile on her lips, knighting her gloating generals and showering them with jewels and titles and kisses. He could see her men fastening bronze chains round anything that flew. He could see the trees drooping down in sorrow, their leaves just barely tinged with red, with autumn, with the coming of September.

"I understand what you mean," Ell said finally. His whiskers whipped in the sour wind. He straightened his back and his scarlet tail. "You mean defiance. I know all about Defiance. It begins with D."